SEASON FOR WAR

P. F. KLUGE

FREUNDLICH BOOKS
New York

This novel is a work of fiction. Names, characters, places and incidents are either the product of the author's imagination or are used fictitiously. Any resemblance to actual events or locales or persons, living or dead, is entirely coincidental.

Library of Congress Cataloging in Publication Data
Kluge, P.F. (Paul Frederick), 1942–
Season for war.
I. Title.
PS3561.L77S4 1984 813'.54 84-13734
ISBN 0-88191-017-1

Published by Freundlich Books
80 Madison Avenue
New York, New York 10016

Distributed to the trade by The Scribner Book Companies, Inc.
597 Fifth Avenue
New York, New York 10017

Manufactured in the United States of America

10 9 8 7 6 5 4 3 2 1

For Pamela Hollie

The master-songs are ended? Rather say
No songs are ended that are ever sung,
And that no names are dead names. When we write
Men's letters on proud marble or on sand,
We write them there forever.

—Edwin Arlington Robinson

SEASON FOR WAR

ONCE A LION

·I·

I am near the end now. There are those who would say I am well past it. They may be right. One thing is certain. Things have come full circle for me, here in 1929. I am finishing up where I started out, back in a newspaper city room, surrounded by young reporters covering police, fire, local politics. Their nursery is my old-age home, their pabulum is my terminal gruel.

I sit unnoticed as the daily sprint begins. Reporters go rushing out on stories, disheveled coats and notebooks, shouted instructions, phones ringing, typewriters pounding, crumpled wads of paper bouncing off wastebasket rims. Around mc, calls of "copy, copy" sound like wounded soldiers pleading for water out in no-man's-land.

Undisturbed, I scratch away at yellow legal pads. I sort letters from Jaimc Navarro, Manila cigar magnate, full of venom; letters from Paul Koch, cantankerous proprietor of a broken-down mineral springs in northern California. I have my interviews with John "Dukie" Duquesne, confined to the blind ward of a veterans hospital in Jefferson, Missouri, and with Lefty Diller, doing fine, thanks, as a Hollywood wrangler and bit player. I sift my memories, and theirs, and I put it all together. I covered hundreds of stories, but there was really only one.

The editors know enough to leave me alone. Their policy is to give the old swashbuckler a desk, let him sit and scribble. Father Time, they call me, a newsroom legend whose best work reposes in the morgue. Given half a chance, I tell endless stories to anyone who'll listen, stories of hyphenated conflicts, the Balkans and the Sudan, obscure wars which students memorize for tests and forget who won. Better not to get me started.

Once I was a lion around here, that morning in 1884 I came from Indiana to work as a staff reporter for the New York *Sun*. On midwestern newspapers I had acquired a journalist's manners and wardrobe, the quick study and the facile style, the patina of worldliness. But I was still a believer. I believed in newspapers, I believed in America, and I believed, most of all, in myself.

I had no doubts about my ambitions. I wanted to be a war correspondent, part of the golden age of war correspondents, the cocky self-promoting fraternity that came to include Floyd Gibbons, Henry Russell, W. C. Symington, Richard Harding Davis, Henry Morton Stanley, Stephen Crane. I wanted to create legends and I wanted to be a legend, self-created. To cover naval engagements from yachts, to soar over trenches in balloons, to pitch a tent like an Arab pasha. To insist on discussing strategy with contending generals, and when prisoners of a certain rank were taken, to have them sitting at my table within an hour of capture! No victory would be credited, no defeat admitted, unless I was there to validate them. Wars that I did not attend would remain rumors!

Such were my young hopes, and at the start, there was New York, its cobbled streets, its beery taverns and busy docks. If lives have seasons, then my first months in New York were surely springtime. Springtime for me and springtime of the year. How wonderful it felt when windows slammed upward and taverns opened their doors to the world, and vendors took the street, and elms turned green and each day felt like one long morning! How, in my new suit, I walked this street and that, sniffing, pacing, building a nest in a city I would claim and hold forever. This will be mine, I said, looking at a tree, a pier, a park bench, and this, and this, and this. Forever!

•II•

Paris, 5 May 1884

Dear Edwin,

I hardly know where to begin. So much has changed I almost despair of catching up, especially with you. I find that I am coming home without knowing why. Because school has ended, I suppose, but so much more has ended at home. Milton will seem like a ghost town to me. I will not stay long: I can't picture myself in Milton. And I know that if I can't picture something happening, then it will never come about. What I can picture, dear Edwin, is you waiting for me at the dock in New York, when the *Columbia* discharges me. Can you indulge me for a few days before you pack me off on the train to Indiana?

Yours ever,
Lucy

If I was a small town's scholar, orator, and newspaper editor, Miss Lucy Hammond represented an older tradition in Milton, Indiana: the small town's queen.

Her father, Carter Hammond, was a pillar of the Indiana Republican party, a patrician lawyer who presided over the fortunes of an entire county from the front porch of a manor house on River Road. I gathered that Hammond might have enjoyed a larger career, more corporate, more national, if he had moved to Indianapolis. As I came to know him, though, I saw he was a self-limiting aristocrat, one of those men who commits himself to one small corner of our democracy and makes it his.

Carter Hammond took an interest in the town's bright lads. Our friendship started formally with an invitation to tea, but soon I was welcome to come when I wished, whether to borrow books, have a toddy, or debate what he called the "issues of the day." Once he found that I edited a school newspaper, Hammond delighted in dropping hints about "big stories." He loved telling me "where the bodies are buried."

After my parents died, I drew closer still to him. It was with his support that I attended Kenyon College, his alma mater, and with his indulgence that I graduated after four dissipated years, and with his letter of recommendation that I obtained my first journalistic employment. On returns home, I lodged with him on River Road. That is where I met Lucy.

Her reputation was substantial. Going forth to eastern schools, returning on holidays, she already was what I hoped to become, an adventurer in the outside world. Her New York clothes, her volume of Browning, her smattering of French, all signaled that she was several steps ahead of me, an impression she did nothing to discourage. It is fair to say she treated me fondly, and it is also fair to say her fondness was laced with condescension. She made me feel poor, provincial, and young, all of which I was.

So long as we met in Milton, she would have me at her green-eyed mercy. But things had changed now. Carter Hammond had died while I was in New York, she in France, at school in Grenoble. Now we were both out in the world. I was in it to stay while she, her letter said, was Indiana-bound. I wanted to see her. Equally, I wanted her to see me.

•III•

Lucy Hammond paused outside the customs gate, glancing left and right, too rapid a scrutiny for her to find me in the crowd of passengers and porters. I wondered if she'd recognize me at all, what with my walking cane, my new suit, and a mustache I had just coaxed out onto my upper lip. She had dressed a little dourly for her coming home: black boots, dark brown skirt, white blouse, and brown velvet jacket. My impression, and we later laughed about it, was that the outfit was a penance for her sins in France.

The crowd thinned out and, anyway, I could hold off no

longer. I walked toward her, slowly, pompously, the image—so I thought—of a polished boulevardier. As soon as she saw me, she laughed.

"Why, Edwin, you fop!" she said, holding my hands as she appraised me. "How long were you spying on me?"

"I'm a reporter, Lucy, not a spy."

"Is that so?" she said. "You're making your way, then?"

"I'm only beginning," I responded. I don't know how she took it: as a confession or a boast. "And you, Lucy?"

"As ever." She shrugged. "Are you sure you have time for me?"

"I'm at your disposal," I answered with a courtly bow that made her laugh. It pleased me to find I could amuse her.

Relentlessly tipping a tribe of porters, I sustained my impersonation of a competent New Yorker and got Lucy, her steamer trunk, and myself into a carriage headed for the Brevoort, and it was on that ride that I made the kind of audacious guess that served me well in journalism.

"This was almost the nation's capital," I rattled on. "It was a very close thing between New York and Washington, and it appears to me, dear Lucy, that somewhere in France you have left behind a lover . . ."

Her head snapped up, her eyes met mine. I was ready for anything from a cuff on the ears to a flow of tears.

"Haven't *you* had a lover yet?"

I blushed, astonished by the sudden turnabout.

"Have I . . ." I hesitated. Had I had a lover? Is that what I could call those inept couplings that had highlighted my orientation in the city?

"Of course you have," she answered for me. "It's easier for a man."

"How do *you* know?"

"You'd never have asked, if you hadn't. It's written all over you, the loss of your virginity, like a scarlet 'A.' and I must say . . . but no . . ."

"What? What is it?"

"Your 'A,' " she said, "you wear it rather well."

I'm sure I puffed up my chest, inhaled my cigar, and looked a fool, because she laughed at me. We both laughed. It was a silly, wonderful feeling, as if we'd gone truant from school, and not only had we not been caught, we didn't feel bad about it either!

"Then I take it," I resumed, "that whatever happened is over and you're all right."

She picked up the solemnity right away.

"You may take it, sir, that the 'it' you refer to is over," she said, "and yes, that I'm all right. However . . ."

"Yes, Lucy . . . what is it?"

"However, I can't guarantee 'it' won't happen again!"

By then we'd arrived at the Brevoort. I escorted her to her room, which looked out on the street. That pleased her. Maybe it ran in the family, the legacy of Carter Hammond's front porch.

"Well," she said. "Shall we talk some more? Or have you discovered everything you wanted to know already?"

"I thought you might want to rest," I said.

"Rest!" she retorted, like a child unfairly confined. "Edwin, please tell me what you would do today by yourself. If it appeals to me, I may accompany you. If not, I suppose we can meet this evening or tomorrow."

"You're sure?"

"I have returned from evil Europe with mind and body intact. Not only intact, but in need of exercise. Now what do you suggest?"

"I suggest," I said, "some exercise."

We walked all the way to Wall Street, stopping at Trinity Church, still the tallest building in the city. I found Alexander Hamilton's grave, and it was there, while I was vaporing about the great duel in Weehawken, that Lucy told me about her French affair.

"Have you ever hurt someone, Edwin?"

"No." It was easy to answer then, but what was true that morning still is true. I have come to think of myself as a man who prefers accepting pain to inflicting it. It has been easier to be on the receiving end, contending with hurt in myself instead of confronting it in someone who was less able to endure it, or had more to lose. I suppose this makes me a stoic of the lowest, laziest sort.

"I have hurt someone," Lucy said.

"For good reason, I'm sure."

"Not good, not bad. Sufficient."

"Was it a man?"

A comical, perplexed look crossed her face.

"A man? Was it . . . a man?" she mimicked. "Why, yes, Edwin, I rather think it was. In fact, I'm almost sure!"

We continued south, stepping lively. With every block, every cobblestone, Lucy seemed more herself again, interested in the city and in me, in the person I was turning out to be. By the time we reached Battery Park, her questions had become rather acute. The first picnickers were coming out, and lines of people headed for the ferries. A baseball game was starting up.

"You used to play," she said. "You were good. At least, Father said you were."

"Good enough for Milton."

"Now, I imagine, it's beneath your dignity. As a man of letters, I mean."

"I don't know what you're getting at," I said. "But I write sentences better than I hit baseballs, if that's your point."

"What about?"

"I beg your pardon?"

"I mean, what are your sentences about? What are your themes?"

"Whatever happens. Whatever they require."

"Anything?"

"Well, yes, anything. You never know. That's the excitement of it. A fire. An election. A trial."

"The subject always changes?"

"Yes."

"Then there is no subject."

"The subject is life!" I protested.

"Yes. But what does that mean?"

"All right. It means that I have the ability . . . the talent . . . the knack . . . to obtain information quickly . . . and to communicate that information quickly in my writing."

"Yes, but . . ."

"But it's a trade and it's my trade."

"But what's it all about? What's at the heart of it? Or are you too busy doing things quickly to know?"

I shrugged, despairing. I was writing journalism. She wanted me writing history. Or making it.

I was sure the barely year-old Brooklyn Bridge would please her. The sweep of the harbor, the ships passing beneath the bridge, the breeze that came all the way from Europe, the splendid June sun that spilled upon us: everything was in sufficiency. It was easy to feel that we were at the crossroads of the world, Europe behind us, America rolling off into the future.

"I'm walking here today!" I exulted. "I may walk here fifty years from now . . . if I can still walk."

"And in between walks?"

"What do you mean? My career?"

"Your life."

She had taken my arm, I noticed, and slowed the pace as we neared the center of the span. Something warned me to answer carefully. Her eyes, I think. I stopped walking and, turning slowly, guided her in a circle around me. It was like a dance.

"Any direction," I said. "As far as I go."

"Anyplace?"

"Wherever there's news. I'll be there. I'll meet all the great men . . ."

"Meet them. Take notes on what they say. Write it down and send it off. Is that all?"

"You make me sound like a secretary."

"All these stories . . . are other people's stories. What will your story be?"

It was more than I could manage. She was maddening! She knew my family, my hometown, and it was not only difficult, it was impossible, to think that anyone could have moved out of that background with more forceful dispatch.

"For the record, Lucy," I responded. "Only for the record. Where would I have to go . . . what would I have to do . . . or be . . . to please you?"

"You know, Edwin," she answered, "I'm not sure you can." And she laughed.

"Sit next to me, please," she said. She studied my face closely, brushed back a lock of hair which had blown over my brow. Then, with a fierce little yank, she straightened my tie.

"The world is full of people who are going to love you," she said. "Do you know that?"

We could see the tides change in the river and the sun start tumbling west.

"Do you know that?" she repeated. "Has it occurred to you, in all your planning?"

"I don't know."

She laughed and nodded, some inward suspicion confirmed. "I thought as much," she said. "You ninny!"

·IV·

I had to work, of course, so Lucy spent a good deal of time on her own. It didn't seem to bother her. She relished each day. I went from Park Row directly to the Brevoort and she never failed to have a stock of adventures waiting for me. She busied herself upgrading my wardrobe, which I have always been neglectful of. She wanted to make me "more presentable." Also, she presented me with a smoking pipe, a quality meerschaum, she said would give me character. I have kept that pipe. It was nice, too, coming home from the newsroom to find her sitting with the newspaper, gallantly trying to guess which story was mine.

I was surprised how much she enjoyed Delmonico's. She'd seen more opulent restaurants in France, I was sure, and eaten more complicated food than the oysters we devoured together. And yet, how the dark wood pleased her, the deep carpets, the silverware and candles! Looking back, I believe what captured her was the aura of the place, the gilded atmosphere, the sense of American power. At first she had regarded New York as the capital of a foreign nation, a place that might or might not be worth knowing. Now she seemed entirely at home. She attracted attention as she moved across the room. Give her time —she wouldn't need much—and the town would talk about her.

"Look at me, Edwin," she said as we lingered over coffee. "You are a reporter. A trained observer. Describe me."

"Brown hair," I said. "And eyes that are . . . let's see . . . green, at least tonight. Height about . . ."

"Not that! I am not a missing person. Go deeper . . . if you can."

"Looking at you . . . I can see you're refined . . . educated . . . not like a schoolteacher . . . though . . . not as if you were educated into a particular trade . . ."

"Which only means you don't expect me to *do* anything with whatever I've learned," she interrupted. "Useless knowledge. If not useless, harmless. Continue."

"Very well. A spoiled small-town brat transformed into a cosmopolitan, multilingual woman of culture . . . is that more like it?"

"Continue."

"A woman of charm, passion, education, wealth . . ." I ventured, "with no particular calling or purpose. Intelligent enough to avoid wrong decisions. Too proud to search too hard for the right ones. In short . . . a desperate case."

"Good." She nodded. "Let me ask you this. If you saw me here, or in Milton, or in Paris, where would you say that I belonged?"

"Anywhere you choose," I answered. "You'd fit in anywhere."

"But no special place?"

"No . . . but that's no problem, Luce . . . it means . . ."

"It means I don't *belong* anywhere . . ."

"You're adaptable."

"I wish I were less adaptable. I wish I had to be somewhere. Go somewhere for my health . . ."

"Where?"

"I don't know! What am I supposed to do, Edwin? Just perch gracefully and wait?"

"You'll sort it out," I said, "when you get home. Sooner than you think."

"Will I?"

"You'll make a decision. Or have it made for you."

"Oh, is that the way?" she asked, a little annoyed at my wise airs. She had a right to be. I felt it all the way home, with Lucy beside me, saying nothing, the very slowness of her steps amounting to a plea for help. But it was late, and I left Lucy at the hotel, promising to see her the next day.

I stopped in Peter Conroy's tavern on Hudson Street, took a stool which was becoming my stool, and drank a beer. I breathed the barroom air—I have always loved what happens between beer and wood—and listened to the noise. How glad I was to be a man! A man had freedom. He could move about the world, never stopping, or stopping anywhere he wished. He could succeed or fail at any number of things, make mistakes and learn from them and have a second chance. But a woman —what had she said?—had to perch gracefully and wait. I don't suppose the plight of women concerned me. The plight of Lucy did. And so I drank, which was something else she couldn't do. She couldn't take comfort in sawdust and mirrors and dark wood, care about baseball, dispute politics, peel a hard-boiled egg and tell a joke on Pat and Mike. I guessed there were compensations, but I couldn't think of any that applied convincingly to Lucy.

Conroy trusted me with a pail of beer to go. I stepped across the street, fumbled for my keys, and heard a voice behind me.

"Edwin!"

She came out of a carriage, rushing toward me.

"Lucy, what's wrong?"

She huddled against me. It wasn't a hug, it was a seeking out of shelter.

"I was up on your bridge," she said, "looking for you."

"I was just across the street," I answered, as if the pail of beer in my hand hadn't told her that.

"May I come in awhile?" she asked. "When you need to sleep, I'll leave."

"How will you get back to the hotel?"

"I don't care where I sleep," she said.

"Well, then . . ."

She was the first "company" I had in the apartment that was to be my lifelong residence. It's cluttered now, very much the preserve of an elderly bachelor. Books in the kitchen, food in the living room, cigar butts poked into flower pots. I do not entertain. The night that Lucy came it was more austere: a bed, a table with two chairs. Conroy's beer pail was the sum total of my dinner service. The only luxury had been inherited from the previous tenant. It was a huge, dark, ugly sofa which must have been too heavy to carry into the street. Ranging from itchy gray to oily black, with clawlike feet defiantly planted on a rug, the couch forbade movement or improvement. Whatever rolled beneath it, money or food, was swallowed forever. It was a couch to die on, or be buried in. In the meantime, it was the only place to sit. Luckily, it faced my front window, just far enough from the sill so that I could prop up my feet, drink my beer, and contemplate the city.

We sat down together. Lucy was distraught. I tried to comfort her, placing an arm around her shoulder. Soon she unlaced her boots, lifted her feet off the floor, and nestled beside me. For a moment, I thought she might be going to sleep. That would have made me happy: the closeness, and the trust.

I heard Conroy's closing, with shouted farewells and a snatch of Irish song. I heard a ship blowing its whistle out on the river, and the clop of late-night carriages down in the street. In New Jersey, there was thunder, headed our way, I guessed.

"What are you doing?" she asked. She sounded like a child. I looked down at her, but all the light we had was the vague glow from gas lamps on the street. I reached out and touched the top of her head, the fine smoothness of her hair.

"Thinking," I said. "Watching. Listening."

"Do you mind?"

"Mind what?"

"My being here? And sitting up with me like this?"

"No. Not at all. I often do."

"Just like this?"

"Yes."

"By yourself?"

"Yes."

"I thought perhaps, you brought . . ."

"Not here."

"Oh." Then, after a pause, and in a new key: "Then where do you . . ."

"Wherever I find them. Or they find me. It's not important, you know. It's just something . . ."

"I see," she said. "But not here?"

"No! Why do you ask?"

She didn't answer. She just curled up more tightly, as small as she could make herself. Disturbing her as little as possible, I reached for the pipe she'd bought me and stuffed the bowl full of tobacco. The breeze caught my match just as I held it over the bowl, and the flame flared dangerously close to my mustache.

"You'll get the hang of it," she teased. "You'll be an accomplished, pipe-smoking man."

"Why don't you close your eyes?" I chided her.

"Why should I?" she bantered back.

"Very well, then. Keep them open."

"Edwin?"

"What *now*?"

"There's something . . ."

"What?"

"Come here . . ."

I leaned down to her and then came the plunge from which I never recovered, the flight, the drowning, the shock and discovery of my lifetime, with her open mouth upon mine and our tongues touching. In no time, I felt the beat of her heart. And then, all at once, she burst off the couch and disappeared to a room at the back of my apartment.

I thought she might be crying. Or struggling to compose herself, as I was. I stood up and leaned forward, resting my forehead against the window. The glass felt clean against my brow. I looked down at the lamps and stoops and trees, all the things I'd counted permanent.

"Edwin."

She'd come up behind me, reaching her arms around and joining her hands on top of mine.

"Hello, Luce," I said. I raised her hands to my mouth and kissed them gently. "You all right?"

"Yes," she answered.

I turned and almost died. My hands slid round her waist, up to her shoulders, encountering nothing but warm skin. I touched her hair, caught it, and followed it down, far down, her back.

She stepped boldly back, holding my hands, and stood before me naked.

"Look," she said.

I obliged. I saw her from head to toe. She, who had once been utterly familiar, a few years had transformed into someone beautiful and strange.

"I see," I said.

She turned in front of me, turned slowly in a full circle, a full minute, it must have been. The light passed over her body as the moon rises and sets on an island, catching every bay and cove and curve of coast.

"So there," she said when at last she faced me again.

"Yes," I gasped.

"Whatever happens to me," she said, "*this* is who it will be happening to. I wanted you to see me. So that when you care about me, if you care . . ."

"I care," I answered in a frightened, strangled voice. "You know I care."

"There are great things in front of us. Don't you think so?"

I nodded.

"Great things." She stepped closer, grasping my hands, placing them on her shoulders.

"Yes," I said, lamely adding, "I'm looking forward . . ."

She laughed and I hated myself. With Lucy naked in front of me I was "looking forward" to the future!

"But . . ." She took my hands, palms forward, and holding them tightly at the wrists, passed them over the tips of her breasts. "You don't want to take advantage of me?"

"No . . ."

"Then I'll put it another way," she countered, resting my hands upon her breasts. "May I take advantage of you?"

She did.

The next morning was the start of summer, New York's fierce, odoriferous season. Even today, though I think of Lucy in many places, the rage of July brings about the sweetest of memories, and the city, at that tar-blistering time, is charged with cues and promptings which carry me back to her, and then, the two weeks or so we had. I walk the docks and recall fishermen pulling eels out of the Hudson. I feel the heat in the streets, the open fire hydrants, and it brings back the evening when, returning from Hoboken with arms full of fruits and vegetables, we made a picnic on the roof. And as long as he lived, my tavernkeeper and good friend Conroy loved remembering a night of Calcuttan torpor which Lucy and I shared with him, our last night before she was to leave for Indiana. Drinking places were not open to women, but there was a side room, with a separate entrance and an exit leading out to Conroy's backyard and garden. Mrs. Conroy invited us to join her at a table in the garden, where she was putting up tomatoes, and there we sat, hour after hour, drinking beer while a sluggish summery moon rolled through the vapor overhead. Conroy joined us at closing time and so did some of his trusted regulars. A good-natured restlessness was in the air, an unwillingness to go home, to stay indoors: it was one of those nights when tomcats screech and people sleep on tenement roofs. The pails of beer kept coming. Some of us rolled up our sleeves, put up money, and, past midnight, started pitching horseshoes! We were competitive, raucous, merry, and near the top of my list of regrets is the regret that my life did not contain more such evenings. They happen so easily, by accident, and yet how many of them can we count? We talked about that night for years, at Conroy's, but it never happened again. We never got around to it, somehow.

That night, I was splendid. Half my horseshoes were leaners and ringers which felt like magic the moment they left my hand. I was unbeatable and, at 3 a.m., we departed in triumph, exhausted by beer and laughter. With one arm, I flung my jacket over my shoulder; the other I dropped across Lucy's shoulder and we walked across the street. Our talk was leaners and ringers. Coming up the stairs, she put a hand over my mouth to quiet me, lest our horseplay awaken sleeping tenants. As we stepped into the front room, flooded with moonlight, I heard Lucy gasp, as if something had startled her. She walked over to the window, all covered with silvery light, and turned to me.

"What am I doing here?" she asked.

"Listen to me," I said, moving toward her. I placed my hand on her shoulder, no more intimately than when we had crossed the street, but her heat and sweat excited me. "I could get along without you, Luce. I'll cover wars and I'll have affairs. I'll live all over the world and whoever notices names in newspapers will notice mine. But without you . . ."

"Yes?"

"I'll be the emptiest man alive. You remind me of other things . . . another kind of person I might become . . ."

"Do you want to?"

"Yes." I took my hand, touched her chin, raised her face toward mine. It came up, slowly, tremulously, her eyes welling, but when I kissed her mouth I sensed a deep inward sigh, acquiescence, and, soon, excitement.

"Please," I said. "Let me."

I guided her to the sofa and pulled off her boots. I raised her to her feet again and proceeded, garment by garment, to undress her. My heart was in my throat, and I couldn't trust myself to stop, halfway, to admire the woman I was undressing. To all this, she submitted quietly. She took the moonlight like a tan, arms outthrust, eyes half shut. Finally, I bade her turn in front of me, the slow, luxuriant circle I loved . . .

"Well," she said, opening her eyes the next morning. "Have you been awake long?"

"Awhile," I said. "Thinking."

"About?"

"You know . . . everything."

"Everything won't do, Edwin. It's like your journalism. If everything is your topic . . . there is no topic . . ."

"Very well, then. The topic was you."

"Ah . . ."

"I want you to come back from Milton. When affairs are settled there . . . I want to settle things here."

There were tears in her eyes. At my proposal? At my awkwardness? I still wonder.

"Promise me," I said, not quite sure what I was asking her to promise.

"I promise."

Half an hour later she was on the train to Milton. Things move fast, if you let them.

· V ·

I was all full of her those next few weeks, picturing what our life together could be. At night I saw her naked, turning in front of me, hair tumbling down almost to the cleft in her buttocks, startling breasts beneath my hands. And I saw the look in her eyes, full of pleasure in herself, full of challenge to me, and there was no telling where that challenge would lead.

The career I'd started left little room for wife and family. It was important that I be unencumbered, able to go anywhere with only myself to worry about. But Lucy was not a bar to adventure; she was adventure herself. Lucy was someone who would lead me on, not hold me back. When we talked about journalism, I sensed how different were our ideas of the journalist's trade. I accepted my work as given, but she thought of it as an avenue to other things. She thought of themes and subjects. She sought the center of things yet never ceased transcending them. She had it in her to make my life better, and me a better man. My goals were modest, at least by comparison with hers. Hers were endless.

It took some talking to myself, yet I managed it. I managed to travel from the point where life with Lucy was unthinkable to its opposite: life was unthinkable without her. So, in the end, love prevailed.

Milton, Indiana
August 17, 1884

Dear Edwin,

An extraordinary thing has happened: I am in love. Here, in Milton, at home! And with a Milton man, whose brothers and sisters were your classmates!

Henry Lawson—Captain Henry Lawson—is my husband-to-be!

His return to Milton was as much an accident as mine. His father died not long ago in a tragic accident. Death brought us together and out of these deaths: LOVE.

A pair of prodigals are we, and likely to remain so. My captain is stationed in Arizona, where he commands a troop—or regiment, or brigade—anyway, a group of men who ride horses after Indians, Mexicans, and other ruffians! And—Edwin—the men he commands are black! How I wish you could meet him! I promise you: I will bring you together. With your flair for journalism and his experience of soldier life, the result would be compelling.

You are not here and, alas, we shall both soon be gone. Why the haste? Well, his leave is short and we must soon leave for Fort Monroe, Arizona, where I shall occupy a house on "Officers' Row." How unimaginable! A few months ago I was in France, where everything was finished and polished, and now I am off to a place where civilization itself is still contested. We shall marry in Indianapolis, and our wedding night will be spent in a railroad car, crossing the plains.

Even as I write, my captain paces anxiously the length of the veranda: what noise he makes! He is a tall man, six feet four! His skin is tanned, which I like, and he has a beard and mustache, which I abhor. At first I found it impossible to talk to this tower of a man. Perhaps that made him more challenging. He is shy—a dozen kinds of shyness, midwestern, military, strong man, poor man, and plain Henry Lawson shyness. Still, he *can* be persistent.

Let me confide in you what I have not shared with him: Why I shall share my life with him. I believe that Henry Lawson's life is an adventure and that, joining him, I will become part of that adventure. There is something about him which suggests special purpose, a role to play. Sometimes I think he senses this himself. At other times, I fear his reply would be a snort of laughter or a shrug. We shall see.

I have mentioned you to Henry and hope that sooner or later he may write to introduce himself to my best friend. Frankly, he's no writer. There are whole areas of life he will leave to me, things he needs me for as I need him.

This *must* be my last paragraph and then, out of the house with me. Edwin, I want you to always be part of my life. I think you cannot fail to know this, the many foolish ways I've tried to say how close I feel to you. Please, in your heart, stay near.

Yours,
Lucy

•VI•

Lucy promised Lawson would write, but the letter never came. Never mind. He'd have said he had nothing much to say, or that he liked to look a man in the eye when he talked to him, or some such visceral nonsense.

Of course I knew who Henry Lawson was. How could I have been raised in Milton and not have heard of the farm-boy hero who had lied about his age to join the Indiana Volunteers, been wounded at Chattanooga, and earned a Medal of Honor at Stone Mountain, Georgia? Who didn't know the story of how Lawson had revenged himself upon the Confederates who had ambushed and killed his commanding officer, how he had stalked and destroyed them one by one, or as the tale had it, "eleven up, eleven down"? We had made that grisly hunt a schoolyard game and taken turns at being Henry Lawson.

When I thought about it, I realized their union was inevitable. So ill matched, so unsuited, so mutually incomplete, and thus so ultimately compatible were they, the farm-boy hero, risen from the ranks, pounding horses on the last ragged edges of the American frontier, and Lucy, the lawyer's daughter, demi-Parisienne, pining for a full, adventurous life. She was seven years younger. Yet they were closer than their ages would suggest. His life had been a long tour of duty, campaign to campaign, fort to fort, and his socializing was confined to little pockets of time, leaves and furloughs that aggregated less than Lucy had accomplished in a French season. No, they had caught each other at just the right time. Coming together, there was no keeping them apart. I know that. And I concede that had I been in Milton myself, the outcome would have been no different, only more painful and humiliating. Lawton would have defeated me without trying; without catching my name, he'd have brushed me aside; he'd have won without knowing the game was on.

It was remarakble how Lucy's letter changed things. How the city flattened for me, the streets narrowed! How my apartment became a cell, my employment a penance! All my passions, all my prizes, were drained of meaning. I will not linger on the days—and nights—of pain and anger. All my imagined revenges! They were not unique. Any rejected lover could have recognized himself in me. What was unusual was what followed: a sense of loss that was almost like mourning. Lucy was lost and I have spent the rest of my life measuring that loss, like an amputee awakened from surgery who takes, not seconds, but years to reach out for the part of him that is missing, dead and gone. I now know that what was lost was more than romance with Lucy, or partnership with her, or the possession of her splendid body. What was lost was the man I might have been. I became . . . what I became. With a vengeance. I became the sort of journalist Lucy feared. I made a career out of covering wars, which I reviewed as entertainments, or followed as hunts, or analyzed as contests, but always from the sidelines, never caring. That was a promise I made myself: never to care. I only wish that I had kept it.

THE BUFFALO SOLDIERS

• I •

Paul W. Koch
Indian Hot Springs
Helenville, California.

August 15, 1928

Dear Morrison,

I guess I should tell you how it is with me these days, so if one of your letters comes back marked "deceased" you'll understand. The spring of 1910—I forget the date but it was around the time Mark Twain croaked, so you could look it up—I had a stroke. For a while, I might have been sharing a cloud with old Mark Twain himself, but here it is 1928, and I'm still sitting in a wheelchair. I keep my legs under a blanket all year round, but not so they stay warm. They could freeze on me, I wouldn't know it. I hate the sight of them, is all. They're already dead, see, nerves gone, muscles shrinking down to nothing, meat coming off the bone. Talk about having a foot in the grave. I've been up to my waist in it for years! Sometimes I feel like an old tumbledown mansion, where they only heat half the rooms in winter. Half dead, half alive. Upstairs, dreams and memories. Downstairs—nix.

Okay. Begin at the beginning.

Maybe you already know that Mrs. Lawson was behind your coming to Arizona. By 1885, let's face it, the handwriting was on the wall for the Apaches. I mean, it was never really a question of who would win, was it? Well, we were always hearing from some correspondent who wanted to go on the trail with us and our answer was always no. Each commander was in charge of setting the ground rules for his outfit. Hell, there were some who damn near begged for coverage; they'd throw in a horse, a telegraph operator, and an occasional squaw to get their name in the papers. And it worked. Ask General Custer. Ask Teddy Roosevelt. Blood wins battles. Ink makes reputations. But Lawson wasn't like that. So you kept sending letters. And I, not knowing who you were, kept turning you down.

One morning, I'm sitting in headquarters, smoking my morning cheroot, at peace with the world. The Boss was over at San Pablos, where things were getting restless the way they usually got restless when spring rolled around. So there I was, feet up on a clean desk, blowing smoke rings out towards the parade ground, and in marches Mrs. Lawson.

"Lieutenant Koch," she said, waving a bunch of letters in my face. "Are you responsible for these?"

Now, I liked that lady from the day she arrived till the day they dedicated the statue, which is about three times as long as I liked any other woman I ever came across. She was easy on the eyes and, believe me, that was something. The army women in Arizona were like the damn landscape—dry, rocky, and not worth fighting over. Most posts, the Commanding Officer's Wife was called the COW. Get it? And what a misfit herd it was. Somehow the word got out that if a woman couldn't get married anyplace else, if maybe she struck out in a leper colony, she should try her luck on a hell-and-gone army post. It must have worked for the first one, because she kept inviting all her ugly cousins, and before you knew it, it was open season. That's one reason I liked officering a black outfit. You didn't have to contend with so many predatory women, only whores. But back to Mrs. Lawson, who, as I was saying, was easy on the eyes.

"Did you consult with Captain Lawson about those letters?"

"No, ma'am. The policy was set before we heard from this Morrison gent. I just made up some reasons why having a reporter tag along would be a real bad idea . . ."

"Mr. Edwin Morrison of the New York *Sun* is my friend," she announced. "I asked him to come. Those letters were written at my urging."

"I'm sorry," I said.

"Then he can come?"

"If Mrs. Van Doren can bless this post with a Christmas visit from her cousin Millie that lasted six months . . ."

She laughed at that. Millie Van Doren had made my life miserable. I was still getting knitted woolen things in the mail from her, which are very useful in Arizona, round puffy things that reminded me of small domestic animals. Slippers is what they were supposed to be. Bedroom slippers.

"The point is," she said, leaning forward confidentially, and I'm not sure she knew what her figure did to men, because she could breathe wonderful life into a long-sleeved, high-necked, candy-striped gingham blouse, "the point is that Mr. Morrison is a journalist. He will want to accompany any column that sets off from here . . ."

"Go out in the field?"

"It would be for our own good if he did."

"How's that?" I asked. It seemed we'd done okay so far without a reporter in tow. I wondered why the devil anybody would want to visit a black cavalry unit at Fort Monroe, Arizona. Look at this, I thought, nine in the morning and a raw steak in the middle of the parade ground wouldn't pull a dog out of the shade.

"Mr. Morrison is a very important journalist," Mrs. Lawson told me. "I can promise you that his presence here would be an enormous boost to all of us."

"A boost?"

"Most certainly. He can secure the attention we deserve . . . the recognition . . ."

"He's that good, huh?"

"Every bit that good. Now, if there are any obstacles in his way I want them removed."

Two weeks later, the Boss was back from parts south: six weeks in the saddle, all along the Mexican border. They'd buried a family of Mexicans, burned a few wicki-ups that had been emptied in a rush, and shot at some Apaches who maybe had something to do with the dead Mexicans. That's the kind of war it was and we'd been in the Territory too long to blame ourselves if it wasn't the Battle of Gettysburg. It was a new kind of war, or an old kind of war, or no kind of war at all, we never made up our minds. War of movement, war of occupation, war of attrition, colonial war, guerrilla war, call it what you want, if you didn't come home dead, you came home dead tired.

"Koch."

The Boss was standing in the doorway one night while I was hacking out some reports. In his hand he held a lit cheroot. He was the only man I ever knew who could smoke cigars, one after the other, all night long. And he did it in such a delicate way. Me, I chewed cigars. If they came with a paper ring, I smoked the ring along with the tobacco, it was all the same to me. Still is. If I got a box of Marsh-Wheelings in the mail some morning I wouldn't mind. Anyway, the Boss was oddly gentle with cigars. He smelled 'em, licked 'em, snipped off the ends. And the butts of his cigars were in perfect shape when he got done, while mine looked like they'd been run through a meat grinder.

"Sir?"

"This Morrison."

"Yes?"

If he felt excitement at your visit, he hid it pretty well.

"Coming," he said.

"Yes, sir."

"You take care of him. Or Van Doren . . ."

"I'll handle it," I said. "I'll keep him busy."

"Good." He nodded and turned out the doorway, but I heard him mutter, "Pain in the ass."

So there you have it. That was how you got to Arizona.

More later,
Paul W. Koch

•II•

Lucy's letters started coming as soon as she arrived in Arizona. Just when I should have been trying to forget her, Lucy refused to be forgotten. She treated her marriage as a part of a plan we had made, a fraction of some vast agreed-upon design we all shared. So we conspired, she with officers, I with editors. All the time, I wondered why I was heading in her direction, when every line of reasoning pleaded with me to stay away forever. Looking back, leafing through the journal pages that follow, I think I wanted to test myself, test my ability to care. Or not to care.

ARIZONA JOURNAL

JUNE 2, 1885

The train halted at an adobe station where husbands waited for wives, teamsters for salesmen, deacon for preacher, Sergeant Dennis "Lefty" Diller for me. He apologized for not carrying my bags, pointing to a knee injured "in the field." He was picked off third base in a post baseball game, I later learned.

My head still aches at the memory of that drive out of Tucson. There was no half hour of cool early morning, no pink light, no morning dew. The land was like the floor of an oven, a dirty oven, littered with charred crumbs and blackened crusts of past bakings. First impressions can be wrong, I know. But for me, the place was dead, incapable of growth, impervious to seasons. The sun passed over like a hunter, and whatever grew was fair game. Even the plants, brush and cactus, were like the bristles popping out of a dead man's face inside a coffin.

The track we followed was a channel among rocks. The rocks grew larger as we neared the mountains, and were piled into heaps, till I felt like we were passing through some Titan's quarry. In one such place, I saw some horses ahead of us, blocking our way.

"Horses," I said.

"Right," Diller acknowledged.

"Apache horses?"

"Nope."

"Wild horses?"

"Nope. Negro horses."

The horses were tethered to an oak tree that looked like a piece of driftwood. Now I could see reins and saddles and blankets with U.S. markings. And then, joking, stretching after a nap among the rocks, came some of the black cavalrymen Henry Lawson commanded. "Swarthy Ethiopes." Their blue woolen shirts, soiled trousers, canvas leggings, scuffed boots, were like Diller's. But these soldiers were black—black, that is, and brown, and in one case reddish brown and freckled—and that sufficed to make them remarkable. They mounted their horses and turned in front of us. One said hello, the others merely nodded, and then they were gone. Diller left enough room for their dust to settle before we followed.

"Why did they meet us here?" I asked. "Why didn't they come into Tucson?"

"Ever been a soldier?"

"No."

"Been around soldiers?"

"No."

"I'll put it this way. When a soldier goes into town there's two things he's looking for. And I don't mean the church and the library. And our boys ain't no different. Only they are."

"You mean . . ."

"I mean that Tucson ain't set up for colored trade. Only us white noncoms go into Tucson. The buffalo soldiers meet us by the Rockpile."

"Buffalo soldiers?"

"Yeah. 'Cause they got that nappy buffalo hair. Meet us out at the Rockpile because it ain't worth dyin' for a beer and a poke."

Diller steered us through a plain of boulders, across dry riverbeds, and finally down into a canyon. At the bottom was a bona fide river, with our escort's horses wading and drinking while their riders watched us come, smoking pipes and laughing at our creaking, cursing, tortuous descent.

Coming down into the canyon, I felt we had plunged into a pool of cool air, pine-scented, and the sight of the river down below amazed me. It was a wide western river, pebbly and shallow, with islands of grass and brush all through it. Indeterminate banks showed me that nature had not yet made its final choice of channel. No Wabash, this unnamed stream, and yet it delighted me. Invigorated, I looked around and saw that we were at last among the mountains. The sun slanted against the peaks, turning boulders into piles of plums and oranges, bright and sharp against the bluest possible sky. And down below, along the river, there were pines and aspen, oak and cottonwood, and grassy meadows.

Finally there were some lights down the river, and the smell of woodsmoke; horses tethered along the back and the sound of someone singing. Our escort veered off to the side and Diller deposited me in front of a row of dwellings against the canyon wall.

I jumped off the wagon, wondering if Lucy was watching for me. This was the moment I had acted out a hundred ways. I'd tossed off epigrams and jokes. I'd confronted her with anger, cut her mercilessly. I'd scattered prizes at her feet and walked off laughing. I'd promenaded past her with the world's most beautiful woman on my arm. And for all my performances, the applause was pain . . .

"Up here," Lucy said. She was standing in an open doorway. The light behind her showed me her silhouette, not her face. I stepped onto the veranda, bags in hand. I didn't want to embrace her.

"Edwin . . ."

"Hello, Lucy. Do I salute?"

"As you were," she answered softly.

JUNE 4, 1885

Fort Monroe is less a fort than a lonely little colony, possibly penal. No stockade, no ramparts, no sense of hostility or siege. The barracks and houses have the canyon wall to the back and *the river to the front. The sole access is along the banks of the river. One way is Tucson, the other to San Pablos Reservation, the justification for our otherwise mystifying presence here.*

The "Officers' Row" which Lucy wrote about consists of three one-story adobe houses, each shared by two white officers and their families. The roof is thatched brush, in which insects abound and snakes take cover. Windows, doors, and floors are wood, but the internal walls do not reach to the ceiling and are in any case so thin as to make privacy a myth. We share our quarters with Lieutenant Koch, much sought after as a housemate because of his bachelor status, but his nightly snoring would wake the dead.

The troops, the blacks, live in a ragged line of tents which runs at a right angle from Officers' Row. Some tents have been turned into commodious dwellings, with wooden floors and benches. Others look like they were pitched, or half pitched, yesterday. Various corrals, pens, and sheds sit behind the black men's tents.

The military headquarters, Lieutenant Koch's domain, is down by the river and so, too, is the town: an aggregration of tents, shanties, and huts containing domesticated Indians, post traders, laundresses, scouts, drummers, and drifters.

That is Fort Monroe: minimal, marginal, and ad hoc. It's hard for me, it would be hard for anyone, to regard this place as the harbinger of an advancing civilization, this lost and awkward backwater! Passing among this gathering of outcasts, I wonder whether these are the people who will win the West or those from whom it will be won.

Lucy has worn herself out keeping me busy. Like a child dragged into a museum, I have been made to pause before every point of interest. With Lucy, I have called on each of the three other white women on the post, Mrs. Presley, Mrs. Van Doren, Mrs. Conaway, to sample cookies, admire quilts, leaf through scrapbooks detailing intimate histories of families I will never meet. And when Lucy has flagged, Lieutenant Koch has been there to arrange lessons and demonstrations of all kinds: horseshoeing, marksmanship, tanning, cooking. Even the handful of troops has been infected with keep-the-visitor-occupied. I need only pause before the most innocuous of objects—a wooden bucket, say—and there is a black face in front of me, instructing me that this object, made of oak, bound with copper, is a bucket, a two-gallon bucket, used for hauling two gallons of water, etc., etc.

But Lucy is the biggest disappointment. I'll put it simply. She doesn't want to be alone with me, to engage me in conversation, to meet me on any emotional level. Her memories of New York are vague, with no more resonance for her than the pictures in Mrs. Conaway's scrapbook. She wanted me to come; her greeting confirmed it. Yet since then, she has seemed a helpless fraction of her former self. I grant that our relationship could not have resumed at the same level of intensity we knew in New York. But has time, or marriage, or distance so diluted the tie between us that I become a bothersome houseguest, to be passed from neighbor to neighbor, sight to sight?

JUNE 7, 1885

We have gotten word that Lawson's column will return later today, so I must now rush to complete my impressions before the Great Man's arrival.

I have talked, at last, to Lucy. It happened thus: Last night, Koch surpassed himself. His snores were Gatling bullets, mortars, cannons, all combined, a veritable Waterloo. I lay in bed, hands folded behind my neck, staring at the ceiling, with insects falling on my sheets. I would never again be able to justify traveling so far to visit Lucy. The effort I had made, I would not repeat. She was still the closest person to me in the world—but not as close as she had been. Estrangement. Marvelous word! The process of becoming strangers.

After a virtuoso performance from Koch, I heard Lucy stirring in the back room, which was her bedroom. The front room, where I slept, was kitchen, parlor, and everything else. I heard Lucy brush open the hanging curtain that divided the two rooms.

"Edwin . . ."

I opened my eyes and saw the Lucy I had lost: standing over me, she was wrapped in a bathrobe far too large. Lawson owned it, and her.

"Would you like to sit outside awhile?" she asked.

I slipped on my own robe and followed her onto the porch. We sat down on a wooden bench that Koch had made.

It was chilly, almost cold, and I felt parts of my body that had been bludgeoned by heat come back to life. Almost as soon as she sat down, Lucy jumped up and disappeared inside the house.

"Now we're all set," she announced when she returned. She unfolded a blanket, placing half of it over me, half around herself. She drew her feet up onto the bench.

"And now . . ."

From her side, she produced a bottle and two tin cups, into which she decanted a healthy dollop of sherry.

"Do you do this often?" I asked.

"This is the first time," she said. "But I think it's nice."

"Yes."

"It could get to be a habit," she said. Then she raised her cup. "To your visit."

"To my . . ."

"No," she corrected. "To your being here."

I nodded and we drank. I knew what was happening: this was Lucy's effort to re-create the mood which had united us in Manhattan, sitting on my couch, watching a thunderstorm rumbling over New Jersey. Now we were together again. I started to say something.

"Shhh," she whispered, covering my mouth with her hand. I let the sentence go.

With no lanterns, no campfires, not even the moon itself for competition, the stars shone undiminished. I felt like some rummaging field mouse sticking his nose out of a burrow, sniffing eternity. What egotists are we, to decorate the heavens with beasts and kitchen implements, signposts and markers, when all there is is eternal time and infinite distance!

"So," Lucy finally said. A one-syllable word, hanging in the air, relaxed and pleasant as a benediction.

"So," I echoed contentedly.

"It's been disappointing, hasn't it?"

"Not now it isn't."

She moved over, snuggled close. "You and I are very much alike. It's never hard for me to know how things are with you. I can tell. I know what pleases you. And what hurts you, too."

"Yes," I said. "I suppose you do."

"It frightens me sometimes—our being so compatible."

"Why?"

"The way we could fit together, fold into one another, you know . . ."

"Yes," I said. I knew.

"So easy, it would have been, so natural. In New York it seemed so right . . ."

I turned to look at her. I forgot the stars. I wanted to see her face when she remembered that moment.

"It would have been a mistake, though," she said. "You knew it even then, I think. You asked me to stay . . . sort of . . . but your heart wasn't in it."

My heart?! My God, where was my heart?

I sipped some sherry, too hurt and too angry to respond. What I had come to see as weakness, she saw as my moment of strength! She thanked me for my fortitude. And this would become the agreed-upon version of that life-changing encounter: that I, being strong, had saved Lucy from—myself!!

"So it worked out well," I said. "You found someone who . . . who what?"

"Who was nothing like me, nothing like you," she answered. She sounded firm and confident. We'd negotiated the morass, we were on high ground, moral and marital terra firma, stamping our feet and kicking the mud off our heels. "I found someone who was unlike anyone . . ."

"And that was the attraction? That he was so different?"

"Of course not. Not just that."

"There was more?"

"Oh, certainly."

"What, then, Lucy?" There was something in my tone I didn't like the sound of but it was hard for me to stop. "So far —let's see—you have told me that this person's main attraction was that he was not like me and, appealing as that sounds . . ."

"No, Edwin, please!"

"If you could only be more specific. Was it that he was tall and I am not? That I am a writer and he's a soldier? That he rides a horse? Carries a gun? That I live in New York and he patrols this invaluable frontier?"

"No! No!" She covered her face with her hands.

"Then I must confess you have me at a loss, Luce. In New York you gave me to understand we had a future together . . ."

"We do! Edwin, we do!" she cried. "Don't you see? I love you both!"

"Excellent," I snapped. "You love us both. Him you love by marrying. Me you love by leaving. He shares your bed. I receive letters . . ."

She reached out a hand to calm me, but there was no holding me back. I have rarely felt so entitled to anger, so determined to enjoy it.

"It didn't take long, Luce, did it? Back in dull old Milton? You worried about having to perch and wait. But the waiting wasn't in you, was it? Not if it meant waiting for me. Not with the cavalry in town."

I was all right as long as I didn't look at her. I carried off my anger well, till I risked a look at her face, and saw those Lucy eyes. Then my anger was broken, and a sense of eternal loss replaced it.

"I took my time," I said. "Too long. My fault."

"Took your time?"

"Falling in love with you. Admitting it to myself. Preparing to tell you. Planning for it. I took my time. And . . . in the time that I took . . . you were gone."

I was prepared to leave it at that.

"I'm not gone!" she said, her firmness surprising me. "We are going to be part of something. You and I and Henry! You and I need each other, Edwin. And we need him."

"Do we . . . ?"

"I knew it from the moment I saw him . . ."

"When was that?"

"Do you want to know?"

"Yes . . . tell me how you fell in love . . ."

"The story won't . . . harm you?"

"It won't harm me. Hurt, yes. Harm no." It was one of the few times I ever gave Lucy a direct order. "Tell it."

She was probably the only native of Milton, Indiana, who had never heard of Henry Lawson. Her private schooling in the East and her two years in France spared her the knowledge of his war record. The first she saw of him was when she came downtown one day with Mrs. DuPre, the Hammond housekeeper, and saw "this giant" sitting in the park, surrounded by an audience of children and old men. Children and old men: the ones who thought the world was still in front of them and the ones who knew that it had already passed them by!

Lucy asked Mrs. DuPre who was holding court and was rewarded with the DuPre version of "eleven up, eleven down." Her account was so excited, so adolescent, it made Lucy laugh. She guessed that Lawson heard her laughing. He looked her way and nodded.

The following day, she received his letter, an awkward composition about how family deaths had brought them both home to Milton, yet, despite the sadness, he dared to hope that he might ride by and present himself. The next afternoon, he came. They sat together on the porch and found that their feelings about Milton were remarkably alike. They loved the downtown faces, well-known streets and houses, the look of the river, the change of seasons, the curve of the roads, what Lawson called "the lay of the land . . . always knowing you can find your way home in the dark."

When their touching celebration of country comforts expired, Lawson shifted around in his chair and Lucy wondered what else they had to talk about. Lawson started to say something and stopped, waving his thoughts away.

"I'm bored to death here," he finally said, with a grin that won her heart. "I can't wait to get the hell out!"

They laughed together like conspirators planning an escape.

"How about you?" Lawson asked. "You planning to set up housekeeping here?"

"Certainly not!" Lucy replied. In another man such directness would have offended her. You expected a man to talk of a variety of things, some serious, some frivolous. Not Lawson.

"Going to go back and learn some more French over there?"

"No," she said. "That's over with . . . I don't know what's next for me." Who was this improbable man? What was she doing, being attended on by local war heroes? How would she ever get him to leave? Not that she necessarily wanted him to go!

"Yeah," he said. "Well . . . so." He sat back in his chair as though he had brilliantly summed up her life's complexity in "yeah" and "well" and "so."

She couldn't resist mimicking him, delivering the words as if they were the first she'd learned in a foreign tongue. "Yeah . . . well . . . so."

Next morning he was there at dawn, awakening her, shouting up to her bedroom window that he always woke up early and anyway didn't she know that was the best time to go riding, when the day and the horses were still fresh? He didn't mind waiting while she "fixed herself up." He plopped himself down on the porch and lit a cigar while Lucy rushed into her clothes, wondering how on earth he had got her to hurry.

Of art, culture, history, he was innocent. Whatever Lucy knew was news to him. Atlanta was the largest city he had ever seen. And yet, he was not complacent. He knew there was a larger world outside, a huge arena where he would be counted on to play his part. He knew it and so did Milton, Indiana. Every face acknowledged it. Lucy had thought of herself as local royalty, Carter Hammond's girl. Her they respected: Henry Lawson they adored. He couldn't pass a farm without being waved in for a meal.

Late one afternoon they improvised a picnic. They rode along the river to a secret place. Lawson had lots of such secret places, springs and caves and berry patches and Indian mounds. This time he took her to "the cove," a sandy bend of river fringed by reeds and cattails and shaded by willows.

"All these places I've never been to!" Lucy exclaimed when they arrived. "I feel I never lived here until now."

"Glad you like it," he said, spreading a blanket and opening the wicker basket she had brought. "I was saving it for last."

"Last?"

"I'm leaving next weekend, Luce. I got orders. See, I don't live here anymore. I live at Fort Monroe."

"It must be nice, not having to decide where to go," Lucy mused. "You just count on history to carry you along.

"History?" he asked. "Yeah. I guess. You ride it or it rides you. I don't know."

While they spoke, he fumbled with the champagne. He tried to joke about it. "For years, when people said let's have a toast, I thought they were having a party with warm pieces of bread."

How he botched it! The cork gave way, the contents exploded, a geyser of sweet foam.

"It's a drink," Lucy teased him. "Not a weapon."

"Tastes okay," he said, licking his lips. "Tastes sweet." He leaned over and kissed her on the mouth. "Here's to you. Is that all right, for a toast?"

"Sounds fine," Lucy said. "The taste is pleasant, too."

"I want you," Henry Lawson said. That was his whole case, his entire pleading.

"Yeah?" Lucy said, mimicking him. "Well? So?"

"Every way, I want you. I want you to come back with me to Fort Monroe. Married, I mean."

"You're leaving in a few days," she responded.

"That's not an answer," he said.

"I only met you."

"Nor that."

"We just kissed!"

"Yeah. Well. So?"

When next she spoke, it sounded to Lucy like someone else was talking. She hardly recognized her voice.

Yes, she loved him. But during the weeks in Arizona, Lucy had detected some weaknesses . . . no, not weaknesses, but absences, and these absences were tied to the very qualities she loved. He assumed the future was his, was theirs, so he declined to think about it: it would come to them. He lived without design and had no clear idea where he should be two, five, ten years hence. More than once she recalled his offhand comment about riding history or being ridden by it.

"The Army is all he knows," she told me on the porch. "And this Negro crew. He's content to ride off with them forever. It's . . . it's heartbreaking how happy he is, with the simplest things!"

"*Why change him?*"

"*Because I am not simple, Edwin, and you are not, and the world is not a simple place. That's why we need you . . . I want you to make him great.*"

"*You want a hero. It that it?*"

"*He is a hero. I want the world to know him. Am I asking too much?*"

"*Of me or him?*"

"*Of both of you. There's greatness in him, but you have to bring it out. We have to launch him, Edwin.*"

The way she looked at me, implored me, implied we were in it together, always would be, I had no choice.

•III•

APACHE HOSTILITIES IMMINENT

**Captain Lawson's Cavalry
Anticipates Savage Campaign**

by EDWIN CARTER MORRISON, *Staff Correspondent*

Fort Monroe, Arizona Territory — Returning to post after six weeks' patrol of hostile territory, the 25th Cavalry, commanded by Captain Henry Lawson, reports that a new outbreak of Apache violence is probable.

"The war's not over yet," commented Captain Lawson, the tanned, towering Civil War hero who led a column of Negro cavalry from one Apache stronghold to another. "The spirit of resistance continues to beat in the Apache heart. They are armed, brave, well led. They will not easily yield."

Sources here estimate that one thousand Apaches are now contained on the vast San Pablos Reservation. Feared and shunned by fellow Apaches, the San Pablos tribe are reputed to be the fiercest fighters in the Southwest. And the daring reconnaissance by Captain Lawson indicated that their warlike mien has not been altered by well-meaning efforts to turn them to "the white man's way."

"Indians do not become white men and that is that," one soldier told this writer. "They will not stay on the reservation as long as they can wander on horse. They will not raise cattle as long as they can hunt. They will not farm as long as they can forage. They will not keep peace as long as they can kill. War is the Apache way."

Wandering freely, striking and vanishing, even the tiniest band of hostiles can paralyze an area the size of New England. The Apache does not stand to fight his pursuers. Pitched battles are avoided. He attacks only when vastly superior, then scatters, and reunites in mountain fastnesses no white man has ever seen. And then, when weary of this bloody sport, he returns to his reservation, where he can eat government provisions, sleep under U.S. Army blankets, chuckle and negotiate and await the outbreak of another predatory season.

OUR FORCES IN ARIZONA

The 25th Cavalry has the unenviable assignment of patrolling the unmapped mountains and deserts of Apacheland. Scarcely two hundred Negroes, led by a handful of white officers, are positioned to withstand the force of an angry Apache nation. The "buffalo soldiers"—so called because of their bisonlike courage and stoical endurance of pain—are isolated and ill equipped. Their horses, some of them joke bitterly, have clear memories of Gettysburg and Bull Run. Black-powder single-shot Springfield rifles are even older. Uniforms, supplies, food, are all outdated, late-arriving, and in short supply. But what they lack in provisions, the Negro cavalrymen make up for in grit.

GALLANT LEADER

More than twenty years have passed since Henry Lawson became Indiana's youngest Medal of Honor winner. His heroism at Stone Mountain can be recited by a whole generation of Hoosier schoolboys. But Appomattox did not end Lawson's service. Since then he has fought a dozen obscure combats against elusive but nonetheless vicious adversaries. Small these wars may be, and little known, but they are opening up a nation.

Great in stature, short in speech, Lawson is impatient with textbook stratagems and blackboard feints and ploys. He maneuvers best in the field, where his tenacity has earned the respect of three races: his own, the one he leads, and the one he fights.

Make a man a hero? It was easy. With no competition on hand, no editor to double-check me, no audience of angry readers to criticize my work, I was free to take certain liberties which are either amusing or appalling, depending, I suppose, on whether one expects to find the truth in newspapers. To me, my first Lawson article is a masterpiece of precocious conjuring, particularly compared with the journal entries that follow. Most artists live through what is real, then write lies. But journalists write lies from the beginning. Then, sometimes, they live the truth. My journal . . .

JUNE 7, 1885

And so they came, Henry Lawson and his soldiers, came at the most absurdly romantic time, when pink and orange splashed the canyon walls and twilight crept over the parade ground, when crickets and owls claimed possession of the river. They came at the time when storybook soldiers always manage to return, riding through the evening cool toward home, where lanterns glow and food is cooking and lovers wait.

Everyone was waiting on the banks of the river. There were our local Indians, housebroken perhaps, but how did they view the cavalry's safe return? There were civilian loiterers, unidentifiable scruffy types. And to one side was a group of merry Mexican ladies. I guessed they were the buffalo soldiers' whores. Presto, Fort Monroe had become a community, full of life, strength, purpose. I sensed it in Lucy's riveted downriver stare, in the Negroes' dark-voiced muttering, in the whores' expectant chatter. I didn't envy them, each woman servicing a medium-

sized tribe of Africans in a single night, but, so far as I could tell, they regarded the prospect just as cheerfully as Lucy awaited her reunion with the heroic Lawson. And what, I wondered bitterly, would be the difference in their couplings? Watching, listening, who could tell?

They approached at a walk, two abreast, in a column a hundred yards long, and the only noise came from dogs and horses. The riders were silent. They were black. I'd known they were black, but there was something ominous and shocking about them just the same. Dusty and tired, their not very uniform uniforms in tatters—some were bare-chested—they were a menacing procession. Black soldiers, black American soldiers, and I could not look at them without wondering where it would end, and what dark powers had been unleashed. You didn't have to be a Southerner. An abolitionist would have wondered, too. Free was one thing, armed and free was something else. Could anyone know what was in their hearts?

Henry Lawson was near the end of the column, chatting with a raggedy little Indian scout. You wouldn't have thought that this was a man at the end of a trail, climaxing six weeks' absence from his new bride. No, he was bantering easily, as if he were somewhere in mid-journey, passing time as amiably as possible. Even after he spotted Lucy, after he smiled and waved, it was as if he'd glimpsed a comely piece of landscape, a passing attraction. He finished what he was saying, then trotted toward where Lucy stood. I stayed a few feet behind, not wishing to intrude.

Lawson wore a blue woolen shirt, sand-colored pants held up by suspenders, and scuffed boots. Atop his head was an incongruously merry straw hat, a Mexican sombrero. Dust was all over him, from the brow of his head to the corners of his eyes, all through his beard. I had to admit: six foot four, on horseback, he was awesome. Here was the man who had changed my life a few months ago, changed it without knowing me then or recognizing me now. And that, I guessed, was the essence of the man: he lived without regard for or knowledge of consequences. He scooped one person up, brushed another aside, all without calculation, without malice. Malice was for men like me.

"Hello, darling," he said to Lucy. He reached down and touched her head, ran his hand around to the back of her neck. "I'm back."

Lucy nodded, touched Lawson's arm, as if to cling to him. At that, he laughed a little and drew away. He seemed surprised to discover that a cigar had been lodged in the corner of his mouth throughout this tender moment. He took it out, examined it, and tossed it away.

"We could've gone chasing forever," I heard him say. "But I was out of smokes."

He winked at her. Maybe it was their private joke. Being out of cigars might mean missing home or needing Lucy's love. Then again, maybe it meant he was out of cigars.

Lawson galloped off to the parade ground and looked on as one of the other officers dismissed the men. The column disintegrated, officers greeting wives, soldiers leading horses, stowing guns and knapsacks. Wanting to give Lucy and Lawson their privacy, I found Koch. He was talking to Lieutenant Billy Presley, notebook in hand, like a waiter taking down an order.

"Routine reconnaissance," Presley resumed after we'd been introduced. His wife was on his arm, tugging impatiently. "No contacts."

"Nothing?"

"Saw Contreras wandering around. Said he was looking for lost cattle. Had a note from the agent, so there wasn't nothing we could do. You know."

"No action, then?"

"Naah. But they're ready to blow."

"Anybody special?"

"Contreras maybe. Lot of talk goin' round, Lobito says."

"How long you give it?"

"Be soon, I bet. Lobito thinks so."

"Okay," Koch said. "I'll write it up."

Presley was led off by his wife, who was full of tales of round-the-clock combat with insects, heat, menacing blacks, bad meat. Presley nodded wearily and permitted himself to be ushered, like a man condemned, to his nuptial couch.

I watched the parade ground empty. Soon I had it to myself. Horses to field, officers to ladies, men to whores, and myself unclaimed. Well, I could stand that. But being hungry was another matter.

Treading firmly on the steps up to the Lawson porch, and

vigorously clearing my throat, I knocked on the door I'd accustomed myself to opening as I pleased.

No response.

Another knock. I glanced in the window. They were not in the front room.

I sat down on the bench, feeling more alone than ever, and a good deal hungrier. At last, Koch came walking across the parade ground. Living alone, he rarely cooked. A connoisseur of beans, he took his meals among the blacks. The cigar he chewed on as he greeted me was enviably postprandial.

"What are you doing out here in the dark?"

"Just sitting."

"Where are they?"

I gestured over my shoulder.

"Forgotten all about you?"

I nodded.

"Can't blame them." He sat down beside me. He liked to keep company, this odd bandy-legged, paper-shuffling, tobacco-smelling little solitaire.

"Smoke?" he asked.

"No, thanks. I . . . uh . . . haven't eaten yet."

"You better come with me," Koch said.

I didn't know where he was taking me. To the Mexican brothel on wheels, I hoped.

"No army's any different," Koch said. "Charlemagne and Roland and El Cid. Back to the Crusades, I'll bet. Maybe they were headed for the Holy Land. Maybe they wanted to die for Jerusalem. But I'll bet my last dollar there was a pussy wagon in tow."

"What do you do, Koch?"

"I'm no different . . ."

"But you're . . ."

"What? White? An officer? Better? Smarter?"

"Then you . . ."

"I cut the ribbon on the whorehouse. And every one of them buffs who tups tonight, I get a dime. And the dimes add up. About one every ten minutes . . ."

"You rake off . . ."

"A lot of dimes. Which go into a camp fund. For baseball

bats. Beer from Tucson. The Christmas party. Mrs. Presley. The candles she puts on her tree, the presents underneath—sewing kits, shaving soap, pomade . . . they're earning them tonight . . ."

By now I saw we were headed for the Negro tents. Resting, shaving, washing, the black men who hadn't seen me before regarded me with surprise. We paused before four of them who were on their haunches around a campfire.

"Where's Eccles at?" Koch inquired.

"He be here. Pouring off some water."

"Eccles goin' to the wagon?"

"Not him."

"What's he saving it for?"

They laughed at that. Four black men, relaxed but cautious. They didn't rush to introduce themselves, yet I didn't think they minded my being there. And they obviously got along with Koch.

"What about you men?" Koch asked.

"We ain't saving nothin'."

"It's in a good cause," Koch reminded them. "Christmas party. Got to put something in the stocking."

"Oh yeah."

"We puttin' it in . . ."

"Believe in a full stocking."

"Favorite charity. Fixin' to donate a couple times, after coffee."

"That's the spirit," Koch said. "Give all you can. Give till it hurts."

"Yessir. Till then."

The lines had been rehearsed, the laughs were all on cue. But it was an act they'd performed before and by now they'd settled comfortably into their lines.

"Whoremongering again, Koch?" I saw a yellowish black man, gaunt and wiry, with a refined scholarly face. He wore wire-rimmed glasses, the first I'd seen on a black man. I suppose I'd thought that this only recently and irregularly literate race hadn't to contend with poor eyesight.

"I brought a guest," Koch said. "His name's Edwin Morrison. Out of New York City."

Eccles stepped around to our side of the fire and extended a hand.

"Benjamin Franklin Eccles," he said, shaking my hand. "You're a long way from New York, mister."

There was a directness in Eccles that the others didn't have. They were careful—whether from military training or slave-race caution, I couldn't say. Nothing was by chance. But Eccles looked at me the way I looked at people I interviewed.

"He hasn't eaten," Koch said.

"Sit down, then," he said. "You too, Koch."

"I ate already."

"That doesn't stop you from sitting."

"All right."

"It's ready," Eccles said after tasting a spoonful of stew. "I'll get a plate for the New Yorker."

While Eccles stepped into the tent, the other four soldiers introduced themselves: Junius from Nashville, Aaron from Mobile, Wilson from Cleveland, and—a long-standing joke—Cleveland from Toledo.

"I'm from Baltimore," Eccles volunteered as he double-wiped the knife and fork he handed me. "Which is why I know how to cook. My father cooks on the railroad."

"Cooking isn't all he does," Koch added. "Eccles here is a writer. Best in the Territory."

"Against no competition at all," Eccles said.

"Till now," Koch gleefully announced. "Morrison here is a correspondent of the New York Sun. Full time, paid for, and bona fide!"

That shook Eccles. He'd been spooning some stew onto a plate and, for a fraction of a second, he stopped dead. He shot me a glance which went deep, as if Koch had announced I was a Confederate.

"Start in now," he said, handing me a plate.

"Morrison's going to do a bunch of write-ups from down here . . ." Koch continued. "Make us all famous."

"Famous for what?" asked one of the others.

"Openin' up the frontier," Koch said. "Chasing Indians."

"Catchin' Indians?"

"That, too. If you can."

"How long are you staying?" Eccles asked.

"Till you go out again," I answered. Another writer in camp bothered him somehow. "What kind of writing do you do, Mr. Eccles?"

"It's nothing much," he replied defensively, stirring the stew. "I write letters about where I am and the things I see. What happens to me and my friends. And how I feel about them. That's all."

"And where do these letters go? Are they published somewhere?"

"Yeah," he said.

"Where might that be?"

"Newspaper in Baltimore."

"That must be the Baltimore Sun," I said.

"No. Not the Sun. I tried them. But I send my letters to the Sentinel."

"The Sentinel? The Baltimore Sentinel? I don't believe I ever . . ."

"It's a newspaper for colored people."

"I see."

"They don't pay me anything," he added. He minimized his writing. And yet, I have been on too many stories with other reporters to miss the resentment.

"It would be a pleasure to look over some of your articles, if you have them," I said.

"Yeah, why not let him have a look-see," Koch prodded. "Morrison here, I'll bet he'd be glad to share some tricks of the trade."

"No, no," I interjected, "I'd be the one who'd be learning."

"I'll look around," Eccles answered without enthusiasm.

Over coffee, Koch led the group through some well-rehearsed jocularity about Gonzáles' whores, Mrs. Presley's wardrobe, and prospects for an upcoming post baseball game. White officers were to be pitted against buffalo soldiers. That was the idea, but there was a built-in shortage of whites and some blacks would have to cross the color line. They debated whether it should be Fowler, who looked white, or Artis, who was half Irish, or Eccles, who thought white, or "Dukie" Duquesne, who was neither black nor white but animal.

·IV·

JOHN "Dukie" DUQUESNE

Interview at Veterans Memorial Hospital, Jefferson, Missouri, December 7, 1928.

DUQUESNE: I was the camp devil. I got locked up, tied up, dressed down, busted down, knocked down. I can't count the times I made corporal. Old man Koch, he used to say fighting Indians was just an excuse for keeping Dukie away from decent folks . . .

E.M.: And yet . . . you were friends . . . you and Lawson . . .

DUQUESNE: We were two of a kind. That's the whole thing. Two of a damned kind. We both knew it, from the first time we met. Somethin' in my eyes was sayin', I'm gonna give you hell, man, I'm gonna take you to the wall, I'm gonna leave marks on you, and his eyes answerin', well, let's don't stand on ceremony, let's get on with it. The time and the place. Name your poison. Choose your weapons. Like he'd been waiting for me to come along.

E.M.: You're saying there was some kind of a fight?

DUQUESNE: Happened after we raised hell in a Tucson cathouse. Boss rode in and got us out of jail. But when we got back to the fort and stood down, he calls me out, real nonchalant. We walk down the river, him and me, a mile or so. He was whistling while he walked. "All right," he says, looking around. "This will do." I turn and see he's pointing his revolver at me. "Take off your shirt, your pants, your boots." Now, I don't mind tellin' you I was scared. I stripped and piled my clothes on a log. "I know just what you're thinkin', you son of a bitch," he says. "You're thinkin', maybe he shoots me once, maybe he shoots me twice, but so help me God, if I get my hands on him, he's dead. Am I right?" I nodded. He was right. His balls would've been like egg yolks. I'd've held on to his throat till his face turned black as mine. "You're not so hard to figure, Dukie," he says. "Neither am I." Then—you know what?—he slips back his suspenders, unbuttons his shirt, stacks his clothes next to mine, puts his revolver on top, and walks over to me, so our chests is touchin'. "Okay, Dukie. No guns. No uniforms. No rank. You, me, and the stars." I still wasn't sure. "I want this real bad," he says, and it seemed like there was something burning in his eyes. "Just as much as you do, Dukie. I'm aching for it. I can't wait." I guess he couldn't. He no sooner finished than he lifts his knees right up into my balls, not the worst shot I ever took, but enough to drop me onto my knees, fold me over, knock my breath away. "That's so you can say I started it," he says, stepping back. I guess he thought I'd wait awhile, collect myself, stand up, and march toward him, holdin' out my fists like a proper boxer. Well, it was my turn to surprise him. I didn't care about waitin' for the pain to go away, I wanted to spread it around some. That's how I am when I get hurt. I jumped off my knees, landed my head in his stomach, knocking him backward. Now we were even. The both of us caught our breath, got to our feet, and he walks toward me, smiling, saying, "Damn, Dukie, that was very . . ." And slugs me with a haymaker right I should've picked off, if I hadn't been waiting for the last word of his sentence, which was ". . . impressive." After that, we went at it pretty good. If you'd seen it, you'd've thought it was strange, because we fought like dogs, do, say, or roosters. I mean, we'd knock hell out of each other for a while, then we'd break off, walk around in circles, talking and preening, before we crashed together again. Oh my, what a pair we was. So long ago. Oh my . . .

E.M.: Who won?

DUQUESNE: Well, at the end, we was on the ground, legs tangled together, rolling over, first him on top and then me, and our hands were locked and what I did was bang him on the head with my head, which hurt me as much as it hurt him. You know how that feels. Well, he ups and does the same thing to me, and he ain't too pleased about it neither. Then I repeated and he repeated, another miserable exchange. Finally, I'm about to bang him again when he starts laughing, kind of a giggle almost, like a kid, and I see that it's kind of comical, so I laugh, too. We're both laughing, hugging. We pull each other up and walk over to the river, flop into the water. Like a pair of kids . . .

E.M.: After that . . .
DUQUESNE: After we lay in the water awhile, he says, "Dukie, stick with me, and you'll get a fair shake. I promise. Do it my way. We'll cover some ground. Have some fun." And me—though I could hardly believe it was me talking—I say sure. From then on, I was with him all the way. Beginning to end. I feel guilty . . . about . . . about him being dead so long already.

• V •

ARIZONA JOURNAL

JUNE 9, 1885

Let the record reflect: The night of Lawson's homecoming I slept on a cot in Koch's office. I made sure it was well after sunrise before I walked up to Officers' Row. Lucy was on the porch waiting for me.

"I was in the camp last night," I volunteered. "We got to talking . . ."

She nodded—we both decided to leave her abandonment of me at that—and motioned me inside.

Lawson was sitting at the dining table, wearing only his pants. Suspenders were over his bare chest, inadequate to cover scratches from the campaign trail, as well as a bruise or two more recently obtained from Lucy.

"Put your shirt on, Henry," Lucy commanded, "and say a proper hello to Edwin here."

He got out of the chair as ordered and shook my hand heartily enough.

"Hello there, Edwin. Glad you made it out okay."

"Glad to be here," I returned.

"Everybody treated you all right?"

"Just fine, thank you."

"Well," he said, "that's good." He pulled down his suspenders, slipped a shirt over his chest, and hoisted his suspenders back up. Nothing was tucked in, nothing buttoned, and he was still barefoot.

"How about an eye-opener?" he asked.

"A what?"

"You look like you could use one." And with a lewdly affectionate glance at his wife: "I sure as hell could."

"Is it a drink?"

"Yes, sir."

"So early?"

"Early's when you drink an eye-opener," he countered with a wink. He then assembled a kind of cocktail consisting of whiskey, water, bitters, and sugar, which—since I declined—he swallowed at once.

"Well, well, well," he commented, pausing as if we'd already spoken for hours, exhausting every possible topic. "I guess we'll be having breakfast before long. You'll breakfast with us?"

"Yes. Lucy . . ."

"Good," he said. "We'll have time to talk some more."

He stepped outside to the front porch, greeted a pack of dogs, put his feet up on the railing, and commenced to whistle. Taken at face value, nothing he'd said ought to have made me feel uncomfortable. But there was an undercurrent of hostility, I am sure of that. His invitation to breakfast, for instance. Until last night, I'd taken every meal at his house. I'd taken those meals for granted, and so, I'm sure, had Lucy. Now he'd made clear that he was the one who did the asking, one meal at a time. And happy as he sounded to "talk some more," he made it sound like the sole purpose of my visit was to have a conversation. When the talk was over, which wouldn't take long, the visit would end.

Lucy came in from the back room, carrying plates and cups, and found me standing alone, indecisive.

"Can I help you, Lucy?"

"Edwin," she said louder than necessary, "do please keep my husband company while I prepare the table."

That left no choice. I went outside and sat beside him. He moved aside, like a grudging passenger on a streetcar. Apart from that, he didn't acknowledge me.

"Nice morning," I said.

"Not bad."

That was that. I decided two could play the same game. I wouldn't break the silence. Behind us, I could hear Lucy setting the table. The plates and silverware landed hard.

"So how's things in Milton?" Lawson finally asked.

"I don't know. I'm a New Yorker now."

"You ain't been back?"

"There's no reason to go."

"Say that again."

"You were back for your father's funeral, Lucy tells me."

"Yeah." It seemed I had angered him. "The old soak got drunk in town and fell asleep in his wagon, which was shrewdly parked on a railroad crossing. He caught the train all right. Closed casket . . ."

He broke off, chewing on some emotion which he hadn't quite swallowed, and then Lucy summoned us to the table.

"Do you remember our Sunday breakfasts?" Lucy asked with a cheerfulness that seemed forced.

"They went on for hours," I said, turning to include Lawson. "We talked, we joked. There were stories. Reports. Even quizzes."

"Henry, there was a metal roof on the house," Lucy said. "And as the sun warmed it, it would expand. It would crack and groan. At night it would make the same sorts of noises as it cooled and contracted. Now, my father always said the night sounds were different from the morning sounds. He insisted he could tell the difference. And I wanted to test him, but all my tests involved keeping him locked in the cellar! For thirty-six hours!"

"Yeah . . . well . . . so," Lawson responded, determined to be gloomy. "My house it was 'them as eats the fastest gets the mostest.' That was our daily grace. Sit together? Talk? Hell, we went to the kitchen when we were hungry and took what we could find. We didn't dine. We foraged."

With that, Lawson sank—or should I say plunged!—into a doleful silence, while Lucy and I persevered as cheerfully as we could. Lawson's plate was empty in no time. While we were still pouring coffee, he sat like a child anxious to be excused or, to be more accurate, like a host eager for company to leave so his house would be his own again.

"Find out what you wanted yet? For your write-up?" he finally asked.

"It's not a question of finding out," I explained. "It's not questions and answers. It's a matter of seeing things. Of being here."

"Oh."

"I hope you don't mind."

"It's up to you, I guess," Lawson said, sounding as if he wished it were up to him. With that not very cordial exchange our meal ended. Lawson retired to the back room, from which he soon emerged, boots on and shirt tucked in.

"Where's my hairbrush?" he asked Lucy.

"You had it," she said.

"I don't have it now. If I did, I wouldn't be asking." He stamped around the room, lifting chairs, yanking back the curtain, looking in all the wrong places, probably on purpose, till Lucy couldn't bear it anymore.

"Oh, Henry!" Lucy pushed herself back from the table, disappeared into the bedroom, and came out immediately with the hairbrush. Lawson took it without comment and was gone.

JULY 1, 1885

I have been as unobtrusive and undemanding as possible. Often, I take my meals among the Negroes. At night, I creep into bed quietly and late, leave early. When Lawson and I meet, I go out of my way not to give offense. All in vain, because my very presence here offends him. I can see him flinch whenever he comes upon me. It's all he can do to nod and say good morning. Lucy persists in hoping for a change. But any reasonable hope died yesterday.

I had gone to look up Koch for a second cup of coffee, as I usually do around the middle of the morning. Entering, I found I had intruded upon some sort of conference. The white officers were there, and the black noncoms, and my grudging host.

"Well, well, the press has us cornered now," Lawson called

out. Koch disagrees, but it sounded sarcastic to me. I backed off, but Lawson would have none of it.

"No, please, Morrison, come on in. There's no secrets in this group. Here, take my chair. I insist."

He pushed me into his seat at the head of the table. He straightened out the papers, acting like a dutiful secretary.

"Does everyone here know Eddie Morrison?" he asked. "Better get on the right side of him because Eddie here spells double trouble. Number one is he's family. Well, not family, but friend of family. Friend-in-law. And number two is that he's with the New York Sun. So there. You fellows better watch yourself around this lad. He's poison."

He leaned over me, the ape, and hung an arm around my shoulder, simulating friendship. I could smell the whiskey on his breath.

"You know everybody here, Eddie?"

I nodded but there was no stopping him.

"But you haven't been properly introduced. Polite society, my wife tells me, it's not just names and handshakes, hell, what good is that? No, sir, what you do is tell each person something about the other person. That way, if you drop dead all of a sudden, they have something besides you to talk about. So, let's see . . ."

I checked the table. Everyone was embarrassed. But I wasn't sure if they blamed me or Lawson for what was happening. Surely he was the instigator. But the whole thing wouldn't have happened if I were not there.

"Start with Lieutenant Van Doren. Used to be a Quaker. Doesn't like to fight unless he's had a chance to talk with the enemy first."

I'd met Van Doren. An affable, dreamy fellow whose commitment to black troops was an expression of ideals. The butt of Lawson's elephantine joking, he looked at me as if this were all my fault.

"Then there's Buddy Conaway." He glanced at the pudgy Alabaman, whom sex and food constantly preoccupied. He loved to boast about what his plain, pale, mute wife and he had accomplished in the kitchen or in bed. He was shameless in his talking. His idea of a lovely time, he said was "to fuck and fry bacon." Right now, he was picking at some skin that was peeling off his forearm, scrutinizing each patch to see if he would discard or chew on what he molted.

"Buddy's got this attachment to lost causes. The Confederacy was one. Now there's us. We're thinking about loaning him to the Apaches, if they'd have him."

Conaway feigned a salute.

"Then we got old Billy Presley. The head-scratchin', shit-kickin', slow-talkin' pride of Tennessee. Don't ask him where he was during the war, 'cause up in those hills it was over before they heard about it."

At least they could have a laugh on Presley, a lean, sardonic mountaineer who greeted every mishap with a "That's wonderful!" or "Ain't we lucky this morning." He'd have clowned his way through the Book of Job.

"Lefty Diller, camp brewmaster. If it lives, it dies. If it dies, it rots. If it rots, it ferments. If it ferments, you can drink it. If you can't drink it, he will. And Paul Koch, in charge of protocol and perjury."

He turned to the blacks. "Lewis Fowler. Benjamin Franklin Eccles. In an honest army, they'd be generals. In a real war, they'd shine. But when you fight a half-assed war with nobody watching—almost nobody—it's another story. So there you have it, Eddie. You have the floor. Shoot."

He was so ignorant! I would never interview officers en masse, and I would never interview anyone without preparation. I was very careful that way, planning things out, first question to last.

"What's the matter, Eddie? You got all this wisdom sitting in front of you. A command performance!"

"This isn't how I . . ."

"Thought you wanted to know how we do it in Arizona. War on the frontier! Red Indians! How we find 'em, how we chase 'em, how we run 'em to earth and bag 'em! Aren't you working today?"

"I'm working every day," I responded, struggling to keep my temper. "I keep my eyes open. I watch and I listen."

" 'I watch and I listen.' Don't you ever do nothin' yourself? You spend your whole life keepin' track of other folks' affairs?"

"I guess that's all the business for today," Koch interrupted. The meeting dissolved, Lawson leaving ahead of the rest. Eccles was the only one who lingered.

"You have a harder job than I thought you did, Mr. Morrison," he said.

I granted that.

·VI·

Paul W. Koch
Indian Hot Springs
Helenville, California
September 17, 1928

Dear Morrison,

About that baseball game. Do I remember?! Hell, until a few years ago I could've dug up the scorecard. I know I saved it. I saved everything. Eccles' newspaper columns, Lucy's Christmas cards, Herman Biddle's prescription for arthritis. Now I don't have anything that won't fit into a coffin. Just memories. They'll fit.

Okay. Play ball. The first thing is we weren't kidding about it. See, other outfits could go into town for fun. Or, often, they'd invite the local gentry out to see a parade or hear a military band. Well, that was out. Sometimes we sang for the ladies. "Annie Laurie," "After the Ball," "The Girl I Left Behind Me." No lie, some evenings still, I don't know whether it's the light slanting at a certain angle, or the time of year, or what I ate for supper, anyway, something inside me kicks off, and I can sit and hear them, all those dead voices in their evening serenade. It's a long ways for voices to carry.

But singing wasn't enough to keep our bunch occupied, those long weeks we were waiting for the Apaches to make a run for it. Baseball was just the ticket. And we had a hundred and a half horny black horseback riders to choose from. Sometimes Van Doren—he was the umpire—told us to relax, take it easy. We were playing for fun, he reminded us. And we reminded him back, winning was more fun than losing.

Koch remembers. So do I. Picture an outpost in a canyon with no name, and a dusty bare-earth parade ground with tents and adobe houses all around it, horses picketed beyond latrines. Now, the spectators: a hundred black soldiers, a handful of white women, and the usual clutter of hangers-on and passers-through, Indians and Mexicans who might not understand balls and strikes, but could sniff humiliation. Perhaps if Lawson and the other officers had presided from the sidelines, it would have been a less intense contest, an all-black kind of thing, where you admired athletic stunts and speed but didn't bother about the final score. But he was in it, so it was a war . . .

> Lawson's team was the home team. I don't remember all the positions, but I'm sure the Boss played first, Diller, Conaway, and Presley made up the infield, and the catcher was Harry Church. Outfield had to have Duquesne in center. And for sure the pitcher was Birmingham Mack. He was one of the nicest fellows we had, one of your Bible-reading type of blacks, teetotaler. He ran to fat, that special way black people do, with his ass looking like somebody pumped air into it and the air was rising, and a gut spilling pork and beans all over his belt. But, boy, did he throw smoke!

All the others played in uniform. My pants were part of a three-piece suit, herringbone, my shoes were made for sidewalks, and—though a pen had leaked ink over my heart—the shirt was one I had worn to the office. The first time I delivered a pitch, my pipe dropped onto the ground. Oh, I was comical.

> Every other team, a guy like Dukie would be batting cleanup, knocking in runners. Putting Dukie first was Lawson's way of saying he didn't care a hoot about finesse. He was out to club you to death from the opening bell. So there stood Dukie. I remember turning to Lobito—Lawson's guide, he never missed a game—and said, "Watch Dukie tear a new asshole in that little guy."
>
> And then, your first pitch. Dukie hadn't seen anything like it. Where did you learn to throw that junk, those slow, nibbly, dipsy-doodly butterfly balls? Hell, sitting in a

wheelchair, I could still whip it in twice as fast as you did.
Dukie laughed and laughed, just ignored the first two strikes. Then he got serious. In comes your pitch. Dukie swings a mighty swing, and plop, your ball lands right on home plate, like a turd dropped from some low-flying bird, and the whole place erupts.

Lawson ragged each of my victims as they returned from their frustrations, suggesting they trade their bats for butterfly nets. But that didn't make him any less formidable when he came to bat at the end of the third inning. The crowd hushed as Lawson dug in. He nodded at me. He even grinned as if to say, nice job, better than expected, but now it's over.

Lawson crowded the plate. His bat could reach all the little edges and corners of the strike zone. I did what was necessary. My first pitch, faster than usual, I aimed at his head.

Falling backward just in time, he hit the dust, dropping the bat, but not before the ball ticked the edge of his bat, lofted softly into the air, and into Eccles' glove, for a totally accidental out. I'm sure no one had ever thrown at Captain Henry Lawson. But he sat in the dirt and laughed and the others joined him. He got up, brushed himself off, and gave me a little mocking bow, which added to the spectators' amusement.

By the fourth inning, the game began in earnest. And I discovered that I was part of a team. It's not a feeling I've had often, living and working by myself all these years. I can't remember all their names, those sons of slaves, but I saw them snatch home runs out of space and turn bullets into double plays, and whenever I faltered someone trotted in to say, "Let 'em hit it, Mr. Morrison, us niggers'll catch it." They usually did.

"How you feeling?" Eccles asked before the last half inning began. We were one run ahead.

"Let's see how it goes."

"You'd be leaving with a lead. We come out ahead, you're the winning pitcher. We lose, it's on me."

"I know, but . . ."

"Anyway, what's the difference between eight and nine?" he asked, reaching to take the ball out of my glove.

"One inning," I answered. I kept the ball.

> Well, God dropped all his other projects and you were able to get past Buddy Conaway. What was it? Six balls he fouled off before you got a third strike past him. But Lefty Diller jumped all over your first pitch with a shot that got to centerfield so fast he didn't have a chance to try for second. Birmingham Mack was the next up and I figured all old Mack had to do was avoid the double play, because Presley, Lawson, and Duquesne were next and you didn't stand a chance of getting past them in one piece. Old Mack knew he couldn't run fast enough to beat out a double play, not with them thin darky legs and that pork-choppy body of his. He took the cue from Lawson, swung at three balls, missed every one of 'em, bowed to the crowd, and made way for the heavy lumber. Presley, Lawson, and Duquesne: it sure as hell wasn't a law firm!

Presley, the rangy, rawboned hillbilly, was delighted it fell to him to deliver the crushing blow. He ignored my first two pitches, slow wobblers that he could have smashed, but there was always the risk of lofting a harmless fly ball. No, he wanted me to come in fast. I did not. What speed was left in my arm, I was saving for Lawson. When Presley saw yet another slow ball floating toward him, he looked disgusted, like a child who unwraps a Christmas present and finds a toothbrush. He swatted the ball down the right-field line, a double. Now Diller, the tying run, stood at third, Presley was at second, halfway home, and Henry Lawson was at bat.

"Call in the dogs, piss on the fire, and let's go home," Dukie shouted. "Now we gonna see who's boss!"

And then Dukie had his triumph of wit. Inside that evil ebony head a joke was born. He folded over in a paroxysm of laughter, hardly able to deliver the newborn humor. The game came to a stop while all eyes focused on him.

"EdWIN is gonna EdLOSE! EdWIN is gonna EdLOSE!"

He danced up and down the foul lines, jigged in front of the crowd, exhorted them to join his cheerleading. Some remained silent, but when the black monster stood right before them, staring and waving his arms, there was no denying him. So, under pressure, the cheering mounted: "EdWIN is gonna EdLOSE!"

Your first pitch was a honey. You took an extra step off the rubber, cross-fire style, and sidearmed a strike. Second time you come in slow with a cow-pie pitch, but the Boss jumped on it and hit about the longest shot I ever saw. Four hundred feet and still rising when I saw the last of it. And funny, even though it was foul, that blast took the heart out of you, it seemed. You stood there, holding the new ball, kind of juggling it in your palm, walking on and off the mound, and Dukie said you were stalling, waiting for dark. I suspected he was right.

Eccles hustled out and talked to you. But it was no good. Your next pitch fell six feet in front of home plate, ball one. The next one, Eccles had to jump a yard off the ground to catch, ball two. The third was even worse, it went behind the Boss, ball three. Eccles shook his head, disgusted, stood up, and signaled for an intentional ball four.

"Just lob it over here," Eccles shouted, "and I'll pitch to Dukie. That's final!"

"Well, okay," you said, "if that's what you want."

Dukie was bouncing up and down, pleased as punch to be coming up with the bases loaded. Lawson looked over and laughed at his clowning. You wound up. Eccles stuck his glove way out of the strike zone. Then he scooted back into a crouch. And before Lawson could move, you whipped a bona fide fast ball into his glove.

It couldn't have lasted more than a second but there was a silence that seemed to go on forever and it only ended when our Quaker umpire, Van Doren, said, "Strike three. You're out, sir."

Yours truly,
Paul W. Koch

Bat in hand, Henry Lawson came striding out toward the pitcher's mound, and our victory celebration suddenly died.

"I want to talk to you," he said. He didn't need to add: alone. My teammates vanished. He led me off, and no one followed.

There were water tanks and shower stalls out behind Officers' Row, but usually the men at Fort Monroe went down to the river, which, shallow though it was, had some waist-deep pools. Lawson's was the farthest upstream. We passed some other bathers—enormous muscular figures bobbing in and out of the water, lying naked on banks, squatting, like man just emerged from primeval seas. Nods. Splashes. Salutations. Smell of cook fires. It felt like a small town, a place where people knew me and I knew them. They called out to us as we passed, laughing about the game, splashing water on each other, joking among themselves. It was all so boyish and so innocent. It was . . . if I could put it in a word, a boyish word . . . it was fun, the sort of fun men leave behind when they grow up and move on to other things. Not here. Here they were staying young forever, so long as Lawson was the Boss.

I had thrown a baseball at his head. I had tricked and humiliated him in front of his troops and I had helped defeat his team. And his response was to throw his arm around my shoulder and treat me like a long-lost friend. It was beyond understanding. But it was good to know that, for whatever reason, he didn't hate me anymore.

Lawson's pool wasn't much larger than a bathtub, but the water was wonderfully cool. We stripped off our clothes, lowered ourselves onto the sand-and-pebble bottom, soaked and drank and tilted our faces toward the reddening sky.

"This is the life," he said. "I'll remember this."

And then, with no prompting from me, he continued. "It's funny, the things you remember. In the war, I saw it all. Every kind of wound. Put your finger anyplace on your body. Anyplace. I guarantee you, I've seen that place when it's been shot up or shot off, stabbed or clubbed, bleeding or starting in to rot. I haven't forgotten any of it. Can't. But there's a difference between what you can't forget and what you remember. One week in autumn we bivouacked in some apple orchards in the Shenandoah. It was like chilled cider, breathing the air. And a time in Tennessee, in bluegrass, just when things were coming up green, you could smell the earth, it gave you strength just standing on it. And down in Georgia, right after we took Atlanta, the first time I saw an ocean! I got a horse and rode along the beach for miles, right where the waves come in. You know what? I didn't know you could do that. I didn't think it was possible. Oh, that was something!"

I waited for him to go on. I could have listened for hours.

For the first time, I saw the man that Lucy had fallen in love with. I could see how she would respond to stories like this. Even if they were only moments, she would want to share them.

"Lucy told me about New York last night," Lawson suddenly announced.

"About . . ." A desperate hope: about Brooklyn Bridge, the Cloisters, Delmonico's.

"By God, she really served it up on a platter, didn't she?"

There was absolutely nothing for me to say.

"I'd've kept after her if I was you," he said. "I'd've never let go. You did. Didn't you?"

"I did," I said, feeling as if I'd pronounced a sentence on myself.

"Now she's mine. And I'm keeping her. I guess you figured that one out, too."

"Yes."

"But what she told me . . . last night, she said there's love and there's love . . . there's some feeling for you she's not about to bury . . . she was asking, hoping, I'd try to share some of that feeling. I said I'd try."

He paused, reached out for a pair of cigars in his shirt and some matches. We lit up and leaned back, enjoying ourselves immensely.

"Those niggers downstream are all the family I've got. All I really want. But there's no reason you or Lucy should be the victim of that. It's just me . . . I worried about you."

"Why?"

"I kept hearing about how much I need you. I didn't even know you. What did I need? But Lucy thinks I need a journalist pushing me to reach the top."

"Do you believe that?"

"She does. As for me . . . what I want . . . what I want is what I got . . . I want to keep her . . ."

He lifted his arm out of the water and offered his hand. We shook.

"I guess we're in this together," he said. "Might as well be friends."

"Might as well," I said.

·VII·

ARIZONA JOURNAL

JULY 5, 1885

I must be the luckiest man alive. It's all coming together . . . Lawson, Lucy, the buffalo soldiers, and now, just in the nick of time, a war! It happened like this:

We were sitting out after supper. Suddenly Lawson tensed, glanced at Koch, stared across the parade ground. I saw two men coming, one Duquesne, the other Santos. (Lobito Santos, or Santos Lobito, I don't know; Lobito means little wolf.)

Lawson stood up to receive them. "Well?"

Santos came closer, nodded to us, bowed to Lucy. The report he gave was accompanied by a disturbing, incongruous smile.

"San Pablos. Hall dead. Mrs. Hall. The kids."

Santos had a boy's voice, high-pitched, erratic, nearly comical.

"What happened?" Lawson asked. "How'd they die?"

"Bad, boss. Real bad. You gonna see."

"Who did it? Contreras?"

"Yes. Him and . . . maybe sixty others. And . . . uh . . ."

"What?"

"They got this crazy man with them. This kind of magic man. His name, they call him, the Singer."

"The Singer?"

"Boss, he's making magic for them."

Twenty minutes later, all of us were sitting in Koch's office. There was a special feeling in the room. Part dread, I think. Part some sort of martial challenge. And part of it a delicious yearning tension, almost sexual. It had something to do with death. Not the deaths that Lobito waited to relate. It pertained to deaths to come. Our own, perhaps.

"Okay, Santos," Lawson began. "I want you to tell what happened."

"Lieutenant Koch here, he is giving me some mail for Agent Hall," Santos said. Koch later explained that Hall had a religious

streak: "He was always receiving boxes and boxes of Bible stories. I had to see this stuff got over to the reservation because the Apaches got very restless when they were running low on religious literature."

"What did you see at the reservation?" Lawson pressed.

"What kind of garden it is, you can't eat nothin' from that garden. What you call that kind, Boss?"

"A flower garden," Van Doren interjected. "Roses."

"Yes! They was in the garden."

"Roses?"

"No. The Halls. Now, Mr. Hall, they tied him to this . . . this where you make the water come out of the ground . . ."

"Pump," Lawson said.

"And they make a fire around him and they . . ."

"What about Mrs. Hall?" Lawson interrupted.

Santos faltered. I suppose he was let down at not being able to tell the whole story. He told me later, and it was his kind of comedy. Picture Hall, tied to the pump, wood and straw crackling into flames, howling when he started to feel the heat. Santos was impressed by Hall's screams, and if I'd asked him how he came to be in earshot of all this, he'd have laughed and said he heard it from a cousin. I gather he had lots of cousins. But the really comic part was when the dying agent groped for the pump handle and pulled it up and down. Santos—or his cousin—said it looked like he was masturbating. At last some water came, splashing onto the chest of a man whose legs were burning. Screaming and steaming, Hall died.

"Mrs. Hall?" Lawson asked.

"She dead, too."

"Did they rape her?" Billy Presley asked.

Santos wasn't sure what rape meant.

"A rape is when a man forces a woman to let him take his pleasure with her," Van Doren offered. He spoke slowly, carefully pronouncing every syllable, but Santos only shrugged.

"A rape is . . ." Lawson gave up. "Oh, hell, tell him, Dukie."

Duquesne stepped forward and punched Santos on the shoulder. Pay attention to this! And he proceeded to stick the middle finger of his right hand in and out of a tunnel formed by the bent fingers of his left hand.

Santos nodded. "Oh yeah, Boss. You bet they do that thing."

"And the children?" asked Van Doren.

"Ah, them little kids . . ." Santos was rolling now, but Lawson had heard enough.

"The kids are dead, right?"

Santos nodded.

"Who's the boss man? The number one?"

"Maybe Contreras."

"Contreras broke off the reservation before, and we brought him back before. He never killed the agent. We catch him now, he gets sent to Florida. The whole tribe goes."

"I try to tell you, Boss," Santos said. "They got this . . . this Singer fella. He been away for years, Boss. I don't know where all. People say in the desert. Others say across the water. Some say . . . the sky."

"The sky? Up in the sky?"

"What they say."

"So he came back from . . . from wherever he went. What did he do?"

"The Singer call people together at night," Santos said, his voice at a whisper. "He sits in front. He don't move. He don't say nothin'. Long time. Then he sing. But it ain't him singing. Other voice. Lot of different kind, maybe animal, maybe gods. Voices of the dead, they say."

"And the voices . . ." Lawson was like a father, hearing out his child's ghost story.

"They say now is time to chase the white man out of our land. The white man and everything he bring. His tools, his clothes, his everything. All got to go. And then, the dead wake up. Animal come back to land. Nobody be hungry, nobody be hurting, nobody be sick. Everything be like it was before . . . before you."

Lawson nodded. You could say he was just trying to encourage Santos, nodding like that, but I swear there was more to it. More than yes, go ahead. More, even, than yes, I understand. He'd never admit it, but a part of Henry Lawson savors the world that Santos was describing.

"A hundred little fights we've had so far," Lawson said. "A hundred chases. Sometimes we find 'em. Sometimes we don't. But we're still here."

"The Singer don't care, Boss. He don't care what you got, what you try. You not able to touch his people. Not with bullet. Because this time, they got magic. They got voices. Dead and living coming together to beat you. The animal and the god. They all against you now. They don't want you round here."

When Santos was gone, Van Doren said the Apaches had finally gone over the edge, a military situation had taken on irrational overtones. Diller said he'd heard of Great Plains warrior-priests taking control of hemmed-in tribes for one last charge. Conaway said it was all a crock of shit, what kind of priests tied up people and burned them? Koch said that's what priests were famous for, which earned him a dirty look from Conaway. Lawson asked what Eccles thought. Eccles said it was going to be rougher than usual out there. Lawson agreed.

·VIII·

My Arizona journal ended when we rode off toward San Pablos. With some pages, I attempted to stanch a wound. It wasn't much good for that. The blood slid off the paper, or the paper off the blood. A metaphor for the literary life, I think. With some, I lit fires. A second metaphor. And a third: with some pages, I wiped my backside. From these important uses, I saved enough pages to scratch out my stories. Couriers took these dispatches back to Fort Monroe, where they were conveyed to Tucson, then telegraphed to New York. No more moonlit melancholy, no maunderings about love, no local color. There was a war out there, if we could find it.

Someone had buried the Halls in shallow graves with makeshift crosses. Someone else had found those graves, pulled the bodies out, and toyed with them some more. Then it was the dogs' turn. Dukie shot one that was running off with an adult shinbone in his mouth. Billy Conaway said it was a wasted bullet: the dog, at least, would bury the bone, which was more than you could count on from Apaches.

Lawson's plan was to leave Clement Van Doren and a dozen others at San Pablos to show the flag, make sure the dead stayed buried, and prepare for the wholesale removal of the population to Florida upon our return. After we made camp around the ruined Hall house, Lawson turned to me. I had vomited when Dukie shot the legbone-carrying dog.

"Eddie, come on," he said. "You look like you could use a ride."

I nodded. I needed something. I mounted up and joined Lawson. Eccles was there, and Dukie, too. The land we rode through was what Billy Presley called "look away" land. He meant that your attention was always far off, drawn to the sky, the mountains, the horizon. By day you watched the sun; by night, the stars. It was a land of distances. That was Billy's way of saying that, wherever you were, the immediate surroundings weren't much: rocks, brush, dust.

"There's nothing here!" I exclaimed, gesturing at a landscape that perfectly reinforced my point. "Where do they live? I wrote there were a thousand Apaches here!"

" 'They are ill discoverers who think there is no land when they see nothing but sea,' " Eccles said.

"Who the hell was that?" Lawson asked.

"Sir Francis Bacon," Eccles replied.

"Ill discoverers. I like that. Eccles, you figure Eddie's an ill discoverer?"

"Could be."

"Let's see."

There were three hours of daylight left that afternoon. They ended when I rolled off my horse, handed the reins to Dukie, and fell asleep with a plateful of salt pork in my lap. Someone lifted me up, carried me off, and rolled me in my blanket. Someone strong. I remember my head against his shoulders and the smell of sweat. It must have been Dukie.

Oh, what a ride! We had made a game of it, a boy's game, and Lawson was the biggest boy of all. Chasing across desert against the setting sun, Lucy was right, that was what he loved. Whooping, laughing, wheeling and turning, we galloped up hillsides, down arroyos, over creekbeds. We scared up prairie dogs, we chased after deer. Birds flew in front of us, shooting into the sky as we approached. And Lawson kept his word. Before long, there were Apache dwellings, wickiups, rounded contraptions of skin and wood. They sat in gullies, under cliffs, in the cleft of hillsides, in unlikely, lonely places, never more than a half dozen structures, a few pens and lean-tos, and some pathetic scratchings that passed for gardens, with melons, squash, and corn. It's hard to convey the impression those desolate dwellings made upon me. They weren't villages, they were hardly houses. Next year, next season, they'd be gone. They were like moths' tents in fruit trees, wasps in the rafters of a barn. Oh, I don't know. But it made me wonder, a man who walked the Brooklyn Bridge, what to make of them, or what they made of us.

We encountered an old woman carrying a load of firewood. We almost missed her. She could have been a grotesquely shaped tree, lightning-struck, she stood so still. The only thing that moved was her mouth, her toothless mouth, endlessly chanting.

"I'm pretty sure she's cursing us," Eccles said.

"We flipped her upside down, I bet she's wearing Mrs. Hall's panties," Dukie said.

The crone must have sensed Dukie was talking about her. She aimed a vicious-sounding sentence at him.

"Witch!" Dukie said. 'Why you gumming away at me, witch?"

It sounded like she was listing diseases she wanted poor Dukie to catch.

"Florida, witch! That's where alligators gonna chew your leathery ass. Florida! You heard it from me! Florida!"

The last we saw of her, she was standing her ground, spitting at the tracks our horses had made.

"You know you're coming in at the end of something," Lawson told me as we rode home. "We're packing them off in a train, the whole kit and caboodle. That's policy. A year from now, you might come back and the place'd be empty."

The ride had relaxed him, and now, our horses slowed to a walk, he pulled out a cheroot. In later years, when I tried to remember what he was like when the going was good, this was the picture that came to mind: the four of us at sunset, darkness in the east, a closing vault of purple in the west, riding home together.

"I guess some of them'll dribble back. But they'll be broken then, like all the rest were broken. The wildness'll be out of 'em. Right now, the reservation is just an idea. Sanctuary, home base. A game they play, rushing off, riding back. A few years in Florida'll break that pattern. When they come back, they'll stay put. You come here then, you'll know you're on a reservation. Like you were stepping into a cage, you'll know it."

"Henry," I finally said, "how do you feel about it?"

"Who you asking?" he responded. "Are you a reporter putting a question to Captain Henry Lawson of the Twenty-fifth Cavalry, Colored?"

"No," I said. "Not like that. It's just us . . . talking."

"Okay. It's late in the day for the Indians. About this time of day, I'd say. Look around. Just a little purple smudge in the west—you can barely make it out anymore—that's Contreras and the rest. Fading away."

I'll be damned! I thought. A metaphor!

"Now, there's going to be a lot of talk back and forth—you can hear some of it already—about us and the Indians, the rights and wrongs of it. Put Van Doren on one side of the room, Conaway on the other. You ever hear them go at it?"

I nodded. I saw Buddy Conaway jabbing the air in Koch's office, denouncing the enemy. Their homes were temporary burrows, shared with vermin. Their industry, their occupation—their whole society was seasonal and predatory. They beat their wives, betrayed their allies, tortured captives, and raised their children to do the same. Their vices were endless. Their idea of military strategy was a knife in the back. Two knives were better than one. That was Conaway, talking like someone in a barroom, piling one charge against another, inflaming himself as he went along, growing so angry he could hardly talk. Or listen. That made it harder on Van Doren, who weighed his arguments judiciously, phrased them carefully, and never won. I could hear him: how the Indians were here first, how we came to their land, not they to ours; how we brought disease, weapons, alcohol; how we seduced and divided and betrayed; and how our attempt to confine them to reservations made as much sense as telling a bird to confine itself to one corner of the sky, a fish to swim beneath one wave. I had heard it all. As for myself, I had no opinion. I was a reporter.

"Yes," I said, "I've heard them."

"Hey, it got dark fast," Lawson said. "I see the lights from camp. I'm starving. You get your appetite back, Eddie?"

"Henry . . . you were saying . . ."

"Yeah. Just that if I was an Indian, I wouldn't be sitting around here waiting to get herded onto a cattle car to Florida, where I could line up for Bible tracts and canned pig for the rest of my life. I wouldn't plead and I wouldn't complain. I wouldn't even care about win or lose. I'd be out there."

"Out where?" I asked, pulling closer. It was dark. I couldn't see where he was pointing.

"Out there, Eddie," Lawson repeated. "Out with the Singer and Contreras and those other maniacs, chasing around with them. Right out there."

This time I saw where he was pointing: to the corner of the night where the sun had set, the part of the horizon where the enemy had gone.

·IX·

Interview with Duquesne:

(We moved into the solarium for this session. A freezing rain had coated everything with a layer of ice, and even as we talked, the explosive reports of branches snapping under the weight sounded from all quarters. "There goes another one," Duquesne kept saying, clapping his hands together.)

DUQUESNE: Just point me in the direction of the sun. There. That feels right. That ain't bad at all. I sure do like the feeling of the sun. You know something?

E.M.: What's that?

DUQUESNE: Women are like the sun.

E.M.: Women are like the sun?

DUQUESNE: Don't laugh at me. I've thought about it. I've worked it out. White women's like the winter sun, kind of pale and weak. Just warm enough to take the chill out of your bones, but you ain't about to take your clothes off and go swimming. Now, your black woman, she's like summer sun, tropic sun, high noon. Talk about sweat!? She'll burn you right up. Turn you into a puddle, boy. But you know what else? There's in-betweeners. Like my little Manila girl. Oh, my, I love to think back on that little girl! She was the morning sun, pink and fresh and mellow, warm you without burning, make you sparkle and come alive . . .

E.M.: We're not in Manila yet, Dukie. We're in Arizona Territory, 1885. The last campaign against the San Pablos Apaches . . .

DUQUESNE: You hush.

E.M.: Hush?

DUQUESNE: You heard me. We'll talk about Apaches, don't you worry. But I just had her pictured fine. Understand what I'm telling you? The only way I see is when I close my eyes and remember. And right then I *saw* her. I saw her fine. I ain't seen her that good in a long time.

E.M.: I'm sorry.

DUQUESNE: What you don't know yet, is you have good and bad days remembering. Some days . . . it's the times I work too hard at it, I want it too bad . . . I don't come up with nothing. It's like I never lived. But other times, she sneaks right up on me. She slips right into the room and puts her fingers over my eyes, like whispering "Guess who?" I can't touch her. But I can feel her touching me.

E.M.: I *am* sorry.

DUQUESNE: Yeah. Okay. What was it you wanted to know about?

E.M.: The Singer Campaign, 1885. We started at the reservation.

DUQUESNE: Where I shot the dog. I guess you could say that was the opening shot of the Singer Campaign. Hah! You better put that down. There was the Boston Massacre with Crispus Attucks. And there was Dukie at San Pablos, blowing away some sag-titted, flea-bitten bitch fixing to gnaw on a missionary shinbone. I guess I got a place in history, after all. Not sure I want it, though. That was a mean campaign, beginning to end.

E.M.: Yes?

DUQUESNE: That first night there was something nasty in

the air. Eccles sniffed it, and so did I. We were out with the horses and we heard some shots . . . we headed where the shots come from . . . Now, the nearest Indians to the Halls was about a mile away. Outside this wickiup is a fire with a man layin' in it. You could smell his hair burning. I hate that smell. Hate it. Like singeing feathers off a plucked chicken. I hate that smell!

E.M.: He'd been shot?

DUQUESNE: Oh yeah. Fell right into the fire. Inside was Conaway and Diller. And a woman. Do I have to draw a picture for you?

E.M.: Well . . .

DUQUESNE: Well, Diller had an arm around the woman's neck and a revolver shoved in her mouth. Conaway was just finished giving her a poke, pulling out and wiping off his cock with his bandana, joking about crabs . . . That was Conaway . . . war was his license to fuck. It's all he talked about. He had this plain dumb wife back at post, the kind of woman should never've been let out of a barn, and each morning, there was Conaway, down on the parade ground, wanting us to know what he did to her, what he got her to do for him. He wanted us to know. And out on the trail, some poor woman or other . . . well, he was the first on line . . . So there he is with that woman and he sees us looking in, does Conaway, and he looks at us like he knows there ain't nothing we can do. He smiles at Eccles, knowing how hard it was for him in particular to see what they were up to. Then he shoots the woman. And I guess he figured he'd never pay the price. But Eccles remembered . . .

E.M.: He did?

DUQUESNE: You know he did. You remember the last you saw of Buddy Conaway?

E.M.: My God! That was years and years . . .

DUQUESNE: Like I say . . . Eccles remembered.

E.M.: One other thing. I've been wondering. How did you feel about serving in a white man's army, fighting Indians under white officers and . . .

DUQUESNE: Stop right there. I heard that question a thousand times. Wasn't none of us didn't ask it.

E.M.: And the answer?

DUQUESNE: Depends. If you'd ask us, the answer we'd give might not be the truth. The answer we gave each other, spoke out loud, that could be bullshit, too. It was complicated . . .

E.M.: But at this late date?

DUQUESNE: All right. Me. Just me. I was a believer, for all my cuttin' up. One: I believed things was better than they had been. Two: I believed things was gonna be gettin' better . . .

E.M.: Okay. Well, after you left San . . .

DUQUESNE: Wait a minute. There's a three. Three is: I don't believe in one and two no more.

• X •

Statement of Thomas Henderson, Nice, France

I am the only survivor of the so-called Henderson Tragedy, and though I can't dine out very long on that distinction anymore, my knowledge is unique. Forgive me if I make my account as brief as possible. No handkerchiefs, please, it was all too long ago. Everyone who died then would probably have died by now anyway, so please . . .

I'm not sure how it all started, but I'm inclined to thank your dashing General Custer. In 1873, I think it was, he hosted the Czar's son, Grand Duke Alexander, on a buffalo-hunting, Indian-watching tour of the Dakotas. Take that, combine it with Wild West shows, Buntline novels, beaver hats, vivid imaginations, nouveau riche boredom, cap it off with Custer's spectacular quietus at the Little Big Horn, and you have the ingredients of the so-called Henderson Tragedy.

My father, Marcus Henderson, mill owner from Birmingham, England, a wealthy, robust, and rather odious man, in 1884 began organizing an expedition to the Wild West. He and eight other predators thought themselves sportsmen. I was drafted for the hunt; having doubts about my manhood, my father reckoned the safari would do me good. He was half right: I came into my full estate as a result.

My father—a passionate arranger and organizer—managed everything: trains, tents, hotels, guides, cooks, porters, a taxidermist, and a photographer. Buffalo were becoming hard to find, but we decimated one of the few remaining herds, somewhere in Montana. In Wyoming elk were plentiful; not as plentiful, however, after we passed through. Around Yellowstone, we assassinated an ancient, amiable grizzly foraging in a patch of blackberries. His teeth were as brown as tobacco, as smooth as cobblestones. When I suggested the grizzly had been felled by a coronary, just ahead of our fusillade, no one was amused.

After the "tragedy," people asked why we moved into arid, inhospitable, and game-poor Apacheland. My response, to newspapers, military authorities, and the British Consul in San Francisco, had to do with mountain lions. I was lying. My father and his friends were bored. No one said it outright, not around me, but I recall the drift of conversation. They talked about Apaches, talked about them in an inflamed, primitive, nearly pornographic way.

We arrived in Tucson in time to hear about the events at San Pablos. What luck! What cheer! What a collective conspiratorial gleam when we at last set out after "mountain lion!" That was what we were hunting, if anybody asked. That's the word they used when I was with them. Tell me, Morrison, I've meant to look it up, but, as usual, laziness prevails: by any chance, are male and female mountain lions respectively known as "bucks" and "squaws"?

Our guides were two Apaches, not of the San Pablos group. I wonder what they made of our caravan! The only thing we lacked was camels! The kitchen and larder accounted for two wagons. A dozen mules were weighed down with tents and chairs and carpets, guns, polo mallets, fishing rods, bear and buffalo skins, swimming trunks, smoking jackets. We were only going to be here once, my father said, so we might as well do it right.

Like a carnival, a circus, a Vanity Fair, our tents blossomed in the desert. The scent of creamy soups, smoked fowl, roasts, and rum cake and fresh-brewed coffee, brandy, and cigars must have betrayed our presence for miles. So did our target practice, our skeet shooting and—here my father surpassed himself—our fireworks! Yes! What a gorgeous display—comets, candles, sparklers, blossoming, spraying the sky with color, their blasts ricocheting off the dark mountains! I've often wondered what the Singer, Contreras, and the others made of this display, since they were almost surely in the neighborhood to see it.

Now, Morrison, pay attention. The great moment approaches. We were sitting in the shade of a long, rectangular tarp. Our tents were twenty yards away on one side, the horses, cooking tents, and wagons an equal distance in the other direction. As he sat down to lunch, Roger Lanning, my father's partner, suggested that we consider leaving the next day. It was clear that he represented a consensus and had been chosen to speak because of my father's business relationship with him.

"It's been a splendid hunt," he began. He was a likable, clubby old pirate. "We've accomplished everything we said we would, and more. Thanks, I might add, to you, Marcus."

There were cheers and approbation all along the table, bearded, beaming faces, tanner and healthier-looking than they had been in years.

"Now, this last gambit, this matter of 'mountain lions,' was worth trying," Lanning continued. "I'm sure none of us regrets having come here. But we knew all along that the chances were these 'mountain lions' might never come into view. We've given it a good try, but now is the time to make an ending. I'd like, if I may, to propose a toast to the conclusion of a grand hunt!"

Up went the glasses. Mine had grape juice.

My father arose. I believe he was resigned to leaving—and to regretting it to the end of his days. He'd make me regret it, too, I believed.

"Thank you, thank you," he began. "I'm glad to say that I've done everything possible to provide for the success of this hunt and . . ."

He paused, perplexed, but that was to be expected. My father's emotions usually were strangled somewhere in his throat. One waited patiently for him to recover; it was like attending to someone with a stutter. But now, hesitation and puzzlement led to a convincing imitation of dismay.

"My God!" he said. "Look!"

From a table set for luncheon, laden with cheese and nuts and olives and peppers, glasses and pipes, cigar cutters and snuffboxes, we saw a dozen Apaches spread out in a line near the cooks' tents.

The diners took their cue from Roger Lanning, and no one was better acquainted with my father's knack of arranging extraordinary surprises.

"Bravo!" he shouted. "Bravo!"

There were bravos up and down the table. Henderson had done it again, another of those singing, souvenir-buying shows that had enlivened our stay in the Dakotas!

"Splendid, absolutely splendid!" Judson Smoot exulted. "I must quick bring out my crossbow. These fellows will be fascinated!"

Now my father looked behind him at our tents, where a dozen—make it two dozen—more Apaches stood.

"Oh my God!" he whispered. But his friends still thought he was acting.

"This must have set you back a bundle," Hendrik Cartwright said. "How many of them did you ask for?"

"A smaller number would have sufficed," Albert Lloyd reflected. "But maybe they're needed for the dance. Is that it, Marcus?"

"You don't understand," my father said. "You don't get it."

"Oh, stop it, Marcus," Judson Smoot demanded.

"Are they going to do anything?" Cartwright asked. "Or just stand there? Are we supposed to do something? Some kind of protocol welcome?"

"I must say," Jacob Leopold whispered, "that the costumes are on the drab side. Compared, I mean, to what we saw among the Sioux."

Cartwright agreed. "All those cast-off army uniforms. No bows and arrows, no spears. Just those tacky rifles. I can't see a thing to buy."

"It's the American influence," Leopold opined. "All the flavor drains out of them in no time."

I used to wonder why they waited so long. Why did they watch us nibble and banter at the table? Why didn't they swoop *right in? I suppose they saw that we were unarmed. Gentlemen didn't carry guns to lunch. However, I believe the main reason is that we were as strange to them as they to us. If it had been our luck to arrive three hundred years before, they might have worshipped us. A hundred years previous they would have gawked, fingered, traded. But those days, alas, were gone.*

Throughout all the chat, while the full horror of the situation dawned upon him, my father remained standing. Assuming he was still tongue-tied and sensing that someone had to welcome the Apaches, Hendrik Cartwright arose, glass raised.

"Gentlemen," he said. "Welcome. Thank you for coming. You look perfectly splendid. You may begin . . ."

They began. A rifle cracked, a bullet spun Cartwright around, smashed him against the table, and pitched him to the ground.

I had been sitting opposite Cartwright. It felt rude, like I was making fun of a dinner guest who'd spilled some gravy, harping on the mess he'd made, but I arose and leaned over the table to see what had become of him. I half believed—the others did, too—that this still might be something my father had arranged. Then I saw that a bullet had caught Cartwright in the eye. All around him, like a secret cache of eyeballs, lay dozens of stuffed olives.

"He's dead, I think," I said. The whole group seemed to be waiting for my report. And still there were some who suspected that I was in on my father's prank. Even the Apaches seemed to be waiting for further instructions.

"Do I take it," Jacob Leopold began, drawing himself up in his chair and addressing my father rather judicially, "that you have no . . . uh . . . arrangement with our visitors?"

"No," grasped my father. "No. No."

"You didn't invite them?"

"No! It's them . . . the mountain lions!"

"Ah," Leopold returned, sinking low in his chair. "I see."

"What about the guides, the cooks . . . all the rest?" someone asked.

Judson Smoot tamped down the last bowl of tobacco he would ever smoke. He knew it.

"I don't know about the guides," he said, blowing out the match he used to light up. "Perhaps they were more closely re-

lated to the San Pablos faction than we were led to believe. That or the prospect of booty . . ."

He glanced around the camp, puffing away serenely. There was a terrible stillness everywhere.

"As for the others, I should say they've died already. Very quietly, too."

Then came the moment which made me admire Judson Smoot forever. Keep in mind, dear Morrison, that when I returned to England, and after a minimal mourning, I was asked to tell this story at least a hundred times. I always obliged. Indeed, I took parts. I acted it out. And Smoot's line was always a smash.

"I wonder," he remarked, contemplating his reeking briar, "if anyone knows how peace pipes work."

By now my father had recovered. "Our weapons are in the tents," he observed quite wistfully. "We'll have to get past our visitors."

"We can't . . ." Leopold ventured, "negotiate?"

"No," my father said. Drawing a deep breath, he said, "Gentlemen, drink up. Lunch has been delayed. I'm sorry."

He glanced at me and winced at the reminder that I was there. "You follow me." Then, to the group: "Is a count of three agreeable?"

I wished—we all did—that he might have proposed a count of one hundred. Or ten. Even four would have felt much better.

"One."

"Three is such a cliché," Smoot remarked.

"Two . . ."

"Good luck all," someone murmured. (Your article, I believe, changed this to "Tally-ho!")

"Three!"

Two were shot before they left the table. Their hearts weren't in it, I suspect. They preferred dying with a glass of wine in front of them, shot from a distance by someone they didn't have to see. It's interesting how character revealed itself. Smoot, for instance, strode manfully toward his tent, as if he could order the Apache who was waiting there to step aside. Leopold walked forward slowly, eyes on the ground like a seaman forced to walk the plank. Lanning stepped to the tent, bowed to his execu-

tioner, and motioned him inside. "After you, please." My father grabbed my hand, made a bulldog rush which ended in a headlong tackle of the warrior who stood outside. Unsportsmanlike, my father kicked him in the head, smashing his face like he was stamping out a fire. Then he flung me toward the back of the tent, seized his rifle, and fired through the open flap.

Now the war was on. Shots and screams were everywhere, theirs and ours. I could tell from the firing that at least one other member of our party had gotten into his tent and to his rifle. So there were two left alive. Three, counting me.

Then, after a few minutes of bedlam, there came an odd stretch of silence. For a brief, heady second, I hoped the Apaches had withdrawn, shattered by our plucky resistance. Then I realized what was really happening: they were gathering for the kill.

That tent! Those canvas walls, shielding us completely yet protecting us so little! Oh, if they were only fortress walls, stone or even wood, walls to shrug off a siege. Yet I watched them billowing in the wind, watched shadows flit outside, and I knew that our ramparts were like paper, no more use against knives and bullets than another layer of skin. I began to cry.

"Now, Tommy," my father said. He faced out the flap. "Here's what you're doing to do. If worse comes to worst, I'm going to pull up the stakes and cut the lines that hold up the tent. I want you to crawl under the cot, under the blanket, build yourself a nest, and it"ll all come fluttering down on you. You could be safe there."

Whimpering, I complied. Towels, bedrolls, blankets, I stuffed them all around me. How permeable they felt!

"Is anyone left but me?" someone shouted. It was James Worthington, the barrister. He was a courtly, gentle, rather fussy man whom a life of privilege seemed to have spoiled thoroughly. When he missed a shot, he sulked. If a proposal of his was not immediately accepted, he pouted. People always had to make things up with him. How had he gotten to his tent? Then I remembered. He'd been there all along. He never ate lunch, always napped and awoke complaining that the evening meal was late.

"Over here, James. It's Marcus Henderson. How are you faring?"

"Oh . . . fine," he answered. "Nothing wrong with me yet."
"That's good!" my father boomed out encouragingly.
"This quiet . . . it doesn't mean they're gone?"
"Doubt it," my father responded. "Better keep your guard up a while yet."
"Yes. Of course."
Another moment passed. It seemed a great deal longer. But it wasn't long enough to convince me that we'd live. We'd wrapped ourselves up in canvas the way a frightened child pulls a sheet over his head. Yet nothing in the world had altered. And now the tent felt like a shroud.
"Oh . . ."
"What's that, James?
"They've . . . uh . . . set fire to my tent. Yours, too?"
"No. Not yet."
"It's getting smoky in here. It's going fast." We heard him coughing. "Marcus?"
"Yes?"
"I'm not coming out. Do you understand?"
"Yes, I . . ."
A shot rang out. My father turned to me. "Well," he said. He started at the edge of the tent, pulling up stakes, cutting ropes. Our world grew smaller. The tent settled down over me, and the last I saw of him he had grasped the main pole and was tugging at it, rocking one way and the other.
I am guessing what happened next, but I cannot be very wrong. The tent came down. My father was draped in canvas, like a statue about to be unveiled. I believe he wanted to work his way out from underneath so that he could draw attention from me and make his last stand in the open. Whether a bullet found him first, or a knife, I cannot say. Both were employed against him, quite redundantly. I picture him faltering, dropping to his knees, struggling forward under canvas. I see him just managing to reach the edge of the tent—the bloodstains suggested he came that close—and reaching out his hand.
A thorough pillaging would have resulted in my capture, but the Apaches already had more swag than they could carry; our wardrobe alone would have slowed them to a crawl. And there were corpses enough to enjoy. I'm sure you don't expect me to describe the mutilations. Such refinement, such finesse, such

variety from such a simple race! I take it as evidence of the humanity we all share! And I leave it at that.

• XI •

"A textbook example of war reportage," my account of the Henderson Tragedy can be found in any number of anthologies. It was the kind of story that writes itself. All the elements were there: English eccentricity, foolishness, wit, and pluck. Indian bestiality. A malleable, traumatized youth. And those mutilated corpses, spread out on the ground, arranged in the shape of an arrow, pointing where the Singer had gone, defying us to follow: a gauntlet flung into the face of an outraged nation! The only problem was Lawson: I couldn't decide how to involve him in the story. A few years before, and in similar circumstances, the press had savaged the reputations of Reno and Benteen, the two officers who might perhaps have rescued Custer. Seen from one point of view, Lawson was a loser, a latecomer, just in time to bury the dead. I could have finished his career on the spot. On the other hand, I could cast him as the now even more determined pursuer of the Singer and Contreras. But if I did that, he would have to deliver the goods.

I found him sitting on a knoll, waiting for the burial. Wrapped in sections of cut-up tents, the Englishmen lay in the trench. Troops were rolling rocks down onto their bodies. A cruel interment, this avalanche of boulders, but soil alone might not hold them. We knew.

"Some story," he said, "You hit the jackpot."

"Well, you never know what editors will do," I cautioned. "But from here it looks like the biggest thing since Custer. Henry, these were all prominent people in England. The outcry will be tremendous."

"Yeah. Me and my niggers could end up looking awful bad."

"Is there anything you want the piece to say," I called out after him, "or not to say?"

He stood up, gently stepping on his cigar, heading to where funeral services were about to begin. "Don't write me up a hero yet," he said.

"Don't write me up a hero yet." For years, people accused me of concocting that incomparable line. Late at night, third brandy, or an editor calling me into his office, "Come now, Morrison, I'll never tell . . ." Yet, just like that, Lawson tossed it off, the line that made him famous.

A newspaperman, any newspaperman, can tell when someone is making a remark that he hopes will become a quotation. The words hang in the air so! I spent an endless afternoon off Gallipoli as the virtual captive of an English admiral who was determined to go down in the history books. He released one flatulent observation after another, ponderous nonsense about tides of power, sands of time, and—when one bloody boatload after another came out from shore—"Cargoes of devotion." After each comment, he eyed me hopefully, watched the movement of my pen, and even repeated himself to make sure I'd got it right. And Lawson, poor Lawson, hardly noticed.

To be sure, I dressed up the scene a little. For one thing, the black troops were hardly the "dusky mournful ranks" that I described. Ragged, restless, scratching, and whispering was more like it, and someone broke wind thunderously during Birmingham Mack's closing prayer, the space around the guilty party rapidly widening. Also, I wrote that Lawson had ordered all the debris, tents and trunks and all, to be burned. That was true, but the fire was over hours before the funeral and no "angry clouds of smoke" blew over the gravesite, no detonating firecrackers punctuated the eulogy, and no English hunting dogs sniffed and bayed morosely at the grave. There was some sort of canine in the area—I heard some barking, maybe it was sad barking, maybe not.

CASA DIABLO

• I •

Sixty Apaches didn't cross a desert without leaving traces and these were sixty careless Apaches. The arrow of corpses had been followed by a dozen smaller signs. The desert was littered with discarded booty from the English camp, things the Apaches had broken or didn't know how to use: shoehorns, an egg timer, and a polo mallet that wasn't any good for hunting. No, the tracking was disturbingly easy. But the trail was long.

My shoes split, soles separating from uppers. Cord held them together. My suit soaked and dried a dozen times, so that there were concentric deposits of salt and dirt spreading from my armpits, my waistline, the backs of my knees. And my skin, the cause of amused comment among the black riders, was worst of all. I had pictured myself returning to Fort Monroe, indeed New York City, *tanned* and *leathery*, but I turned out to be the kind of man who reddened, peeled, and blistered, unevenly and in patches. My nose, red as a cherry, felt like it would pop out of my face.

I don't know where the savagery began, whether it was something we did to them or they to us: judgments like that were not required of me. But the Singer raid was a frenzied effort to destroy everything that the white man had brought to the Indian lands. So little time, so much to destroy! A rancher who had been staked out in the sun, his body smeared with molasses to attract ants. A prospector, so badly butchered that his dog, unwilling to stray, had nonetheless commenced to gnaw on his more impersonal parts, pieces that were scattered farthest from the dead man's head. And finally, that unfortunate wagonload of settlers, California-bound, six of them, all dead, but one of them—the oldest, the leader—crucified. We rode into that tableau at dusk, against a pink and orange sky. Lobito Santos waited, staring up at the cross, uncertain whether reverence, anger, or hilarious laughter was expected. He ran toward us as we rode in.

"See what they done, Boss?" he shouted. "They cross him up! They cross him up!"

After a dozen raids, fifty spectacular executions, the Apaches' trail led up into the mountains, where there were no white men to kill.

"They're up there, huh?" Lawson asked Lobito Santos. "You sure?"

Santos nodded.

"All of them?"

"Yes," Santos said, pointing to a trail that curved and hairpinned up the slopes. It traversed fields of loose gravel. It wound around boulders, cut through fringes of pine and juniper, hugged cliff edges, plunged across canyons.

"Santos, what do you think? They expect us to follow them up there?"

"Maybe no," Santos answered, clearly hoping that Lawson would decide to camp down in the flatlands.

"I'll bet they don't," Lawson said.

There it was again, that peculiar smile whenever Lawson talked about the enemy. Sympathy? Empathy? He liked to think about them, he liked knowing they were there, liked being near them. He took more pleasure from their living than from their dying. Santos put it to me this way, when we talked about it once: Lawson was more a hunter than a soldier.

"They come down, Boss, sooner or later."

Lawson humored him. "What goes up, must come down."

"Yes."

"Sure. They get tired of lying around, right? They get tired of talking, run out of whiskey, they come on down."

"Yes."

"And if that don't work, we could wait till winter, right, because no way do they spend winter in the mountains. All we have to do is sit. I mean, hell, they're not doing nobody any harm up there."

Santos nodded.

"We could make us a nice camp. 'Situation under control.' No sleeping in saddle blankets either. Build proper quarters. Doilies on the dining table."

Now Santos knew he wasn't going to win.

"And then when they come down again, and raise hell again, we chase 'em again, from, say, April first to November fifteenth. That'll be the season."

Lawson placed both hands on his scout's shoulders. "Tomorrow morning."

"I go to the hills from whence cometh my health," Birmingham Mack pronounced that night, but the amens were halfhearted. Behind us, downhill, the desert stretched out forever, rolling away beneath the stars. But now we sensed the mountains, the dark bulk in front of us, like the shoulders of a monster. We felt the slight tilt of the ground when we spread our blankets. An ominous chill in the breezes that came down to us. Night birds. Coyotes we hadn't heard for weeks. And echoes. Every shout, every bark or whinny made an echo which sounded like a warning.

Lawson sought me out that night. I was wrapped in my blankets, wide-eyed, thinking about the morning.

"Hello, Eddie," he said, squatting down beside me. The cooking fire had burned down to embers. "Have a taste."

We sat a moment, enjoying the last of the fire, and some brandy. I didn't want to talk to him about the mountain and the morning. They were both too close.

"What do you guess Lucy's doing now?" Lawson asked.

"Well, it's late. She could be sleeping."

"Nah. She gets by on five hours when I'm not home."

"Reading? Visiting with Mrs. Presley?"

"You know what, I bet she's sitting out on the porch, on the bench, looking in our direction."

"That could be."

"Sometimes I can feel her thinking about me. I can feel it like a current."

"She cares."

"I guess she does." He nodded. "But that's not it. Sure, she's pulling for me and all, but the feeling I get is . . . madder than that."

"Madder?"

"Well, hurt, say. Hurt that we're apart. That she's not with me. That's the message. You know, the morning we left Fort Monroe, I leaned over to kiss her goodbye. She asks me a question. 'You know what the hardest part of all this is?' And I said I guessed it was my leaving. You know what she said? 'No, Henry. Not your leaving. My staying.' "

·II·

One hundred and fifty men left Fort Monroe. After dropping a group at San Pablos and sending a detail to Tucson with Thomas Henderson, there were perhaps ten dozen of us who filed up the mountain trail the next morning. And each man, each survivor, I should say, has a drastically different account of what befell us at ten minutes after two that afternoon. The time of the attack is all we have in common: we were stretched out over a mile of hairpin trail, some ahead, some behind, yet those in the rear directly above and out of sight of those in front and below. I was toward the front, with Eccles.

I heard a horse neigh on the trail above, and an annoying

shower of stones came rolling downward. That had happened before.

"There's men below . . ." someone started to shout, but a scream interrupted him. A man and a horse plunged over the trail and into the ravine below.

"What the hell . . ." I started to ask.

"A snake?" Eccles wondered, but suddenly there was a second scream on the trail above, and Eccles gave me a look which was horrified and comical at the same time. Perhaps an animal feels that way at the spring of a trap or the hoist of a snare: mortally afraid and very foolish. Eccles looked at me: "Two snakes?"

I put the story together later. Birmingham Mack, near the rear of the column, leading a mule laden with provisions, turned around to see if the man behind him—Cleveland from Toledo—was attending to his proofs of the existence of the Deity. Birmingham Mack was accustomed to silence from the men he attempted to reform, but after his third "You follow?" Mack turned and saw that Cleveland from Toledo had not followed at all. His place was taken by an Apache who was about to jump off a rock and knock Mack out of his saddle. There was no time to fire: Mack just managed to swing his rifle like a club, stunning his assailant with a blow on the neck. Then Mack shot him.

"I only winged him, caught him in the right shoulder," Mack lamented. "Biddle could've fixed him up in no time. But the fella keeps coming. He's got a knife in his left hand. 'Now don't you do that,' I says to him, but he raises his arm, fixin' to come at me, and I shoot him in the leg. 'Now I *told* you not to do that,' I says. I didn't want to kill nobody. And he keeps coming and I keep warning him. Four times I shot him."

With our Z-shaped column strung out against a mountainside, the Apaches had attacked from above and between our lines. Horses screaming, skidding off the trail, cavalrymen dodging rocks that the enemy rolled down from above—the rocks were worse than the bullets, everyone said—the first few moments were a horror. In all, four men went tumbling down the hillside. Four others were overwhelmed at the middle of the column, just behind me. They bore the brunt of the attack, and when it was over, the "Z" had lost its diagonal: we were two lines, upper and lower, with only corpses to connect us.

Between the two lines was one hundred yards of boulders, gravel piles, mesquite, juniper, and Apaches. You could hear them in the not quite silence that followed the first attack. Footsteps. Grunts. Whispers.

"Hold my horse," Eccles said, handing me the reins. "I'm going to check the column."

He scuttled past, dodging on his hands and knees. Ten minutes before, we had been a column of soldiers, a moving line of men and horses. Now we were a broken line, isolated bundles of death and pain. But when Eccles came back, we were a column again.

"We've got to get off the trail," Eccles said when he came back. "The upper line moves down and the lower line moves up, except for some men who hold the horses. We meet in the middle."

"That's where the shooting came from."

"Correct."

"So we're attacking."

"Yes," Eccles said. "Maybe."

A shot rang out then, Lawson's signal. We climbed up and they clambered down. Stumbling, tripping, cursing. It was a small miracle none of us shot each other. There was no one else to shoot: the Apaches had vanished.

"Stupid! So goddamned stupid," Lawson raged, chucking a handful of pebbles at a nearby stump. "We didn't even see them. Can you beat that? Four dead and seven wounded and we never laid eyes on 'em. What the hell kind of a way to fight is that?"

I tried to solace him: something to the effect that any column moving through this kind of terrain would be vulnerable. He shouldn't blame himself too much.

"Me? I'm not blaming me. I'm blaming them!"

"Them?"

"The damned Apaches! What'd they do, Eddie? They take the easy pickings and they run for it!"

Incredible! Dressing down the enemy for his failure to annihilate us! All this while dead were on the trail, while Diller lay on a stretcher, half his nose shot off, while another man was screaming as Biddle attempted to cut a bullet out of his abdomen, pleading with him to leave it in, please, God, leave it in, let it be, don't touch it!

"They never follow up, Eddie, that's the whole story, they don't put in an honest day. They win an early victory, they loot, they leave, they lay up someplace. They quarrel among themselves. They got tired, they get drunk, they want to go home. And that's what makes 'em losers."

The other officers had walked over and caught the end of Lawson's tirade. None seemed surprised. Lobito perched on top of a nearby boulder, parroting every comment. "Never put in honest day . . . never fight the last round . . . go home early."

"They had their chance to finish us," Lawson said. "And tonight it's our turn at bat."

"Tonight?" Billy Presley wondered aloud. Who wouldn't? We'd taken a beating in broad daylight. What chance would we have in the dark? "What's that about tonight?"

"We're going after them tonight."

"Uh-huh," Billy Presley said. "I see."

Perhaps it came from living with Ellie Presley, but Billy had a wry, understated manner. He took the part of a rustic simpleton, eager to please, never insubordinate, but falling just short of clear understanding.

"We did real well today," Presley continued. "Folks lining up to see that one Apache old Mack shot and now we're gonna go up there in the dark and give 'em some more hell . . . That it, Captain?"

"Now, listen," Lawson said. He knelt down and the others stooped around him in a circle. He reminded me of the ringleader in some schoolyard contest. "This is how we're going to get them."

•III•

At dusk, with the enemy still likely to be watching, the defeated 25th Cavalry piled its dead and wounded onto horses and turned back toward the camp they'd made the night before, leaving the Apaches in possession of the mountains.

Two miles down the trail, while half the column, and all the horses, continued the retreat, the other half turned back toward the scene of their earlier defeat. But this time they stayed off the trail. One group worked its way below, the other stayed above, thirty men on each side, picking their way. First the highs, then the lows, advanced. Between them the trail was empty, like a stream shining in the moonlight, with Lobito darting from one bank to the other, keeping the groups together.

Past midnight, Lobito spotted the Apache camp. A lazy, sloppy, victorious camp it was, with fires still burning and no sentinels, with deep sleep and a full moon and not even a watchful dog to see the two columns fan left and right and form the jaws of Lawson's trap.

Remember tonight, I told myself. Remember the silent sprint toward the slumbering camp, the race between our thirty men and Eccles' thirty, the race across the silvery meadow to see who could reach the wickiups first. Remember thinking that this was what it was like to feel alive, in the paradoxical imminence of death. Remember thinking, even as I ran, that this was a cliché. Remember retorting, out of breath, that it was true anyway. Remember finding food and hides, warm fires. Remember the look on Lawson's face—the anger and frustration and the glint of admiration—when he knew the camp was empty.

Lobito Santos saw them first: high on a ridge in back of the camp, three or four Apaches. One of them held a torch. Two others turned—I never reported this—revealed their naked buttocks to us. A fourth Apache shouted at us in a high, querulous voice; his short speech ended in a laugh.

"The Singer," Lobito said. He was frightened.

"What'd he say?" Lawson asked.

"You are thief and fool and not strong and sleeping with your mother and he is asking . . ."

"Yes . . . what?"

"Not good." Lobito was trembling.

"What?"

"He is asking . . . how are your wounded soldiers? And where are your horses?"

"Oh my God," Lawson said, appalled. "Oh my God."

In another five minutes we were rushing back toward a camp we would be too late to rescue, with the Singer's laughter ringing in our ears.

·IV·

DUQUESNE: Some night that was. You know, for years later, moonlight scared me. I always got spooked by a full moon, 'specially when I was in strange country. Darkness I could handle. But moonlight scared me. Moonlight was just enough light to do wrong in . . .

E.M.: Maybe if you started from the beginning . . .

DUQUESNE: I tried to sleep. But sometimes you're too tired to sleep. And the moonlight didn't help. And Diller was moaning. I'd slip off for five, ten minutes, and there'd be a noise . . . I'd jump right up again. Around three in the morning, I get up to take a . . . you know . . . a dump. Put that anyway you like. "Visit the latrine." That sounds stupid, too, you don't "visit" no latrine. There I am with my suspenders at my elbows and my pants around my ankles. My friend, not only am I unarmed, I am defenseless every which way. And then . . . I can laugh about it now, but when it happened, it shut my asshole *watertight* . . . I'm squatting in the shadows and two, three, ten Apaches pass right by. And they were so quiet! They didn't say nothin', they didn't move nothin', drop nothin', hit nothin'. They moved like the wind. Like ghosts. Like death . . .

E.M.: What'd you do?

DUQUESNE: I hoped that the Apaches would come in whooping and wake folks up. But no, not that night. I watched. Watched them work through the trees. They carried guns, but they was holdin' knives. I saw the moon bounce off them knives . . . I saw . . .

E.M.: Yes . . .

DUQUESNE: They stepped out from between the trees, knives in their hands. Not a sound. It was like nothin' else I ever saw. It was like something religious, a sacrifice, maybe, a ceremony. They walked right in and they stood . . . they stood over these bumps on the ground . . . blankets where folks was sleeping, only they were just these bumps that already looked like the bumps of fresh-dug graves . . . They kneeled down, the Apaches, and they lifted up their knives and . . . they stabbed the bumps . . . in the moonlight. It was like a ceremony . . .

E.M.: A ceremony.

DUQUESNE: Till somebody screamed . . .

• V •

When I awoke around midday, I started writing my account of the Battle of Apache Pass, which I would send with the wounded back to Fort Monroe. Eccles found me hard at work.

"A courier came out from post," he said, handing me an envelope.

"Let's have a look," I said. I was still a young enough journalist to fear rejection. I tore open the envelope and pulled out the clippings of my first two stories, the killings at San Pablos and the Henderson Tragedy.

"Look at this!" I exulted, dangling the inky columns like they were some prize trout. "Page one."

While Eccles read what I had written—and there was a trace of envy in his curiosity—I found a note from the editor, who had reluctantly consented to my trip. Fine job . . . keep it coming . . . stay as long as you like . . . delighted you have this story to yourself so far.

I passed the note to Eccles. A more mature reporter might have kept the kudos to himself, but I couldn't resist spreading my success around.

I started shuffling through my notes, organizing and outlining. I had pages spread out on the ground in front of me. Pebbles were my paperweights.

"You mind if I ask a question?" Eccles said. "I know you're busy."

"Go ahead," I said, not looking up. I *was* busy. I was feeling pressure. It was the kind of pressure newspapermen profess to hate: the deadline. Secretly, they love it. They know in their hearts that more time wouldn't make much difference, wouldn't make their stories any more timeless or true.

"Well, I was wondering how you're writing up what happened to us the last few days."

"The Battle of Apache Pass, you mean."

"That's what you're calling it? Well, who won?"

"Who *won*? We did, of course."

"We did?"

"No question about it."

"How can you say that? They ambushed us up there. They dodged us. Then they ambushed our boys down here. They had everything their way. How do you write up something like that?"

"Here's how," I said. "The Twenty-fifth Cavalry under Captain Henry Lawson et cetera tracked the fleeing Apaches into their mountain stronghold. Audaciously forcing their way up a trail that no white man . . ."

I broke off to glance at Eccles' expressionless face. "That's a convention. Everyone knows it's a colored outfit but you can't say 'up a trail that no white or colored man ever climbed.' "

"All right. What then?"

"While on this treacherous mountain trail, the cavalry encountered desperate et cetera opposition, a sneak attack from concealed snipers . . ."

"Snipers? Sneak attack?"

"They hid behind rocks, didn't they? So they're snipers. And they caught us by surprise. We weren't expecting them. That makes it a sneak attack."

"What about what we tried to do to their camp? Was that a sneak attack?"

"No, that was a well-laid ambush."

"Which failed?"

"Because the enemy had already retreated, abandoning their secret et cetera stronghold to Captain Lawson's dogged, stalwart et ceteras."

"Yeah, but they retreated down here and raised hell with us some more."

"And we remain in possession of the battlefield."

"And they're free as the breeze."

"Eccles," I said, "the Apache newspapers may be entitled to print a different version of events. But I work for the New York *Sun*. And I doubt that our Apache subscribers will complain . . ."

"But the truth is . . ."

"That they have their version and we have ours, which makes this no different from any other war or any other newspaper that's ever been."

Eccles walked off smiling. At me? With me? At the time, it didn't matter.

Lobito never had seen Lawson so grim. Being fooled by Apaches was one thing; being bested by other units was another. And the odds were we would be bested: General Erwin Gottschalk had taken three fresh units out in the field, five hundred men who wanted the Singer as their prize, all of them competing against one cuffed-about colored outfit. Half our men were wounded or were occupied caring for the wounded. Our horses, never the best, were nearly finished. The Apaches' grass-fed ponies held on forever; our grain-fed veterans of Shiloh quickly wilted. This was the question Lawson put to Lobito Santos: Take sixty men, sixty horses. Was there any chance of finding the Singer? Or should the whole column trudge back to Fort Monroe and settle for honorable mention?

There were so many places they could have gone, Lobito said. In the mountains alone, there were a half dozen strongholds as good as what we'd seen. There were desert springs that only the Apaches knew. South was Mexico, where they could hole up for months if they got past General Gottschalk. Who could tell about such people?

Yes, Lawson said, I know all that. I know the odds. But we have one chance left. One roll of the dice. So tell me, Lobito, where do we go?

Lobito told him.

·VI·

From the New York *Sun*, September 15, 1885.

CAPTAIN LAWSON'S CAVALRY CORNERS APACHE RENEGADES

"The Singer" Overtaken, Negotiations Pending

by EDWIN CARTER MORRISON, *Special Correspondent*

Casa Diablo, Arizona Territory — Captain Henry Lawson's tortuous three-month-long pursuit of Apache renegades led by a warrior-priest called the Singer appears to have ended triumphantly.

With his force cut in half by deaths, wounds, and exhaustion, and with several fresh U.S. columns in pursuit of the wily enemy, Lawson risked his last strength on a desperate gamble that the Apaches would be found in Casa Diablo, a sacred canyon filled with thermal springs to which the Indians attribute spiritual properties.

Arriving at dawn after a two-week forced march, Lawson's column surrounded a two-mile-long, 200-foot-deep canyon and sealed off the only trail leading down to where a mountain-fed stream runs a gauntlet of scalding cauldrons bubbling from beneath the surface of the earth.

At first light, clouds of sulphur-scented steam obscured the cavalry's view into the place the Spaniards called "the devil's house." After hours of anxious waiting, when morning's mists finally dissipated, Lawson learned that his hunting instincts had been vindicated. The devil's house was tenanted by the raiders who have slain close to fifty soldiers and civilians since their outbreak from San Pablos Reservation last July 4.

On sighting the cavalry, the Apaches surged up the trail leading out of the canyon. For the first time in the long campaign, the terrain favored the white man. Hemmed in by a narrow upward trail, the Apaches were readily picked off by Lawson's black sharpshooters. One after another tumbled back into the canyon, their lifeless forms sometimes landing in the kettles of scalding water that earn this place its name.

After the failure of their main escape attempt, the Apaches mounted smaller, stealthier escape attempts at night. All have been rebuffed. Lawson's veterans patrol the rim of the canyon night and day. The Apaches, who rebelled at the vast confines of San Pablos, now see their hunting grounds dwindle to a tiny, bubbling canyon. Here, their warrior spirit will likely be entombed.

"Have you got them?" I asked. "Have you really got them?"

We were walking along the canyon rim. Down below, we could see Apache campfires. Later in the night we heard singing and chanting: the death song of a race. The Apaches had stepped inside a cage.

"I keep looking for something," Lawson said. "Anything. Another trail, a tunnel, a cavern. I say to myself, there's got to be a way out. But I can't see it! Damn!"

He kicked a stone over the edge. We listened to it land down below, like the first handful of soil on a coffin.

"You know," he said, "there were times when I thought it would go on forever."

"Yes."

"And . . . you know what else? There were times I kind of wanted it to."

"I thought so. You did a good job, Henry."

"I suppose. Then why don't I feel better?"

"I don't know. I wish you did."

"Me, too."

On the morning of the fourth day, Lawson showed me a message he'd received by courier from Tucson. The other units, plus a swarm of high-ranking officers and politicians, were on their way. Reporters were coming too. Time, which we had thought was on our side, was about to betray us.

"You've got to do something!" I urged. "If those others come here, they'll claim all the credit."

"It'll be rough on them down there, too," Lawson said. "Those officers aren't gonna wait for the Apaches to admit they're beat."

"They wouldn't try to storm the canyon, would they?" God forgive me, but my blood pulsed at the prospect of describing such an assault.

"Nothing like that," Lawson said. "They'll lob shells into the canyon till it looks like the bottom of a stewpot. When the Apaches make a move, they'll run into Gatlings."

"You could tell them that. Send Lobito down."

"They'd kill him."

"Then shout down. Tell them what's coming. If they surrender they get . . . you know . . . fair treatment and a just trial and most of them will join their people at . . . a new reservation in Florida . . . down there, they haven't got a chance . . ."

"Some choice," Lawson said. "Go to Florida or get blasted to kingdom come."

He drew deep on his cigar and sent a little blue circle wobbling out over the canyon.

"Eddie, they just might turn down Florida."

Lobito Santos shouted himself hoarse. The only words I recognized—a dozen times at least—were "Captain Lawson." And not half an hour after he finished, four men started walking up the canyon trail. The man in front carried an Englishman's white underpants as a flag of truce.

"Contreras," Lobito whispered.

"And the other three?"

"Luciano. Big Pete. I don't know the other."

"Is it the Singer?"

"No. The Singer ain't coming." Lobito said it with such finality I wondered how he knew.

Lawson, Lobito, and I waited for the Apaches at the top of the trail. Around the canyon was a fence of cavalrymen. Sixty guns were trained on the men who came to parley.

There was an exchange of names when they reached the top.

"This other fella, he is calling himself Jacinto. Boss, he was with the Englishmen. He was a guide."

We moved off to a campfire. Lawson motioned for everyone to be seated. How the Apaches heeded Lawson! To them, Lobito was detestable. I was regarded without interest. Their eyes were on Lawson. Nothing he did, lighting a cigar or tugging at his beard, escaped their notice. They were like beaten animals trying to attach themselves to a new master.

Contreras spoke for the Apaches. He wore good military boots, light brown cotton trousers that were nearly new, and—what greater incongruity!—an English maroon velvet smoking jacket. Getting dressed, he'd incriminated himself enough to hang a dozen times.

He began a long speech. To hear it, you'd have thought he was calling on the four winds, Mother Nature, and all the gods to bear witness to the justice of his cause.

"He is asking, Boss, you got any cigarettes, anything to drink? They all out. They had English whiskey, but that crazy Singer broke the bottles. So what you got? they ask."

"That's all they said?"

"No. You are a great warrior and they are feeling good because they know you are a fair man and do the right thing."

"All right. No drinks." Lawson walked over to his saddlebags and dug out his cigar box. He was down to a half dozen and cast me an extraordinarily pained look when he dug into his precious supply.

"Tell them to take the rings off before they light up," he told Santos.

Thanks and nods. Now their allegiance to Lawson was complete. If he'd proposed a joint raid into Mexico, they'd have followed joyfully.

"All right. Ask them if they understood what you said. Ask them if they've come to surrender. Because that's what we're here for. The rest of it, I don't need to hear."

It didn't make any difference. Contreras delivered the speech he was determined to deliver. A fine job of oratory, it seemed, but Lobito Santos was not equipped, or inclined, to do it justice.

"All bullshit, Boss," he said when Contreras had made a dignified conclusion and sat down immensely pleased with himself. "All bullshit . . ."

"Just boil it down for me."

"He say everything was good till the Singer come. He say the Singer crazy, the Singer bad, the Singer got magic. The Singer make them fight. They got no choice. They don't want to hurt nobody, they don't want no trouble, but whenever the Singer speak, they got to do it, because he got magic. Contreras say he is happy you come to take them away from this bad man the Singer."

Lawson asked Lobito to confirm they were now prepared to surrender.

"Oh yes. They happy you come. They do what you say."

"They're not surrendering to *me*," Lawson cautioned. "They're surrendering to the United States government. Tell them that."

Lobito translated what Lawson said, at least he tried to, but the response was much the same.

"They say they gonna do whatever you want. You the Boss, not this crazy Singer."

"Do they understand that they will be punished? That they will have to pay for what they did?"

Lobito tried again and came back with another declaration of loyalty to Lawson.

"Damn it, do they know they'll be shipped two thousand miles away? That they might never see the West again? That they might . . ."

"Hold on, Henry," I interrupted. Somebody had to. "Aren't you forgetting? The point of this discussion is to bring them out of the canyon. Not to seal them in . . ."

"Okay . . . okay. Lobito, tell them I want them out of there now. Weapons, horses, loot, everything they've got."

When Lobito translated Lawson's request, the Apaches conferred among themselves. The discussion was short.

"Contreras say the San Pablos people lay down their arms and put their lives in the hands of Captain Henry Lawson. That they are your children now and anything happens to them, it's up to you."

Lawson wasn't pleased.

"Look at them, Eddie," he said. "Four charmers, puffing away. Indians and niggers . . . I do real well, don't I?"

"Just let it be, Henry. Let it end."

"Sure. It ended."

·VII·

"Where's the Singer?"

Lobito Santos put the question to the San Pablos Apaches. They were our prisoners now. They counted on us for protection and tobacco.

Contreras' cigar was long finished, but he wore the butt in his mouth and the paper ring on his finger, for these were important gifts from Captain Lawson.

"Boss, I'm telling you, this bullshitter is bullshitting," Lobito insisted. "I'm gonna tell you what he say. He say the Singer still down there someplace."

"He won't surrender?"

"Boss, he say he is wanting to talk to you. Just you. He is gonna surrender to you . . ."

"The Singer alone?"

"Boss, this bullshitter, he say so. But maybe he got plenty friend down there. You go, they gonna kill you for sure."

"What do you think?" Lawson asked me.

"He's right. There's no room for discussion. None."

"That's true."

"No doubt about it, it's a ploy. If you want to be the last white man killed by the last fighting Indian, then go down. Otherwise . . ."

"Since you put it that way . . ."

While I watched, dumbfounded, Lawson started walking down the trail, and into history. It was probably his most famous moment, but there was no coaching from me. He simply set off down the trail, without a second thought or a last word, without leaving instructions or messages behind.

Oh, I admit that I worked that scene hard. By the time I finished, I compared Lawson's descent into that thermal valley with Orpheus' journey into Hades. I called it "this fatal promenade," a "rendezvous with evil," and—oh, joy!—"one-man invasion of hell."

I was the man who watched him go: never was my whole life more completely captured in a single scene. I watched him walk along the creek, skip over steaming pools, and finally disappear into a copse of pine trees. I watched. And when I couldn't see him anymore, I listened. Twenty minutes after Lawson disappeared among the pines, we heard a single shot.

Twenty minutes was an eternity. I don't mean that in a literary way. I mean that it was a small grove. It didn't have twenty minutes of walking, stalking, hunting in it. The two men must have found each other in two minutes, or five. What then? And what about after the shot, what about those ten minutes before Lawson emerged, the Singer's body unceremoniously slung over his shoulder?

At first, there was wild cheering from the troops. From the Apaches . . . I watched Contreras closely . . . there was resignation. They were already beaten, I supposed.

Some of the soldiers rushed toward Lawson when he reached the top. But as soon as they got to within six feet of him, they stopped in their tracks, as if repulsed by an electric charge.

"Dukie!" Lawson shouted. "Where the hell is Dukie!"

The Singer hung over Lawson's shoulders. His face rested against Lawson's stomach. I searched it for an expression. I might as well have turned out his pockets for a last will and testament.

Dukie rushed over, panting and enthusiastic, but one look from Lawson calmed him down.

"Take this," Lawson said, "and bury it. Bury it where no one can find it. Even you."

Without a word, Dukie shouldered the corpse and walked away.

·VIII·

Paul W. Koch
Indian Hot Springs
Helenville, California

November 10, 1929

Dear Morrison,

To pick up where we left off. As soon as the wounded started coming back, along with your reports, we could feel the excitement spread. The stir: brass in Tucson, Kansas, and finally Washington wanting *daily* reports on Lawson's progress. Can you beat that? And the commanders leading the other columns demanding to be posted on Lawson's whereabouts, so they could "coordinate" operations! Coordinate, that is, the way six dogs chasing one bone coordinate! Politicians and reporters and big-game hunters and a couple actors, everybody wanted to get into the act.

That's when Lucy Lawson set up shop. A couple newspapers sent some fellows out, and there was nobody else around to interview. I used to sit in on those sessions, which she conducted out on our front porch. I heard her telling people all about her husband, his habits, and funny stories from around the fort, plus things he'd mentioned from past campaigns. And you know something, once she got cranked up she really had a flair for it. The stories got better and better, yet every time she told a story, she made it sound like she'd just remembered it. And she worked up these little teasing introductions—"I shouldn't tell you this" and "My husband would be very angry if this came out" and "You won't find this in the official report but . . ." When Lucy got up and looked at the horizon, she gave off a certain kind of sigh, and when she was coming up with a confidential-sounding yarn, she sometimes touched the reporter on the hand that held the pen. "Oh, wait, you mustn't write this."

Once I teased her, told her she'd done some kind of a job. She frowned, asked me, what did I mean by "job"? I said, you know, "the treatment." She told me she didn't have the faintest idea what I meant. That was the last time I tried to rib her.

Well, the word came that Lawson had killed the Singer in some kind of duel. At first we expected that there'd be a formal surrender ceremony down at Casa Diablo. That's what headquarters was planning on, a huge "do" with General Gottschalk presiding. Imagine my surprise when Van Doren sent a message that the whole bunch had arrived back at San Pablos! The prisoners would be kept under guard there until we were ready to ship the whole caboodle East. Lawson and the boys would be back next evening. That got me hopping. First message was to Gonzáles, to haul out the pussy wagon, the boys were coming home. Then I contacted Washington . . .

Koch could not know . . . he never will . . . that Lawson's decision not to await the other columns was my doing. I urged our immediate return to base. I told Lawson our rations for troops would be rapidly depleted when shared with our famished wards. If we failed to provide rations we would have to allow them to hunt, with horses and guns, and there was no telling what that might lead to. I doubt that Lawson suspected my true motives. This was my reasoning: The other columns had reporters in tow. These reporters were tired of writing color pieces on cavalry life and interviewing soldiers who hadn't seen Apaches in months. They were behind, they were anxious to file, and when they found Casa Diablo deserted, there was a good chance that they might leap at a sensational disappearance. Vanished Apaches! Missing cavalry! Another Little Big Horn! I assisted them in rushing to this conclusion by penning a letter, unfinished and unsigned, which described a fictitious trooper's intimations that the Apache surrender was a ruse. They were restless, they weren't to be trusted, they conspired in whispers, they eyed their captors' guns and horses, and any minute . . . There the letter ended. I dropped it on the ground five minutes before we departed for San Pablos.

Lucy had pictured something special: a victory parade, with Indians following along, with speeches, flag raisings, promotions, medals, I don't know. But when I told her that the renegades would be dropped off at San Pablos, under guard, she was dismayed. "You mean Van Doren gets to keep them?!"

A few days' captivity reduced our dreaded enemy to a contemptible, bedraggled pack of camp followers. Their complaints were endless, their problems insoluble, their pathetic dependence more annoying than their earlier hostility. Lawson had been at least halfway right when he suggested they should have ended it all at Casa Diablo, singing their death songs and walking into bullets. As it was, we dropped off the whole depressing bunch and rushed away, as if fleeing the scene of a crime. Only then, with the enemy no longer clinging to our reins, did we begin to taste victory! It was races and target practice, songs and jokes, up and down the line. We were a great bunch, each and every one of us, the hardest fighters, the longest riders, and our Boss was the best in the West.

> Lucy was afraid you'd come in like a bunch of raggedy transients crowding into a boardinghouse dining room, elbowing and goosing each other. She had me ride out a couple miles and warn you there was gentry in camp. And that night she planned a party . . .

We were like a winning baseball team, reluctant to leave the field. Opponents gone, bleachers emptied, darkness coming on, we wandered around the parade ground, unwilling to let go of the glory. And I was part of it. I remember the looks the buffalo soldiers gave me, which seemed to say: *Don't forget me, don't you dare, because I won't be forgetting you.*

Eventually, I found myself sitting in the river, soliloquizing. I wasn't quite drunk. I was wondering whether journalism was raw history or history was stale journalism, when I saw Dukie towering over me. God! Those pile-driver arms, that gleaming head, that broad chest!

"How you doin'?" he asked.

"I'm just fine."

"And you're plenty clean, right?"

"Cleaner than I've been in months."

"I'll bet," he said.

With that, he reached down, hooked one arm under my knees, another around my shoulders, and pulled my naked body out of the river as deftly as a mother scoops a baby out of the bath.

"Now don't you make no fuss."

"But what are you . . ."

"Stop kicking! It's not gonna hurt a bit."

I saw that the whole 25th Cavalry, minus officers, was watching, laughing as he carried me along. Indeed, they fell in behind us. Whatever was happening, they were all in on it.

Dukie paused while someone wrapped a kerchief around my eyes. That blindfold was my only clothing!

"Hold up a minute," someone whispered. "Line ain't formed up yet."

A line? Ah, so that was it! I was going to have to run a gamut. What would it be? Belts, branches, paddles, or bare hands? Well, soon enough I'd know.

"Does the Boss know about this?" I burst out indignantly. "Because when he hears about it . . ."

"Orders is orders," Dukie responded. And with that, he threw me into the air—it felt like I was ten feet high—but before I hit the ground there were other arms to catch me, and throw me, and so I was passed along, like a bucket of water headed toward a fire. Which, in the end, is what it turned out to be. The last time they tossed me, I landed soft, on blankets and pillows, a cushioned platform of some kind, sweet-smelling. While someone held my hands, preventing me from undoing the blindfold, someone else leaned over me. My body got the message first and passed the news to my brain. The someone poised above me was a woman. Her breasts brushed lightly over my amazed stomach, her nipples loitered playfully around my navel. Off came the blindfold: I was inside Gonzáles' wagon, two wagons, actually, placed side by side, a tiny island of sheets, blankets, hanging curtains, soft light, muffled voices, and women's bodies. They had brown eyes, Indian cheekbones, straight, long, glossy hair, full bodies, equal to the hard use made of them, and they spoke no English. Communication was impossible, and so, for me, was self-denial. "No saying no," Dukie had shouted from outside. He was right. The spell that Lucy had cast on me in Manhattan, a year before, was finally broken. When I stepped out of the wagon, a hundred men were there to cheer me, a hundred men who'd put me to the front of the line and who now separated me from a couple of my fellow journalists, dark-suited and furtive, who waited at the very end. I bowed, saluted, and walked away. And that was why I came late to Lucy's party.

The party was pretty much over my head. I was the last person the news boys wanted to jaw with. Lawson was the star of the show anyway, or at least the co-star. Because it was *her* night, when all was said and done. Beautiful women are rarer than military heroes, at least around army posts, and I never saw her looking any better than she did that night. She wore a maroon dress of some velvety material you kind of want to write your name on with your finger, and a black lacy shawl over her shoulders. Did we ever talk about that lady's neck? I'd hate for you to leave it out: the smoothness, the lines, the taper, everything signaling nobility up north and all kinds of kingdoms to the south. I caught one of the reporters calling it a "gorgeous isthmus"! Can you beat that? He made me think of Panama.

I quietly entered the nondescript little cottage which Lucy had managed to transform into an exotic salon and inserted myself among a group of reporters.

"Did Lawson *kill* the Singer?" one of them asked.

He was William Charles (W.C., "Water Closet") Symington of the Chicago *Tribune*, a round, short, white-haired little man wearing a once-good suit hopelessly deformed by pockets bulging with pipes, pens, pencils, wads of paper. I studied him carefully, connecting the famous name and the florid face.

"That's what I reported," I answered warily.

"But you didn't see it?"

"I reported that as well."

"Oh yes, a prize piece of obfuscation. 'One shot sounded, one man walked out alive.' That's not bad, but the facts remain painfully obscure. Was it a duel? Was it an ambush? What happened?"

"I don't know."

"Ah. Well, did Lawson *say* that he killed the Singer? Did it occur to you to ask him? Being a reporter . . ."

"He didn't say so, not in so many words. When he came out carrying a dead man, it didn't seem necessary to ask, 'Did you kill him?' "

"Not necessary?! Tell me, was it necessary to find out who the dead man was?"

"He was the Singer."

"Who said so?"

"The Apaches. And our guide."

"Who is also an Apache?"

"Why, yes . . ."

"Marvelous. And tell me, what kind of wound or wounds were on this alleged Singer?"

"Captain Lawson wanted him buried immediately. He handed the body to one of the soldiers."

"Who placed the body in an unmarked grave. Well, that's that."

"We didn't lay the dead man out," I burst out, embarrassed and defensive. "We didn't put him on display. No scalps. No ears, no souvenirs."

"That rhymes," Symington said. "No ears, no souvenirs. You missed your calling."

"What do you mean by that?"

"It means, Morrison, that I can hear you huffing and puffing behind every poetic paragraph, every rhyming episode of this cottage-industry campaign of yours."

"What *are* you gentlemen carrying on about?"

It was Lucy, with Lawson at her side. He looked handsome in uniform, but after weeks of seeing him in the clothes Lucy made him pile outside the door, it was like seeing some dead dirt-poor farmer in an undertaker's suit.

"Ah, there she is!" Symington exclaimed. "The only decent interview this month. And I'm not sure what we even talked about."

"You took notes!"

"All those cunning anecdotes! If they weren't true, they certainly ought to have been. Life imitates art, and you, Mrs. Lawson, are an artist. But no man could live up to your description of your husband."

"Don't be too sure, sir. Have you met him?"

Symington introduced himself and shook Lawson's hand. There was something consummately professional in the way this yellow-toothed, whiskey-mouthed old-timer who had drunk with Grant appraised Henry Lawson. He measured him in a glance. I am sure he could have forecast the whole course of Lawson's career from that moment on. Like many journalists, he knew a lot. Like them, he kept it to himself. All he said, to no one in particular, was: "Impressive."

"Impressive?" Lawson looked at Lucy as if to ask what it was that impressed him. Her dress? His uniform? Symington caught the puzzlement.

"Interesting," he added. Now there was no question but that he was talking about Lawson. "It'll take time, but it'll be interesting."

That left Lawson at more of a loss. After another look at Lucy, he gave up and tilted the contents of a whiskey glass into his mouth. But when he turned back, Symington was still staring at him.

"Now, what were you talking about?" Lucy asked, attempting to break the stare that Symington had fixed upon her husband. "Was someone being congratulated?"

It was another second or two before the old professional's eyes left Lawson's face. Lucy had started to repeat her question, a little louder.

"I hear you perfectly, Mrs. Lawson," Symington responded. "I was congratulating this youngster on his coverage of this . . . this Singer business."

"Singer business." Not a war, not a battle, it was a commercial transaction. Maybe he was right. I didn't care about it then, but now I realize that our chase of the Apaches was really a process of eviction. They were our quarry. They were never people. When we gave them human qualities . . . cleverness, ferocity, speed . . . it was the way a hunter talks about a deer or fox. There could never be a truce. The hunt would be over when the beast was tamed or dead.

"I waited for every word he wrote," Lucy said. I wished she were less enthusiastic. "I saw every dispatch. Even now, what he wrote is all I know."

"I should leave it at that," Symington responded, "and consider myself lucky in the bargain."

He started to excuse himself. He bowed low to Lucy, nodded to me, and took Lawson's hand, which he did not release.

"A word of advice," he said. "I can't resist it."

"Sure," Lawson said, amiably enough.

"Pick your wars. Pick them very carefully."

"I never thought there was much choosing when it comes to wars," Lawson commented, with the air of a plain fellow who had heard a bit too much highfalutin nonsense. "They happen, see? Somebody starts them up. You fight until they're finished. So I don't understand about the picking."

Symington nodded, bowed, started to leave. At the door he gestured for me to follow. He was waiting for me on the porch.

"You must think yourself a clever boy," he said. "That letter you dropped on the ground at Casa Diablo led me to one of the most spectacularly erroneous dispatches I've ever filed. You made me look bad and you had better pray, young man, that you never cover a war with me . . ."

"I'm sorry . . ."

"No, no," he interrupted. "I'll make you sorry, if I have half a chance to do it. That's a warning, which is more than you gave me. And I'll give you another warning, too."

He leaned close to me. I smelled his whiskey, his tobacco, and his sweat, and I feared he might embrace me, not from fondness, but to spread another case of whatever in the world it was he suffered from.

"Stay away from the gallant leader, Morrison. And stay away from the lovely wife."

• IX •

Koch's letter resumes.

The big shots said good night. Mrs. Van Doren and Mrs. Presley siphoned off some of them for dinner, and the rest hotfooted it to the pussy wagon.

When I saw the table Lucy set, I nearly cried, what with the flowers, the good china, the wineglasses and silver, and the candlelight, which was supposed to make everything intimate and romantic, even though you and the Boss had several weeks of similar intimate and romantic lighting behind you. Just looking at Lucy put a lump in my throat. I mean it, watching her put an apron on top of her dress, and a padded mitten to hold hot pots, doing the best she could to treat us three bozos like we were proper gentlemen! As we sat down, I said about a dozen silent prayers: that you wouldn't knock over your wineglass and that the candlelight wasn't bright enough to show up the purple bruises on your neck and that Lucy wouldn't notice your fly had been half buttoned all night long—that I wouldn't blow my nose in my napkin—or that Lawson wouldn't throw his chewed-off bones out the door to the dogs on the parade ground, wouldn't empty his wineglass like it was a canteen, wouldn't be so tired, or get so drunk, that he'd break her heart by accident. Later that night, I figured maybe half my prayers were answered. Nobody spilled anything, but the dogs outside ate pretty good.

"This is beautiful," I said when we sat down, trying to start things off nicely. "This how they do it in Paris?"

"Not every day," Lucy said. "And not quite like this, ever. I hope the chicken's not too . . . muscular."

"Looks top-notch to me," Lawson said. To him, hot beans were top-notch. "What is it?"

"*Coq au vin*. Chicken in wine."

"Did you drown him in it? Or was he dead already when you put him in?"

"Henry!"

"Joking, dear."

We started in to eat and, well, the chicken died fighting, that was for sure. Still, we made out just fine for a while. . . .

"What a peculiar gentleman that Mr. Symington was," Lucy said.

"I'll say," Lawson snorted.

"Is he well known?"

"Yes, he is," I answered. "About as well known as any American journalist right now."

"I almost wished we could have made another place at dinner," Lucy said. "There was something about him. Something in his eyes."

"Yeah," Lawson said. "Wool."

"Henry . . ."

"You want to feed him, you can give him my place, Luce."

"Why are you so hard on him?"

" 'Pick your wars.' What's that supposed to mean? Say 'yes'? Say 'no'? Say 'maybe'? If there's a war, you go. He ought to know that."

"He was saying—I think he was saying—that there are good wars and bad wars," I ventured.

"Sure," Lawson said. "The ones you lose are the bad ones. That what he meant?"

"Not that. Something else."

"Well, what? Because if a so-called bad war happens along, I'd like to know ahead of time. Wouldn't you, Koch?"

"It's all the same to me," Koch said.

"That's the damn point," Lawson said. "When you're a soldier it's all the same."

"You mean you feel the same"—I was sticking my neck out now—"after every war you win? After every battle?"

"Sure. If you win."

"You feel the same after Casa Diablo as after Stone Mountain? Feel the same shipping Apaches to Florida as seeing the Army of Northern Virginia lay down arms at Appomattox Court House?"

That stopped him.

"Well, no," he said. "No. Not by a long shot. Saving the Union's one thing. Making the West safe for trespassers is something else."

"But they both were victories, weren't they? Yet you admit it yourself, there's a difference."

"Okay," Lawson conceded, "I'll grant you there's a difference. But it had nothing to do with my being there or my not being there. That doesn't change. That can't change!"

By the time he finished, he'd raised his voice. Lawson almost never spoke that way. He regarded me with some irritation, as if to say, all right, you caught me out. So what? Now what?

"This is all a little beyond me," Lucy said.

"Me, too," Koch seconded.

"And me most of all," Lawson said, good humor returning. "Eddie, what the hell are we arguing about anyway?"

"Beats me," I said, throwing up my hands. "Anyway, the Territory's at peace and I'm out of business here."

"You're leaving?" Lucy asked.

"The day after tomorrow," I replied. "The war's over."

I glanced at Lucy to make sure she caught what I said next. "It's been a good trip. I think I accomplished everything I set out to do."

"But I haven't heard a thing about what happened," Lucy protested. "Now, please . . . sit back . . . I want to hear it all. Start from the beginning. I don't care how long it takes. Everything you didn't put in your articles. Everything."

"That's a tall order," Lawson said.

"I'll be patient," Lucy countered. "Coffee's ready. If it takes all night, I'll cook breakfast, too."

She looked hopefully from me to Lawson and back again, while Lawson and I exchanged glances ourselves, like a pair of students reluctant to recite.

"Well?" Lucy pleaded. "Isn't anybody going to talk to me?"

"You say you read my articles," I began.

"Of course I did. And so did thousands of other people who had the price of a newspaper. I had thought—perhaps I deceived myself—that I was entitled to something more from the lips of the two men I chiefly care about on earth."

"What was it you wanted to know?" Lawson asked.

"I haven't prepared a list! I'm not a reporter and I'm not a fellow officer. But I will not be contented with . . . scraps! Does it occur to you, to either of you, that the nights while you were away left ample time for wondering?"

"We came back, didn't we, Luce?" Lawson asked. That was a gigantic misstep.

"Does that imply that if you had *not* come back, if you were dead or missing, I would be entitled to a full account—from someone else, of course—but since you have returned, it's business as usual, until your next adventure?

Koch's letter resumes.

. . . As soon as she started asking those questions, I knew we were headed for trouble. I sympathized with Lucy. Many were the nights we'd conjectured about where you fellows were at. And she was no dummy either. It wasn't: I hope he put on dry socks. She understood cavalry operations, sensed how Apaches fought, and she could read a map as well as I could. Still, I'd seen the Boss come in more times than she had and I knew the last thing he wanted to talk about was what had happened. He wanted to plunge himself into what our late President called "normalcy." He wanted to talk about food, pitch some horseshoes, sink his teeth into a *Police Gazette*.

"Was it all so awful you can't talk about it?" Lucy pleaded. We heard her, but Lawson and I were still looking at each other and Lucy's voice came to us from another place. I think both of us must have realized that, though no one had planned it, there was something between us that Lucy could never share. She, the most adventurous of us all, might be condemned to live on the edge of our adventures. She'd have to be satisfied by what we gave her: secondhand accounts, when we were in the mood.

"Oh hell," Lawson said, leaning back in his chair. "No point in keeping secrets. There's some times we had were plain glorious. Eddie, am I right?"

"Oh yes," I said. "There were lots of moments I'll remember. Not just the ones I put in my stories."

"Well?" Lawson said. "What are you waiting for? Spin the lady a yarn or two."

I told Lucy how we roamed across the reservation at dusk. I told her how I trembled when the Apaches caught us on the mountain trail, and how exhilirated and alive I felt that night we rushed the Apache camp. I worked hard—it was as close as Lucy would ever get to the reality of a campaign—and I talked well, tossing off landscapes, characters, vignettes, and strategies.

"My God, you spin a yarn!" Lawson exclaimed when I settled back triumphantly.

"You were there. You made it happen."

"But you tell it with all the trimmings! 'Four horsemen silhouetted against a blood-red sky'! That's terrific! If Koch said it, it would be 'Returned to camp, p.m.' And if I said it, it would be 'We rode home on account it was getting dark.' "

"It's all in the telling," I said, pleased to have made Henry Lawson appreciate the power of language. Lucy appreciated that power, too. Too much.

"You need to have Edwin with you all the time," she said. "And it did him good to be out there with you. You each have something the other lacks."

Perhaps Lucy didn't mean it to come out that way, but she

had turned me into a Park Row Boswell and made Lawson a coarse and unpoetic warrior.

"Yeah, well," he said. He looked out the door. A silence descended on the table. I lacked the strength to break it. Only Lucy could do that, with a kiss or a joke. An apology would do. But it was Lawson who finally stirred.

"Well, that would be nice, having Eddie come along," he reflected. "But he's leaving, so I guess I'll have to muddle through without him and get help wherever I can find it."

"Well, it looks like we're in for a spell of peace," Koch said, apropos of nothing. "We're out of business, too, once we get those fellows on the train."

"Peace," Lawson said. "Ain't it wonderful?"

He got up and went to the cabinet that contained his liquor. He brought out some brandy and stepped around the table, pouring each of us a drink, ours into glasses, his own into a dented tin cup, the very same he used for his morning eye-opener and carried with him in the field. Ugly as it was, he planted it on Lucy's tablecloth.

Now he faced her, took her hand, as if he were about to pull her off someplace. It felt like Koch and I ought to be someplace else, yet if we had not been there, the moment would never have happened. They needed witnesses.

"Understand, Luce? When I had nothing to do, I thought of you. And when I was scared, I thought of you. Not a minute that I didn't miss you. And—hear this—not a minute that I wanted you to be there. Maybe that doesn't make sense. So be it. I can't sort it out."

"Neither can I," Lucy said.

• X •

It is surprising how effectively friendship and even familiarity compete with love. Friendship overwhelmed me my last day at Fort Monroe. As I was brushing my suit, polishing my shoes, packing my bags, one after another of the buffalo soldiers sought me out. Sometimes there were letters to mail, small presents, arrowheads and buckskins and such. They gave me addresses. If I am ever in Birmingham or Port Charles, Gainesville or Ashtabula, I will be well hosted in the colored quarter. I do not believe they would have done this for any visitor.

Eccles found me in Herman Biddle's barber chair. He watched Biddle deliver a point-by-point inventory of the defaults and malfunctions of the white man's physiognomy: I felt like an unsavory specimen in some tribal medical school. My hair was thin and flimsy; my beard couldn't make up its mind what color it should be, and my skin, my "Chalk-asian" skin, was a battleground of pigments and pustules. If I were a slave on an auction block, I wouldn't bring ten dollars: I lacked the strength for field work, adroitness for kitchen service. And yet, Biddle ended his performance with a gift, a green glass jar, wax-sealed, containing a salve to rub on anything that felt poorly.

"I hear you're leaving soon," Eccles began when my shave and haircut were ended.

"Yes."

"The war's over and we won it and so that's the end of it." He seemed to be going out of his way to make our parting as unemotional as possible.

"That's right," I said, "but I'm not sure I would put it exactly that way."

"How would you put it?"

"I would say, I'll remember this trip. Not just the campaign. The people. The personal side. Like it or not, Sergeant Eccles, I'll remember you."

"You will?" The least sentimental of men himself, he seemed startled to find that I was capable of feeling.

"I'll remember you as the most persistent interrogator on the frontier, for one thing."

"I like to make sure I understand things."

"I've gathered that."

"I like to keep the record straight, so other people understand."

"Well, all right, then. Good luck."

"Goodbye," Eccles said, shaking my hand. And with his free hand he presented me what I'd requested the first night at Fort Monroe, clippings of his articles for the Baltimore *Sentinel*. Odd! He gave me no errands to run, no letters to mail, no address. He didn't want me to meet his family and he didn't threaten to look me up back East. Yet I felt a tie to him . . .

That night, I joined Koch for a final round of pinochle. With Koch, there were no ceremonies. It was curious that the most sociable man at Fort Monroe should be the loneliest. We smoked cigars and played cards as usual and the only thing that made the evening any different was a nonchalant remark of his about the controversial French penal colony off Guiana, Devil's Island. Koch said he thought it would suit him fine there. He couldn't understand what all the complaining was about, living on an island in a warm place. He could spend his life in prison cheerfully, he said, if it weren't for the other prisoners. At the end I gave him my remaining cigars and stepped out onto the parade ground, where Lucy found me.

"You've been avoiding me," she charged.

"You're right," I said. "I have. Where's the Boss?"

" 'The Boss' is sleeping," she said. "You'll have to talk to me alone, if you haven't lost the knack."

We sat on the grass at the river's edge. How familiar everything had become! I knew the river by heart, the rocks, the overhanging branches where we hung out our clothes, the deep pools that were good for swimming. I could tell the time of day from the way the sun slanted into the canyon, its color and angle as it hit the sandstone walls surrounding us. I knew what light shone in what tent; every tent was someone's address. Full moons were like a holiday and when nights were dark I could find my way without a lantern.

The fort was part of me. And so was Henry Lawson. The man who had taken over Lucy's life had changed mine, too. I wouldn't have expected it. He wasn't a reader, his knowledge even of military history was slim, and he wasn't a fluent talker or a ready socializer. Moreover, I doubted that I would ever mean as much to him as he meant to me.

"Are you sorry you came?" she asked me. "Are you sorry you're leaving? Is there more love in your life? More adventure? Will we see you again? Are you happy?"

The way she looked at men when she spoke, I felt that she could have answered all those questions for me. Better answers than my own.

"Very well, Luce. Since you asked. A word about Henry. A word about Lucy. Last, a word about myself . . . I was prepared, I was anxious to dislike your husband. He can be rude, coarse, sullen, and he drinks too much. That's not all. He's supremely inconsiderate. Not deliberately, not maliciously, but naturally inconsiderate, which makes it worse. He doesn't notice people the way he should, doesn't read them carefully or try to figure them out. He looks at them and then he looks past them, and one of these days he'll regret that, because just when his eyes are scanning the far horizon, someone will hurt him . . ."

"Who?"

"Some officer he trusted. Some polite nonentity whose name he didn't quite catch. An old friend he took for granted. Or you . . ."

"Me!"

"Yes. You frighten me, Lucy. It sounds odd, I know. Men aren't supposed to be frightened of women. But all the things you want for him . . ."

"For all of us," she corrected. "For you, too, Edwin."

"You keep saying that. You say we're all in it together. But you're the one who wants things. Henry doesn't know what you want. I don't know. And I don't know that you do either. But somehow, you're the pilot of us all. And I for one am afraid of where you'll take us. I'm afraid of what you'll do to get there. I'm glad to be going . . . glad to be leaving you . . . and I never thought I'd say that . . ."

"But you're not sorry you came . . ."

"I wrote the stories you wanted."

"No one asked you to lie," she said. "It cost you nothing. It may have helped your career as much as Henry's."

"I said it was all right, Luce. I did it. Assignment completed. I wrote up a hero . . ."

"You're leaving tomorrow. Is that the note you want to leave on?"

We walked together in silence. Arm in arm. We were almost to Officers' Row.

"No," I said. "When I'm with you, Luce, I have a feeling my life is in your hands. I don't want to feel that way. I want to get out of your life for a while . . ."

"Yeah . . . well . . . so," she said when the silence had grown unbearable, and her mimicking of Lawson made us both laugh.

"Oh hell," I said. "I wonder how long it will take me . . ."

It was hard to say it.

"For what?"

"How long it will take for me to find someone like you to love."

HOME LEAVE

·I·

Darling Edwin, please come soon.
All the boys are listening
For your martial tune.
We cannot fire a bullet
And we cannot sign a truce
Without the Sun's *man present.*
What's the use?

It was the making of me, that little ride with Lawson. Within months of my return from Casa Diablo, I was off to London, my base for the next dozen years. While America surfeited itself with peace, I was its representative in foreign conflicts. I covered a dozen wars, or pieces of wars, in Africa, the Balkans, the Far and Middle East. Small wars, but splendid stories nonetheless. I was very good in the Sudan.

It seemed to me that I had left Lucy behind. I had learned not to care or, at least, to keep my caring in the past. But it turned out that one love was all the love that was in me. There was no one else to follow Lucy. I accepted this, with time: I even welcomed it. My romantic life was a handful of foredoomed affairs and a modest commerce with prostitutes, none abused. Perhaps I preferred such transactions to the risk of hurting, or loving, or caring. My love for Lucy was in the past. Yet it was the only love I had. I came to regard it as a life not lived, a road not taken. Sometimes I wondered how things might have been.

There was no news in a place like Camp Sherman, Oregon, or Fort Riley, Kansas. I was able to cruise the world in search of wars, but the Lawsons were the prisoners of a peaceful nation. I didn't like to think about what the Army had poor Henry doing: drills and practices and paper exercises were not his forte, nor was military politics. I wanted to remember him as he had been, and might never be again, the heartbreakingly naïve horseman against a blood-red sky, smoking a cheroot, talking thoughtfully, with Dukie and Eccles to keep him company, and Apaches over the horizon.

In letters, Lucy sounded far away, interested in my accomplishments, informative about events and people at Fort Monroe, but never revealing how her life was turning out. As for Lawson, he scrawled his greetings at the bottom of each letter, sentences like "Give 'em hell, Eddie" or "Sound like you're having a whale of a time" or, in an attempt at humor, "Wish I was there," which I took to be an inversion of the standard "Wish you were here."

Every now and again, I would receive a letter, a present, a small something from the 25th Cavalry. Once it was a letter from Herman Biddle, a testy note chiding me for my silence and demanding a full report on the state of my health, not omitting any evidence of "Chalk-asian deterioration." It reached me in Khartoum. I kept hearing from Sergeant Eccles, too. Every year or so, I'd get a packet of his newspaper columns. He wasn't a writer: I'd known that from the beginning. But his failure was interesting. He had read too much. He was writing too hard, overwriting, and the result was florid, prolix, and stentorian. His voice was buried under an avalanche of books. There was so much yearning in the man, credos on the responsibilities and opportunities of the black man, the black soldier, and—for this was the recurrent theme—the black officer. So much yearning! So little warmth! All he wrote by way of personal communication was "Mrs. Lawson shows me your writing. No response to this is necessary."

I save the most amazing gift for last. One morning in London, I found a long cardboard cylinder waiting, with a return address at Fort Riley, Kansas. I tore the package open and pulled out a cane, an oak walking stick, festooned with carving the way a carnival freak is covered with tattoos. It was the ugliest thing I had ever seen, but when I turned the tortured wood around and saw the letters cut into the handle my heart was in my throat: *to Morrison, from Dukie.*

·II·

My newspaper insisted that its overseas representatives return to New York every few years, whether to refresh the correspondent's knowledge of the newspaper or to reassert the paper's dominion over the correspondent, I cannot exactly say. My first such return came in 1890. I enjoyed it, I must say, but was soon anxious to be gone. After I walked the bridge, spent a few nights sitting at the window of the apartment I insisted on retaining, after I dealt with publishers and editors, dined and dissipated, I felt the itch for war. I lacked conventional ambitions, New York style: the *Sun* had nothing I wanted, nothing more than it had given me, and that was a dangerous position for a still-young journalist to be in.

One afternoon, I was told that a visitor who declined to give his name was in the lobby. Normally, I would have insisted on a name: New York was full of cranks. Normally, too, the porter, William Jenkins, a cantankerous veteran of Shiloh, would have obtained the name: to him, every visitor was an anarchist bomb thrower. But this time, Jenkins practically tugged at my sleeve, pulling me out of the newsroom, into the lobby, where Henry Lawson, massive and gray-bearded, stood waiting.

"Boss!" I shouted, loud enough to turn the head of every tout and drummer in the lobby.

"Hello, Eddie," he responded. He'd expected big-city formalities, and here I was, hugging him!

He was older, no doubt, tall and massive as ever but lined and weathered and . . . aged. The difference between then and now was the difference between a new mountain, raw and jagged, and an older peak, worn by glaciers, with forests creeping up toward the timberline and rocks slowly turning into soil. Still, he looked splendid in civilian clothes—I'd often tried to picture him out of uniform—and here he was in a white suit that Mark Twain might have envied.

"What are you doing here? When did you get in? Where's Lucy?" I overwhelmed him with questions. "And who's in charge of the Twenty-fifth?"

"Hold on, hold on," he said. "There's time. Any place we can sit?"

I led him into the newsroom. His presence was daunting: he still had the magic. When he sat at a chair I pulled over to my desk, the nearby reporters found cause to stop work and eavesdrop. I'm sure they recognized him. I had made his reputation and he mine, and they were curious how that worked. Was I his mouthpiece? Was he my dancing bear?

"See this?" I said, lifting Dukie's unspeakable walking stick. "I swear, I think about you people whenever I pick this up. What with his name touching my palm, it's like a long-distance handshake."

"Oh yeah." Lawson inspected the cane, with all its scars and ridges. "Dukie got drunk and I had to put him in the guardhouse. He started in to carving, paperweights, whistles, cook spoons, chessmen, I don't know what all."

"Oh." I was disappointed. Silly, but I liked thinking my gift was unique.

"That was the first thing he made, though," Lawson added. "I didn't tell him to. He just sent it out and said, would I ship it along to you?"

"Ah." My self-image restored, I asked again about his visit to New York. He had come East, he said, "to talk to a man about a railroad." He tried making light of it, but I sensed that this foray was an attempt to escape from a stagnating military career before it was too late. But it already was too late: the trip had been a failure. Lawson didn't appear to be looking forward to returning to Kansas and breaking the news to Lucy. Nonetheless, he was leaving, he said, that evening.

"Tonight?" I asked. "This is all I get to see of you?"

"I'm sorry, Eddie," Lawson said. "I guess we could have had some good times. But I wanted . . . I wanted to have something to cheer about."

"Have you seen the city?"

"Not much." He shrugged. "Mostly the inside of my hotel, waiting for messages. I ate there. I walked over to the docks once and looked at all the ships. The comings and goings. That's really something. I wouldn't mind crossing the ocean sometime."

It broke my heart, how time, and the city, and some businessmen who weren't fit to hold his reins had humbled him. And how readily he accepted the beating. He sat in his hotel room waiting for messages. When they didn't come, he went for walks alone.

"You should have called me."

"I'm sorry . . . I promised I'd contact you right off. Lucy said you could set things up, plug me in . . . but this damn railroad fiasco ripped the heart right out of me."

I understood: the appointments and presentations, interviews and dinners, and ultimate disappointment. He wanted to fail alone, without reporting back to me, without my offering to write letters and pull strings. With Lucy waiting breathlessly, there was no reason he should have to anatomize defeat in my presence also. It was a miracle he had visited me at all.

"I'm glad you looked me up," I told him. "I'm really glad."

"Yeah. Well . . ." He was touched, I could see. There'd been nothing in his letters to indicate that he felt much of anything. But he was softer now, vulnerable and human. Losing did that to him.

"We talk about you sometimes," he said. "You'd be surprised."

"You and Lucy, you mean?"

"Us, too, sure," he answered. "But the men. The old-timers. They never will let me forget that damned baseball game."

"How long have you got, before your train?"

"Till ten o'clock."

"And you've got nothing to do till then?"

"No," he replied, shrugging. "Nothing cooking."

"Have you got much to go back with?"

"Like . . ."

"I mean, to carry."

"Oh. No," he said, another apology. "Just me."

"All right, Boss," I said. I stressed "Boss." "Let's march."

Lawson must have told the story of the next few hours around a hundred campfires, until it became part of the oral history of the 25th Cavalry: the Manhattan Campaign, when Morrison took the Boss in tow and, together, they rampaged through the finest shops in Gotham, the best of everything, first class all the way. A busy afternoon of shopping, that is all it was, but Lawson made it sound like the Sack of Rome.

I had intended to send back gifts to Lucy. Then, thank God, I realized that Lawson couldn't go back carrying my gifts and his empty-handed defeat. That meant presents from both of us, and then it got out of hand, because Koch had to have cigars, and Eccles might fancy a leather-bound journal. Herman Biddle couldn't be ignored, so we rushed to an obscure medical supply house to purchase a floor-to-ceiling chart of the human anatomy, muscles, bones, nerves, viscera, and all. And Dukie—well, that was the moment I learned of his great weakness, a passion for sweets, especially lemon balls.

Our last stop was a bookseller. I lost track of Lawson while I browsed, unable to decide what to send Lucy. It was like selecting a handful of volumes to salvage from a shipwreck. When I had the stack down to a half dozen, I glanced up, suddenly conscious of having neglected Lawson. Curious: in any other store I would have let him fend for himself, but here I felt responsible and guilty.

I saw him shambling between shelves, hovering over display tables, as if something might reach out and ambush him. I had directed him to the history section, thinking he might find something military. Grant's *Memoirs* was an obvious choice, and Elizabeth B. Custer's three volumes on her husband's campaigns had been much acclaimed. But Lawson drifted into the children's section.

"Boss?"

By now, offices were emptying; pedestrians crowded sidewalks, carriages and wagons of all sorts fought their way down streets, and Henry Lawson gazed out at them as if they were part of a parade that he could never join.

"Don't worry about me, Eddie. I haven't broken anything."

We ended up at Goddard's restaurant, packages and all, in a booth which commanded the dining room and bar. Lawson was easily the most striking figure in the room, yet he stared out like a child on his first visit to the city. When I had thought of them, I pictured what Lucy was missing. I'd taken Lawson for granted. Now I saw that there were cravings which the camaraderie of the 25th Cavalry could not satisfy. Maybe he wanted to be known in a tavern, get into arguments, stand a round of drinks, wager on a baseball game. In civilian clothes, he looked like the sort of man who moves well through clouds of smoke and jovial crowds. But the ticket to Kansas was in his pocket.

"Know something, Eddie?" he asked after several minutes of beery silence.

"What's that?" I said.

"You should have married her."

"What?!" It was so out of the blue, so calmly uttered, as if he were saying the beer was good or the weather might change.

"It's not that I don't love her. And I'm not going out of my way to do you a big favor. It's just that . . . that love isn't everything."

"I can understand you're down, Boss. But it was just a job. One job. You wouldn't give up so fast if you were trailing Apaches."

"Yeah. That's where they should put me. With the damn Apaches. On a reservation, or in a Wild West show. I shouldn't have been in such a rush to wind up that war."

"Well, I'm sure things wouldn't be any different if Lucy were with me."

"But you could bring her here, at least, or London, put her in with a better class of people, women she could talk to about something other than post housing . . ."

"That I could do," I conceded, accepting Lawson's hypothesis. "I bring her to London, install her in lovely quarters. We hire servants, buy furniture, we entertain. People entertain us. Even when I'm overseas, *especially* when I'm overseas, she's besieged with invitations for dinners and weekends. Our world is crowded with friends, filled with conversation, pervaded by good humor and good company and . . . Henry?"

"All right." He nodded.

"You take my point?"

"Yeah. Sooner or later you'd wind up in the soup, too."

"In the soup. There's always something else. Something would be missing. The openness of the frontier, the far horizon, the western sky at night. All the stars . . ."

"But, damn it, there's more to it than that!" Lawson said. "It's not just missing the city when you're in the country, or vice versa. It's something, she doesn't even know what it is."

"Is that so unusual? We've all got a case of something missing."

"Lucy figured that I could do it for her, do it for the both of us . . ."

"Do what?"

"Catch up with that missing something. Sniff it, stalk it, track it, hunt it, hell, kill it, screw it, I don't know. *I was the man.* Am I right?"

I had to nod. I wished I could convince him he was nobody special, an ordinary chap moving from youthful hopes to middle-aged compromise and an old age commingling memories and regrets. But the essence of Lawson was that he stood above the ranks, an outsize figure, expected to play a special part. Anything could happen to him . . . anything had better!

"Yes." I had to say it. "I believed it."

"So did I," said Lawson. "So did I. I believed . . . I believed I could do *anything*! . . . But times like these . . . hell, I'm a soldier. I'm not bloodthirsty. But, let's face it . . ."

He hesitated, swallowed more beer.

". . . I'm a soldier, Eddie." It sounded like he was saying "thief" or "outlaw." "Not a staff soldier or a War College lecturer . . . a fighting soldier, field-level commander . . . you know. Lucy keeps on about all the soldiers who move on to other things. Look at General Grant, she says. He went all the way to the White House. Robert E. Lee lost and still he wound up as a college president someplace. But I didn't join to move up. I joined to be what I am!"

"I know. But these are peaceful times . . ."

"Ain't that the truth." Another beer. "*Rest in peace.* See it on gravestones all over the land. You ever think what it means to rest in peace? It means *rest*: you don't do nothing. And peace: nothing gets done to you. Know what else it means? It means you're dead . . ."

We motioned for another round and sat together drinking. I suspect that Lawson was grimly satisfied that I accepted his tale of stagnation, disappointment, and failure without trying to jolly him out of it. That would have been a mistake, and I guessed it was the kind of mistake that Lucy made repeatedly: pathetic attempts to penetrate the gloom in which he wrapped himself, disturbing the peace with rumors of a promotion here, a civilian opportunity there, all beside the point, because what Henry Lawson needed was a war.

"You know what I wished I'd been?" he asked, wiping foam off his beard. "A mercenary."

"A mercenary?"

"Like the Hessians, or the Irish, or the Polish Guards."

"Sell yourself?"

"It's not for the money, Eddie. It's so's to . . . to be what I am. If you're a soldier you belong in a war. You really do. It don't matter what the war's about. It really don't. Wars are like storms. Who knows what makes an ocean angry? Wars are war. And any of those wars you write up—let me ask you—wouldn't it be better if I was there? Faster? Cleaner? Wouldn't I be better for being there? So call me a mercenary. You're kind of a mercenary, too, aren't you? With your pen?"

"I suppose I am."

"You don't care who's in it?"

"No."

"Or who wins?"

"Usually not."

"And if there's peace all over . . . you're out of business, am I right?"

"Yes." I looked up, surprised by his shrewdness, and we

both laughed. "I can't take you with me, Henry. Anyway, there's Lucy. What about children?"

"She says she can't have 'em."

"Can't?"

"A woman like that? You believe it? Sometimes the 'can't' sounds a lot like 'won't' to me. Maybe she figures I'm enough to handle. And having kids . . . it would be like letting me off the hook. She doesn't want that yet. She still wants a miracle."

"You mean a war?"

"Yeah. A war would suit her fine."

Henry Lawson's visit unsettled me. After years of living alone, it reminded me that I had a kind of family after all. There were people with whom my life was linked, people who remembered me and talked about the time I'd shared with them, and used visits, letters, small gifts, to keep the memory alive.

The day after he left I walked the bridge, thinking of the woman I had loved and the man who might be counted my only friend and a troop of black cavalrymen who thought of me as their proxy in the world. I guessed I loved them all. I wanted what was best for them. Standing at the bridge railing, staring west past barges, docks, and factories on the Jersey shore, I saw a spectacular, unsubtle summer sunset, orange and red, so that it seemed there was a vast conflagration over the horizon, a bonfire all across the land. It looked to me like there was a war out there, and I couldn't help hoping I was right.

THE NICEST PEOPLE ON EARTH

• I •

Paul W. Koch
Indian Hot Springs
Helenville, California

February 23, 1929

Dear Morrison,

If you believe that the Civil War was fought to free the slaves and the Great War was to keep Huns from raping Belgian nuns, then I guess you figure that we went to Cuba because somebody sank the *Maine*. As for me, I put the *Maine* right up there with the Easter Bunny.

The century was ending, and that gave all of us a funny feeling. Do you have any idea what I mean, Morrison? When you grow old in a century that's different from the one you were born in, you feel like kind of a leftover. It was scary, starting something we knew we'd never finish. We talked about Jesus coming again, and Halley's comet.

We talked about weapons and inventions, battleships and airships, and it wasn't the kind of talk that made a bunch of horse soldiers feel they had a real tight grip on the future. We even talked about New Year's Eve, 1899, and how to celebrate it. In bed, asleep, was my idea. Reading the Bible. Drinking. Screwing. The Boss said maybe we'd ride over to Fort Sill, Oklahoma, where Geronimo and some of the other Apaches were confined, and whoop it up with them. Hell, he said, they were retired, we were retired, and the new century wasn't going to have much use for either of us. The only one who didn't join in in all this chat was Eccles. He didn't have to. We all knew he was looking forward to it, all full of "The Negro in the New Century," "Dawn of a New Era," etc. You'd have thought the turn of the century was his personal graduation ceremony.

Here's what happened with Eccles. There were towns all over Kansas, farming towns that had started up after the Civil War, and we were expected to help them. There weren't any Indians to fight and, fortunately, no strikes to break, but now and then we'd throw in a couple days' "happy labor" putting up a school. I daresay there's a dozen all-white farming towns around Kansas that thought well of us, asked us back, fed us generously, and thanked us kindly, so long as we got our niggers back to post before dark.

A few weeks before Christmas, 1897, Eccles arrived with a request from some preacher in Nicodemus, Kansas, that we send representatives to attend the dedication of a new town hall. Well, the Boss thought it would be fun to take a trip, Eccles, Dukie, me, and him.

And it was fun. It was the sort of thing we did too little of anymore. I remember riding through the snowstorm, the horses' breath steaming and the flakes melting as they hit my face, and how we crossed a frozen river and camped on the bank and sat there fishing through a hole in the ice, passing around a bottle of applejack. I remember how, while we were out on the ice, the snow stopped falling and the clouds peeled off and the sky was all stars and the ice on the river was all silver and the fields rolled pure white into the horizon, and I'll tell you this, Morrison, we didn't miss a war right then.

Well, what we didn't know about Nicodemus was that it was one of a handful of all-black ex-slave settlements, with black schools and mayors and sheriffs and all. When we filed in, the whole town was waiting for us, like we were somebody important. You know me. At official ceremonies, I duck off to the back of the room, rear pew, but there were seats up front for me, for Dukic, too, and when the preacher introduced us, he told all about us, where we were born and our careers so far. But it was Eccles he asked to say a few words. And Eccles was ready. Here's that famous speech.

A FAIR SALUTE

Remarks at Town Hall Dedication, Nicodemus, Kansas

Sgt. B. F. Eccles
The Twenty-fifth Cavalry

New Year's has an extra significance for the Negro soldier, a meaning which may not be apparent to our civilian cousins, who mark the annual departure of the hoary old year with a cheerful toast and the hope for better times to come. The Negro soldier has been leading our race's march away from slavery, our climb out of the pits of bondage, our painful journey from darkness to daylight. For us, each year that passes is another step forward. And it matters little whether "dogs of war" roam the country or peace smiles upon a sleeping land, for our campaign for justice and equality has known no pause, no ceasefire, no truce or armistice.

Mocking voices may inquire: who opposes us, who blocks our path in this supposedly peaceful and fair-minded nation? Well, a soldier had better know his enemies. They are as many as the drops of rain, as myriad as the winds of summer, elusive and pervasive as smoke. There are the slavemasters of old, lords of field and factory, who buy by the hour the life they once purchased by the pound! There are the false friends, "supporters of the freedman," who would have us march forward, but oh so slowly, a step at a time, along the paths they choose for us, but their paths are narrow, their pace is deadly, and, were our eyes not so downcast, were we not commanded to plan every step, observe the lift and the landing of each single toe, we would see that we are losing ground, not gaining it, parading in the dark, in small, slow circles. But now I come to the deadliest enemy of all: our own people, the ones who are patient, accepting, believing. They croon obedience, they preach subservience, they counsel an eternity of patience.

Against all these, the Negro soldier is our first line of defense. Unequivocally committed to the nation, he must be equally committed to the advancement of his race. That he can fight, he has demonstrated, and that he can die. That he can obey is known. What remains to be shown, and it must be shown soon, is that he is fit to command. To this end, we must press forward, in peace and war. Ladies and gentlemen of Nicodemus, the time for measured steps and moderate voices is passing, the era of mute obedience and blind hope. To those who say slow, I say faster. To those who say never, I say ever. To those who say a little at a time, I say everything. I say it to you. I say it now. Our time has come. Thank you!

It wasn't such a barn-burner, when you analyze it. I guess you had to be there. Eccles had brought a dress uniform, which made him look like a prince. The rest of us had on what we'd worn when we were ice fishing. No medals, sash, saber. But Eccles shone, and those black farmers loved him like he was Hannibal, fresh off his elephant.

"Some speech that Eccles made," I said to the Boss later, wondering how he felt, but all he did was light up a cigar and blow a smoke ring out across the room. Maybe he was hurt, maybe he was angry. It could be he was surprised. Then again, maybe he saw it coming for years. Maybe his heart was breaking. If so, he kept it quiet.

Well, it turned out that one of the men in the audience had a connection with a black newspaper in St. Louis. He obtained a copy of Eccles' speech, but Eccles insisted he didn't know the man had anything to do with a newspaper, and if you believe that, I've got some choice land in Florida I want to talk to you about. The white newspapers picked up the story and the War Department got into the act and it was a mess. By the time the *Maine* sank, there were all sorts of demands, debates, petitions circulating among black troops. Other outfits got nastier, but we were remembered as the place where the virus broke out and the Boss was the one who got blamed for it. Lucky, in a way, that near-beer war came along when it did.

• II •

E.M.: What did you think about the Spanish-American War?

DUQUESNE: That was when things started turning queer. So far, the fighting we'd done was all-American, see. Every step led from here to there, and we'd always headed west, more or less. But now they were talking about going east, to Cuba, and fighting Spaniards! That felt queer. It felt queer when they put us and our horses on a train and we headed back east, through all the land we took, and you know what was the queerest thing of all?

E.M.: No. What?

DUQUESNE: I tell people this happened, they don't believe me, but I swear it did. We stopped, our train did, in this here little town in Oklahoma, see, and they told us we got to wait for a train to come in from the east before we can leave. Well, those trains got pretty ripe, there wasn't no Pullman cars and smiling porters. Horses and soldiers, we was all livestock. So we all piled out and just sat in the sun, stretched in the grass, smoking, jawing, wondering what the hell was waiting for us in Cuba. We talked about snakes and monkeys and señoritas and I recall somebody mentioned "sugar fields" and I was trying to figure out what a field of sugar looked like. Was it like a lawn full of candy? Did you dig it off the ground, pick it off trees, or what? That was something I wanted to see! Dawson, Jamaica Dawson, he tried telling me they send the niggers into plowed-up fields with sacks of jelly beans, lemon drops, pralines, and sour balls they stick into the ground about six inches apart and I pretended I believed him and he said the hardest part was when it come time to harvest taffy, on account they pulled it out of the ground, which is what they call a taffy pull. Of course I'd heard of that . . . Finally the train comes from the east and pulls off the main track onto the siding and we all stand watching to see who gets off. We're looking for skirts, for gentry, but you know what comes off that train? Apaches! There they was, some of the very ones we'd trailed, Contreras and Big Pete and finally Geronimo himself, back to Fort Sill from a Wild West show at an exposition someplace, with suits and boxes and luggage that had hotel stamps from around the world. They was headed west, we was going east, going to the same damn state of Florida we'd shipped 'em off to a dozen years before for punishment! Mister, I'll never forget that moment! "Boss, you know who that is?" I ask. Lawson says, "I do." There wasn't no doubt they recognized us, the way they stared across the tracks. "Maybe they're wishing us a nice trip to Florida," Lawson said, "and we could be wishing them a pleasant welcome home." But not one of them was smiling. Those Apaches, a smile would've broken their faces. Maybe we was all aching for a chance to do it again. "What do you say, Dukie, let's go someplace," Lawson said. "What do you mean, Boss? You know where we're headed to." He laughs a little but he's still looking across them tracks, where the Apaches is waiting for a detail to escort them back to Fort Sill. "Go over and tell 'em we'll give 'em a day's head start," Lawson says. "Fresh horses. No mortars, no Gatlings, nothing heavier than Springfields. Everything like it used to be, trail 'em into Mexico if that's where they head. Think they'll go for it?" The Apaches were still on us: them snake eyes that burned like coals, them hunting eyes which wasn't never gonna be farmer's eyes. "They'd go for it, Boss," I said, "on the spot." "I bet they would," Lawson said. The Boss turned away from the Apaches and looked straight at Eccles. "Goddamn," he said. "Sometimes I wonder. Doesn't anybody wind up happy?"

•III•

Koch's letter, 1928:

When we got to Florida—Tampa Bay was supposed to be the staging area for Cuba—we had to build our own camp in a palmetto swamp, where half the men came down with fever, myself included, and when the camp was built, they signed it over to some college boy volunteers. The day before we were supposed to sail for Cuba, they decided to send us to the Philippines. They took our horses, some of which they butchered, others they sold, and put us on a train for San Francisco, and by the time we got through all of that we knew that, whatever his faults, that pain-in-the-ass Eccles wasn't wrong. The Boss drank heavily on the train west and not much that Dukie could do about it, but I decided there was one final contribution I could make to the morale of this scuffed-up, crapped-on, black-and-blue outfit. I resigned from it, retired, which I did as soon as we got to San Francisco, and by juggling this and juggling that, I saw to it that Eccles got my job, and made a lieutenant as well, which the self-righteous son of a bitch never even thanked me for. They were supposed to have a rip-roaring party the day before they sailed, combination bon voyage and retirement, but for once the ship —the *President Buchanan*—came early, which was lucky, because an angry tot with a can opener could've put the thing on the bottom of the bay, so the sooner our horseless wonders got off, the better. I came down to the dock that last morning to say goodbye, and by God, the Boss had them all lined up for me to review, right by the gangplank, and I shook hands with each one as he stepped on board. I started in by making jokes and saying, "Step it up, you niggers," and they gave back as good as they got and I thought I had it under control until, when they were all on board, I stepped back and I could see that they were all along the railing, more than a hundred of them, just waving to me. That's when it got to me. The last I heard was Dukie shouting he was going to bring me back a girl who did the hula-hula.

Know something? All those years in the Army, I saw a

lot of homesick soldiers. It came and went like flu, and sometimes it seemed everyone was down with it but me. Home cooking, home loving, spring planting season: you never knew what would start it. And I never felt the least bit homesick. Every place they sent us was all right with me, and not one place I'd pay a quarter to go back and see. But I'll tell you one thing, Morrison, and be sure you put it in: standing on that dock in San Francisco, watching the Boss and his boatload of niggers go sailing out to sea, I knew right off that homesickness and me were going to be getting well acquainted.

Yours truly,
Paul W. Koch

·IV·

With American lives at stake (though not in great numbers, and surely not for very long), thc amused and ironic tone which dominated my Balkan dispatches might be out of order, and likewise my cheerful ignorance of politics. I had better do some homework. I looked over the reportage on Cuba and the accounts of the fall of Manila. It was appalling stuff: skirmishes blown into battles, accidents become atrocities, armed bandits turned into insurrecto heroes. There wasn't much to choose from, so I picked the man I knew. It had been thirteen years and he said he was leaving shortly for Egypt "to do something about the Nile." (It sounded like he might dam or divert it.) But W. C. "Water Closet" Symington said he would see me, just before he sailed.

R.M.S. *Albertine,* New York to Southampton: porters showing passengers to cabins, excited children exploring promenades, bon voyage parties in every other room, all the flurry of a transatlantic crossing, which W. C. Symington told me was to be his twenty-third.

"It usually takes a day or two before they find this bar," he told me.

He was sunk in a chair in a lounge off the first-class dining room, where we could see the Statue of Liberty catching the last sunlight on the tip of her torch. W.C. hadn't changed much since Fort Monroe: white hair, nicotine teeth, reddish angry eyes, and a body that made a first-class suit disreputable the minute he put it on. He ordered drinks. We had the room to ourselves. Like most journalists who invaded other people's privacy professionally, he defended his own territory fiercely. Whenever some cheerful passengers came looking for a drink, Symington scowled and said, "Lifeboat drill, five minutes, lower deck."

"Well, we work for different newspapers," he said after drinks had come. "That is, I assume we do. You haven't come about a job . . ."

"No."

"And it's not shop talk you're here for. After that dog-and-pony show you cooked up in Arizona, I saw that I had very little to teach you. You're as much a mountebank as I am, boy."

"Thank you."

"Well, then . . ."

"Manila. 'Oriental America.' I'm headed that way, I wanted some background and I saw from your dispatches you'd just been . . ."

"The professional response should be that the story said what the story said."

"I read every word."

"And you want more?"

"Background. I've got friends over there."

"Ah, yes! I remember! You were connected to the famous Lawsons. Major Henry and . . ."

"Major, did you say?"

"You didn't know? It arrived while I was there. It took time coming, didn't it?"

"He's not the kind of officer who rises in a peacetime army."

"Evidently not. I heard someone joking that they must have put his promotion in a bottle and let it float across the Pacific."

"He doesn't care much about rank," I said.

"Ah, but his wife does. The Belle of Manila staged a small orgy of self-congratulation, at which, I'm happy to say, I got gloriously drunk. So did the new major. But not with me, alas. He keeps his distance. He suspects I know things that he doesn't, which is true enough, true enough."

He motioned for another round. He'd been at it for some time before I arrived.

"What's happening over there?" I pressed. "I wouldn't ask if I didn't care about them . . ."

"Then you've made an amateur's mistake, my boy, and nothing good will come of it. Never care. Never. Never care about them and never let them care about you. You ought to know."

He lifted his glass, drained it, motioned for another. It was no use trying to keep up. While the steward replenished his liquor, he stared out the window down the Hudson, past the tip of Manhattan, to where the Statue of Liberty was falling into darkness, a silhouette.

"Sometimes I hate to hear myself talk," he suddenly remarked. "Do you know what I mean? I'm tired of being an insider. I'd like to just read newspapers and believe them. But this business takes it away from you."

He sighed, and drank. "Twenty-three crossings. The Atlantic doesn't mean a thing to me. Half of Europe works itself to death to come over here. Half of America wondering how things are over there. Who wouldn't trade places?"

Another swallow.

"Correspondent reflects on melancholy life. All right, Morrison. It's another dog-and-pony show, the Philippines. The Filipinos welcomed us as liberators from the Spanish, the aristocrats and friars. They set up a government which we won't recognize. We say they're not ready, we're staying . . ."

"Are they ready?"

"For self-government? Who ever is? Were we? Seems to me we had a Civil War not long ago. Well, we're saying they're not. We're saying that if we don't take over, maybe the Kaiser will, or the Emperor of Japan, I don't know. Meanwhile, there's missionaries who won't get to first base, and politicians who figure the Pacific is an American lake, and businessmen crowing about new markets that are mostly fantasies. So what the hell? We're there and we're staying, and if they don't like it now, they'll learn to like it later. Because, after all, we are likable. That's the bottom line, Morrison. We're a nation of the nicest people on earth. Didn't you know?"

I ignored the cynicism. Time was short. I'd already heard the first call for visitors to leave.

"What kind of war?" I asked. "Short and sweet, like Cuba?"

"We weren't fighting Cubans in Cuba. We were fighting Spaniards. This'll be something different. Long, small, and very dirty would be my guess."

"Like the Indians?"

"We outnumbered the Indians. There are ten million Filipinos. And seven thousand islands to fight on. They won't stand and fight, I think. It could take a while. Too bad for your friends the Lawsons."

"How much did you see of them?"

"The woman is the handsomest American in town. And she knows it. She queens it some."

"And Lawson?"

The second bell sounded and Symington seemed happy to hear it. He behaved like a fortune-teller who'd turned up some bad cards. He emptied his glass and lurched to his feet.

"You've got to go!" he said. "I'll walk you out."

He took my arm. He needed it, to steady himself. We made our way toward the gangplank, where we encountered a traffic jam of hugs and tears and last-minute promises. For us, a handshake sufficed.

"Gottschalk hates him."

"Who?"

"Erwin Gottschalk. General. Running the show. Goes back to Arizona. Probably would've happened anyway, though. Different styles, you'll see. Nobody's fault."

We waited for the crowd to sort itself out, leavers separating from stayers.

"You know what went wrong with this country?" Symington asked. "We ran out of three things. We ran out of land. We ran out of Indians. And we ran out of ideas. Goodbye, Morrison."

• V •

I remember the forty-five-day voyage from San Francisco to Manila that began the last year of the last century. I had a book in mind, several books, and if I had written as much every day on board as I did in a day's hard filing at the front, I would have had a decent-sized volume by the time the *Winfield Han-*

cock slipped into Manila Bay. And if I had occasion to write, I also had a chance to read, for I had selected good company to go voyaging with me: Thackeray, Tolstoi, Swift, and Scott. But they were cold-weather thinkers, brisk and clearheaded and transcendent. As we plowed slowly into warmer seas, what overcame me overcame them: sweat and mold, monosyllabic torpor, so that the partnership we struck in a Fifth Avenue bookseller's ended in wordless apathy somewhere west of Honolulu. What got to them got to me: heat and humidity and the sheer size of the Pacific.

We came into the islands at night. They were dark shapes, sometimes marked by points of light that were lower and lesser than the stars. Then there were boats: fishing boats, barges, scows, and lighters, all crowded with cargo, dogs, stevedores, naked children. People looked up at us as if we were envoys from another world. Engines stopped, anchor cables went rattling over the side. And then came the smell of the islands, not just wood fires or stagnant water, rotting wood or garbage, but that great greenhouse vegetable smell, primal ooze and fallen blossoms. I had never felt so far from home.

Before dawn, all the harbor craft converged on the *Hancock*, crowding against us, tangling lines, jostling for position. I thought of my visit with Water Closet Symington, staring past his drunken face at the Statue of Liberty, lifing her torch into the sunset. At dawn in a different harbor I espied the remains of Admiral Dewey's victims, a ring of green scum around the upturned bottoms and gulls picking at the blackened keels.

"Mr. Morrison, please?"

I opened my eyes to see a frail, yellowish man, white-suited, hat in hands, a Latin, probably a Spaniard, and, if so, a perfect example of what happens when a race strays too far from home, and stays away too long.

"Yes?"

"Please come with me," he implored.

"Where to?" I asked. I realized I had already adopted the manner of a winner speaking to a loser: it was easy to be imperious, and this man invited it.

"I am Jaime Navarro. I come from Mrs. Lawson."

We alit on a quay in the Pasig River, near Fort Santiago, where Old Glory was flying over stones that had been piled on one another not long after Magellan's ship sailed around the world. Magellan had died somewhere in these islands, I recalled. In a way, it was sad that we'd made such short work of the Spaniards. It was a slap in the face of our discoverer, just a slap, but we didn't know our own strength, we Americans, and it sent them stumbling backwards halfway across the world. Had we meant to hurt them that much?

"You speak English very well," I said. It was odd how patronizing a modest compliment could sound.

"Oh no, not very good," he countered, as though flabbergasted by my kindness.

"Where were you born?" I asked.

"In America," he answered softly.

"Where in America?"

"Here," he said, gesturing at a street crowded with oxcarts, passenger carriages, drays, ponies. The human traffic was also mixed: white-haired Spanish ladies fresh from Mass, civilians in tropical suits, ragamuffin children with black hair and dark eyes, Chinese scurrying on Chinese errands, young women in twos and threes, with puffy white blouses, bright-colored skirts, holding umbrellas to defend against rain and sun alike. There were soldiers, too, our boys, some in white duck uniforms with brass buttons, others in the blue woolen shirts, suspenders, and cotton trousers I had seen on the frontier.

"This is America now," Navarro persisted. "No?"

"Correct," I said. He must think that we were an easy people to know, straightforward, unsubtle, easily charmed, a nation of easy winners. I guess that the Lawsons could take credit for that.

Manila was a mixture: old as the stones in Fort Santiago, new as the puddles in the streets of town. There were red-roofed houses with balconies and patios that befit colonial rule, but there were many more nipa huts, wooden-floored thatched-roof contraptions lifted off the ground by stilts. They reminded me of bamboo cages or beach houses, built to last between tides.

"Soon we are at the house of Major and Mrs. Lawson," Navarro told me.

"The Lawsons' house, you say?"

"Yes."

He gestured down the road, which was the shore drive, curving around the edge of Manila Bay. Dogs and roosters dodged in front of us, naked children played in ditches where women were washing. Men glanced up from mending fishnets and nodded at Navarro. They were not greetings. They were acknowledgments.

"You mean *your* house, don't you?"

"Sir?"

"Mrs. Lawson's letters gave me to understand that the house was your property, or your family's," I said, feeling needlessly contentious. "Isn't that true?"

He nodded, but he smelled a trap.

"Then the house is yours," I said.

"Yes," he acknowledged, "and no."

"What on earth does that mean?"

A fatalistic shrug, a bit of a sigh, an appeal for me to understand, if I could, the complexity of things.

"The house belongs," he said, "to those who live in it."

·VI·

The road curved inland, brushing the edge of rice fields, making room for the bougainvillea-covered wrought-iron fence that cropped up on the right. After several hundred yards we came to a gate, which two American soldiers, white and dressed in white, swung open, and drove into a courtyard dominated by a house that Carter Hammond of Milton, Indiana, would have loved on sight. It was a rambling two-story stucco painted a light yellow that might have been objectionable in temperate climates but here seemed perfectly in keeping with the crushed-coral drive, the rioting flowers, the bright green lawn that rolled like a carpet to the edge of the bay, where Lucy was waiting for me in a hibiscus-covered gazebo just above the beach.

Surely, Lucy had seen me coming and arranged herself, but never mind, she took my breath away. She was seated on a wicker chair, with flowers and sea behind her. She was wearing a simple white shift, trimmed at the edges with black and gold, and around her neck she wore a golden pendant. She looked handsomer than ever. This was the crest, the moment of fullness, and she knew it.

She raised her hand to touch my mouth. She leaned forward. How I sensed the movement of her body behind that oh so simple dress! She took my head in her hands, running her fingers over each feature, the way a blind person reads a stranger's face.

"There's one thing you must know," she said. "I have never been happier than I am now."

"Ah." I had to do something to break this sudden intimacy. "Does that mean that my coming has made you happier than ever? Or are you warning me not to ruin this blissful state? I can go . . ."

She laughed, and it was good to hear that low conspiratorial laugh of hers again.

"Oh, Edwin," she said, "you're so dear."

Before I knew it, she had whirled around in front of me, a quick reprise of the erotic turn she had once performed whenever I desired, but this time it was fully clothed, and broad daylight, and she ended with a laugh.

"No comment?"

"None necessary," I said. "It speaks for itself."

"Don't be so sure of that," she said. "Come on now. There are other things I have to show you."

She led me outside the gazebo, down a path to the sea wall. The tide was in, Manila Bay lapping right up against the stones.

"Cavite. Manila. Corregidor." She pointed them out. "Did you see the Spanish wrecks? Admiral Montoyo's fleet! They raised three of them for refitting, but I hope they leave the rest. Henry loves it here."

"You mean the Philippines?"

"I mean this particular spot. He comes out here after dinner. There's his hammock. He says he can't get over it, having the Pacific Ocean— 'the biggest damn thing on earth!'—right in his backyard!"

"Where is he, Luce?"

"A village north of here, facing the Filipino lines. He comes home whenever he can. He wants to see you, Edwin."

"I'm glad."

"Come see the house!" she said, grasping my hand and pulling me along, like a child anxious to show his parent some magic castle. And once we entered, I saw that it was indeed a castle. She showed me to every window, insisting I contemplate the view, and each was like a bright and happy painting, blue and green, sea, and clouds, and palms, two or three such paintings in every room, a gallery of them up and down the hall. She made me touch the wood in the walls, mahogany and teak, told me how the house breathed and sighed at sunrise and sunset, much as the house in Milton had done. The smallest things delighted her: how table legs sat in cans of water to prevent columns of ants from attacking food! She asked me to admire a servant who polished the floor by skating back and forth across it with coconut husks under his feet, and this same servant, at Lucy's request, broke into "A Hot Time in the Old Town Tonight." It had been played so often by military bands, she said, that many Filipinos took the tune to be our national anthem.

"Now," Lucy said, "the best is last! The bedroom!"

Again she grasped my hand and led me along, like a lad being ushered to his first bedding. It was a bold gesture, our past intimacy notwithstanding, and I wonder whether it was because of that history, or in spite of it, that Lucy wanted to show me where she slept and loved.

Her bed was a remarkable production, an enormous platform of cool sheets, teak bordered, with a vast billowy mosquito netting overhead.

"It's not as if we really needed a mosquito net," she said, parting the curtain to sit on the edge of the bed. "But I love the look of it. The way it settles over me when I sleep, like a cloud. The way it rustles in the wind. I half expect my father to step into the room, part the curtain, to make sure I'm all right. Under here, I almost believe in guardian angels. See how silly I've become, Edwin? Who ever loved mosquito nets?"

"Your guardian angels brought you to the Philippines, then? And sank the Spanish fleet?"

"I believe they did," she said. She bounced off the bed and ushered me onto a terrace that gave out onto the garden.

"And the war that's brewing. Guardian angels again?"

"I can't picture guardian angels on the Filipino side," she answered. "Popinjay government. General José So-and-So and Emilio Something Else. Such wrongheaded little chaps! They seem determined to misunderstand us. We came here in their best interests, after all . . ."

"Is that so?"

"Of course. And if there is a war, I guarantee you this, Edwin, the native forces will quickly be dispatched."

"That's what Henry says?"

"Henry says as little as possible. But I have other sources. We're not at Fort Monroe anymore, thank God. This is Manila, and Manila is a town that loves to talk. I've been cultivating it."

Behind her smile, I heard a warning, and the warning was for me. Lucy seemed to be saying that while I was an older version of the man I always had been, she had changed materially. She was a woman of power and opinions.

"I can't depend on Henry to make things happen," she said. "I accept that. Edwin, this is his chance and I might as well say it's his last chance. We've got to put him over the top. Make him a name to conjure with. If Roosevelt did it in Cuba . . ."

"Roosevelt was Assistant Secretary of the Navy before the war. His name had been conjured with for some time."

"That just means we'll all have to work harder, won't we?" she responded. Those green eyes, that knowing little smile! The sense that she had a plan and a place for all of us!

"You've finally brought it together, haven't you? The sword *and* the pen."

"Only don't ask me which is mightier," she replied.

"And a war of course. We're none of us any good without a war."

"Which will be small and practically painless and, thanks to you, splendidly reported . . ."

If I had not loved her, and thought that she loved me, I would have said she was using me. In Arizona I had done about as much as one man could to advance the career of Henry Lawson, but the kind of newspaper fame that I conferred was fleeting. It didn't compound automatically, and

Lawson wasn't the man to exploit it on his own. Now Lucy wanted more. Maybe I could accomplish what she wanted. But I hoped no one was watching me too closely.

·VII·

Sr. Jaime Navarro
Manila
The Philippines

March 15, 1926

Dear Morrison,

From the moment I saw you I knew you were a fool, and never more of a fool than when you attempted to be subtle. I was inclined to reject your offer without comment, but then I found that your letter, once I passed its rudeness and fatuity, started me thinking about the past. For several days I have been all full of the people and places you asked about. I have your letter to thank for that, I admit. I discarded the list of questions. I do not propose to be interrogated by the likes of you. Take what I give you and be thankful for it.

The first Americans! That is how I think of them, the new race and the new century arriving together. They swept into our stagnant islands, our sleepy, senile empire, like a fresh wave. So strong were they, so full of life, they were not merely victorious, they were victory itself, the statue come to life. And you thought I hated them!

Morrison, I was ecstatic when they took our house! Move into the stables? Gladly! I'd have camped on the beach to be near them. Lawson, a leader, many times a hero—and yet, so unspoiled. I would watch him splashing in the sea water I had been taught to shun, building fires on the beach, sleeping out of doors—unthinkable to me—carrying all the enjoyments of childhood into adult life. Every day, he amazed me more. At dawn, sometimes, I would find him working in the garden, sweating like a peasant, and he would shout out, "How you doin', Jamey?" In the middle of the day, just as I arose from my siesta, sluggish as an eighty-year-old, I would see his giant figure, bearded and bare-chested, streak across the garden, straight out to the sea wall, and hurtle off the edge, splashing into the bay! Marvelous man!

I laughed just now, Morrison, because I remembered one morning when he raced past me, just as I have told, and took his dive, but I knew, alas, that he had gravely misjudged the tide. Fearing that injury had come to him, I rushed to the sea wall. He was stretched out in a morass of mud and rotting sea weed, unhurt, but filthy. He gazed up at me, I down at him. "The tides, señor, they go in and out," I said, as if it were my fault for not having advised him earlier of this. "The tides? Yes! The tides!" He looked at me, looked at himself, and commenced to laugh, laugh uproariously, rolling around in the mud like a beached whale, laughing till the tears came, till he fought for breath, and I laughed along with him, at first politely, then with a heartiness that almost matched his own, as if laughter were a language he was teaching me.

Now, when I speak of Mrs. Lawson, I speak as a man who admires women, needs them, but has seldom enjoyed their company. Thus, I pay her a rare compliment when I confess that to be with her was an almost constant pleasure. Her husband was awesome: one stood back to admire him. His wife one studied more closely, watching for moods, hints, nuances. I enjoyed talking with her, planning the house, discussing menus, shopping in Manila, gossiping. What I admired about her was her approach to things: her assumption that with diligent application and ample study, everything could be learned, anything could be accomplished. She had come to a new place, whose history and culture and politics were a tangle. Seven thousand islands, hundreds of languages, dozens of peoples, rights and wrongs, piled on one another forever. Yet she set out to master the place as though she were perfecting a recipe. Every day, another step, another lesson. I can still hear her saying, "Now, Jaime, let me get this straight . . ."

Now, I shall tell you a story which illustrates the quality of this marvelous woman. For most of their married life, my parents slept in average-sized beds in separate rooms. Conjugal duties were performed in one room or another and then they slept apart. I do not think this speaks ill of them. I have never savored the romance of rolling up against a sweating haunch on a hot night or having one's sleep punctuated by a lover's snores or awakening to find the mouth one kissed befouled by the odors of a night's digestion. Ah, but Mrs. Lawson desired a large, an enormous bed, and together we searched Manila for something that was, as her husband eventually put it, "about the size of a parade ground." Finally, I learned of such a bed, inspected, priced, and endorsed it heartily, yet she insisted on seeing the item before she paid for it. This perfectly reasonable stipulation appalled me. The bed was indiscreetly located in a brothel, not the largest, but the finest in Manila, the Casa Rosa, or Pink House, where this bed had been the stage, or should I say the arena, for entertainments without precedent since Babylon.

You can imagine my agonies, my circumlocutions, as I tried to inform, or avoid informing, Mrs. Lawson of the nature of the institution. "A house of entertainment." "A residence of unmarried women . . ."

"Then it's a brothel, isn't it?"

"Yes," I said.

"Forgive me, señora, for my subterfuge, but I knew that if you learned how this admittedly still magnificent bed had been despoiled, you would never permit such furniture in your home. Perhaps if I take the measurements and engage a cabinetmaker . . ."

"Suppose we have a look at this great bed," she suggested.

"You mean . . . go to this place?"

"Yes," she said. "Now is fine."

I insisted upon preceding her into the lobby and there I sought out the justly celebrated proprietress, Señora Antonia Valdez Lee. Half Spanish, half Chinese, striking and moody, the body of a siren, the mind of an astronomer, she presided over extraordinary combinations.

It started badly. Señora Antonia denied our conversation about the bed, wasn't sure she wanted to dispose of it. She wondered aloud, to the amusement of the half dozen charmers who surrounded her, what kind of woman would require such a playing field. These were not welcome portents, but there was nothing to do but take Mrs. Lawson by the arm and usher her inside.

Now: the great moment. Mrs. Lawson nodded at the

girls, said, "Good afternoon, everybody." She advanced directly to Señora Antonia. They stood before each other, staring. God knows what measurements they made, what signals passed between them! I took a seat among the lovelies—we were all one audience now—and, despite my dismay, I considered myself fortunate to witness such a meeting. Nothing would have surprised me. If the two women had lunged, tearing at each other's throat, I would have understood and never dreamed of interfering, no matter what. And if they'd smiled, Antonia loosening a strap, Lucy answering by stepping out of her shoes, if they had disrobed and made tumultuous love before us, I would have thought it natural and wonderful. Ah, I would have loved to watch them make love! I wonder if I was the only one who pictured this, or did something similar enter their minds also? I cannot say, but I assure you of this: they spent a long while looking at each other.

"I'm Lucy," Mrs. Lawson said at last. She stepped forward, extending her hand, which Antonia took and held.

"Antonia Valdez Lee. Please, your last name?"

"Lawson," Lucy responded without hesitation. "Wife of Major Henry Lawson."

Antonia nodded, pleased that Lucy was not ashamed to give her married name.

"And you are the lady who requires"—Antonia smiled—"a large bed."

"I do," she acknowledged.

"For your own use?"

"And my husband's."

"Is he sick?"

"No. He is very well."

"You have been told what kind of place this is?"

"Yes."

Mrs. Lawson was smiling in what I took to be a particularly American style, signaling confidence in her power to transform anything. "It doesn't bother me a bit . . . if it's a good bed, that is."

Antonia laughed and led Mrs. Lawson up the stairs. When they came down, twenty minutes later, they were arm in arm and smiling. Extraordinary beauties! To have known them both was a blessing; to have seen them together a miracle.

I wonder if they met again. I suspect they did, though

I cannot confirm it. Two such women, on the same island, at the same time, I cannot imagine their staying apart! But I can certify that the bed arrived, compliments of Antonia Valdez Lee. I wondered whether Mrs. Lawson would confide the bed's origins to her husband. The major took pride in his house and was happy to lead visitors on a tour of every room, not excepting the boudoir, which he saved for last. Word must have spread around Manila: soon wives were as curious as husbands about the Lawsons' bedroom. More than one proper husband blushed uncontrollably at the sight of that bed. The questioning expressions, the puzzled glances, the shocks of recognition! It lasted until one of the visitors—he was Britain's longtime consul—ended the game.

"Pardon me," asked the Pacific representative of Queen Victoria. "Where on earth did you obtain such a commodious bed?"

"In a cathouse," Major Lawson replied delightedly.

"A what?"

"My wife found it for me."

Why do I tell you this? Because it pleases me to have Mrs. Lawson remembered in this way. She had other sides, not all of them as becoming: manipulative, political, imperial traits. Still, when I recall such meetings as the one at Casa Rosa, I cannot think harshly of her. I picture that last morning, when she left the islands forever, with a coffin for company, all in black. At the height of her grief, she ordered me to arrange for the return of that bed to Casa Rosa, where it gave good service. I always asked for that bed. And, dear Morrison, I wonder if time has made you perceptive enough to grasp the moral? It is precisely as I told you the first morning we met, when you interrogated me about whose house we were approaching. It is with beds as with houses, as with islands: we are all renters, transients, temporary occupants, and nothing that we have do we keep forever.

·VIII·

In the late afternoon, low tide, the beach came alive, with boats returning, fishermen casting nets in low pools, children emerging from nipa huts and wading out into the waves. And there was Lawson, riding the way he had ridden along the Georgia coast at the end of Sherman's march, vaulting over fishing boats, kicking up sand, racing just ahead of breaking waves, a moment of unfailing happiness for him, and transcendent grace. I knew then that, whatever we did, we were incomplete without him.

Trousers soaked, beard dripping, he galloped down the beach, leapt over the sea wall, jumped off his horse and into Lucy's arms, lifting her off the ground and whirling her around.

"Hello, darling," he cried out, setting her on her feet and embracing her.

"Eddie!" he shouted, and pulled me into his bear hug. I had never seen anyone so happy to see me. "We finally made it! Three damn Hoosiers at the end of the world. Or the beginning. Hell, I don't know. Luce! I brought some eats."

He held up a string bag in which a five-pound fish was dying. "They don't come any fresher. Here you go, Jamey."

He tossed the sack to the Spaniard, who carried it off. "Ten minutes," Lawson shouted after him. "Make it nice." Then, to me, "How about a cold one?"

"How about a shower first?" Lucy interjected.

"What for?" Lawson asked. "I haven't hardly talked to Eddie yet."

"Henry, you need a shower."

"Take it with me?"

"Henry!"

He scooped her up and ran across the lawn. "Make it twenty minutes!"

I heard Lucy laughing while the Boss carried her upstairs. The servants were laughing, and I laughed, too.

The sun crashed into the sea, its wreckage on the water, and Jaime Navarro was cutting up a fish, flinging entrails over the sea wall, where birds caught them before they hit the stand. After an hour with Lucy, Lawson came across the lawn, barefoot, wearing a long white cotton shirt and white trousers, carrying several bottles of beer and two steins.

"So!" He planted the beer on the table with a finality that hinted that at last we men . . . or boys . . . could settle down to serious talk. He picked up a couple of pieces of raw fish, dipped them in a sauce of soya, lemon, hot pepper, and swallowed, urging me to emulate him. I managed.

"So," I responded, "how are you, Boss? How the hell are you?"

He raised his hand and gestured at the sea as if he owned it, at Cavite, at Manila. He pointed to the palm trees above, the house behind us, the whiff of cooking meat and the sound of foreign voices drifting from the kitchen. He drained half a glass of beer, smacking his lips.

"I'm in paradise," he said. "Beats Fort Riley. Beats Fort Monroe. Not for publication, it beats Milton, Indiana. There was a world out here. Islands. Oceans. How come nobody told me? I saw my first volcano a week ago, smoking and rumbling. Boulders the size of barns. I rode half a day across lava fields. Why were they keeping me in the dark? Or wasn't I listening? All this good stuff!"

"It sounds to me," I said, "like you've staked a claim. How are we ever going to get you back home?"

"I don't believe you will," he answered.

"It's that good?"

"Either that or I'm getting soft. A long time, I did what I was told. Fought Southerners. Chased some Apaches around the West. It was all one long march. And this is where I stopped marching."

"And the war?"

"Won't amount to nothing. Wait. You'll see. It's just for appearance' sake, so they can say they put up a fight. A one-day war."

"And Lucy . . ."

He lay back on the grass, with his arms behind his head, and took a deep breath. "That's the best of all. Ever since we came, she's been happy. It's like someone had been saving up our luck, and gave all of it to us at once."

"You were due, all right. All those years on Officers' Rows."

"It wasn't that bad for me. But I sensed she felt that life had let us down somehow. Or I had let her down, I don't know. Nothing was coming true for her. She'd ask me sometimes what I was looking forward to and I couldn't say. But here . . ."

Lucy came out across the lawn.

"You've known her longer than I have. You've seen her in a lot of different places. Can't you tell? She's never been better, has she?"

"No," I said. "Never better."

"She still wants to make you great," I said. "You know that."

"Yeah. Well." The long Lawson pause. "I'll settle for happy."

That night we were happy. We ate well, drank more than we should have. There were accounts of Europe from me, tales of the 25th Cavalry from Lawson, talk of servants and markets from Lucy, the same kind of conversation I'd heard around a dozen other tables: war stories, home talk, colonial tempests. But I remember how, at the end, Lucy proposed what was to be "the absolutely last toast."

We obediently raised our glasses and waited, while she half started a sentence, broke off again, reconsidered.

"Maybe if we had some music it would come out a little easier, Luce," Lawson said.

"Wait . . ."

"Been waiting . . ."

"My arm's starting to hurt . . ." I said.

"I want to get it right!" she cried.

"There's always breakfast," Lawson said. "After coffee we could . . ."

"This *matters* to me, you boors!"

"Okay if I change hands, Luce?" I asked. "This one's getting tired."

"All right!" she said. "Now I have it."

"Hurray!"

"Out with it, before you forget."

"Glasses together," Lucy commanded. "There. Don't dare move until I'm finished."

"Can't promise . . ."

"Edwin!"

"I'll do my best. Proceed."

"Very well. I wanted to say that I love you both . . ."

I waited for more, wondering if this would be the night when all was declared. It would be a mistake, I thought, to say everything, but I suspected it was coming. The look in her eyes said as much.

"I love you both . . ." She repeated it, searching for something more. "I . . ."

She looked from him to me. This was the moment. She was charging out into strange territory, ahead of the pack, far beyond the lines, and while I watched for the outcome, her husband came rushing to the rescue.

"We both love you, Luce," Lawson said. "Eddie, am I right?"

"Right you arc, Boss," I said.

·IX·

"The famous Morrison! In my office! War must be on the way!"

General Erwin Gottschalk, Lawson's commander in the Philippines, was not the kind of soldier history loves. If Lawson was a Custer, Gottschalk was a General George McClellan. From quartermaster to headquarters, he made his way unnoticed by the press, unloved by his troops. If you asked him about the progress of a war, he would talk of numbers of troops, lines of supply, lost equipment, bottlenecks, snags, and schedules. He would iterate chains of commands, grouse about civilian interference, complain about remoteness from Washington. He might talk for an hour and never mention the enemy. Just as surely, the enemy would never know his name.

Surrounded by sycophantic aides, imprisoned in a dungeon of paperwork which he declined to delegate, preoccupied with water treatment, mayoral elections, a shortage of schoolbooks, a surfeit of syringes, he was the image of the armchair general whom all lovers of sprightly journalism have learned to detest.

There were jokes about him: if he were reincarnated as an animal, he'd return as a tick; if an army traveled on its stomach, Gottschalk was invincible. But he was not stupid. At some point, he had made a rational judgment about armies and war. Armies were constant, wars were occasional, and if, as the immigrant son of a Saxon butcher, you valued security, then you counted on the constant army, not the sometimes war. Yet even in war you could prosper. Men like Lawson or Custer or J. E. B. Stuart could dash and prance. They could win a war quickly or they could lose it. But this might be a long war, and Gottschalk was going to fight it his way, surrounded by wooden filing cabinets and long conference tables, with formal dinners and hot lunches, tours and reports. Gottschalk was a stayer.

"You think there'll be a war?" I inquired.

"The ingredients are here, I think. A variety of armies, a variety of generals, and, most important, a variety of newspaper correspondents."

"The role of a correspondent . . ."

". . . is crucial. I remember, years ago, spending dreadful weeks riding hither and yon over Southwest deserts in search of a mysterious Indian named the Singer. All I ever knew of this undoubted villain was what I read in the newspapers! What a life! What a dramatic death! And for all this, I had you to thank!"

He was having too good a time to be interrupted. He turned to his aide, Captain Erickson.

"You know about Casa Diablo, Erickson? . . . No? Ach, you should go. You visit Waterloo. You visit Gettysburg. Then you should not omit Casa Diablo. The fatal canyon! The hellish cauldrons! The one-man invasion of hell! The tiny forest where an American officer and a brutal Apache conducted their fatal interview, their duel of honor! Poetry!"

Ponderous as his irony, he hoisted himself out of his chair, walked to the window. It was late afternoon, and a military band was rehearsing somewhere.

" 'The Poet and Peasant Overture'!" He looked at Erickson. "No?"

Erickson nodded.

"You made him, didn't you?" Gottschalk suddenly asked.

"Made . . ."

"Made. Created. Concocted. Sculpted."

"What?!"

"Henry Lawson. But a word of advice, Morrison. The same picture . . . don't try to paint it twice."

Lucy was waiting in a carriage outside the main entrance to Fort Santiago, chatting with half the headquarters staff. I could tell that her visit was a special treat for young officers. They served up their secrets to the Belle of Manila, they stood in line to tell them.

"How was your interview, Edwin?" She didn't introduce me to the officers, but I sensed she'd already told them who I was. You develop an instinct for that sort of thing. A keyed-up politeness, a heightened articulation: people behave differently around journalists.

"Wonderful," I said, not wanting to report in front of an audience. "Most informative. And yet, such a modest man . . ."

"With good reason," someone interjected. I ignored it.

"The right man in the right place at the right time, that's the whole secret of leadership," I pontificated. "Lawson in the field. Gottschalk in headquarters. And these men here."

Let them chew on that, I thought, lifting myself into the carriage, nodding to Navarro, who flicked the reins.

"How was it really?" Lucy asked. "A ghastly man . . ."

"I'd watch myself around him," I said.

"What did he say?"

"I'll tell you one thing, Luce. He's in no rush. No rush to start a war and, if a war starts, in no rush to finish it."

"I can't picture a war here," Lucy said. "I really can't. I hear the talk. I know the names. I'm familiar with the issues. And yet . . ."

"What?"

"It seems so unnecessary . . . such a misunderstanding . . . like a letter delivered to the wrong address . . . that small a mistake . . ."

"It's not a letter sent to the wrong address. It's an army."

"No," she said, shaking her head. "You're wrong." After years of accepting my expert guidance in world affairs, she had staked out some territory which she called her own. And she was willing to defend it.

"I'm wrong?"

"I think so. I've been here longer than you, Edwin. I've talked to people, studied it through. We belong here. I know it. I'm more convinced about this place than I ever was about Arizona. I feel it in my bones. This is where our lives were headed. Everything else was marking time. You'll see."

"Perhaps."

"Perhaps you've seen too much already. Too many wars. You can't see the differences."

"That's true enough. I can't."

That night, anyway, the evidence was all on Lucy's side. There was no sign of insurrection at Luneta Park. It was Easter Parade and Fourth of July: dozens of carriages idling through the seaside park, cabs open to catch the breezes off the bay, a parade of fashion and good manners, along a path decked with flowers, flags and lanterns, while on the bandstand, the U.S. Army musicians played the sweet, nostalgic music that warmed the general's heart.

Was this an occupied city, this playground, this merry-go-round, with carriages trailing laughter like perfume? Was this a garrison state, whose general, the least bellicose of men, could be prevailed upon to enter the bandstand, bow to his audience of adoring retainers, heft the baton, and launch into a lush rendition of selections from *Die Fledermaus*?

• X •

All the old-timers were waiting for me at Lawson's headquarters. There were Dukie, Herman Biddle, Billy Presley, Lefty Diller, Buddy Conaway, Jamaica Dawson, Benjamin Franklin Eccles, and others whose names I'd forgotten, but I recalled them in that famous baseball game, remembered their laughter as I exited the whore wagon, could still picture how they rode when we went into the mountains after Contreras and the Singer. They pretended they just happened to be there when we rode in.

"Looks to me like an old soldiers' home," Lawson groused. "Anybody on duty today?"

"EdWIN is gonna EdLOSE!" Dukie cried, laughing, and even Eccles smiled.

"You going to write us up again?" Diller asked. "Don't forget my nose."

He modeled his new nose, a miracle of ivory, gum, and plaster, which might have been chiseled off a Roman statue.

"Oh hell," Lawson said. "All you old-timers come upstairs. We'll have a taste on Eddie."

Lawson guided me through some of the war stories I'd regaled him with the night before: massacres in Africa, punitive campaigns in the Sudan, flabbergastingly inept offenses in the Balkans. Then, when I flagged, he steered the conversation around the room. Billy Presley was obliged to report Ellie's death two years before, but his delivery was more dutiful than mournful, and I gathered he was recovering nicely around Manila. Dukie said he wanted to take me to the cockfights, Jamaica Dawson asked if I could buy him a meerschaum pipe, and Herman Biddle wondered where a man could find an up-to-date book on phrenology.

After an hour, they left, joking, clapping me on the shoulder, glad to have me back. Soon the balcony was almost empty. Dumpling Grimes, who had replaced the retired Birmingham Mack as quartermaster and orderly, cleared away the empty glasses. He was heavier than Mack and, if it were possible, even sunnier-dispositioned. While Eccles and Lawson reviewed papers, I stepped to the veranda railing. The departed friars had situated their rectory so there was no doubt about who ruled the town. From here one could see over miles of rice paddies, a landscape of terraced squares in which all seasons were contained: in one place, spring; in another, harvest. Closer to town, there were groves of bananas, gardens full of squash, beans, corn, okra, tiny plots which suggested that each family provided for itself, one day at a time.

Along the main street were a half dozen one-story shops, Chinese-operated. They were sorry-looking places with inhospitable owners who wore pajamas all day long and slept whenever they wished. Their goods might have been salvaged from a shipwreck: once an item was sold it was never replaced, but very little was ever sold, so the shops and owners endured forever, somehow.

Religion was two-story buildings. Commerce, much reduced, was one. The rest of life was nipa huts: wooden piles, wooden floors, rattan sides, thatched roofs, impermanent as a pile of raked-together leaves. They were airy and elegant compared to the Apache wickiups at San Pablos, but still they were the homes of another race that was content to sleep below the roosters and above the pigs, to dine a little before the dogs and the goats, to bathe a little upstream from the oxen. And their islands had become the keys to the Pacific. I'd said so myself.

· XI ·

Behind the Lines
FILIPINO MILITARY LEADER VOWS ULTIMATE VICTORY
Sun's Correspondent's Exclusive Interview in Insurgent Stronghold

by EDWIN CARTER MORRISON, *Staff Correspondent*

Manila, The Philippines — The lines of battle are drawn here, in the rich plains of Luzon, just north of Manila. Sentries face each other across a no-man's-land, waiting to report—possibly to discharge—the shots which will mark the opening battle for these islands which are the keys to the Pacific. The trenches, miles of trenches, yawn like open graves ready to accept a mass human offering, and if this observer's reading of the situation here is not amiss, the trenches will soon be filled.

By now, the issues standing our mission in the Philippines are familiar. The men who face each other are beyond debate. Relations between the two armies, which were amicable at the time of their joint deposition of the tyrannical Spaniards, have deteriorated drastically. Shouts of "Amigo!"—Spanish for friend—greeted the first Americans, and were accompanied by smiles, flowers, food. But now "amigo" means enemy, a word laced with irony, a midnight shot on a dark street, a stab in the back.

This correspondent arrived determined to visit those Filipinos who so staunchly resist "benevolent assimilation" by the United States. The trip was made two nights ago. An American who had become acquainted with some of the insurrecto force in happier times agreed to escort me through the lines at night.

We stalked through fields that will know no harvest this year. On hands and knees we crept through jungle thickets. Tangled vines and creepers made the passage endless. The sound of night creatures—frogs, birds, insects—made a racket that seemed sure to invite both armies' wrath. A stone would have perspired.

At a river, the enemy kept his rendezvous. We heard a low whistle, which my escort answered in kind. "Amigo?" he asked. "Amigo" was the answer from across the river, but I did not like the sound of this "amigo." We waded into the river. I have never felt more vulnerable, more conscious of the whims and accidents that rule our lives.

"Where are they?" I asked as we stepped dripping onto hostile ground. Soon I saw. On every side but one, the river side, stood a Filipino soldier clad in white shirt and trousers, and with every Filipino soldier was a Filipino bolo, a gleaming, razor-sharp machete, a portable, personal guillotine.

In a moment, my helplessness was compounded by a blindfold and our guides, or captors, led us through enemy territory. It is a strange sensation, to be led through a hostile camp at night. I lived as if every moment were my last. Though my eyes were shrouded, my other senses worked overtime: I noticed the smell of burning wood, the mutter of alien voices, the whinnying of horses, the very texture of the ground, now swampy from rain, now hard-packed by marching feet.

When the blindfold was removed, I found myself in the Filipino headquarters, a tent with a half dozen rebel officers who were studying me as if they might shortly be polled on my life or death. Some looked as if my death were already decided and all that remained to be discussed, with enthusiasm, was the method of my execution.

I was introduced to General Sergio de León, the fiery

youthful commander of this sector and chief spokesman for the others. Fluent in English, a onetime representative of the rebel junta in Hong Kong, de León introduced me to the others, none of whom admitted to being anything less than a general, of which this fledgling army has no shortage.

The thrust of de León's statement to me will be familiar to those who have followed the utterances of Aguinaldo, Mabini, et al.: that U.S. officials promised independence in return for cooperation against the Spaniards, that this promise was repeated by Admiral Dewey upon his arrival and, since then, has been delayed, withdrawn, and ultimately reversed. This alleged change in policy constitutes a betrayal and *casus belli*.

At the conclusion, the whole insurgent leadership regarded with me a discomfiting stare, as if they expected an immediate high-level review of our patently misguided policy. It disappointed them that I was not President McKinley. They thought a debate could win a war. I inquired about troops, supplies, ammunition, and guns.

"We spoke to you of issues," de León snapped. "You ask about bullets. A quartermaster's question. Or a spy's."

"A fair question nonetheless," I said, "on the eve of battle."

"You will know *how* we fight, *when* we fight!" the peppery little general responded. "Is there no interest in *why* we fight?"

Wishing to assure myself safe conduct back through the lines, I promised de León I would report what he had said, and anything more he cared to add. This concession seemed to mollify the group, who then consulted about what their "message to America" should contain. It was as if these verbose generals were searching for a magic formula which would make 20,000 U.S. soldiers, sailors, and marines disappear!

"Why do you deny to us what you fought to achieve for yourselves?" de León asked. "Your liberty, your free nation, your constitution which we read, your history which we study, why do you betray them here?"

I scribbled away, more stenographer than reporter, but I knew that these notes were my ticket to the other side of the river . . .

They don't write them like *that* anymore. It's just as well. I'll admit this much: if leaving something out or putting a little something in made a good story better, if nobody got hurt and the chances were I wouldn't get caught, then I didn't mind raising my journalism to the level of fiction. Here, dear friends, is what really happened.

It was Eccles, not the thoroughly puzzled insurrectos, who blindfolded me, at my request, with his very own bandana. My description of the jungle was a flight of fancy. We were never obliged to crawl, although I did stumble a few times. The river was only a foot deep, I confess, and when I reached the far side, the "bolo-wielding enemy" extended a hand to lift me up, and gave me a shoulder to steady myself while I put my boots back on. Despite my protests, the Filipinos made me remove my blindfold, which I did, but only after I had taken a few steps, enough to give me some sense of what a longer walk would have been like. As for the insurgent generals, I telescoped a leisurely two-hour chat into what read like a tense twenty-minute audience. I omitted our cordial, meandering discussion of U.S. presidential politics, Freemasonry, and military music, plus the fact that we were drinking. I omitted—no one would believe it!—that General de León took me on a tour of his camp, displaying a captured Krupp field gun serviced by Spanish prisoners, which he thought might intimidate the Americans. He led me through the trenches as if the very extent of excavations—the mere ability to dig—might entitle the Filipinos to victory. At our farewell, he embraced me.

There was one another incident I did not mention in my dispatch. Soon after we crossed the river and waved goodbye to our smiling hostile escorts, we were shot at. Eccles pushed me onto the ground and threw himself beside me.

"Those sons of bitches!" I cried. "They smiled and shook our hands and now . . ."

"Morrison?"

"Yes."

"Those shots came from our lines."

"Oh." I assumed it was a mistake, the risk one always runs when crossing lines. "Let's identify ourselves."

"Good idea," Eccles said, cupping his hands to his mouth and shouting, "Twenty-fifth Cav here."

The answer was a rebel yell and a few more shots. "All the niggers on one side of the river," someone shouted.

"That's how it is," Eccles said. "We'd best just wait a while."

Crouched together on the ground, we stayed silent. I knew that Eccles wasn't the kind for small talk and it surprised me when he spoke at all.

"What did you think of it?" he suddenly inquired.

"Of what?"

"That speech I made at Nicodemus, Kansas. You heard about that?"

The man's single-mindedness was amazing. He might at least have pretended that we were friends! He could have asked about my health, or commented on his own, and I'd have been delighted to hear him wonder about the weather.

"Oh yes," I said, pretending to stifle a yawn. "That. There was a little something in the newspapers."

"And . . . Well? . . . What do you think?" It took more than a yawn to discourage him. It took a perfectly equivocal answer, which is what I gave him.

"I couldn't see what all the fuss was about."

"She hates me for it," Eccles said. "She's the one. Not him."

"You mean . . ."

"The Queen of Sheba. It was all right in the old days, when there wasn't much of a choice. Better to have her husband running a pack of slaves than a crew of drunken Irish or garlic-chewing Italians. But lately she's gotten ambitious. She figures that with Eccles and Dukie around, he doesn't go far. She came to me after Nicodemus, said didn't I feel ashamed of myself, didn't I care what people said, didn't I know how many dinner parties I ruined for them? Was this the thanks they got, after all they'd done for 'my race'? She about cried, she was so mad."

"Was the Boss there?"

"No."

"And you never talked to him about it? Before? After?"

"No."

"How many years do you have to serve together before you do?"

"I've been waiting. I thought that he would *see*. I hoped he had a plan . . . something that included all of us. But you know what? The Queen of Sheba's the one who does the planning. And her plans don't include us."

·XII·

DUQUESNE: I never did figure out what that war was all about. They called it the Spanish-American War, but I never shot no Spaniards. Only Spaniards I saw was some poor bastards scraping around Manila. They might still be there, hanging around the docks. No, our enemies was the Filipinos. Some Filipinos, that is. They was called revolutionaries, insurrectos, banditos. Flips, amigos, gugus. Know what else they was called?

E.M.: No.

DUQUESNE: Niggers. Yes, sir. Don't know how it looked from Washington, but from where I sat, it was open season on niggers . . .

E.M.: You hated it.

DUQUESNE: Yeah. I should have. Had every right to. But dumb old Dukie . . . falls in love . . . And you know something? That's the place I think on . . . blind old me. I just set in a chair and go back into the past. And the memory of my Filipina . . . that's the place I'm most comfortable. It's where I like to go . . . Philippines way . . .

E.M.: In spite of everything?

DUQUESNE: Yeah. Sure, lots of us hated the place. Hot weather, bad strategy, a war you couldn't find, but it dragged on forever, eight thousand miles from home, and after the first couple battles, who gave a damn? Lost three times, four times the men we lost in Cuba, fought ten times as long, and who the hell cared? But I loved it. Hot weather didn't bother me none and I liked being in farm country. I liked bamboo and coconuts, bananas, papayas, things I never heard of . . . soursops, mangosteens . . . But it wasn't just the food. It was the feeling of the place. Evenings I'd walk out into the rice paddies, just me, and there was a thousand little ponds and terraces, and each pool would catch a piece of the sunset . . . It was a well-made world out there . . . I loved it . . .

Goddamn eyes that are only good for crying . . . if you can't see you shouldn't have to cry . . .

All right. The first time I went to cockfights was an accident. I wanted to know where all these men with roosters on their arms was going . . . I walked in and there was roosters staked out, ready to fight, roosters that had fought, bloody, feathers missing, trailing guts, owners spitting into their wounds to make them real, and there was lots of dead roosters all over. I was the only American in a whole bunch of Filipinos and some of 'em was insurrectos . . . I won a couple bets and then I lost one on purpose, and I made a point. I found the guy, paid him, shook his hand. They got used to seeing me there, and when I was in town, folks smiled at me and I started knowing folks by name and picking up the language pretty quick . . . Well, one night some guys from other units dropped in. They lost some money, claimed the fights was fixed, started to tear things down . . . What are you gonna do with people like that? It was me against four of 'em, right in the ring, in the middle of the guts and shit and feathers. I won. After that I was a person of some importance at Kablaw's cockfight pit . . . That was her daddy . . .

E.M.: Whose?

DUQUESNE: Teresa Kablaw. Teresita. Her mother was María, her father Alexandro. She was the oldest of a bunch of kids, big-eyed, barefooted little tan-skinned kids. They all called me "Mr. Doookie . . ." Say, Morrison, you still listening?

E.M.: Right here.

DUQUESNE: For a minute I thought you'd walked away . . . wouldn't that be dumb, sitting talking to myself . . . ?

E.M.: I've been here all through, Dukie.

DUQUESNE: You remember that peach brandy up top my dresser? Pour me some. You, too.

E.M.: Don't mind if I do, Dukie.

DUQUESNE: Mr. Doookie . . . Boss used to say never take a drink till dark . . . if he could see me now. Here's to you, after all these years. This is really for a book?

E.M.: Yes.

DUQUESNE: Okay. One night, after I run the cockfights, she waits for me down the road. She kind of takes my hand and leads me off down this trail. She didn't say nothing. I'm thinking maybe someone got hurt. But she don't tell me nothing. She takes me through rice fields, into trees, and before I knew it, we was walking in a kind of jungle, ferns, bamboos, and all, and where we ended up, it was kind of a spring, a grotto. All around the water, it was like a garden, with cocoa, coffee bushes, bananas, and a couple big old mangoes overhead, so that only little chunks of moonlight got down to the surface of the pond, which was all covered with water lilies. She sat me down on a rock right at that edge and sat beside me and I was pleased she'd showed me this beautiful place, which I'm sure none of the other Americans even heard about, or ever would, if it was up to me. I say thank you, little sister, I like it here. She makes that face she was always making when I called her that. She sits me down and lifts my legs and pulls off my boots. She sits on my lap, pulls my suspenders off my shoulders, and then she's unbuttoning my shirt . . . Okay, a swim's okay, little sister . . . She unbuckles my belt and signals I should take my trousers off . . . She turns her back to me while I take off my trousers and my socks . . . she's all of a sudden naked, and without her even turning around, I can see that she's a woman . . . She laughs at me, teases me, because she ain't wearing anything, but I still got my drawers on . . . She points at them . . . off! . . . and without staying around to watch, she dives on into the pond, a quiet little dive, hardly made a splash, light as a leaf off a tree, and I try to copy her dive, which results in a belly whopper that drenched an acre. That splashed her, so she splashed me back. I caught her and she kind of folded into me, floating and cuddling, with her legs tucked around in back of me . . . and then . . . in the water . . . moonlight . . . water lilies . . . all touching . . . we come together . . .

Know something, Morrison?

E.M.: What's that, Dukie?

DUQUESNE: I wish I could go back, just one day, and you could pull the plug on me tomorrow . . . go swimming among them flowers one more time, spend one night in that little house we shared, wake up and see my little girl sweepin' down below, getting the earth ready for me to step on it . . . Mr. Doookie . . . Mr. Doookie . . .

SCHUTZENFEST

• I •

We heard the war start, Henry and I. It began while we were up on the veranda, enjoying some Cagayan cigars after supper, staring down into the road and wondering how long it would take a couple of dogs, one male, one female, to come unstuck.

"Mister Dog is headed north and Missus Dog is headed south," Lawson commented. It was a small town, and Lawson was a small-town boy.

"It's the female's fault," I said. "The muscles contract. She won't let go."

"Could be she can't let go," Lawson replied, puffing contentedly.

"If someone got a bucket of water . . ."

"Naah. How would you like a bucket of cold water thrown on you? Ever think about that? The way those dogs look to us, maybe we look like to someone else."

The first shots sounded tentative. We'd heard shots before at night. Remembering the sound years later, I think of the cranking of an automobile on a cold morning. This time the engine responded. We heard it catch, up and down the lines, a crackling racket that soon became a roar in which individual shots were lost.

"They won't be able to negotiate this away, Boss," I said.

"Sounds that way," he said. He walked over to the balcony. "The dogs split up."

"Boss!" Lefty Diller came racing down the street. "It's happening! All over the place."

"Well, that's just fine, Lefty."

"Ain't you coming?"

"In a minute, Lefty."

He took his time pulling on his boots. I believe he enjoyed those last minutes of peace.

"No fire discipline," Lawson murmured as he listened to the roar from insurrecto lines. "They're not careful, they'll be wasted in the morning."

There it was again! The old Lawson habit of counseling the people who were out to kill him, opening his shirt like Marshal Ney and ordering his nervous executioners to aim for his heart.

"How's it feel, Boss?" I asked. "I've covered lots of wars. But I've never fought one."

"It feels like . . ." He drank his whiskey, glanced at me, looked away. "Not like I expected."

"How's that?"

"All my life I've been waiting for the war worth fighting. The absolutely right one. The perfect enemy, the great occasion, when you show the world who you are . . ."

"And this . . ."

"Are you kidding me? It's a sideshow."

"Boss," I said, "I want your permission for something."

"What for?"

"Sideshow or not, we may never have another chance like this. Tomorrow, I want to stay close to you. When it's over, I'm going to write a piece that will make a name for you and the Twenty-fifth."

"She got you to write me up a hero one more time. That it?"

"Yes."

"Whether or not I am?"

"You are if I say you are. That's the way it works."

"Call me stupid," he said. "There was a time when I thought that . . . that this wasn't all arranged . . . cooked up ahead of time. You maybe did something that was special and folks noticed and the word spread and you know . . . like that."

He sat a moment, probably wondering what he was letting himself in for. You'd have thought that he was doing me a favor.

·II·

"Boss, they can't shoot!" Diller exulted. "They can't shoot for shit!"

We didn't believe him, but after half an hour of walking in easy range of the enemy trenches, the incredible truth was clear. Though deadly with bolos and industrious in their fortifications, equipped with flags and uniforms and bands, led by a hierarchy of officers whose self-importance rivaled that of the German General Staff, the Filipinos were the world's worst shots.

There were several explanations. For one thing, as Lawson had noted the night before, they lacked fire discipline. They shot at the first Americans they saw, betraying their position before they knew how large a force they were facing. In trenches, they tended to lift rifles over their heads and pull triggers without exposing themselves or venturing to aim. And, we soon learned, the insurrectos had no very clear idea of how to aim a gun, how to align the front and rear sights, either or both of which they frequently removed, so that their rifles became little more than wands to wave in the direction of the enemy. And this goes to the very essence of the war, the enemy we destroyed. They were dreamers, our so-called little brown brothers, unprepared for battle. We were a young nation but they were younger. Too bad we had to kill them, for the killing made us old.

I stayed with Lawson in the first wave, Dukie on one side, Lefty Diller on the other, smelling victory with his ivory nose.

Eccles and Buddy Conaway brought up the second wave, who passed and repassed us as we alternated our advance. They came up behind us like a stampeding herd, leapt over our prostrate forms, and rushed forward screaming. And Eccles was as far in front of his line as Lawson was in front of ours. We were fast, but he was faster; if we covered fifty yards, they went for sixty. Eccles ran, Diller muttered, as if his career depended on it. I laugh as I remember puffy, alcoholic Buddy Conaway lagging, out of breath, flopping down beside us, giving Lawson the saddest look in the world and saying, "Boss, that nigger's dangerous!"

When we were in front of the Filipino lines, less than a hundred yards to go, the enemy broke. Was it our more accurate firing? The sight of bayonets? The hellish shouting that we made? I cannot say, but I saw the insurrectos leaping out of their trenches and fleeing to the rear. They were easy targets then. The handful who stayed fared better: they lived an extra minute.

The plan had been that when the first line came to within fifty yards of the enemy, it would wait for the second line to join it, so the combined force could be brought to bear in the final assault.

I was on the ground next to Lawson when it happened, when we saw that Eccles wasn't waiting for anybody. He rushed ahead, bounding up the slope, hurdling the insurgent trenches. All around us there was cheering, from our men and from his, from flanking units. And Lawson had a look on his face I will not forget, in which hurt and pride were mingled.

"Eccles didn't wait!" I cried.

Lawson said nothing. He rose to his feet, wiped the dust off his slicker, and, I must say, he looked a little foolish, like a baseball player who has been caught off base. Then he walked toward the battle that was over by the time he got there.

The Filipino position was a charnel house. I saw lovingly prepared trenches turned into open graves, littered with dead and dying, our pathetic opponents, who had tried to fight a war without learning how to shoot. Some lay motionless, others twitched and quivered, like fish pulled out of a stream and tossed onto a riverbank, ignored while anglers rebaited their hooks. I saw Buddy Conaway firing at retreating foes while Lefty Diller administered a dozen coups de grâce: he loved the bayonet that morning. In back of the trenches, they were stripping General de León's body: they took his saber and his boots and they rolled him into the trench.

The units on our flanks moved forward now, finishing what we had started, but our sector was quiet. I wanted to be with Lawson when he caught up with Eccles. We found him at the last line of enemy trenches, gazing north across the rice paddies. I could still see insurgents making for a line of jungle perhaps a mile away, little white-clad figures who never looked back. The Filipino Republic, the insurrection—it had all fled that-a-way.

"Lieutenant Eccles!" Lawson shouted in a parade-ground voice.

Eccles turned, and I will never forget the expression on his face. Knowing him, I had expected a look of stubborn pride: do what you want with me, I'll take my punishment, but don't expect apologies. But what I saw—think I saw—was pain, disgust, confusion. Lawson must have seen it, too.

"Come here a minute," he said, much more softly. "I'm not going to hit you."

Eccles and the Boss stood together, speaking in whispers. When they finished, Eccles nodded and Lawson started walking back toward town.

"Well, Boss?" I asked when I caught up with him.

"Well, what?"

"What did you do about Eccles?"

"I told him to set up new lines. Bury the dead. Inventory the weapons we took and destroy what we can't use. Send the captured flag to General Gottschalk, with compliments. And prepare papers for my signature. I'm putting him in for the Medal of Honor."

Eccles had seen the enemy starting to break and, sensing their vulnerability, had struck without delay. Who could blame a young officer for grasping the chance to turn a battle into a rout? It was the brave, the enterprising, the *only* thing to do and the Army needed officers who could think on their feet. That was what Lawson said to anyone who asked him. I heard him defend Eccles half a dozen times, the first time as vehement as the last, and he always made it sound like the very question was foolish and would not have arisen if Lieutenant Eccles were white. He wasn't wrong about that either, he didn't have to feign conviction against people like Galloping Joe Gibbons, the professionally colorful ex-Confederate in the next sector. ("I hear your niggers beat you to the hen coop, Lawson.") Even with me, he never deviated from that line of defense, never budged or wavered. And I will go to my grave not knowing whether he believed what he was saying. Anyway, Lawson forgave Eccles, or tried to. That was his nature. I could not. That was mine.

My account of that first charge was the longest I ever wrote, more than four thousand purplish words. Words like *courageous* and *stalwart* for the Americans, *feisty* and *stubborn* and *plucky* for the insurrecto troops, *doomed* and *misguided* for their leaders. The battle was an *event* or *contest* divided into *episodes*, all leading to the moment when the day was carried, the field captured. Henry Lawson was all through the piece, and Lieutenant Eccles did not appear at all.

• III •

I finished my dispatch and strolled into Lawson's office, to find Lawson and Lucy sitting together. I knew right off that something was wrong.

"Have I interrupted you?" I asked.

Lucy started to nod, but Lawson motioned for me to sit.

"Lucy here came out to watch the battle. Jaime drove her. She was parked with the other gentry at the railroad trestle. There was diplomats and businessmen and some Filipino upper crust who wanted to make sure who'd win and . . ."

"General Gottschalk was there!" Lucy interrupted. "When he saw what happened, he offered condolences. 'The race is to the swift,' he said!"

"That's what this is about, Eddie," Lawson said. "My performance wasn't up to snuff. My wife thinks she married a loser. Seems that I should have tripped Eccles on his way up to the insurrecto line. Or grabbed the flag ahead of Creeper Simmons. Or pulled the boots off of General de León's body before Dumpling Grimes rolled him into the trench . . ."

"I shouldn't have to plead with you to do what's in your best interest," Lucy said. "I shouldn't have to arrange everything for you."

With my dispatch in my pocket, a dispatch trumpeting Lawson's triumph and omitting all mention of Eccles' courage, I felt uncomfortably like one of the things that Lucy had to arrange.

"You knew what I was when we were married," Lawson said.

"And I dreamed of what you could be."

"And I'm not living up to your dream. Well, goddamn!"

"We won the battle," I interjected. "Isn't that the point?"

"That is not the point, Edwin, and you know it."

"To thine own damn self be true," Lawson groused.

"A recipe for failure," Lucy retorted. "Follow it and you'll remain a boy forever. Oh Lord, why do I waste my time . . ."

"Why do you?" I couldn't help asking.

Lucy turned upon me. Lawson was out of it. This was for me. "Sometimes I think I've gotten things quite wrong. Terribly wrong. I think that I've allied myself, not with two men, not with even one. I feel surrounded by boys . . . fighting boys . . . writing boys . . . lovely little boys who love me back . . . exceptional little boys . . . but boys. The kinds of boys who grow old, not up."

With that, she left. Lawson was the first to react.

"She could be right . . ." he said.

"She could."

"Yeah . . . well . . . so?"

• IV •

" 'The future of the Philippine Islands is now in the hands of the American people,' " General Gottschalk read aloud, fork in one hand, newspaper in another, " 'And the Paris Treaty commits the free and franchised Filipinos to the guiding hands and the liberalizing influences, the generous sympathies, the uplifting agitation, not of their American masters, but of their American emancipators.' "

He put down the newspaper. "President McKinley. It seems that everyone has his own version of events here."

Gottschalk believed in a hot lunch. Or, as he had put it when we sat down, he "subscribed to the concept of the *table d'hôte.*" At his invitation we were dining at the Hotel del Oriente. I had long finished, but Gottschalk dissected a grilled fish with a surgical delicacy his gross appearance belied. He enjoyed dissecting things.

"And what is your version of events?" I asked.

"What we have here, Mr. Morrison, is a *Schutzenfest.*"

"A *Schutzenfest?*"

"Yes," he said, refolding his napkin in the original creases after he dabbed the corners of his mouth. "You know the phrase?"

"No."

"Well, it is German. Of course you gathered that. *Schutzen* means to shoot. And *Fest*—well, that is a kind of . . . picnic. So, altogether, a military picnic."

"*Schutzenfest,*" I repeated. I confess, I rather liked it. It was precise, it was arrogant. And it was playful.

Gottschalk leaned back while a waiter filled his cup. "All these Spanish churches. Monstrous cathedrals in every hamlet. They should have built good bakeries instead. So."

"So?"

"I have read your work, Mr. Morrison, and I confess that I'm puzzled. Not surprised, not disappointed. Puzzled. You take a rout and you make it a duel. You take a slaughter and turn it into a joust. It's all so . . . so medieval!"

He broke off while the waiter displayed a tray of tropical fruit. Gottschalk was not impressed.

"A pineapple is a fruit. A cut-up fruit is not dessert. Desserts are *made,* not grown. Often they are baked."

The waiter retreated.

"Now, Morrison, I appreciate poetry as much as the next man, but its presence in your work . . . I don't know what to think. I am a reader. I am a collector. I have—call it a blessing or a curse—a long memory. Looking back, as I have done with some assistance from my aides, I find this . . . poetic . . . strain enters only when you treat of Major Lawson. Not with Russians and Turks, Italians and Abyssinians, French and English. Not then. But when Lawson comes galloping into view, something happens. Tell me, what is it?"

"You study my work too closely," I said. "More closely than it was meant to be."

"Can I help it? Does an actor read reviews? I witnessed the battle you describe. I saw a rampaging Negro unit easily destroy Filipino positions. But in your account . . . Lawson . . . Lawson . . . Lawson . . ."

"He was their commander," I reminded him.

"And I am his. So?" He had me there.

"You weren't on the lines."

"True enough. But Lieutenant Eccles was. And yet there was no mention of him. No, Morrison. There are men above and men below, but everything is Lawson, Lawson, Lawson, and I am mystified."

"Then mystified you'll remain," I sighed.

"No!" he snapped, his anger surprising him. I watched him contain it, staring out to where a gaggle of Filipino hansom drivers squatted in their horses' shadows. When he faced me, he was himself again.

"No," he said. "The mystifying is over. And the mystery. And the mythmaking. All over. I'm warning you, Morrison . . . I have weapons."

"What weapons are those?"

He smiled, dabbing his lips with a napkin. "The truth."

• V •

Los Baños, Caloocan, the Tuliajan River. Malinta, Polo, Meycauayan, Marilao, Bocaue, Guiguinto. American victories along the road north, but who remembers them? I have trouble distinguishing one from another, trouble even pronouncing the names, and if I don't remember them, who does?

Our campaign had all the subtlety of a wave washing over a

sand castle. What did we compare it to? To shooting fish in a barrel or ducks in a gallery, to cutting butter with a hot knife, to smoking wasps out of rafters. Sometimes we flanked them, sometimes we ran right over them; either way, we won. But we couldn't make them surrender.

We'd had high hopes for the capture of Aguinaldo's capital, Malolos. The war was supposed to be over once we took it. I attended a conference with Lawson, Gibbons, Wheeler, Wheaton, Arthur MacArthur, and Gottschalk himself devising a strategy to end the war, an elaborate flanking, pinching, encircling movement which was marvelous on paper and might have prospered on the plains of Poland.

"It's all over my head," Lawson muttered with his unfailing tactlessness.

"Lawson is quite hopeless, beyond a certain point," Gottschalk countered. "If he knows what a flank is, he learned from his magnificent wife."

Lawson was right, however. One village was mistaken for another, a road turned out to be a river, and what looked like a lake turned out to be a dry, crack-bottomed mud flat. One column got lost, one was delayed, and a third—Galloping Joe Gibbons'—galloped off in the wrong direction. We took Malolos, but the decisive victory eluded us.

During this period, my writing dwindled. Part of it was a result of Gottschalk's intimidation. I'd always known that my coverage of Henry Lawson was one long impropriety, but now I knew that other people were watching. There was more, though. I began to sense that the words I'd lavished on him had done more harm than good. Whether or not he was a hero was not the point. The issue was that I had called him one. Not the praise of a poet, not the esteem of his fellow officers, not the loyalty of his troops—all of which he deserved—but a journalist's inky hyperbole is what I conferred. I made him a popular hero and it has taken me the rest of my life to realize that popular is what a hero never can be.

·VI·

"You wander out onto a battlefield, you get killed," Lefty Diller was saying. "We take that damn chance every day. Am I right?"

"Not the way the gugus shoot," Buddy Conaway said.

"How they shoot, that ain't the point," Diller persisted. "It could happen."

"And you could maybe get hit by a meteorite," Conaway joked. "That could happen."

"So what the hell were they doing out there anyway?" Billy Presley asked. "Back of the lines is where they should be, at the hospital tent maybe."

"I'll tell you one damn thing," Diller said. But he broke off abruptly as soon as he saw me. He didn't even try to change the subject, he merely stared at me, as if he expected me to leave, the sooner the better.

"What are we talking about, Boss?" I asked. He'd been drinking every night, usually with this same crew of whites. In the old days, that wouldn't have happened. Had the Eccles incident changed things, after all? And where was Dukie hiding?

"It seems"—he spoke slowly, the cup of whiskey in front of his mouth and his eyes off in the distance—"that two priests were found among the Filipino dead this morning. Unarmed. Holding crosses."

"Can't see a cross at a thousand yards," Diller interjected. "Can't tell a priest from nobody else."

Lawson nodded and drank. "Morrison knows that, I'm sure."

"Well, I'm making sure he knows it," Diller said. "Some gugu priests want to administer last rites, let 'em wait until people are dead. They want to pray for victory . . . well . . . too bad."

"You're not upset?" I asked.

"Hell no."

"Then why were you talking about it?"

"Hey!" Diller shouted. "You go after catfish, you catch a trout, that's worth talking about!" He emptied his glass and got to his feet. "I'm going to sleep. And I don't expect to have no trouble sleeping."

Presley and Conaway left, too. In a moment, Lawson and I were left alone.

"You sure can kill a party," Lawson said.

"What's going on around here?"

Lawson handed me a piece of paper.

I wish I'd saved it. It was a little like a wanted poster, addressed to "Negro American Soldiers" from "the People and Government of the Philippines." Half the poster was words: "Why are the oppressed black people of America shedding their blood to keep Filipinos in bondage? Why struggle to enslave us here when you suffer so at home? Join us in a common crusade for freedom and dignity!"

The words were predictable. But the illustration—it must have been a newspaper photograph originally—was devastating. The flickering lighting, the grinning rustic faces, the ominous tree, the broken black body hanging from a limb.

"Jesus!" I exclaimed. "Where'd they get this anyway?"

"The Filipinos?" Lawson said. "Probably sent to them by one of the anti-imperialist clubs back home. Who knows? Does it matter? The real crime wasn't in the sending, anyway."

"Who found this?"

"You know who."

"Eccles."

Lawson nodded. "He didn't say nothing. He just passed it over and looked at me, his face in front of mine, right in the eyes. Not angry, not sad, just like he was waiting for me to say something or do something that would change things."

"And?"

"What I am supposed to say? That it's a great country, with all its faults?"

Dumpling appeared with a fresh bottle of rum. Stumpy legs, rippling belly, empty and benign face: I wondered how he would look on a rope, hated myself for wondering.

"Everybody was right but me," Lawson said.

Was it the fire that gave his face the ruddy glow? The smoke that made him wipe his eyes? The rum that caused his hands to tremble?

"I was the only one who believed . . ."

•VII•

DUQUESNE: We come into a town one time, it's kind of odd, everything looks familiar. We're bone-tired, we're hot, we got fever and diarrhea, we got bites from snakes and bugs, our shit is full of worms, and it's starting to rain so the road is damn near a canal and huge balls of mud are sticking to our horses' hooves, and some people we couldn't see took shots at us, but it wasn't worth chasin' em, anyway they missed, and the Boss looks over at me and he says, "Dukie . . . haven't we captured this town before?"

E.M.: Bad times, Dukie. I remember.

DUQUESNE: We were sliding around in the mud on what everybody but us called a nigger hunt and it was enough to make you wonder—Herman Biddle was the one who said it . . . "if we ain't gone out of our way to wind up stupid."

E.M.: What do you remember of Eccles around then?

DUQUESNE: He saw the Filipinos falling apart at Los Baños! What was he supposed to do? Curtsy? Bow? Wait for white officers and white reporters? Bullshit! And anyway, they didn't give him no medal . . . didn't no blacks get that medal . . .

E.M.: Was he changing, do you think?

DUQUESNE: He was strange, let's say. He started collecting them nigger postcards the white troops had. Souvenirs, he said. He had enough to fill a book.

E.M.: I never saw them. Postcards?

DUQUESNE: Like there'd be a picture of some trenches full of dead Filipinos and the caption would say, "Can our boys shoot? Well, count the dead niggers." Or a picture of Negritos with blowguns and spears, and it would say, "The nigger cabinet." Or a dirty one, two white boys with their hands on some woman's tits, and it would say, "Take up the white man's burden."

E.M.: And he collected them? He sounds cold . . .

DUQUESNE: I guess he does. But I'll tell you. One time, somewheres north of Malolos, Eccles and me come upon some of Galloping Joe's boys who'd got ambushed by some insurrectos on a switchback trail that led down to a river. Soon as we rode up, we saw Galloping Joe motion to us we should come over double-quick. "Got something to show you," he shouted. What they showed us was something they had shot. He was a short little man with nothing but a loincloth and a spear. He was less than five feet, black as ink, kinky hair. He don't look nothing like a Filipino. I guess he was a Negrito, one of the hill tribes. The poor little bastard carried a kind of shield which was animal skins stretched over a bent piece of wood, and that might have helped him against sticks and stones, but was no use at all against a Springfield rifle. The shots that killed him had tore right through them animal skins and plowed on into his chest, and the little guy had a confused expression on his face, like "What the hell goes on here?" "This one of your scouts, Lieutenant?" Galloping Joe asks, and everybody's laughing. Eccles shakes his head, says nothing. "What the hell is that little black bastard? A man or a monkey? I can't tell." One of the others bends down, pulls back the little guy's lips, so we can see his teeth is filed to points. "Now, you *sure* it ain't one of your finest?" Gibbons asks. And Eccles, he says, "Maybe so." They're all cracking up, wondering if they should bury it or stuff it and keep it in a trophy room. And while we're riding back, I notice Eccles is crying. See? With him, you never knew what was going on inside . . .

E.M.: What ever happened to your little girl, Dukie?

DUQUESNE: When I got back she wasn't there . . . I asked all around the village, folks I knew, shopkeepers, farmers, folks from the cockfights. Nobody knew where she was, at least they wasn't saying. The cockfights was closed . . . that was policy . . . and the family had moved off . . . That little house of ours, you remember I told you about it? The ladder had fallen to the ground, the roof was on the floor, there was chickens picking for bugs in the thatch . . . A house like that, it goes to pieces fast with nobody living in it . . .

E.M.: And so you . . .

DUQUESNE: Don't think I left it at that. I wasn't letting go so easy. I asked everywhere, priests and officials and guys from other units. I offered a reward even. Oh, that was funny . . .

E.M.: Funny?

DUQUESNE: Oh yeah. The word got around about Dukie, it

followed me wherever I went. One big sorry nigger in search of a lost little native girl. If found, please contact Sergeant Doookie. Sergeant Doookie . . .

E.M.: I think we should probably stop.

DUQUESNE: I ain't got to the funny part yet. See, they made a joke out of it. Not so much our men, but the other units. In some bar or cathouse, a soldier would drag out some poor bitch and say, "Is this her, Dukie? Is this the one?" Or I'd be sitting out someplace, trying to get my head straight and along come the boys and a bunch of whores they was taking to the beach and they'd march 'em past me, drunk and giggling. The women didn't know nothing. "Is this her, Dukie? We think we found her this time . . ."

·VIII·

In my memories of northern Luzon, it is always raining. True, it was the wet season. But the image of rain goes deeper. The whole affair was inclement. It should have been "rained out," postponed, rescheduled for a better day, with more spirited teams, a livelier audience, a cleaner field. Rain. It came at us out of low locked-in skies, a few large drops spattering through the leaves, and then the downpour, which flooded roads and filled trenches and turned us all into refugees. Then, when it should have cleared, when the clouds were mostly spent, it lingered: drizzling days, mold and rot, earth, mud, and horizon blurred together. It seemed we had lost the sun forever.

Lawson's dream was turning into nightmare. A cavalryman who dreamed of gallant short campaigns found himself in a guerrilla war, protracted and ugly. He used to say that any war he was in was worth fighting, and this war proved him wrong. But, still a cavalryman, he galloped right toward the doom he must have known was waiting.

I remember, for instance, the incident of the sniper. He had picked up the column one morning as we broke camp, firing from a bamboo thicket a few hundred yards across some untended rice fields that were turning into swamp. He missed, but he kept following the column, and kept firing. Sometimes we saw him, rushing to keep pace with us, racing ahead for cover —trees, swamp grass, bamboo, banana plants—firing and missing and sprinting to the next location, more like a mascot than anything else. It continued all morning. It became a joke. And then, early in the afternoon, it stopped being funny.

"Damn it!" Lawson shouted after yet another harmless shot. He dashed off the trail, splattering through the swampland.

Eccles and a few others roused themselves to follow, but Lawson motioned that they should remain behind. The whole column paused to watch, feeling more awake than they'd been for weeks. "The Boss is worried about his afternoon nap," someone suggested.

Lawson made straight for the bamboo copse where the sniper had hidden. Two more shots confirmed his presence and then, seeing Lawson, he panicked, sprinting up a slope. He fired another shot from inside a grove of banana trees. He wasn't aiming, only praying he could evade the maniac pursuer his trivial plinking had provoked.

The Filipino was headed toward the top of the ridge, where jungle began. Lawson dashed ahead. When the Filipino emerged from the banana grove, Lawson was waiting for him.

Lawson and the Filipino studied each other. Lawson sat as if he were posing for a still life. He waited while the Filipino dropped to his knees, raised his rifle, aimed.

"Oh my God," Diller said. "He's standing still for him. He's giving him a free shot!"

The shot rang out and everyone waited for Lawson to tumble to the ground. Instead, he dismounted and walked toward where the insurrecto was struggling to reload. A trained soldier might have managed, but the insurrecto botched it, fumbling cartridges, scattering them on the ground, trying to attend to his Mauser and keep an eye on the giant striding toward him, calm as if he were asking directions to the next village. When Lawson was twenty feet away, the Filipino must have realized the reloading would not be successfully completed. He dropped the Mauser, drew out his bolo, and got to his feet.

They circled each other, Lawson holding his Colt, the Filipino with his bolo. The circles grew smaller and smaller.

"Finish 'im off, Boss," Dukie pleaded. "Do it!"

At twenty feet, even ten, a bolo stood no chance against a pistol. After that, it was an even proposition. At five feet, the bolo wielder had the advantage. They were that close now.

The men who were watching could only guess what happened next: Lawson was under no obligation to report. Diller thought he saw Lawson nod his head, and maybe smile, as if he were saying, "That's enough shooting for today. Now get out of here."

The circle widened. Lawson was showing mercy, breaking off the engagement. He stooped down to pick up the discarded Mauser. That made sense: Mausers were more important than insurrectos.

"Look out, Boss!" Dukie screamed.

The insurrecto didn't want Lawson's mercy. He came charging forward, his bolo slashing toward Lawson's head. The Boss ducked down and the force of his charge carried the Filipino past him, head over heels. He came up hooking the bolo at Lawson's throat. Lawson ducked again, grasped the blade, and the two of them rolled down the slope, right to the edge of the swamp.

"Why don't he use the pistol?" Dukie pleaded. "What's the matter with him?!"

They rose and fell together, tumbling backward into the water, six inches of water, a foot at most, but deep enough for a man to drown in. Lawson was on top, the insurrecto was in the water. When the uneven struggle was over, Lawson folded the man's hands over his chest.

At last, the Boss staggered to his feet, standing in the water, steadying himself. He tossed the Mauser into the swamp. He examined the bolo, testing it for sharpness, threw it in the water too. He mounted his horse, galloped through the swamp, up the bank, down the road. An hour later we caught up to him in the center of a village that was probably hostile but this afternoon it was frightened to death, and no wonder. There was Lawson, a foot taller than a man ought to be, and twice as dirty, sitting in a fountain outside the Catholic church, muddy, bloody, well armed, and very, very drunk.

"Well, Eddie, how'd you like it?" he asked while Biddle ministered to the slash across his forearm. "Gonna write me up a hero one more time?"

My writing was over, however. The next morning I awoke covered with sweat, trousers befouled, barely able to move. The fevers and infections which are the islands' best defense against foreign invaders had selected me. Sick as I was, I was grateful for the chance to leave.

I can recall bits and pieces of the weeks that followed, after Lawson deposited me at a railhead and left Eccles as my escort to Manila. I recall watching the buffalo soldiers break camp, watching them ride out into a morning fog, and I wondered if I wasn't left to care about them, who would? I recall riding on a flatcar through rice fields, with Eccles tending me solicitously. I'd snubbed him for weeks, but now I couldn't deny the friendship he was finally offering.

"Are you coming back to us," he asked, "after you get well?"

"I'm ready to leave," I sighed.

"I thought you were here for the duration. Don't you want to be in at the finish?"

"The finish? When it's finished, you tell me, Eccles. I'll pass the word along."

He fell silent, looking across the rice fields. "I read what you wrote about that first battle."

"Looking for your name?"

"What I want you to know is I don't mind your not mentioning me. And I don't miss that medal either."

"Now that surprises me."

"You remember that time in Arizona, after the 'Battle of Apache Pass'? We talked about how you were going to write up this big victory, even though we both knew the Singer whipped us good. Ever since then I've been thinking about all the people who never get their story told, all those people, those tribes and armies that just get lost . . . drop out of history."

"You mean the losers."

"I mean all the ones who never find a voice. The Indians, the Filipinos . . ."

"You *do* mean the losers . . ."

"And the blacks. When I got to the top of those trenches, it's what I thought of . . . it's all I've thought of since then . . . I keep thinking about the ones who go down silent . . ."

If I replied to him, I don't remember. I sank into another fevered sleep. A sleep of dreams. I dreamed of Lucy, naked, turning voluptuously before me, turning into Dumpling Grimes, who danced a jiggly hootchy-kootchy. I dreamed of Lefty Diller warning me about Eccles. "Watch that alley-cat skin, them piss-colored eyes." I dreamed of a Mexican woman moving the tips of her breasts across my chest, her dark nipples circling mine. I saw Lawson, naked in a pool, laughing at some fornicating dogs and shouting, "Pick your wars, pick your wars!" And at the very end, at the station of Manila, I saw something that was not a dream at all.

"You look dreadful, Morrison. I believe I'll fill in for you a while . . ."

Whiskey breath. Yellow teeth. Wrinkled suit. W. C. Symington, headed north.

"Gottschalk's sending you, isn't he?"

"I'm just an old hack after a story. I take help where I find it."

"Stay away. Please."

"He'll love me, Morrison. He'll eat out of my hand."

"Poison."

"He'll never know."

"Why are you doing this to him?"

"Him? Lawson?" Symington laughed at me. "You still don't have it, do you, Morrison? I want the organ grinder, not the monkey. I want *you*. It's nothing personal. I'm a whore, you're a whore. We both lie every day. But I hate myself for it. I sold myself a little bit at a time. You get a better price that way—but that's not the point. I was able to tell myself—for years—that there was part of me, some inner fortress, some personal redoubt, that believed in truth. All of which makes me pathetic now, I know. But you. You were a whore from the start. You took to it easily. Too easily. I don't like that."

I saw the old man staring at me. I expect, when I die, to see someone looking down on me like that.

"And you did it for a woman, Morrison. You were a whore for love. I like that least of all . . ."

• IX •

MAJOR LAWSON HAS DOUBTS ABOUT U.S. STRATEGY IN "THIS ACCURSED WAR"

by W. C. Symington

Luzon, The Philippines — After months campaigning against the stubborn insurrectos, a leading American soldier, Major Henry Lawson, has his doubts about our strategy and purpose here.

In an exclusive interview with this correspondent, the well-known, much-decorated veteran of the Civil War and the Indian wars termed recent efforts against the insurrectos "a mess" . . .

• X •

Lucy raced into my room, ripped aside the mosquito netting, shattered my nap, shoved the newspaper into my hands. I knew my convalescence—my weeks of mornings in the garden, afternoons by the sea, evenings with Lucy at Luneta concerts—was over. My sickness might linger, but it had been overtaken by a greater illness than my own.

"He always has been one to speak his mind," I said, handing back the article. "At least that hasn't changed."

"No, he hasn't changed." Lucy's apparent calmness deceived me. She was calmly launching an indictment. "It's a point of pride with Henry. Wars come and go. Times change, politics, policies. Not Henry. Henry is constant. Henry is *a* constant. He looks at me sometimes, when he's a little sad or a little drunk, and he asks me if he's still the man I fell in love with. I tell him yes and it never quite dawns on him that that's the whole problem."

"It's a hard time he's having. The war up north . . ."

"You'll have to fix this fast," she said, as if I'd never started to speak. She didn't interrupt: she never heard.

"Fix?"

"Oh, come now, Edwin, you must have a way of cleaning up the mess that Henry's made. I hate to ask you but . . ."

"Luce. Listen. There's nothing I can do for Henry. The hero-making's over. We need a rest from heroes."

"One more story. The taking of some village, perhaps, or capturing an insurrecto chieftain . . ."

"No! I couldn't. I shouldn't. I can't! I won't!"

"I can," she said. Calm. Imperious. Formidable. And there was no love in her, not for me. Because Lucy had loved me before she used me, I thought that the loving mattered more than the using. I doubted that now.

Not even Lucy could spare Lawson all the consequences of W.C.'s article. His comments had been extraordinarily rash, and in America the *Journal* jumped at the chance to discredit a soldier who had been discovered by a reporter for a rival newspaper. They kept the story alive for weeks, soliciting comments from other officers. On the whole, Lawson's colleagues were discreet, and none more discreet than General Gottschalk, who sympathized with "the rigors and sufferings of Lawson's long and difficult campaign."

Lucy neglected me entirely the next few days. She was at Fort Santiago in the afternoon, alone on the Luneta at night, courting Gottschalk and his equally loathed wife. I'm sure Lucy had a hand in the "clarification" that was attributed to Lawson the week after Symington's story:

> I do not claim to have been misquoted, but I have been misunderstood. The fault is mine. The statements were made in a time of extraordinary stress. They reflect the failure, which is my failure, to see this war ended as quickly as all of us had wished. That our goals here are difficult of accomplishment does not mean they are unworthy. I yield to no one in my determination to see our stewardship here well and peacefully founded.

The statement was only part of Gottschalk's price. Lawson was to come to Manila to occupy a "less strenuous" position on the headquarters staff. The 25th Cavalry, Colored, was folded into a larger force under Captain (now Major) Stanley Erickson. And with the war on Luzon turning into a small-scale guerrilla hunt, Gottschalk made his last move. He transferred the 25th to the garrison at Balangiga on the island of Samar.

·XI·

We were all very careful with each other when Henry returned from the north. We took walks and drives, gave and were given dinners. I think the reason things went so well was that we knew in our hearts they wouldn't last. So we muddled along, enjoying what time we had. As before, Lawson came home "from the office" at dusk, splashing along the purple shore.

Evenings were on the dull side. Lawson didn't enjoy the Luneta. He saw too much of Gottschalk during the day to sit through a Gottschalk-conducted concert at night. "Ten hours of him calling the tune is plenty." Lucy and I went to the concerts together. She made no secret of it: with or without Henry, the Luneta was the highlight of her day. Whatever happened to Lawson, she was still the Belle of Manila, invincibly social and endlessly conspiratorial. It was for Lawson, asleep at home, a bottle beneath his hammock, that she conspired.

"I have just performed a miracle," she announced one evening. Turning to Henry, she added: "On your behalf."

"For me?"

"A commission is coming here from Washington to prepare a report on the Philippines. The operations of the civil government, military plans . . ."

"Reports of torture," I interjected. Lucy didn't hear . . .

". . . with some judges and two senators and a university president . . ."

"Yeah . . . well . . ."

". . . and I understand that this commission will make a request . . . it may already have been made . . . for an interview, which will also be a dinner party . . . with America's *foremost fighting soldier*!"

"Oh no!" Lawson groaned. "I've had enough of this."

"You have not!" Lucy cried. "Why do you refuse to grow

up? Why do you let subordinates upstage you, and why do you defend them when they do? You ignore your friends' advice. Why? You alienate those superiors on whom your future depends! Why?"

Henry just shook his head back and forth, like a patient refusing medicine.

"You say you want to stay here when the war is over. Yet you act as though your whole ambition was to land in a Wild West show. Why is the sum of all your happiness to romp forever with an obsolete pack of black Indian fighters?"

That hit home. "They're my men," Lawson said. "I knew them before I knew you."

"It's pathetic!" Lucy said, slapping her hand on the table and turning to me. "He cannot bear to be separated from that gang of black men."

"You're right there," Lawson said.

"Tell me, Edwin. When you find yourself among a group of men . . . on a newspaper, or a ball team, or in the Army . . . where is it ordained that you're obliged to stay with them forever . . . and *never* move on?"

"I guess you get attached," I said.

"Oh God!" Lucy cried. "You, too! You're part of it, too! You're part of the gang! And you! . . ."

She faced Lawson, angrier than I had ever seen her.

"I know it hasn't been your kind of war. You keep saying to everyone 'it don't amount to much.' Perhaps not. The battles aren't big enough. The enemy won't stand and fight. The weather is bad. But one thing I'll never forgive you for, Henry Lawson. When things turn bad . . . you make them worse!"

"So what's this great opportunity?" Lawson asked, finally softening.

"It *is* a great opportunity!"

"All right," he said. "All right."

·XII·

The visiting commission's reception for Henry Lawson was on the grounds of Fort Santiago. The Spanish bulwark where Gottschalk ruled had lovely gardens, orchids, plumeria, bougainvillea, and hibiscus, which the good general oversaw as carefully as his pet orchestra. There were battlements where guests could stroll across the river, passing before cannons that had been unable to stop our coming here.

Lucy and I entered together, arm in arm, and I sensed a shudder of excitement when she saw the people who were waiting. There were Gottschalk and his staff, all in dress uniforms, and the commission members, in crisp tropical whites, and several dozen "Americanista" Filipinos anxious to testify to the importance of our inevitable victory.

The 25th Cavalry was shipping out to Samar that afternoon and Lawson said he wanted to see his boys off before coming to the party. It seemed little enough to ask. With their departure, one phase of his life was ending, and this evening marked the beginning of a new phase. He was "clearing the decks" for his new career, he said.

I remember circulating through the crowd with Lucy. I remember how, after half an hour or so, we caught each other glancing at the gate, waiting for Lawson to make one of the splendid entrances that came so easily to him. I'd seen how he could dominate a room by stepping inside, how he would pick Lucy out of a crowd and head straight for her and greet her with a hug she said embarrassed her, but we all knew better. "Howdy, darling, home from the wars!" But this time he didn't come, and the room was whispering. I heard the beginnings of doubt, its immediate suppression, its quick return. Theories, hypotheses, excuses. I saw dinner begin and he still could have had his triumph, arriving late and breathless, in time for cigars and coffee. But there was nothing. I remember waiting, hanging on while people left, commission members, Lawson's future, Lucy's happiness draining out into the night. I heard Lucy apologizing . . . I apologized, too . . . and I wondered why we were apologizing. I remember leaving. God knows what they said when we were gone. Lucy asked our driver to take us to the military docks.

We heard the party from half a mile away. Horseshoes clanging, raucous laughter, bits of song. The dock was covered with beer and buffalo soldiers. America's most famous fighting soldier was pissing off the edge of a pier, no doubt proclaiming how he loved pissing into the biggest damn thing on earth. Lucy wept all the way home and I held her in my arms, dry-eyed and wondering.

·XIII·

In the days that followed, Lucy never left home, Lawson never came home. And something inside repeated what my editors had been cabling for weeks: I should leave. The war had petered out. The newspapers were already calling the insurrectos "bandits." In China, the armies of a dozen nations were carving up an ancient empire. In South Africa, England was entangled in a war of particular brutality. Compared to these, America's plodding campaign against the stubborn Filipinos was penny-ante. No use pretending otherwise, benevolent assimilation had turned out to be bad news.

I didn't know how to say goodbye to Lucy; I was saving that for last. I took a bundle of Henry Lawson's clothes and went to call on him for one last time. I waited outside his office in Fort Santiago, observing a stream of busy officers and benevolently assimilated Filipinos.

"Come in, Mr. Morrison," General Gottschalk said as soon as he saw me, and I knew it wouldn't save me to protest I had not come to see him.

"Are you at work today?" he asked, settling behind a desk piled high with papers. No doubt he relished a full desk: a clean desk was like an empty plate.

"I'm leaving," I told him. "Manila to Cape Town."

It sounded like a ridiculous trip, the oddest combination on the planet.

"Well, then, what I say to you will seem irrelevant. Nevertheless, I will say it."

"Please," I said.

"In nature there is a tension between tall, handsome, heroic figures like Major Lawson and . . . well . . . such as myself. I look at myself, Morrison, truly I do, and I think, no, such a person should never have been born. And in society there is a tension between noble, inarticulate types—'men of few words'

—and those of us who, let's face it, love to talk. And in the military there is tension between field commanders, active, dashing, combatants, and those of us who preside over . . . over . . . this."

He gestured at his desk. As he gestured, he glanced at some of the papers, and frowned.

"The point, General?"

"The point is that I want you to know that I have nothing but the highest regard for the major, for what he is and what he represents, for his courage, his . . ."

In the hall, there was a heavy tread, a door opening and slamming shut, Lawson coming late to work. Inside his office, he sneezed and the sneeze formed itself into a word that could have been heard over on Corregidor. "Hooorse . . . SHIT!"

Gottschalk smiled. "Splendid man. I suppose you know why he's back here."

"He was somewhat indiscreet . . ."

"Somewhat indiscreet?! 'We leave a trail of hoofprints and dead mayors'! *Disastrously* indiscreet. I had no choice but to bring him back here. And frankly, I was relieved to do so. With someone like Lawson in the field you never know what will happen. He can cover ten miles in a week or fifty in a night . . . All of which may be the stuff of which folk songs and boys' tales and certain kinds of journalism are made . . ."

"And this is what you wanted to tell me?"

"Not quite. When Major Lawson returned to Manila and came under my protection . . ."

"Protection? Come now! He's a soldier, not a wayward youth."

"No, Morrison. *You* 'come now.' He's a soldier who behaves like a wayward youth. It was this or a court-martial. It was my choice. And I made it for his benefit."

"I suppose you did, General. Knowing Lawson, he'd have picked the court-martial."

"This is not a war of escapades. This is not a war of adventures, or duels, or chases . . ."

"I gather. Too bad."

Gottschalk sighed. "You should both grow up. You . . . *you* know better . . . you should help him see things realistically, instead of embellishing his fantasies. Mark my words, Morrison, you have something to answer for in the fate of Henry Lawson."

He picked a tiny bell off his desk and tinkled for his adjutant, telling him to bring Lawson in.

The Boss stepped in, eyes forward. I saw him before he knew I was there: the shambling walk, the unsteady stance, the redness in his skin, and the scent of whiskey in the morning air. Gottschalk pointed at me, and the Boss turned around to see who was there. He took me in, nodded a little, as if to say, yes, he recognized me, he knew me way back when.

"Eddie."

"Hello, Boss."

"You come to see me?"

"Yes," I said. "The general and I were just getting reacquainted."

"Oh," he answered. "That's nice." It seemed as if he were looking for an excuse to leave. He noticed the bundle of clothing from Lucy. "That for me?"

I handed it over. It was a pathetic exchange in any case, and even worse in front of Gottschalk. Lawson could have waited till we'd left, but he appeared not to care whether anyone saw what had become of him. On the contrary, he wanted them to see.

"Mr. Morrison says he won't be here for very long," Gottschalk said. "Isn't that so?"

"Yes," I confirmed. "I'm going to Africa. Dutch against English. They're giving each other hell, Boss."

"Africa." Lawson said it wistfully, as if he were adding another name to the long list of places he'd never get to. "That must be something."

"I have a suggestion!" Gottschalk interjected. "Major Lawson is in charge, among many other things, of a special program, the Model Villages. You are scheduled to leave today for San Vicente, no?"

Lawson nodded without enthusiasm. "I guess so."

"And to stay the night, no? Well, why don't you let Mr. Morrison accompany you? You'll have time to chat and Morrison will see another side of our program here."

Lawson waited for me to beg off, and when I didn't, he said, "Okay, I don't mind."

We went ten miles up the Pasig River, an alley of banana groves and nipa huts and carabao wading along the banks, and then out onto the large shallow lake called Laguna de Bay, with San Vicente on its far shore. We transferred from a packet boat to canoes to make our landing.

"This is my third time here," Lawson remarked as we were rowed toward shore, where crowds of people waited and a village band was playing "America the Beautiful."

It was our first time alone together. The boat had carried all sorts of officials, a public health officer, a schoolteacher, a dentist, and others, all of whom had wanted to talk to Lawson and have their pictures taken with him. Now he stood at the front of the lead canoe, waving to the cheerful throngs on shore.

"The first time, we killed thirty-five insurgents. Easy. The second visit, they'd killed the mayor we installed. Wrapped him in a flag, Old Glory, soaked it in kerosene, took him to the town square, rang the church bells, and lit him up. But they're a Model Village now."

"What does that mean?"

"We got a garrison here, permanent. We ain't leaving. They noticed. We're happy they noticed."

I watched the Filipinos that day. A lot of Americans didn't like them, thought them children, childish and childlike. They were said to be moody, fickle, and undisciplined. They had a short attention span, never planning today what they could improvise tomorrow. They worked the way they fought, whimsically, sporadically. And yet, you had to admire them. They didn't linger over past defeats, didn't hold grudges. Every day was a new beginning. We carried the past around with us: the older we got, the heavier the burden, till it seemed it wasn't our age so much as our memories that finally crushed us. These people weren't like that. Six months ago, they'd have gleefully butchered every one of us. Now they welcomed us with music. They erected an arch with a bamboo eagle flapping bamboo wings as we passed beneath, onto a main street that was lined with banana trees planted like so many lampposts, decorated with bunting, red, white, and blue. They fed us constantly, not merely pig and chicken and rice and plantain, but ham and turkey and a cake with a confectionary statue of Henry Lawson, sword raised, leading a charge against their own republic. No one ate that statue, no one touched it. They cut around it till it toppled onto a field of crumbs and was whisked away, like the relics of a saint.

The highlight was a debate in Tagalog between two teenage children, one of whom took the side of the Americanistas, the other speaking for the insurrectos. Lawson presided, on a schoolroom chair his bulk made look like a milking stool, while the two beaming, big-eyed scholars orated in a language he could not understand.

An interpreter gave us the gist of it, and it was interesting. The insurrecto lad spoke for independence, basing his argument on the example of the United States, which once had fought just as revolutionary Filipinos now were doing. The Americanista countered that it made little sense to fight the very nation one sought to imitate. One fought Spain, which had come to oppress, not America, which had come to protect. So the great issue of the rebellion came down to this: how could one more quickly become like the Americans?

Lawson applauded both boys, shook their hands, served them cake, and magnanimously declined to choose a winner. Both speakers were marvelous, he told the audience, and he wished all wars could be fought so amicably. Filipinos had known war and peace, he stated, and he could testify that they excelled at both. But the people of this village were done fighting, and done debating. They had made their choice, and he, who had faced them in battle, now had come to win their hearts in peace. He introduced the doctor, the sanitarian, and the rest, and asked the local priest to close the meeting with a prayer.

After an interminable concert by the village band, Lawson and I were escorted to a nipa house which was newly constructed for our use: fresh linen, piles of fruit, and a few slabs of patriotic cake awaited us.

Lawson sat down, tossed me a cigar, and lit one for himself. I didn't know how to begin to talk to him. The day vividly illustrated what had become of him, and it seemed pointless to elaborate. He glanced at me, wondering when the first question would come, and what was keeping it.

"Nice people here, huh, Eddie? Natural-born musicians."

"Do they mean it?"

"Mean what?"

"This welcome. A while ago it was all bolos. Now it's cake and music."

"The cake's pretty deadly," he answered, belching. "Yeah, I think they mean it. Sure. They meant it when they fought us. They mean it now. It's all from the heart."

"What if they came in here tonight with bolos?"

"They'd mean that, too," he said, "but I don't see that happening. We're winning the war."

"How about you, Boss?"

"Me? I've got it knocked. Oh, I'm sitting pretty, that's for sure. I could tour these villages forever. When I die, they can stuff me, stick me on a horse, and I can lead the Fourth of July parade till kingdom come."

I had come to talk. He knew that. And there was a world of things to talk about, but no way of beginning, none that I could find. Lawson didn't want my advice or understanding. He didn't want my company. He was touched I'd come—I could see that, sometimes—but he wished I hadn't. Back in Manila, late the next afternoon, he was relieved when it was time for me to leave.

"Don't suppose I'll see you again this trip," he said. "This trip"—it sounded like I was in the neighborhood every few weeks. He knew better.

"Africa," he said. "I sure would like to see Africa. They say it's open country in the south, plains and the desert. Plenty room for a man to move."

I could hardly bear to look at him. I wondered if this would be the last memory I would have of him. We shook hands, but it felt as though he was already years and miles away.

"Eddie," he said when I had almost gone. "Sorry I let you down. Lucy and you."

"You didn't let us down, Boss," I responded. But the way it came out, I knew he didn't believe me, and I didn't expect to be believed myself.

"Yeah . . . well . . ." His voice trailed off. "So how's Lucy?"

"I'm sure she'd like to see you."

He put his hands on my shoulders; he knew I was lying. "There's nothing that happens to me that I can't stand. Drunk or busted down or broken . . . it's all all right with me . . . Lucy is the one whose heart gets broke . . . and that breaks mine."

He hugged me, patting my back. "Take her, Eddie. You'd be doing me a favor."

·XIV·

Returning late, I saw that Lucy had already retired and I soon did so, too. My time with Lawson had exhausted me. It was worse than attending a funeral, being around him now. In his heart he was dead, gone the way of the buffalo soldiers, of the buffaloes themselves, herds chopped up and habitat destroyed. Lucy couldn't save him and neither could I. Whatever we did, he'd shrug us off and continue waiting for the last shot, the final bell. I went to bed picturing what his obituary would read like.

The trade winds carried rain that night, full, heavy clouds which rolled off the Pacific to impale themselves on Luzon's peaks and pour their cargo into Manila Bay. I awoke to the sound of clapping shots all around the house, a cadre of servants slamming windows upstairs and down. One of the girls tiptoed past my bed and went over to the windows, which she gently closed. I lay back, listening to the rain. The maid came over and stood beside my bed. It was Lucy.

"Come sit with me," she said.

I put some chairs in the doorway leading out onto the terrace, just beyond the rain. At first I put my chair next to hers so we could sit next to each other, just like Arizona.

"No," she said. "Sit over there. That way we can put up our feet."

I put my chair opposite hers, across the doorway. She lifted her feet, placed them in my lap, while my feet reached to the sides of her chair, resting against her bathrobe.

"Trouble sleeping?" I asked.

"Yes."

"The rain?"

"Not just that," she answered. She looked out at the rain a while. "You saw Henry . . ."

"Yes. I don't like what's become of him . . ."

"I don't like what's become of any of us. Him. Or me. Even you, Edwin."

"*Even* me?" I said. "I never claimed immunity. Sometimes I think I was the first to catch it . . . whatever it was we caught."

"Sometimes I wonder . . . God forgive me . . . what my life would be . . . or would have been . . . if Henry Lawson had not come galloping into it."

The galloping was cruel, I thought. Why such a sharp word? *Galloping?*

"And I wondered," she continued, "if you ever think . . . ever picture . . . that, too."

"What your life would have been?"

"And yours . . ."

"If you hadn't"—I couldn't resist it—"been galloped off with?"

"Don't clown, Edwin."

"I was the worst day of my life when your letter came. I wasn't clowning that day. Or was I, Luce?"

"You got over it . . ."

"I didn't die, if that's what you mean. But my life was changed, that's certain. It turned out differently."

"You sound as though your life is over."

"Well, not over, but a good deal farther along . . ."

She fell quiet then, and we listened to the storm rumbling out over the bay, like a great naval battle somewhere over the horizon, imaginary armadas dueling to death. I'd never heard a battle that matched a good thunderstorm.

"You know, Edwin, I love the rain here. In Arizona, it hardly ever rained. The clouds were all headed this way, I suppose. Even in Indiana, it was just so much water coming down, like a regular monthly deposit, enough to keep the farms going for another season . . . You know where Henry spends his nights?"

"No," I answered.

"He didn't tell you?"

"No."

"And nobody else did? It's all over town. Henry is living in a brothel. Antonia Lee's."

I was dumbfounded. Casa Rosa? Casa Diablo! Whether an Apache waited at the bottom of a valley or a mestizo prostitute at the top of the stairs, he felt entitled, at any given moment, to leave us forever.

"How is your taste for irony?" Lucy asked.

"Irony?"

"Yes. We traded, that woman and I. She took my husband. I took her bed. So there we are, Edwin. That's how everything turned out. Time was, I thought there was something special in store for us. Somewhere,we'd find it. Henry had the magic. You had the talent. And I . . ."

"Yes?"

"I brought them together."

"That's all?"

"No. I believed. More than you believed. That was easy. More than Henry, too. I believed we'd be great someday. I believed we'd find a special place which we'd know was our place and a special time, our time, where every day we lived was golden, and every minute, and we'd know it . . ."

She was crying now. Sad tears, and angry. They combined. That was Lucy.

"And now, what am I? A hot-weather Lady Macbeth, it seems. And Henry . . . a museum piece, drunk and broken. And you . . . a too-well-traveled journalist. Oh, Edwin, I'm sorry. I'm sorry for all of us . . ."

"I'm sorriest for you, Luce," I said. "Henry could have taken things as they were. And I could have settled for less. I do. I have. But you . . . What'll become of you . . . ?"

"I've been wondering . . ."

"Sometimes I think we should all go home."

"Not to Indiana?"

"New York at least. The bridge. Draw strength from where we started. I've thought about that lately. Perhaps . . . you should think about it, too."

"What are you saying?"

"I want to make you whole again. I want to be whole myself."

We sat together in silence, and I liked believing she was pondering what I had said about going home and starting over. How at ease we were together, watching the storm light and crackle all around Manila Bay. We had loved each other forever. Would life together be any different?

I felt Lucy's hands touch my feet, her fingers half circling my ankles, slowly moving up and down my calves.

"We're getting wet," she said.

"I don't mind."

When was it? Eleven? Eleven-thirty? Sometime before midnight he came, all the way from Manila, riding out of the darkness and rain, rearing up on his horse, shouting up to our bedroom windows like an unquiet ghost.

"Luce! Eddie! Anybody home?!"

I opened the window, though it was pouring, and stuck out my head.

He looked like a figure from the past, a visitor from Valhalla, defying the lightning to strike him down, electric and majestic. Had we ever really known him?

"Come on down, you two. Make it snappy!"

We rushed downstairs.

"Is he drunk?" I asked.

"I don't think so."

"Is he angry with us?"

"I don't know."

Lawson had stayed on his horse: no dismounting, no coming inside for him. When he looked down at us, I knew he didn't care about what we had promised each other inside the house.

"We got a message from down in Leyte," Lawson said.

"Leyte?"

"The next island to Samar. There's been a massacre. Our boys."

"Why'd they do that?"

"They *got* massacred. In a place called Balangiga. The Filipinos caught 'em by surprise."

"Who died?"

"I don't know."

"Dukie?"

"I don't know who all. They're sending me down to pick up the pieces. I'm leaving tonight. Now."

I heard Lucy gasp. She grasped my hand. I heard her say, "No." No to what? To massacres? To her husband's departure? To mine?

"There's a war on, Eddie. Want to come?"

"No!" Lucy repeated, and Lawson must have heard her this time.

"They were your outfit, too," Lawson said. "I thought you'd want to find out what the hell happened to us all."

"No," Lucy said.

"I'm coming, Boss," I answered. In a moment, we were riding away.

THE MASSACRE

·I·

DUQUESNE: I knew it the first day we saw that place. I knew it before.

E.M.: Knew what, Dukie?

DUQUESNE: That something awful was waiting for us in Samar. I saw signs.

E.M.: What kind of signs?

DUQUESNE: July 5, 1899, they put us on a transport from Manila to Leyte to Samar. It was one of the Spanish boats we hadn't quite sunk, the *Reina del Mar,* which means *Queen of the Sea.* And what happened to the horses on board that ship, that was a sign to me . . .

E.M.: The horses?

DUQUESNE: The *Queen of the Sea* broke down all over the Pacific. The trip took a week, and the horses suffered something awful in the heat. We did everything we could to keep those animals alive. We walked them on the deck, we watered and washed them with our own water, and anyway they died, and I remember how we pushed 'em overboard and we stood against the railing, Herman Biddle and me, and we knew, deep down, something was wrong. We watched them horse corpses floating behind us in the wake, watching for the sharks to find 'em. There was our horses, lost at sea, moving with the waves, and all of a sudden—my God!—the water would explode, the bodies would turn and thrash, almost jump out of the water, and then there'd be a big red blotch we were sailing away from. And I knew that it was gonna be coming down on us . . .

Samar was a monster of an island. When I found him thirty years later, Lefty Diller still shuddered at the memory of its sad, black beaches and sullen coastal villages, its trackless interior, a tangle of mountains, rain forests, cliffs, and gullies, which he would always picture, as would I, through a prism of endless rain.

"It was like something pissed God off on the day of Creation and he took the land he was making and crumpled it up, the way you'd wad up a sheet of waste paper. That island was crumpled up, too. It wasn't no small place—a hundred fifty miles by seventy-five, they said—but the way it looked to me, it was like a fist poking out of the sea. The mountains were fingers and knuckles, punching up into the bellies of the clouds."

Like most villages on Samar, Balangiga sat on a black sand coastline, the Catholic church and convent surrounded by a cluster of nipa huts, and a fleet of native canoes—barotos—drawn up onto the beach.

"It was funny," Diller recalled. "Those people had lived there as long as they could remember. At least, they couldn't remember living no place else. You'd point into the jungle, or up to the mountain someone should have climbed by now, and you'd ask them gugus what was it like in there and they'd shrug. They didn't know. They'd never been there. No reason to go.

"The first thing we did," Diller said, "was we herded all the grown men out in front of the church and had 'em pledge allegiance to the United States. As a ceremony it didn't amount to much—a bunch of gugus hemmed in by American soldiers. Some of 'em said they didn't understand, some said they'd already sworn the oath someplace else. They had to get the priest to talk to 'em before they did it. After that it went off without a hitch, everybody listening to Erickson explain why America was in the Philippines and how we planned to fix up their lives. They contained their joy pretty good. Major Erickson said that meant it was up to us to 'establish an atmosphere of mutual trust.' "

DUQUESNE: You had to hold your nose when you walked through town. Garbage and shit was under the houses and in the streets. A dog died, they let him lay there, so you got to see him rot and puff and burst and rot and nobody gave a damn. Nobody kept gardens, nobody swept in front of the houses, or went underneath 'em, unless it was to take a dump. We boiled our water, but we all had malaria anyway, and dysentery, and prickly heat, and ten kinds of bites. It was a bad village, a bad place.

E.M.: Tell me about Major Erickson.

DUQUESNE: They turned him into "Custer of the Jungle." I didn't like that . . .

E.M.: Well, wasn't he?

DUQUESNE: He was a soldier got stuck with a bad post. If you think that all the dead are losers and all the ones who live are winners . . . if that's how you keep score . . . that's your business. But I got other ways of reckoning . . .

E.M.: Okay, what happened?

DUQUESNE: A lot of people, when they looked back on it, talked about the cockfight . . .

Major Erickson didn't believe in ordering people around, Diller said, unless you asked them nicely first. He tried to convince the town priest, Father Alacrón, that cockfighting was what was keeping them in the Middle Ages. And the priest said, yes, it's terrible, but these people are children. That was Alacrón's style. First a gugu smile and then a gugu shrug. Yes, the village is filthy, the men are shiftless, the women are pregnant, but what is one to do with such children? "We live in a fallen world," the priest said, and Lefty Diller agreed. "Only some places fell harder than others."

DUQUESNE: From the way people talked about it later, you'd think that Balangiga was a powder keg. It wasn't nothing like that. It was boring. Those village people lived on that island like they'd been shipwrecked. They just squatted by the edge of the sea and waited, and when we came it was like we were another bunch of shipwrecks, stranded on the same island, waiting for somebody to come rescue us.

E.M.: What about the insurrectos?

DUQUESNE: That was queer. Right at the start, General Lukban had come down from Luzon with a hundred riflemen and landed at Catbalogan, which was the capital, and set about organizing the island. He executed Spanish priests, recruited soldiers, stashed arms, set up communications, planted spies. When the Americans garrisoned the towns along the coast, all Lukban did was move to the center of the island. No roads, no trails, no maps. It looked like he could stay there forever, doing pretty much as he pleased. Everywhere else on Samar, he was shooting up patrols, burning bridges, killing mayors. But where we were, it was Sleepy Hollow.

When the rains came to stay, the village stank worse than ever, Lefty Diller said. In the morning, cooking-fire smoke and drizzle and stench covered the place, so that Jamaica Dawson's reveille "went off like a wet fart in a steam bath."

"Our headquarters was the old convent. Armory was on the second story, infirmary and office down below, and enlisted men in tents and nipa huts on both sides. Major Erickson believed in teaching by example. Our quarters looked spick-and-span, but the better we looked, the worse off was the town. You'd think that by 1899 people would know to bury their shit and burn their garbage and not wash upstream of where they drank, but at Balangiga those lessons were a few years down the road.

"Someone died of cholera and Major Erickson still couldn't

get those people to clean up their town. He asked for volunteers and nothing changed. If it was just Filipinos, I would've been happy to let the disease run its course, so there'd be fewer asshole amigos in the world. But Erickson was high-minded. Against a clear threat to public health, he decided to get tough. One night, he sent us through the village rounding up every able-bodied gugu male we could find, putting them under guard outside the convent, about twenty of them, and the next morning, presto, we had a sanitation department."

DUQUESNE: I never saw Major Erickson so happy as the night Father Alacrón came to talk over the cleanup campaign. The men we'd rounded up was slow workers, but it looked like Erickson had made his point, because the priest suggested that there were a couple dozen more men in the countryside who owed the town back taxes, and the mayor had already allowed it might be okay to have them work off their taxes by coming into town and helping out. "It's a breakthrough, Dukie," Erickson said after the priest was gone, and he launched right into writing a report to Manila on how things were coming around. That night, he was talking about schools and water treatment and an infirmary and a baseball field. "There's more than one way to win a war," he said.

Saturday, December 31, 1899. Balangiga would start the century with a fresh-scrubbed face. Streams of country people were converging on the town. Most of the newcomers were women, come to join the men who'd already been impressed into the cleanup. Some of the women carried market goods, some brought food for the next day's festival, and only a pair of arriving coffins dampened Major Erickson's high spirits, reminding him that the battle against cholera would reach into the next century. But the major had no doubt about the outcome.

DUQUESNE: It was the last day of a hundred years. It rained all night and drizzled on at dawn. You could hardly tell the sky from the sea, or black from gray, or night from morning. I wondered if I'd ever see a place with seasons again. And I wondered about the new century, how much of it I would see. Maybe a quarter. Half? Never. Eccles, me, and Jamaica Dawson and some others shared a nipa hut next to the convent. Eccles was awake, too, and I had a feeling he'd been watching me. He asked me, what was I thinking? I told him I remembered when I was a boy in Georgia, walking through the cemetery, reading the names and the dates, birth and death. The first one you got at the beginning and the second you don't ever get to know. Most of the graves were pretty new, like from the Civil War, so those folks had died while I was alive. We overlapped. We could have met. But them old graves, they were what really got to me, people who died in 1812 or 1820, around then. And what I was thinking now was that I was likely to be like them, someone who got old and died while the century was still young. It made me feel queer. Eccles asked me, was I scared of dying? And I said probably so, but what scared me now was . . . was being dead a long time, not just me, but everyone I knew and who knew me, the whole bunch of us being gone and no one left to remember, so that our graves wasn't even graves, just mounds of dirt, and our markers wasn't markers, only stones, and no one remembers. Eccles asked me, what's to remember? What did I ever accomplish? What did I want to accomplish? And I told him how good it felt, startin' out with the Boss so many years ago, like we were bound for someplace special. And Eccles asked me, what did I feel about the Boss? Maybe I put it bad, but I said the Boss was someone who would do the best he could for us. "Was this the best he could do?" Eccles asks.

"He stood up for you a couple times," I tell him.

"That he did," Eccles says, "that he did. Like a big kid taking punishment for a little one. It kept me small."

"I don't get you . . ."

"He didn't want to take us anywhere. He just wanted us around for playmates. Playmates, forever. Playing ball and chasing Indians. That's all. Now he's stewing in Manila, shacking in a whorehouse that's for whites only, and we're struck here on the wrong side of a bad war and nobody knows where we went off the track. No more Indians to chase. No more niggers to play with."

•11•

Maybe Erickson was right. As Diller and Buddy Conaway stepped out of the tent they shared and walked over to the mess tent and cook hut, Lefty allowed that he hadn't seen so many people at work before. The age of miracles wasn't over. Not when you could get the gugus to pray and work all in one day. In church, an early Mass was starting.

DUQUESNE: Eccles went away, said he wanted to wash up before breakfast. Breakfast wasn't nothing I washed up for. Dumpling didn't wash up to cook, so why should I wash up to eat? And anyway, I wasn't hungry.

How it began, I saw the police chief, Pedro Elorde, come out of church, and I guessed first Mass was over, except nobody followed him, and I wondered whether it wasn't some kind of town meeting and they needed to talk something over with Major Erickson.

Then I saw the police chief stop in front of the convent and stand next to Jamaica Dawson, like he wanted to pass the time of day, and that was downright odd, because the chief didn't know hardly any English and Dawson don't speak nothing else. Damn, I say, that's really something, they're turning a new leaf.

I guess they did. Because the next thing, Elorde yanks the rifle out of Jamaica's hands and butts him to the ground, and Jamaica is all of a sudden down on his knees and the look on his face tells me he don't think he's being attacked so much as somebody is pulling a trick on him which ain't so funny, but then Elorde grabs that rifle by the barrel and swings it like a bat, and smashes in Jamaica's head. Elorde raises the rifle, fires a shot, and the church bells start to ringing and conch shells start to blowing and the church doors bust open and a couple dozen bolo men rush out like bulls into a pen, and the details that was chopping weeds and stacking wood, and the cook's helpers who was washing dishes, they are all coming at us, wherever they can find us . . .

"I sat there," Lefty Diller said, "wondering whether Dawson had fell asleep and dropped his Krag or Billy Presley woke up with a hangover and started sniping rats. Those tuba hangovers were awful. I never figured it was gugus, because if there was ever a bunch of folks that didn't know shit from apple butter, this was them. Piss in your drinking water, sleep above the pigs, and spend your whole week waiting to see a couple roosters slice each other to death didn't count for much in my book. I guess this was my day to learn there was something I'd missed about the Filipinos.

"I heard screaming and bells and shots out in the square and the sound which I later found out was the blowing of conch shells and I still didn't know what was happening but it sure enough was big. I heard a commotion in the kitchen, and then there were bolo men inside the tent, hacking and slashing, and I saw Lee Artis look up just in time to see a blade come down on the side of his throat. His head went into his hash and his body slid onto the floor. You'd think it was enough to chop a man's head off, especially with plenty others still alive, but this was a gugu, see, and he was bringing down the machete again, wanting to split that poor head into halves and quarters, like a melon, and after I splashed that son of a bitch with coffee I went across the table with a fork, which I made go into his throat, and made it turn. There was fighting all around the tent, plates and knives and forks against bolos, and then they cut the lines and the tent come down on us and they chopped at the men who got caught below. I was lucky. Being near the back, I retreated into the cook hut and there I see our devoted helper Rogelio is holding Private Lynn Mimms in a cauldron of boiling water while our devoted woodchopper Fernando is axing him in the back, and a bunch of other gugus have got Dumpling Grimes cornered in the larder, where he's pitching cans at them, left and right, and I break through to where Dumpling is and heave a few cans myself, but the shelves are damn near empty. 'C'mon, Dumpling,' I say, pulling his hand, and we run out the back and across the square, which is all of a sudden a slaughterhouse, with ten different fights, each in its own location, like a picnic that went crazy."

DUQUESNE: Creeper Simmons and me rushed to the convent, hoping we might be the first to get there, but when we got inside we saw Private Kirby Johnson on the steps, and he was still alive, he was even trying to talk, but a bolo had took off the lower part of his face from the nose to the tip of his chin, and his lips was hanging in a flap over his throat, so he could have kissed his Adam's apple. The bolo is some hell of a weapon. If all wars was fought with bolos, there wouldn't be no wars, that's my opinion. A gun ain't what kills you, a gun only fires a bullet and you can't look at a bullet and get scared, you can't even see it coming, but a bolo . . . a bolo does it all . . . Down the hall, in the infirmary, there's gugus up and down the beds, a dozen beds, jaundice and malaria mostly, and it's like hell in there. Privates Eustace, Charles, Bouchette, and Leppert probably was killed in their sleep, but big old Bobby Glance was out of bed, stuck, bleeding, trying to crawl, and they were riding him and knifing him, and a bunch of others was hacking at Private Dibbs through the mosquito netting. They were devils, those people. They wasn't just fighting and doing a job. They loved it. That was when I look at the Creeper and the Creeper looks at me and it come over me like the need of a drink, or the hunger for food, or the itch for pussy: the need to kill. We run up the stairs and down into the gun room, where we jump a pair of gugus who was just breaking in. I strangled mine. Corporal Samuel Dodd comes up the stairs and two or three others are behind him. Everyone tried to get to the convent. It was that or run for the river. We left Dodd at the gun room and went to the back of the convent, to where Major Erickson, and his aide, Lieutenant Knotts, were billeted, but the police chief and two other gugus were there already, with blood on their bolos, and neither of the officers in view, and they raised their hands to surrender and we shoot 'em and, looking out the back, we saw both officers on the ground, Knotts pretty well bled out and Erickson cut up bad and trying to crawl and a bunch of gugus finishing him off. We finished them and some were women and that didn't bother me a bit. Nits breed lice. I was only sorry I couldn't've fucked 'em first.

Two, three at a time, they fought their way across the square, where comrades were still being butchered, entrails strewn like crepe ribbons unraveled for the new century they didn't live to celebrate. The biggest heap of all was Dumpling Grimes. Billy Presley was the last to come and when he was halfway across the square one of the gugus arose and started to come after him. Diller, watching from the convent, lifted him off the ground with one shot, spun him around with a second, blasted him backward with a third. Presley looked up at Diller, nodding thanks. "Happy New Year," Billy said.

DUQUESNE: You know something? You know what the big letdown is about war? It ain't fair. It ain't a fair fight. That's what broke Lawson's heart in the end. As a kid, playing soldier, dreaming of it, you picture duels . . . matches . . . even-sized teams. But it hardly ever happens, 'less it's by accident. It's a stab in the back or a sniper up a tree. It's an ambush or a massacre. It's two against one, or five against one is better, which is what happened that day. They caught our sentries. They caught us eating breakfast, sleeping, walking on the beach, and some of us they killed when they was sick and a couple they caught on the latrines, who died with their pants around their ankles, tumbling backwards into their own shit. Some boys had run into the river when the shooting started, and a small navy of gugus followed in canoes, caught up and hacked them into bait-sized chunks and come paddling back to shore like they'd sunk Dewey's fleet, jabbering and laughing. We met them on the beach, and we stood 'em in a line, one behind the other, close order, single file. I wanted to see how many men one bullet can kill. Could I shoot through one and get the one behind? The answer is yes. Sounds terrible. It was nothing. Creeper Simmons did the same thing with a bayonet.

The Filipinos withdrew up into the hills, but conch shells kept blowing, warning of another attack. The surviving Americans lowered the flag, loaded the stretchers, attempted to burn the convent so as to destroy the ammunition and guns they were forced to leave behind. There were six barotos, three men to a boat. They pushed into the water while the insurrectos poured down out of the hills, across the town, and out onto the black sand beach, where they waved their bolos, fired their guns, shook their fists, and cursed the fleeing Americans.

DUQUESNE: The sea was calm and the rain was down to a mist, and once we got offshore I glanced back at what looked like the coast of hell and wondered what did we ever do to make those people that mad? They followed us along the coast, stamping and screaming. Once they had us, they didn't want us to leave alive. Three barotos pulled out from shore, coming after us. We grouped together then, like a damn wagon train, and let them come, paddling like mad, firing high and wild, but this was our game and when they were close enough to splash us, we blew them out into the water, and didn't nobody swim away. That drove 'em crazy onshore, but not so crazy they came after us. Then we had another problem. Billy Presley had took a bullet in his shoulder. Not much of a wound, a soft ticket to the infirmary. But the wind whipped up and the water turned choppy and the onshore current was terrible strong and Billy's baroto got sucked inland. Isaac Jameson was with him, slashed across the forehead, and Thomas Reese was on the stretcher, having raised both hands to stop a bolo and lost 'em both, one at the fingers, one at the wrist . . . So it was up to Billy to paddle and he couldn't paddle and all of a sudden he's sliding away, and he gives me this look which is oh shit, and goodbye, and Dukie, I'm scared, all wrapped up together. "I don't want them to get me, Dukie," he says, and I can't blame him, but I don't want to understand him either. "Dukie," he says, "check me out." And I tell him no. After all the blood and shit and pain and rain we'd had that day, I couldn't do it. "You got to help me out, Dukie," he says. The shore is coming closer, and while part of me was praying it won't happen, another part is figuring in a little while he's gonna be out of range. "C'mon, Dukie," Billy says as I raise up my Krag, "I'll never tell."

Finally, they had a little good luck, Diller said. The same *Reina del Mar* that had brought them to Balangiga was en route to Basey, thirty miles up the coast, and found them that afternoon. Before dark they were in the infirmary at Basey garrison, and the news of the disaster was out. It was New Year's Eve. Diller slept right through it.

DUQUESNE: I woke up in a bed at Basey. New Year's Day. It hadn't stopped raining. You'd think they'd start us off with a blue sky, instead of old puddles and last year's mud. I lay there watching the rain drip off the tent flaps. I kept picturing how Billy Presley waited for me to shoot him. We were part of the same outfit for twenty years. Billy was a southern boy, and if he hadn't been a Confederate, it was only because he'd been too young to join. He had a wife who nagged him and when she died he mourned a lot and then he played around a lot. He was a good officer, a fair baseball player, and he never called me a nigger unless he thought I wasn't listening. He was the most cheerful man in camp. The secret, he said, was to always have something to look forward to, breakfast, a clean shave, a cool drink. Keep your mind on something like that and you'd always be all right. I wished I hadn't had to do what he asked me to do, and I couldn't for the life of me see anything out here that made it worth doing. I went to sleep and the next thing I recollect is waking up and the Boss is standing by my bed. "Boss!" I said, and I couldn't keep from crying. "They got us, Boss, they got us!"

·III·

I followed Lawson from bed to bed. Some were sleeping, others started stammering the story of what had happened, and he hushed them, and others saluted, and he returned the salute, and some started in to cry, and he cried, too. He saved Dukie for last, kneeling beside the bed and resting his hands on Dukie's head, as if his touch might make all the pain go away.

It was curious and sad, how little each of the survivors knew, how the great catastrophe broke into dozens of personal disasters. Smashed and shattered, the 25th Cavalry came together for a last review, in alphabetical order: the patrol that was caught coming down from the mountains, the men who were chopped up in the river, clubbed in the mess tent, overrun on the beach, butchered in the infirmary. We knew who died fighting and who died sleeping, who died fast and who died hard. We put it together like a puzzle—a scream here, a shot there, a body glimpsed as it ran or fell and when we finished there were only two pieces missing, two for whom no one could account from beginning to end: Benjamin Franklin Eccles and Buddy Conaway. It was tempting to think they might still be alive, escaped into the jungle, but the overwhelming likelihood was that they had died alone, like the others, in some obscure corner.

"Now I'm gonna tell you about something called the chain of command," Lawson said. "It goes like this."

The War Department in Washington had cabled General Gottschalk to take "all measures necessary" to recapture Balangiga and pacify Samar, Lawson said. General Gottschalk had put it another way in verbal orders to Galloping Joe Gibbons: "Pull out the stops on Samar, do what you have to do and don't worry about the fine points." And General Gibbons had told Major Lawson he didn't care if he turned the island into "a howling wilderness." He added, "The rougher you play, the better I'll like it . . . you know what I mean."

"*You know what I mean.*" Lawson repeated it. I looked around the room and I could see that his beaten soldiers caught the ominous shorthand that passes between men who kill. It meant that the benevolence had gone out of benevolent assimilation, that we were going to fight the kind of war the situation demanded, a war of revenge, the less said about it, the better. They all knew; even the ones who were tied into their beds or wrapped in bandages: this was a campaign to be talked about in whispers.

"You've taken a wallop," Lawson said, "and I'm going to die being sorry I wasn't with you. Not because I could have seen it coming. I might've missed it. Not because I could turn defeat into victory. Maybe not. Just to have been there with you, any which way."

He stopped a moment when his apology, for that was what it amounted to, was done. To the wounded he apologized for not having been wounded. But a deeper regret remained for the dead.

"They're giving me a hundred and fifty troops out of Manila," Lawson said. "They'd give me a thousand if that's what I wanted. All volunteers, bona fide. Everybody wants in on this one. I got a few spots open. If anybody feels in the mood to go back with me that way . . . I'd be grateful."

Lawson always reigned supreme in small groups. He led without seeming to lead, in that shuffling understated way that Americans have made their own, and I suppose the man who said "Don't write me up a hero yet" at Casa Diablo thought that the same magic would work in the hospital tent at Basey. "I got a few spots open. If anybody feels in the mood to go back with me that way . . . I'd be grateful." Good stuff, but the spell was broken.

Not a hand was raised.

"Well," he said, "you got every right. I'm blaming you for nothing. I got to go. Boat's leaving. I don't guess you'll be here when I come back. So this must be the time to . . ."

I didn't see the breakdown coming. One moment he was talking normally, like the man I'd written about for years. Then he had turned away, his voice breaking, and he pretended it was coughing; he sneezed, walked to the front of the tent, and spat out into the rain, and when he turned back, he was himself again. He stood there, staring at one after another of the survivors. I don't think he did that to persuade them to come. He did it because now he knew that it was all over. This was the end of the buffalo soldiers. So he took a turn looking at each man, each rough face, and that was his goodbye.

"You were a good outfit," he said. "When you look back on it, don't think too hard on how it ended."

He walked out of the tent, and most of them never saw him again.

·IV·

One last boat came out from shore: a load of Gatling guns, they said. We had plenty already, but then, excess was going to be the trademark of this expedition. The boat nestled against the *Meade*, bobbing up and down against the side, slamming near and pulling away. Dukie stretched for the lower rung, pulling his way up the ladder, his shaven head gleaming in the rain. Behind him, crotchety and full of complaint, his arm wrapped in bandages, was Herman Biddle.

"You know where we're going, you boys?" someone jeered as Dukie came on deck. "It's rough on niggers down the coast."

It was a southern voice. There were a lot of voices like that in the Philippines; no matter where they came from, the islands brought it out in them. Sometimes, it seemed we were all from the South. And when Dukie heard that voice he pulled himself to full height, scowling. He never looked more cocky and vicious. And then, just when the anger was ready to spill over, a word from Herman Biddle pulled him back. He smiled.

"I already been," he said. "I liked it there, so I'm going back. Right, Herman?"

"Nice place, nice people," Biddle said. "I can't wait."

"They got hula girls and fancy dancers, warm beaches and fields of sugar and plenty coconut wine. And they love us there. Right, Herman?"

"As much as we love them." Biddle broke into an unnerving cackle. "You crackers'll see."

DUQUESNE: I lay in my bed after he left. Till then, I'd been reckoning I could get back to Luzon some way . . . medical leave, furlough, desert . . . and look for my little girl. That's what I'd been planning, but when I saw him by my bed, puttin' his hands on my head, like it was the most valuable thing he owned, he only had to touch it to make it well . . . that changed my plans.

E.M.: But the girl . . .

DUQUESNE: I loved them both. They both loved me. But what it finally comes to . . . it isn't who you love . . . it's who needs your love the most . . .

"*Why didn't I go?*" The question irritated Lefty Diller, though thirty years had passed since Lawson stepped out of the hospital tent, into the rain, and left him forever.

"You could have, couldn't you?" I asked. "I mean, physically?"

"Oh, hell yeah, *physically* I was able," Diller parroted back, still resentful. "And *mentally*, I wasn't. You want me to spell it out for you, Morrison? I didn't go because I *decided* not to go. It was written all over him."

"Lawson?"

"Why'd you think he came? For troops? He had a boatload of 'em, fresh out of Manila and horny for blood. Why'd he want us to come along? Answer me that!"

I had some theories of my own, but this was Lefty's moment.

"He wanted witnesses! Oh, he had you. But you weren't enough. He wanted some of the boys to come along . . ."

"To witness what?"

"What was going to happen to him."

"How do you know that?"

"I got eyes." He pointed to them defiantly. "The Boss was looking for pallbearers."

"And you stayed behind."

"Yeah. It was all over. The next I saw him, he was a statue. And you were in front of the statue, as full of shit as the first pigeon . . ."

• V •

I have read accounts of generals—Napoleon was one of them, I think—who walked battlefields commenting poetically on the attitudes, postures, and expressions of the soldiers who had fallen. He must have picked his battlefield carefully, and carefully timed his visit. At Balangiga, thirty-six hours after the massacre, we walked through town with handkerchiefs over our faces, gagging, retching, averting our eyes from what remained of the men we mourned.

The Filipinos had outrageously mutilated our dead. Limbs had been severed and rearranged, so that legs and arms were switched. Genitals were misplaced. In the mess tent, one man had been smeared with jam, so that ants swarmed over his body. The village dogs and cats had needed no such inducement. It was a village of the dead, a feast of carrion. When Lawson and I entered the square, rats rushed off in front of us, and birds with bloody beaks took flight.

"Eyes and balls," Lawson said. "That's what they eat first."

The rain and heat had done their work, too, so that it was better not to look too closely at this or that pile of human parts. The less one recognized, the better. I kept a cologne-soaked handkerchief over my mouth. Behind us troops were cursing and vomiting as they trundled bodies to the parade ground Major Frickson had wanted to turn into a baseball diamond.

At the convent, we watched soldiers pulling bodies out from under the collapsed mess tent. The smell came up to us. It wasn't much of a goodbye for the buffalo soldiers, passing in review on stretchers, planks, and wheelbarrows. Their elegy was grunts and curses, their last salute handkerchiefs held over their pallbearers' noses.

"The last I saw them was the fourth of July," Lawson said. His eyes were red-rimmed and I felt that if someone pulled that cigar out of his mouth he'd fall apart completely.

"They were supposed to leave the night of the fourth. I went down to the docks to say goodbye. And the boat hadn't come, wasn't gonna come till July 5. I didn't have no choice!" Was I supposed to leave 'em sitting on the dock while I got passed around a party, 'America's foremost fighting soldier'? You think that I could do that?"

"No, Boss," I said. "I understand."

"Why didn't she?"

"It's not that she doesn't love you . . . it's because . . . she wants things for you."

"I know that. But me and these men . . ." He gestured to the square, where the portage of corpses continued. "We went back forever . . ."

Our return had interrupted the insurgents' burial of their own dead. Behind the town, next to the graveyard, was an open trench which contained some two hundred bodies, men, women, and children. Lawson barely glanced inside.

"They get ripe fast, don't they?" he remarked.

"Want us to finish burying them, or what?" Lieutenant Peter O'Connor asked. A ruddy, busy little Boston Irishman, he officered the fresh troops from Luzon.

"No," Lawson said. "Bring up some kerosene."

As soon as the troops came up with kerosene, an old man walked out of the woods. Biddle identified him as Gregorio Villacampos, mayor of Balangiga. White-haired, feeble, and slow to understand—though we had brought an interpreter from Basey—he pleaded to have the bodies buried, not burned, as burning was contrary to Catholic practice.

"What's the Catholic stand on massacres?" Lawson snapped back. "Ask him what happened here."

While the interpreter complied, Lawson glanced at me. "He's shaking, Eddie. They left him because he's old. And if we kill him, what's a year, more or less, to him?"

"Sir," said the interpreter, "the mayor says General Lukban's troops came out of the hills and surprised the Americans. He says it was terrible."

"A terrible surprise. Where'd his people go?"

"They are hiding in the woods."

"And where'd the insurrectos go?"

The mayor said he did not know.

"Pour the kerosene," Lawson said. "Give 'em a good dousing. It's been raining, they're probably wet."

The soldiers emptied one gallon after another into the trench. When it was done, Lawson put an arm around the old man and guided him to the edge of the trench. He made him look down inside, and from the back, they both might have been contemplating what comes to all men. He lit cigars, one for the mayor, one for himself, and for a ghastly moment I thought he might push the mayor, lit cigar and all, down onto the dead bodies and the puddles of kerosene. I never did ask if that is what he contemplated, but my heart says yes.

The mayor turned to face him and Lawson put both hands on the man's shoulders, which could have been the beginning of an embrace or of a push over the edge.

Thank God that moment passed! He saw something in the old man's eyes, in the way he struggled to stop his trembling: at last Lawson reached out and guided the old man away. With hardly a backward glance, he tossed a match into the trench. In an instant, the kerosene took, with an explosion, a sudden whoof, and smoke billowed out of the trench. I smelled cloth, and flesh, and hair.

"Tell the mayor I want to know where they went," Lawson said.

The mayor protested: the insurrectos were strangers, General Lukban, their commander, was from Luzon, and Father Alacrón, their local agent, was another stranger. The insurrectos did not confide in him, they only gave orders which he and his hapless fellow citizens were unable to resist. Surely, Major Lawson understood their predicament.

"Tell him I don't believe him. It's his island. They're on it, someplace. I want to know where."

The mayor shrugged. So did Lawson.

"I guess it's the water cure," he said.

Sergeant Elton Greene, a Montana cowboy, made it seem as innocent and routine as the shearing of a sheep. I thought that torturers hated the men they tortured, *had* to hate them, or how else could they ply their trade? But hate had nothing to do with it. He escorted the mayor into the infirmary, bade him to lie down on the floor, in the aisle. He tied the mayor's hands to the front legs of one cot and his ankles to the front legs of another across the aisle. He smiled, joked, and once, when the old man panicked and struggled, he patted him on the head. "There, there, old-timer."

Sergeant Greene had arrived somewhere Lawson and I could never travel. He treated human beings as livestock, and once you regarded them that way, once you broke that bond of fellow feeling, you were invigorated. You could walk among the grisliest scenes untouched, and accomplish masterpieces of cruelty with a cheerful plowboy grin.

It began with a parody of gentleness. Sergeant Greene cradled the old man's head in his arms and gave him a drink of water out of his canteen.

"It's best to get 'em to drink as much as they can of their own free will," Greene explained. "It starts 'em off right."

When the Mayor had swallowed about half the canteen, he signaled he had had enough. Greene nodded and wiped the mayor's mouth with his own handkerchief, kind as a nurse. Then he raised his canteen again, signaling that the mayor should take a second drink. The mayor wasn't thirsty and it is hard to drink water when you are not thirsty. But something in the sergeant's eyes convinced him to oblige. It was a struggle to swallow now, and he wasted more water than before, but Sergeant Greene held the canteen firmly, and the mayor drained it.

"There now," he said, "you're coming along fine. You've drunk it dry."

He upended the canteen: not a drop fell out. "Like a baby and a bottle."

I saw a shimmer of hope in the old man's eyes. Was this all? Was this the American torture? A kind of humiliating baptism?

"Do I ask him now?" Lawson inquired. "What say, I ask him?"

Greene dismissed the idea. "He'd lie. I'll know when he's ready."

He signaled to some soldiers who were waiting in the hall, and they came in carrying buckets and a funnel.

"It's better not to let them see the equipment until they've had a sip or two. Don't want them to fight you from the start. Ain't that right, amigo?"

The mayor's eyes widened. There were five buckets of water in front of him.

"That's right, señor," the sergeant said. "And it's all for you. Now here's your mommy's nipple."

He fit the funnel into the old man's mouth, and now I felt that we were all part of a grotesque medieval woodcut.

"You can leave if you want," the sergeant said. "It could take an hour."

"That long?" Lawson protested.

"Sir," the sergeant said. "You want it fast or you want it right?"

Lawson winced, nodded, and the operation began in earnest. If Lawson had left, I would have been happy to follow, but this was a scene he wanted to inflict on himself, and on me: gallon after gallon of water forced into the choking, sputtering old man. His eyes bulged, his arms and legs rubbed against their bonds till they bled. Sometimes he choked, once he vomited. He lost control of his bladder and sphincter, but there was always plenty of water of make up the loss, and the clucking, kindly sergeant was there to pour it. We watched the old man's belly distend, like a nine months' pregnancy telescoped into a single hour. How quickly he bloated, how soon his abdomen was tight as a drum! And the water kept coming. The old man must have felt that he was drowning in the open air, drowning from the inside out, in a hospital room with not unkindly strangers looking on. That, finally, was the terror of it.

At last, Sergeant Greene let his hand rest lightly on the mayor's stomach. The touch, the lightest of touches, was agony. His scream blew the funnel out of his mouth, and the sergeant smiled at a job well done.

"He's yours," he said.

"Will he die?" Lawson asked.

"Not unless we ruptured something," Greene replied. "They don't usually die." He glanced down at the old man, who lay in a widening puddle of urine, then looked back at us. "It's not the worst punishment in the world," he said.

In half an hour we knew where the insurrectos had gone. The river which flowed into the sea at Balangiga had its source deep in the heart of the island. If we followed it, it would take us to a place of "high rocks"—cliffs, apparently—from which General Lukban directed insurgent activities throughout Samar.

Greene untied the mayor. We left him lying on the floor, crying, curled up like an incontinent child. That night I looked in, and he was gone. The next morning, we headed up the river.

·VI·

The jungle parted easily, smiling to admit us. Starting at dawn, on foot, with a hundred men and a few supply ponies, we tramped along the riverbanks, through groves of bananas and coconut palms, which some of us harvested en route. The rain was a drizzle, and it cooled us as we walked.

In the afternoon, the terrain grew steep, the river narrowed and we had to cross and recross a half dozen times, but this was accomplished without mishap. The men remarked that the water was cooler and cleaner than they'd have expected, on islands that were "three degrees hotter than hell." No wonder there were no trails into the interior. Why have a trail, when you could stroll up the river, and the river knew the way?

Toward the middle of the afternoon, precipitous cliffs hemmed in the river, which debouched into a rocky mile-long rapids, leaving no dry banks to walk on. Overhead, a tangle of vines and creepers, dead and living trees, made us feel that we were entering a dark, uphill green tunnel. At the end of the tunnel was a waterfall, an eighty-foot cascade over gleaming black rocks, emptying into a pool that looked like the Garden of Eden. That was where we camped.

Dukie, Herman Biddle, and I were part of Lawson's entourage. The other soldiers were strangers to us, but not as strange as we must have seemed to them. They were the usual collection of immigrants and rednecks, Tomasettis and Hatfields, and they must have wondered what brought a citified journalist, two black cavalrymen, and the legendary Lawson together. I sensed they studied us, and it was that curiosity, more than the exotic setting, which made me feel that we were the survivors of another time and place. And the others felt it, too.

"You know what this reminds me of, Boss?" Dukie asked that night.

"What's that, Dukie?"

"That time in Arizona Territory. Morrison was along then, too, and we went chasing after that crazy Apache. What was his name?"

"They called him the Singer."

"Yeah. The Singer. We went up into the mountains after him. The Singer."

It was an apt comparison. All day long, I'd sensed that I'd been here before: not the same place, but the same situation, following Lawson. Then, as now, we had marched uphill, over unknown terrain, to encounter an enemy who outnumbered us and could be expected to know of our approach.

"That Singer was something," Lawson reflected. "The best that we came up against out there. Led us on a merry chase. Lured us up into the mountains. Caught us on the trail, at just the right place, and gave us what for."

He laughed at that. He laughed like it was a comical episode, and no one had died up on that trail.

"And then we came after him at night, sneaking up the trail with half our force, while the rest of the men and horses were camped out down below. Remember? Stalking up the mountain on foot, staying off the trail? And finally sweeping into that village? And it was empty! By God, that Singer made a horse's ass out of me! And then . . . Jesus did he have us! . . . while we're up on the mountain with our thumbs up our asses, he's attacking the camp down below and we have to rush down without our horses! He led us along, he strung us out, he split us up, and then he hit us by surprise. Damn! And you . . ."

He turned to me and laughed some more. "You write it up a victory. The Battle of Apache Pass! Goddamn! You could have fooled me. The Singer had it all his way that day, from where I stood."

While Lawson walked off to relieve himself, the rest of us traded embarrassed glances. In his current frame of mind, Lawson seemed to enjoy telling us our victories were accidents It was to salvage something of our old feeling that, when Lawson returned, Dukie asked the question I had always lacked the courage to put.

"Boss? That Singer?"

"Yeah? What about him?"

"Anyway, we finally got him."

"Oh, sure. We got him at Casa Diablo."

The answer was fine, but there was something in the tone that worried Dukie. His brow wrinkled and he looked around for help.

"What the man means," Herman Biddle said, "is *you* got him, didn't you? Not to put too fine a point on it, you *killed* him. Am I right?"

Lawson walked to the edge of the pool, squatted down, and started chucking rocks into the water. What started as campfire chat, something we could share the way we passed a bottle or spooned out a stew, had changed. A moment of truth had trapped us.

Lawson took a last pebble, wound up, and skipped it across the water three or four times before it sank.

"Where'd you read that, Herman? In a newspaper? In a book someplace?"

"No, sir," Biddle answered firmly. When he chose, he could stand up to any man. "I didn't read it in the newspapers. I was there. And the general idea that day was that you killed the Singer. You found him, you fought, you came out on top. That's what people said and sometimes they said it around you and I didn't never hear you contradict them."

"Yeah . . . well . . ." Lawson turned to us. "So you really want to hear it? All right, Herman. I walked into that canyon, into that grove of trees. I stepped right past him. Understand? He could have killed me or kissed me, we were that close. Only he was on the ground, kneeling, staring. Chanting. And I stared back at him. I wanted to break into his world a minute. I wanted him to know I was there and I wanted to tell him . . . Well, never mind what I wanted to tell him."

Lawson paused. I think we all knew the sort of message that would have passed between Lawson and the Singer. Perhaps something had gotten transmitted anyway, though the Boss never found the words.

"So I stared at him and he stared through me, and that was the only duel I fought that day. I lost. He was staring when I shot him. The hardest part was carrying out the body."

The Boss got up, stumbled into the darkness to relieve himself again against a tree. "Big man, small bladder," he muttered to himself. And then to us: "The Singer and me. We both got cheated that day."

That was his good-night.

"I liked my version better," I said after a while.

"Me, too," Dukie said.

"Let's don't change it now," Herman Biddle concurred. "This late date."

·VII·

Looking in from offshore, it had seemed that the island was formed around a single mountain, with beaches bordering coastal plains, plains yielding to foothills which led up to a central peak. But it turned out there were many mountains, a series of false peaks with unheard-of valleys in between. On the third day, climbing past another waterfall, we saw the river widen as it meandered through a gentle green valley. It was like a child's drawing of "The Happy Valley," with the river curling through fields of rice, corn, sugarcane, tobacco, and banana, with dwellings clustered here and there, and dense green hillsides all around. Though I was not a man to linger over landscapes, the place took my breath away. I watched the rest of the column emerge from out of the jungle, scratched and cursing, mud-coated and spoiling for a fight, and my heart sank, because I knew that this was a place we were going to defile.

"This will be defended," Lawson told Lieutenant O'Connor. "I want two men in front, right and left, about half a mile ahead of us."

"Yes, sir."

"I don't want them engaging with the enemy. I want them to see and not be seen. Can you manage that?"

We were filing through rice country, moist and fertile, when a volley of shots, errant as ever, sprayed overhead from the right. Then we saw the insurrectos, lying prone behind the earthen dikes that separated the paddies, with only their guns and the tops of their hats in view. They were half a mile away, across the river and a broad swath of rice fields. After the first volley, and despite our ragged and inflamed response, they held their fire.

"How about that?" Lawson mused. "They learned to hold their fire. Usually they shoot off their whole load as quick as they can and call it a day."

"They fight the way they fuck," someone said.

"You gonna show them how to fuck?" another soldier jested.

"I wouldn't mind," the first voice responded. "Soon as we clean up this shit across the way."

"Pipe down," Lieutenant O'Connor shouted, but he was smiling and it pleased him to see that his men had spirit. Lawson had disappointed him so far. He didn't live up to his reputation. He was old and he drank and sometimes he didn't seem to care. But O'Connor still wanted to impress him.

"They can't shoot much," he told Lawson. "Frontal attack should blow 'em away."

"Yeah, okay," Lawson said, "but if it gets too hot, I want you to pull back and flank, understand?"

"Yes, sir."

"I'm gonna tell you twice, Lieutenant. If one man gets shot, forget about rushing them. We'll get 'em another way."

Lawson did not join the attack. It seemed reasonable to give Lieutenant O'Connor a chance to show his mettle. We stayed by the river, on a grassy knoll, under the shade of a banyan, like the Washington gentry who had driven out to Manassas for the first Battle of Bull Run, expecting a grandstand seat on an easy victory.

The Americans forded the river with ease and stepped out into the rice fields, firing as they advanced toward the Filipino lines, which were curiously silent. We could see that they hadn't retreated, but they weren't firing. They were waiting.

"No," Lawson said. "I don't like it."

The orderly blue line moved ahead. It looked more like a line of harvesters than men in battle, or like hunters waiting for quail to fly up out of a field of stubble corn.

The Americans were within a hundred yards, well past the normal Filipino breaking point. We heard a shout, a command, a solitary voice from behind their lines, and the insurrectos opened up. The next instant was pure shock.

"Boss, you see!?" Dukie shouted.

The errant volley had been a ruse. Now one after another of our men toppled into the paddies. Some lay still, others struggled to their feet, covered with mud and blood, staggering back toward the river. It was a different war when the enemy knew how to shoot.

"BREAK OFF!" Lawson shouted, waving toward Lieutenant O'Connor. "COME ON BACK!"

O'Connor didn't hear him, or maybe he did. It's a small question. Urging his men toward the line, he rushed ten feet across the paddy and was met with a fusillade that sent him spinning backwards through the mud, as though yanked by a cord from behind. He had an entire volley all to himself.

No need for anyone to call for a withdrawal then! We had a

retreat, a sloppy, sliding, pell-mell race across mud pools and grass dikes. They came back, filthy and indignant.

"They made us withdraw!" Sergeant Greene exclaimed.

"They made you run," Lawson corrected him. "*That's* what I call a withdrawal."

He pointed to where the Filipinos jogged off the field, filing into the jungle, with no apparent casualties to encumber them.

The insurrectos gave us the town, a picturesque and prosperous farming village, which they apparently hoped to spare by not defending. It was altogether different from Balangiga. The houses were clean, the yards well swept and bordered with flowers, and the church, unlike the gross edifices everywhere else, was a whitewashed stucco chapel, perfectly in keeping with the town. In front of the church, our missing scouts awaited us. They were seated in wooden chairs, looking our way as we marched in, and they greeted us with stuck-out tongues and blue faces and bulging eyes, having been garroted where they sat. Their bodies were still limp and warm and I wondered if someone had let them live until they could see our column approaching, hear our distant voices, and then the wires dropped and tightened. How had they done it? One at a time or both together?

We buried them and stayed in town that night. One of our patrols encountered some women—a mother and a daughter, I was told—who were either innocent or stupid. And unlucky. They were certainly unlucky.

"We fucked 'em and we killed 'em," Sergeant Greene reported.

"I don't like that," Lawson said, "in my command."

"Sure, sir," Greene responded, winking as though we all knew that Lawson was only speaking for the record. He intimated that anyone who had watched his water cure couldn't object to rape and murder. Torture had brought us all together.

"I *really* don't like it," Lawson muttered when Greene was gone.

"It's over now," I counseled, "so there's nothing you can do."

"You know what old man Gottschalk said when he gave me

this command? He said it suited my 'unique abilities.' What do you think he meant by that?"

"I guess he was admitting that you could do the job better than anyone else around," I answered.

"So it's a compliment?"

"In a way, I suppose it is."

"Don't you get it, Eddie? He's setting me up."

"What for?"

"A punitive campaign is risky . . . if word gets out that . . . you know . . . it got out of hand down here . . . the boys went a little wild . . . they need a name . . . somebody to blame . . . a punitive campaign means don't fuss about prisoners or civilians, and if women or kids get in the way . . . that's too bad . . . that's what they think I'm good for."

Lawson pulled himself up. "Well, maybe they're right. Maybe that is what I am good for, and *all* I'm good for. But you know what, Eddie? It sure as hell ain't where I thought I was headed when I started out."

·VIII·

We arrived at our destination on January 11, 1900. We knew, as soon as we saw it, that we had found the place.

No more false peaks. This was the top of the mountain, the heart of the island, the place where the river began. We emerged from the rain forest and saw a two-hundred-foot cliff, honeycombed with caves and ledges, which the insurrectos occupied and fortified, beginning twenty feet from the top and extending down to the stream which curved around it. There would be no flanking movements here: on the right was a bare slope, part loose gravel, part sheer rock, and on the left was a waterfall plummeting a hundred feet.

"My God," Lawson remarked, his voice filled with a wonder I entirely shared. Some landscapes are for painting, some conduce to meditation. This was put on earth to be defended. "Cochise had places like this, way back in the Sangre de Cristos. You could hold off an army with a regiment, forever. Secret places. Strongholds. Natural . . . what's the word? . . . citadels.

They got high ground, plenty water. Lots of ammunition. Oh Lord!"

The Filipinos knew we'd arrived. They were all over the cliff, looking our way, and some of them waved at us. They knew their position was impregnable: in the heart of the jungle, they had found the Rock of Gibraltar.

Our men flopped on the ground and gazed at the fortress, then looked at Lawson, unmistakable in his yellow slicker, pacing back and forth, studying the falls, the river, the ledges, caves, and heights. To a man, they expected us to withdraw, and I was no exception. A much larger force might besiege this place, might even somehow assault it, but our numbers were equal and the enemy had all the advantages.

"Well, boys," Lawson said when he returned from his reconnaissance. "What do you think?"

Dukie shook his head. Biddle had nothing to say, for now.

"Eddie?"

"There are two questions," I said. "The first is whether we *can* do it. If the answer is no, and I think it is, then that's the end of it."

"What was the other question?"

"The other question is whether we *should* do it."

"Should?"

"Yes. *Should*. Whether we ought to even try."

"We got orders," Lawson countered. "So where does *ought* and *should* come in?"

"Just tell me," I retorted, "whether you think the war depends on our knocking the Filipinos off some obscure mountain in the middle of the jungle in the center of an island that nobody ever heard of, and in the rain besides. If you think it's important, Boss, if it's strategic, if it really matters to anyone . . . go ahead."

"Wars are fought in lots of out-of-the-way places," Lawson answered. "What makes this so different?"

"This place doesn't count. Your orders were to conduct a punitive campaign . . ."

"Yeah, and so far we're the ones that's taking all the punishment."

"Will it be any less punishing to try and take that mountain?"

"There's a way." Lawson smiled and then I knew that though everything I'd said was true, it would not dissuade him. All his life he'd been looking for this mountain.

DUQUESNE: You had to try and see it through the Boss's eyes. The Filipinos knew we were there, camped right in front of them, and another soldier would say he'd lost the element of surprise, but the Boss would say surprise was for parties. They had as many men as we did, maybe more, but the Boss would say good, fair fight. The Filipinos were dug in on a hillside and we were miles from headquarters and supplies, but the Boss would say terrific, because that meant neither of us had no place to run. And another soldier would say unimportant target, but the Boss had an answer for that one, too. Mountains ain't targets, he would say. People are targets. All of us are targets, we're all somebody's target. He had a point, see, it all depends on how you look at it.

What Henry Lawson did at dawn seemed like madness, unequivocal and terminal. But there also was a kind of logic in his actions, a connection with other deeds and other days. Perhaps that means he was sane—or that he had been mad for longer than I was willing to admit.

The facts are these: With half the troops still sleeping, Lawson and Dukie arose, passed through our lines carrying a white flag, and stepped down to the river. In full view of both camps, he shouted up at the enemy. His voice echoed off the cliffs, awakening all those who were not already awake.

"Hey, up there," he shouted. "Hey!"

The surprise was mutual. The Filipinos popped out of their caves and trenches, Americans pulled themselves from under their ponchos and staggered forward. Lawson stood on a rock at the edge of the stream, with Dukie behind him, waving a white flag, as though he might ward off bullets with it.

A cluster of insurrectos appeared outside a sizable cave well up the slope. From the way they consulted together, I guessed these were the rebel officers.

"Got anybody up there who understands some English?" Lawson shouted. There was a stir among the insurrectos. One of them disappeared and came out with a man in brown trousers and a blue shirt. It was Benjamin Franklin Eccles.

"You okay, Eccles?" Lawson called out. I noticed Eccles translated the question, even though it was addressed to him. Where had Eccles learned Tagalog?

"I'm fine," Eccles answered.

"And Buddy, too?"

"Buddy, too."

"They haven't pulled no funny stuff?"

"No, Boss," Eccles answered. "No funny stuff."

"I came to get you out. We got to save what's left to save, it looks like."

"That might not be so easy, Boss."

"Listen, Eccles, I want you to tell them something. I got an offer to make. We try to take that hill, there's lots of good men who'll be dead. I want to settle things in the old-fashioned way. I want a fair fight, one on one. Right down here, an hour from now. Our best man against their best man, to the death. If their man wins, they get to keep the mountain. We leave. If our man wins, the Filipinos surrender."

Eccles translated the message, which triggered a lively hubbub on the cliff. It was preposterous any way you looked at it. What officer would pin an army on a single man? But Lawson was Lawson, and the Filipinos loved a cockfight.

"They want to know who's your best man," Eccles responded.

"They're looking at him now."

"Dukie?"

"Me."

Another insurrecto consultation followed, which ended when the insurrecto officers stepped back inside the cave. Eccles followed.

"They went for it, Boss," he shouted. "In an hour."

"If you came to argue, don't," Lawson said.

Of course I wanted to argue. I had rushed down to the river with a hundred reasons why an officer in his fifties shouldn't duel with the best fighter a rebel army could offer. They wouldn't fight fair. They wouldn't surrender if their man lost.

Who would? It was an act of monstrous folly. And Lawson didn't want to talk about it.

"But, Boss . . ."

"And if you *do* argue with me, I'll ask Dukie to make you leave. Right, Dukie?"

"You better not argue, Mr. Morrison," Dukie admonished.

Lawson had taken off his hat and slicker and shirt. Suspenders covered a massive chest. He was smoking a cigar and enjoying it, enjoying the whole morning immensely.

I didn't want Dukie to carry me back like a squalling child, so I forced myself to sit down and let the moments pass. Everything was quiet. The rain had stopped and two armies were looking on. How quickly they accommodated themselves to the idea of medieval combat! I tried to look at Lawson, to communicate without words, to remind him that there were people who loved him. He shouldn't forget us, shouldn't throw his life away in a bit of bravado. Yet there he sat, smiling and smoking his cigar. How could he be so content to leave us?

"You're wrong, Boss!" I burst out. "You think they'll do it your way, but they won't! They won't! Nobody does! They don't now and I doubt they ever did!"

A cluster of insurrectos emerged from a cave and slowly picked their way along a trail that would bring them down to the river.

"You got to go, Eddie," Lawson said. "I got an appointment to keep. I'm not planning to lose, but if I do I'm counting on you to . . . uh . . ."

"What?"

"Say what has to be said. Around Manila."

"What should I say?"

"I trust you . . ."

"That won't do!" I pleaded. "I need more!"

"I hate punitive campaigns," he said. "I really hate them. This is better."

With that, Dukie gestured for me to leave.

"Can't you stop him, Dukie?"

Dukie shook his head. I stepped back onto the riverbank, into the middle of an incredible scene: two armies turned into spectators and sports fans. They weren't appalled. They weren't even worried. They were wondering whether Lawson's size would compensate for his age, whether the Filipino nominee would be big and strong or small and sneaky.

DUQUESNE: It was me and the Boss. All my life I'd thought it would come to this, and so had he, I bet, so you could say that a dream, or something, was coming true. That was until Eccles stepped out from behind a rock.

"I'm the second, Boss," he said.

"What'd they make you do that for?" Lawson asked. "You're a prisoner."

"No, Boss. I volunteered."

"I don't get it."

"I'm on their side now. I crossed over."

"What?! I don't believe you. They making you say that?"

"I wanted to be the one who met you here. I thought that you would want that. A clean fight. But they overruled me. They decided to send out Buddy. Sorry."

Eccles nodded and started moving backwards, a step at a time.

"Buddy! That's plain crazy! Eccles, come here!"

"No, Boss. Buddy'll be out directly." Eccles disappeared behind the rocks.

The Boss turned to me, like I could explain things. He'd wanted things to come down to one pure fight, clear and clean, win, lose, or draw. And now . . . Well, I couldn't help him. I was screaming. I'd just seen the worst thing in the world.

Dukie screamed and pointed. Lawson wheeled around, braced for a Filipino onslaught, and then he screamed, too, and dropped to his knees and vomited.

Buddy Conaway tottered forward from behind the rocks. As soon as I saw what they had done to him, I was sick, too, as were most of the soldiers who were near me, a whole column felled by a wave of nausea, while our opponents laughed and whooped it up, firing their rifles in the air.

They called it the necklace and it amounted to this: Buddy wore his hands, his eyes and ears, his tongue and his genitals on a string around his neck. And he was still alive! In shock, shuffling, bleeding, slobbering, arms outstretched, he moved toward Lawson. And Lawson managed to get off his knees and let Buddy come to him. He stretched out his arms and waited to receive him. And then I saw that whatever falsehoods I had written about him, and despite the truths I would never write, Henry Lawson was a hero, a man who held his ground when others fell away, who stared ahead when others averted their eyes, who opened his arms to the worst pain that evil men could devise, who took Buddy Conaway into his arms, lifted him up, and carried the dying soldier back across the river.

·IX·

After seeing Buddy Conaway, no one doubted we were going up the mountain. If the Filipinos' point was to provoke an attack, they succeeded. A ragtag expedition had turned into a crusade, a truly punitive campaign.

DUQUESNE: That night the Boss asked, did I hear what Eccles said? I told him I hadn't heard nothing. We both of us knew I was lying.

Lawson's plan called for the bulk of our forces to mount a night attack on the Filipinos, crossing the river and forcing their way up the cliffs toward the caves. A night attack made sense, for then our men would be less exposed to the Filipinos' newfound accuracy. And in hand-to-hand combat, Americans could be expected to prevail.

That was only part of it. Ten men under Lawson were to make their way to the far side, scale the cliffs, and overwhelm the Filipino lookouts at the top. Then, with control of the heights and a command of the battlefield below, they could pick off the insurgents from above.

"Can I come?" I asked him late that afternoon.

"You want to come?" he asked me back. "Why? You're no soldier."

"There was a time you didn't think I was a pitcher. Remember who won the game?"

"Oh shit." His eyes watered and he glanced at Dukie. "You guys won't never let me forget that game, will you? Jesus!"

"Some game," Dukie said. "Hah! 'EdWIN is gonna EdLOSE!' Remember?"

"That was a million years ago," Lawson mused. "And awfully far from here. What do you think about this one, Eddie? How's it gonna look when folks look back on it?"

"I don't know," I said.

"Well," he said, "is it that I was young then and I'm old now?"

"I think it's more than that. More than growing old. I mean, it's not just us that's changed."

"I used to think that any war was okay . . . so long as I was in it! Maybe I was wrong. But we still got a war. And I'm still here. And they're up there. You sure you want to come?"

"Yes."

"You like my strategy?"

"That's not strategy. It's king of the mountain. It's grown men playing boys' games."

I meant no harm, but as soon as I said it I saw that I might have hurt him. King of the mountain was right on the mark. Lawson was no strategist, we both knew that. But I didn't want to hurt the man who had taken Buddy Conaway in his arms. He fell quiet, looked at me, and, thank god, decided to forgive me.

"Kids' games. Yeah," he said. "Want to play?"

"Yes."

There were eleven of us altogether: Lawson, Dukie, Biddle, myself, and seven of the new men. We left camp as soon as it got dark, turning away from the mountain. We knew roughly where we wanted to go, but there were no trails, and we felt our way through the rain forest, where vines were like anchor cables and ferns grew past our heads. The ground wheezed and sucked wherever we stepped, solid-seeming trees fell apart at the lightest touch. It seemed that we had entered the gorge of a vast, vegetative monster, with birds and monkeys to comment on the rate of our decay. With no moon, no light to guide us, we relied on whispers to keep together and on the dark bulk of the insurrectos' mountain, scarcely darker than the leaking, starless sky. Twice we required one of the soldiers to climb a tree, like a sailor up a mast, to give us back our bearings. After the second sighting, when we were well away from the lines, we turned in toward the mountain, toward its flank. I was glad enough to leave the rain forest behind: though no one could find us there, it unnerved me to be in a place where the earth was mud and rain was sweat and everything raced toward decay, feasting on what had already died. I believed in seasons and in gardens. I loved frost.

We bumped against the mountain in the dark. One moment it was vines and creepers, trees that had branches like roots and roots like branches, so many veins and arteries that would bleed when cut. And then we were out of it, standing at what looked like the floor of a quarry, among piles of stones that the mountain had flung down to keep the forest back. We traversed a slope of loose gravel, crawling forward and sliding back, and arrived at the part of the mountain that was solid: steep, bare, wet rock, a hundred feet of it. There was nothing like a trail. We had to feel our way, clutching for toeholds and handholds, tiny dents and blemishes that couldn't hold a cupful of dirt. Once we ran into a sheer wall, slick as glass, and had to turn. That turn was awful. I'd promised not to think about the height and I was glad that the darkness saved me from seeing how far up we'd come already. But when we turned, rotating on a six-inch ledge, the fear hit me all at once. I sensed the depths below me, the hot air, the light rain, the warm cabbage-like smell of the forest. My confidence vanished, my strength drained, my calves were trembling. I closed my eyes and hugged the mountain, which yielded not at all to my embrace. Then I heard someone gasp and fall, and thought that it was me.

"Who is it?" Lawson whispered. I saw he had one hand on my shoulder, and Dukie held me by the other. They weren't letting go of me.

"Who is it?" Lawson repeated.

"I'm down here," someone cried, a voice from twenty feet below.

"I'll get a rope . . ." someone said.

"I can't see. I can't hold." Whoever he was, he must have been clinging by his fingertips.

"Hold on!"

"Can't."

"Listen," Lawson said. "Whatever you do . . . don't scream. Please. If they hear you scream, we're all dead. Understand? Don't scream!"

"Yes, sir."

Someone had a rope and dangled it over the edge, like a fisherman who knew he'd never get a bite. The rest of us waited. It couldn't have been more than a few seconds. Then we heard a bit of a sigh, and the sound of release, a few pebbles breaking loose. Some of the men thought they heard a thud.

When we had crept to within fifty yards of the lookouts, Lawson signaled a halt. He wanted to wait until dawn to dislodge them. A commotion in the dark would warn the people down below.

We hid in a crevice and listened to the battle. It was a bad time, hearing a battle that you could not see. For it was *not* a battle. Battles were fought in the daylight, for the same reason armies wore uniforms, to distinguish friend from foe, to follow the progress of a fight, to measure gains and losses, and ultimately to permit victors and vanquished to know themselves. Here, at night, we knew nothing. It was a collection of murders, ours and theirs, and it sounded like what it was: sprays of bullets, silences, moans, screams, curses, clubbings, more silence. Our screams or theirs? We couldn't tell.

There were six Filipinos at the lookout and we got to know them rather well as they moved around the fire. There was the cook, poking at a kettle on the fire. From the way he fussed at his food and shooed away the others, I knew he loved his work. There was the jabberer, who kept peering over the cliff, rushing back to report, though it was clear he didn't know anything more than we did. There was a man who urinated a lot. The others teased him: perhaps he had venereal disease. And once, toward dawn, when things were quiet down below, one of the insurrectos sang a song, just part of a song, a little lovely something I can still hum after almost thirty years. It was hard for me to reconcile that melody with the sight of Buddy Conaway and his bloody necklace: that lovely air and that obscene disfigurement, coming out of the same camp. Well, they have their memories of us, and we have our memories of them.

At first light we attacked. We waited until there was a commotion down below and then we fired, each of us at his previously selected target. Five of them were dead right away. The exception was the cook. I admired him. He stayed right at the fire, with the bodies of his comrades all around him, dead before they knew they were being attacked. That knowledge was saved for the cook. He didn't dash for freedom, or lunge for a rifle, and . . . what impressed me more . . . he didn't raise his hands and try to surrender, as any insurrecto being approached by ten armed Americans might have done. He stared at us, shocked at first, and then the shock passed and he made a decision to continue being what he had been: a cook. He dipped a wooden spoon into his pot, stirred a bit, pulled up the spoon, and was tasting what he'd made when we shot him.

The Filipino post was twenty yards back from the edge of the cliff. All of us were curious how our troops had fared during the night and we crept forward on our bellies to have a look.

Good God, what a morning! How had we done? Very well and very badly. On the right our troops had fought nearly up to the lowest caves, but on the left the original Filipino lines were intact. That, I think, is what an officer would report. But what I remember was the plain, random nastiness of it. Everyone who was killed, and some who were still alive, had fallen, ten feet or a hundred, onto stones, so that battlefield was a quarry of bodies, theirs and ours, smashed, splashed, and splintered. And it was still going on: men were firing around rocks, pushing each other off trails, clubbing in front of caves. It was war, or murder, without mercy. On one trail, some Americans had stacked bodies, Filipino and American, and were shooting from behind this tangled, bleeding wall. Further down among the rocks, wounded soldiers crawled from body to body, savaging the enemy. They reminded me of crabs, half crushed, missing a claw, but still feeding on whatever carrion they could find.

"Quick," Lawson whispered, "everybody on the line." In a

moment, our men were ready to open fire and tip the balance in a battle that otherwise would continue until the last man was dead.

"Listen here," Lawson said. "I don't want an opening volley. They'll just duck into caves. I want to get them while they're still in the open. So what we're going to do is plink away at 'em, one at a time, understand, and I don't want 'em to know where it's coming from. And I don't want nobody to miss."

He pointed a finger at the man at the end of the line.

"You!"

A Filipino sitting on top of a rock was blown out of view.

"You!"

A man who had been scavenging rifles and ammunition from dead Americans was spun around, and clattered off the trail.

"You! Over there!"

A burly insurrecto, probably an officer, was shot in the back as he helped a wounded comrade limp toward a cave. The wounded man knew something was wrong. He looked up, saw us, and hobbled up the trail to give the alarm. He was heroic, and he was dead before he could pass the word along. And so it went, a dozen, fifteen, insurrectos shot from above and behind before our luck ran out.

By then, we had gotten careless. Our opening shots were fired from a prone position, but after the first victims had crumpled, almost all the soldiers had gotten to their knees and some were standing, checking their colleagues' accuracy and seeking new targets. The volley which came from down below took out three of us, two of whom tumbled over the cliff. Another volley wounded Herman Biddle in the arm. Those of us who were left turned and saw that someone had detected us, collected a half dozen sharpshooters, led them onto some high rocks, told them where to aim and when to fire. As they ducked for cover, I saw a blue uniform, and dark skin, and the familiar, scholarly face of Benjamin Franklin Eccles.

"Did you see that, Boss?" I cried.

"They spotted us," he acknowledged.

"*They* spotted us!? It was Eccles! I saw him!"

"I saw the sharpshooters," Lawson countered firmly. "I didn't see Eccles."

"He was there! You must have seen him!"

"Dukie," Lawson asked, "did you see Eccles?"

"No, Boss," he answered softly. "I doubt they'd let a prisoner out of the caves."

"I'm telling you," I shouted. "I saw it. Eccles is a traitor!"

"Biddle?"

Herman Biddle was bandaging his arm. He'd been grazed below the elbow and was poking around in his wound, which fascinated him.

"What's that, Boss?" he asked.

"Did you see Eccles down there?"

"No, sir," Biddle answered. He never looked up.

We were down to six men, five if I excluded my unarmed self, but our "plinking" had cleared out the enemy and the very sight of us inspirited the men below. They waved and shouted at us. Lawson rose to full height and waved back despite some bullets that came whizzing by. He was king of the mountain and he wanted both sides to know it.

"We got a flag?" he asked. Nobody had thought to bring one. "Well, Dukie and the rest of you. Bring them Filipinos over here. The ones we killed."

The soldiers got up and began dragging bodies to the edge of the cliff.

"We got to show them who's boss," Lawson said. It took a while. Three bodies came forward and the men who carried them dropped them on the ground, panting. Lawson stared at me. I didn't like the look of him.

"You could help, too," he said.

I nodded and went with Dukie. He took one of the cook's legs, I grabbed the other, and we hauled him over to where the others were piled.

"Now," Lawson said. "One at a time. Roll them over the edge."

"What?!" I balked at that. I had no business doing something like that. It was senseless, gratuitous, cruel.

"Do it!" he shouted. "Like this!" He kicked at one of the dead men, who slid over the edge, and I could hear a cheer from the men below. A shower of bodies delighted them. It wasn't a flag raising: it was better.

"Do it!" Lawson shouted.

There was just one body left, the dead cook, and the others were waiting to see if I would obey. I looked at Dukie and Herman Biddle for support, and found none, and it seemed that if I didn't push the cook over the ledge, Lawson would push me. I'd never seen him like that.

"Do it, damn you! You see it! You talk it up! You write about it! Do it!"

I tried to push the dead man with my feet, but the cook was stubborn: dead weight.

"Pitch into it!" Lawson shouted. "You're always telling me how the world works, you and Lucy, giving me instructions. How names are made, how power works. This is how the world works. Bodies over cliffs. Do it!"

I crouched down and touched the Filipino's hips and shoulders. It was like rolling the heaviest of carpets across a floor. No one helped me. I shoved, cursing myself for weakness and the dead man for inertia and Lawson for humiliating me. Finally the cook went down over the edge. I could not bring myself to watch him land on the rocks, but my countrymen's cheers told me he arrived.

I stayed on my hands and knees, shocked and abased. Lawson kneeled beside me. He was still angry.

"I don't care who sits on this fucking mountain, or who owns this island, or who wins this war. I care about my men."

It was crazy, crazy as all the rest of it, but now at least I knew why Lawson raged at me: it was for seeing Eccles, and saying so.

"I know you care about your men," I replied. "But Eccles is on the other side now. I saw him."

Lawson's head dropped down, his chin on his chest. He closed his eyes.

"Could you be a little less sure?" he asked. "Just for a little while?"

He lifted his head, put his hands on my shoulders, and whispered, "Please . . . Listen, Eddie. I'll tell you something I should've told you a long time ago. Told Lucy, too. Maybe you can tell her. The thing in my life I'm proudest of . . . it ain't this or that battle. Names on maps is all they were, and some not even names. It's the men. My men. The buffalo soldiers. Just being with them . . . that's what made me rich . . . and strong.

That's where the magic was. Not over the horizon someplace. All around me . . . every day . . . Dukie . . . Biddle . . . all of 'em. Eccles, too. I want to bring him back . . . So could you stop . . . could you be a little less sure you saw him shooting at us? . . . Please . . ."

The moment got to me: now it was my turn for my eyes to fill.

"They take a prisoner," I heard myself say, "and put him in front of a squad of marksmen . . . use him as a shield. Insurrecto trick. I saw it in Madagascar and . . . where was it? . . . in the Sudan."

"Thanks, Eddie," he said.

This I admit: the sight of those insurrecto bodies rolling off the mountain had a tonic effect on the battered combatants below. Our men started moving up the mountain, and the Filipinos gave ground. They didn't break and run, but they yielded, filing back toward the caves. Our men were right behind them, sensing that a stalemate might turn into a victory and a victory, with luck, into a massacre.

"Quick," Lawson shouted. "The ropes."

"What?" Even Dukie had relaxed, thinking our job was done and it was time to sit and watch.

"Give me the damn ropes, Dukie," Lawson snapped. "We got to get Eccles out of there. And we ain't walking down the same way we walked up."

We tied the ropes together, secured one end against a boulder, tossed the other end over the side, and now I saw he meant for us to rappel down the cliff, onto one of the ledge trails that led to the insurrecto caves.

"Me first," Lawson said, and I was in no mind to contradict him.

"No, Boss," Dukie said. Before Lawson could do anything about it, Dukie had grasped the rope and slid over the edge.

"Goddamn, Dukie," Lawson said. "Babysitting again!"

But before he could do anything about it, Lawson had lost the second spot as well. Wounded arm and all, spindly and spavined, Herman Biddle had gone down the rope. And then I knew it was my turn. I took the rope.

"I'll follow you down," he said. "That way, if I fall, you'll catch me." Perhaps he meant it as a joke, but it sounded sad. He wasn't anxious to go down the rope.

"I'll be around at the bottom," I said. "You fall, I'll catch you."

I was no mountaineer. The rope immediately cut off circulation in my arms, burned my hands raw, and once it slammed me against the mountain. But I made it to the bottom, and looked at Lawson. I saw him hesitate, right at the edge. With the rope around his waist, he stopped and took in the battlefield below, the harvest of motionless soldiers at the bottom of the mountain.

"Wait for me," he said.

Henry Lawson had his hands full coming down the rope. It was something he had never done before. He looked slow and awkward, old and heavy, and sometimes—whether out of weariness or fear of heights—he hung motionless, like a ripe fruit on a vine, ready for an autumn wind to blow him to the ground. That rope, that cliff, was all he could manage. Yet something more was waiting for him.

It happened fast. Our troops had already taken a number of lower caves, but the cost was high. Shooting from cover, the cornered insurrectos provided each cave with a welcome mat of dead blue uniforms. In response, some Americans had tried smoking out the enemy, lighting bundles of branches and tossing them inside the caves. Now, while Lawson was on the rope, the strategy seemed to be working. We heard shouts from inside a cave: "Amigo, amigo!" Five coughing, scared insurrectos came stumbling out, hands high. When they fought us, they were soldiers. In surrender, they were peasants, white peasant shirts and trousers, barefoot and unarmed.

And doomed. For it was then that Henry Lawson's mountaintop display of falling corpses bore its unexpected dividend. How quickly brutality compounded! The troops emulated Lawson—with living men. Yes, Sergeant Greene was right. There were worse things than the water cure. There was the tossing of insurrectos into the river far below, a boyish swimming-hole prank, except that our troops always missed, landing their victims on the rocks, professing regret and determining to try again. Five times they missed and at the end of it all they looked cheerfully up at Lawson, as if they were counting on his applause.

He hung there, motionless, silent, like a body on a gallows. No scream, no cry, no keening in the wind. But from the look on his face when he finally descended, I could tell that Henry Lawson had come to the end of things. Only Eccles remained. And that was part of the ending he desired.

We waved some shirts in front of the headquarters cave, tossed stones inside, threw our hats in the air, and drew no fire. Reckless, Dukie dashed across the opening. Again, no fire. All that came was a cool, damp, earth-smelling breeze. Was it empty? Had they fled? Or had they gone further inside?

"Wait," Lawson said. He unbuttoned the yellow slicker which had become his trademark in the Philippines and held it at arm's length in front of the cave. Instantly, some shots tore into it.

"It's me they want," he said, grimly pleased.

I had to look at Dukie and Biddle. It was clear to me exactly who wanted Lawson. Biddle looked away. Dukie's eyes met mine and pleaded, passionately, for silence.

"It's me they get," Lawson said. "Dukie, Biddle, and me. We'll bring him out."

"Hold on, sir." It was Sergeant Greene. "Maybe I'm not part of the old guard, but we left a lot of men down on those rocks. This is the headquarters cave. With respect, I think we have a right to join on in."

"We?"

"Our representative."

"Who the hell's your representative?"

"I guess I'll do."

"All right," Lawson said. "In we go. All the way to China."

We plowed into a corridor of smoke, shooting ahead of us, tripping over rocks we could not see, sprayed with rock splinters from enemy shots or, it increasingly seemed possible, our own ricochets. Lawson signaled for us to hold our fire, and we tiptoed forward into a cave that was turning out to be a cavern, a cool and musty tunnel, the intestines of the mountain, with springs and puddles and rockslides along the way. The smoke was behind us, but now there was blackness, a blackness without stars, a blackness that would never yield to dawn.

I still find it hard to describe the terror of that cave. Every fear . . . of being lost, of falling, of darkness and closed spaces, of being buried and being born . . . seized me. And yet there was an uncanny intimacy about it. I never felt so tied . . . so . . . linked! . . . to other men as in that dark passage, groping forward, vulnerable but never alone. I remember Lawson grunting and Dukie sweating and Herman's hands at my back and even torturer Greene in front of me, his canteen clinking against his belt. Good company, on the whole; any company was good.

At last the tunnel dropped away, the walls lifted. We stood up and stretched our arms, temporarily exhilarated by the space around us, but then the roominess intimidated us. We clustered together again, huddling in an unknown void.

Suddenly, a torch was lit and went flying through the air, landing on a pile of papers and wood and rags some twenty feet below. As the fire took, I saw that we were in a room the size of a barn, at about where the hayloft would be, and the fire was burning on the floor of General Lukban's headquarters. The wood that was burning was broken furniture, the rags were soiled sheets and bandages, and the paper was insurrecto currency.

Then a shot rang out: it sounded like an explosion underground. I couldn't tell where it came from or, for a moment, where it hit. Then I felt Sergeant Greene tap me on the shoulder. I turned, thinking he had detected where the shot had come from. I was wrong. But he knew where it had gone. With a troubled expression and a trembling finger, Greene pointed to a hole in his chest, a little above the heart. Then he rolled forward onto the floor of the cave.

"Now it's just us buffalo soldiers," a voice said. "And Morrison."

It was Eccles, sitting in a chair in the corner of the cave, his feet propped up on a cask, his rifle across his lap, his face in shadows except that, now and then, when another bundle of insurrecto currency caught fire, the flames reflected in his glasses.

"Hello, Boss," he said.

"Eccles."

"Dukie. How you doing, so far?"

"Still here. You know me."

"Yeah. Herman, I see they nicked you in the arm."

"I'll be all right," Herman answered.

"You did all right out there," Eccles said. "I should've known you'd find a way up top. I believe we'd've held if it wasn't for that. Didn't know you could climb that way, Boss."

"I did it for you."

"You want me that bad, Boss?"

"Not the way you think. I want to get you out of this mess."

"And what?"

"Get you squared away. Get back to where we were. How things used to be . . ."

Eccles didn't answer, and I couldn't blame him. If he was touched by Lawson's message, or appalled, he had a right to be. There was no going back. The century had turned, and the buffalo soldiers were a cargo of coffins in the hold of a freighter that was in no rush to get to San Francisco. Dead was dead.

"It's all over here," Lawson said. "They're surrendering in droves."

"I'm not surrendering."

"They're gonna be Americans."

"Not me, Boss. Not anymore."

"I can't leave without you."

"I'm staying."

"Then I'll stay too," Lawson said. He walked toward Eccles, arms outstretched. To show he meant no harm? To make a better target? To offer an embrace?

"You do what you got to do," Lawson said.

And Eccles shot him.

Lawson faltered, dropped to his knees, and fell to the ground, face down in piles of insurrecto dollars.

DUQUESNE: In no time I was across the cave, scrambling toward Eccles, and Herman Biddle was right with me. Only it wasn't no corner, it was another tunnel. I bumped into walls, tripped over timbers, banged my head against an overhead rock . . . I got the dent in my head to this day . . . and I don't feel a thing and all the time, Herman tells me later, I'm screaming, one long scream, like my heart had got tore out, which it had been. Well, we're still running fast and don't neither of us know where and all of a sudden the ground ain't there no more, we're knee deep in water, and to one side there is some light, and we get out to it. Then we turn a corner and there's mist and a curtain of water and we're standing in back of a waterfall, and I see Eccles through the water, on the other side of the pool, and . . . it's a funny thing about distance . . . there's something inside, tells you whether you can catch something or not, and killing a man is no different from catching a fly ball . . . You know whether or not you have it. And I had Eccles . . . You draw a circle around yourself, a killing circle. And Eccles was inside. Easy.

Eccles' bullet had caught Lawson square in the chest, and though he was still alive when I came over to him, his shirt was soaked with blood. His mouth was full of blood as well, but he managed to turn his head and spit it out.

"Boss . . ." He was dying and it would take years before I could measure everything that died along with him. All the words came later, the talk of idealism and self-destruction, romance and tragedy, about his having deserved a nobler death, in a nobler cause. But when I held him in my arms, all I could say, again and again, till it sounded like I was crooning, was "Boss."

He had no last words. But he was crying. I saw the tears. I do not think they were tears of pain. The pain was somewhere else. The tears were tears of mourning.

"Boss," I said, "I love you. We all do."

He nodded to that, and wept some more. At the very end, he tried to say something. To say he loved us, too? To thank us for loving him? I cannot say, for something burst inside him and blood, lots of it, came out instead of words. His mourning was over, and mine had only begun.

DUQUESNE: You know where Eccles ran? Right through the damn battlefield, over the big rocks at the bottom of the cliff, hopping over dead men, brushing past stretcher bearers and burial details and bunches of soldiers resting up after the fight. They laughed at us . . . two niggers chasing another nigger after the fighting was done. Maybe they thought we were arguing over something we took off a body. "Where's the hen house?" someone shouted.

I couldn't do much about the blood, but I tried to wipe away his tears. I used my fingers. What had he cried for? For himself? For us? For the 25th Cavalry, Colored? For the century, or the country? For Lucy?

He was an American soldier and an American dreamer. He traveled far, and farther, in search of a dream, a romance of adventure. He thought that there was something out there, just for him, in the West or across the Pacific, which he would find and have and share with all of us. But, at the end, it was a bullet in a dark cave, far from home.

DUQUESNE: Herman and I find him in the river. He's sitting on a rock, watching us come down to him.

"How we going to do this, Herman?" I ask. "Bullet, knife, bare hands? . . . Fast or slow?"

"I don't know," Herman says.

"Wait a minute. There's the garrote. That's something new."

"Yeah," Herman says. "The local custom."

"Or what they did to Buddy. We could give the man a necklace."

"We ain't gonna do him," Herman says, real quiet.

"What?!" I spin around, and I see old Herman's come up behind me and got a Krag in my back. "What?!"

"We ain't gonna do him, Dukie," Herman says again.

"We gonna leave him?"

"Yeah."

Eccles is watching this and his face still ain't moved a muscle.

"Get out of here," Herman says to him. "Go your way, boy."

Eccles hasn't moved. Maybe he figures it's a trick and

Herman'll let him have it as soon as he turns his back. "Shot while trying to escape."

"I mean it," Herman says. "You're free to go. Understand? I won't shoot you. I *can't* shoot you."

Eccles gets up, starts walking away, backing off, which is hard to do if you're walking through a rocky stream, and he falls ass over elbows into the water.

"It goes better if you turn around," Herman tells him. "You see where you're headed that way."

"Is he gone?" Eccles asks. "The Boss?"

"Yeah," Biddle says.

"You killed him!" I shout. "What you have to do that for?!" I'm about out of my mind right then, but I ain't so far gone I can't see what happened next. It was a look, was all, that passed from Eccles to Herman Biddle and back, a message without words, so that when Eccles did put it into words I sensed it was for my dumb benefit.

"I'm sorry. Had to be. You know?"

"I know," Herman says. "You better go now . . ."

Eccles is looking at us and for maybe the first time I see some human feeling on his face and I remember how alone he'd always been and I had a feeling he'd be staying lonely, whether he was one of ours or one of theirs, no matter.

"Thanks," he said, he actually said it. "So long."

We watched him all the way out, picking his way down the river, working his way up the bank, and disappearing forever . . . far as I know . . . in a line of trees up top.

"He killed the Boss, Herman!" I said. "Why'd you let him go?" I was crying now myself. "What'd you do that for?"

"You'll see," Herman says. He's got his arm around my shoulder.

"I won't never see!"

"Yes, you will, Dukie. You surely will. It might take a while, but you'll see."

You know what? Old Herman was right. It took time. It took years. And it didn't happen all at once, it happened slow. And now I see. You hear what this blind man's saying? You hear, Morrison? I see. I truly do. Do you?

• X •

We carried his body on a stretcher back to the village we had not quite destroyed. There we made a coffin to hold him until Basey, where the *Meade* was waiting, and the news of his death was told. In Basey, they embalmed the Boss and transferred him to a better coffin for the voyage to Manila, where General Gottschalk, the other generals, the American civil commissioners, and the Americanista Filipinos all received him. The plan was for a cortege through the streets of Manila, out to the house, where Lucy was waiting. I changed that and, with Dukie and Biddle backing me up, no one dared to overrule us. We took him home the way he loved to come home, along the beach.

I wondered if they remembered him, the people who wandered out of nipa huts, the fishermen, the teamsters washing their horses in the sea, or the wide-eyed children who ran and hid beneath their houses as we passed slowly by. Did they make any connection between this gloomy rainy-day procession, the black caissons and the flag-draped coffin, and the magnificent bearded horseman who had thundered past at dusk and sometimes stopped to buy fish along the way?

Once we reached the house, things passed out of our control. The house was decked in flags, the road lined with carriages. An occupying nation and a beaten republic had come to pay respects. There was music, sweet and mournful, and hushed, important talk: insurrectos surrendering, a peace feeler from the wily Lukban. Discreet refreshments. There was a reception line and it was long, with Lucy and General Gottschalk side by side. She was all in black, of course, and completely composed. Some of the women who embraced her, and a few of the men, broke down. She consoled them.

No one missed us. We went outside, across the lawn, and sat down together on the edge of the sea wall, Dukie, Biddle, and I. The day-long rain relented. Toward dusk, a few weak rays of sunlight slanted in under the clouds and flushed the dripping garden and the listless flags and the vast Manila Bay with a touch of gold. Now and then, some of the mourners stepped out onto the lawn, to stretch their arms, to smoke and laugh a little, to sniff the air, which promised better days ahead. I watched that closing vault of sunset, that realm of warmth and color, as it turned the horizon from yellow to gold, to pink and purple, and finally yielded to darkness. I remembered that brilliant bonfire sunset which I had seen on the Brooklyn Bridge, signaling fantastic enterprises out West, and I recalled that reddish aura which enveloped us the first day at San Pablos when we rode back to camp through Apacheland and Lawson said that *out there*, that was where he wanted to go. And now, seeing that purple trace succumb over dark volcanic mountains, I knew that was where he had gone, out there, and all alone, and I whispered goodbye to him, goodbye and so long, and I knew there was a part of me which still would jump at the chance to travel with him, wherever he was headed.

"The Pacific Ocean. 'The biggest damn thing on earth.' That's what the Boss used to say," Dukie mused. " 'We come about as far from home as you can go.' Where they gonna bury him, Mr. Morrison?"

"Arlington National Cemetery."

"Where's that?"

"Virginia. Outside Washington."

"Oh, that'll be nice. It'll be spring before he gets there, won't it?"

"Yes. It'll be spring all right. It'll definitely be spring."

"I'd like to go with him, back there," Dukie said. "Can you put in a word for me?"

"How about you, Herman?" I asked.

"I wouldn't mind," he said.

We stayed there while the house filled up with mourners. I left them only when I saw a chance to corner General Gottschalk. I cut short his profession of sympathy to put in a word for Dukie and Biddle. He acceded. Lawson had threatened his humanity: I appealed to it. He wished there was more he could do, he said, and then he returned to a group of courteous Filipinos. It felt like Lawson's death was the end of the war season: he was the enemy's sole trophy and once they brought him down they could surrender in good conscience. And the

Americans could accept the surrender. They had gotten Lawson out of their system, too. Now it was time for resident commissioners and provisional governors and host-country representatives and new mayors. Tonight they mourned the Boss and tomorrow they would put him behind them, absolutely behind them, and begin a whole new game.

Lucy saw me while I was still inside. She was surrounded by Americans and Filipinos. Not a uniform in the group. She gestured that I should come over and be introduced. Lawson's coffin was in an empty corner, like a table that they'd all gotten up from. I went back outside.

"Mr. Morrison?"

It was Jaime Navarro, in delicate black, so excited he could hardly contain himself. I wondered if he'd already rented out the house again.

"Yes."

"And these other gentlemen are Private Duquesne and Sergeant Biddle?"

"They are."

"Very good. Mrs. Lawson would like to speak to all of you . . . separately."

"Where?" I asked.

"She is in the garden." He motioned toward the gazebo. "There. Who will go first?"

"I'll go," Dukie said. He got up and followed Jaime Navarro across the lawn.

"Dukie," Herman Biddle called out after him. "You remember now . . ."

Dukie waved his hand. "No problem."

"What was that about?" I asked.

"I been meaning to talk to you," Biddle said. "It's about Lieutenant Eccles. Dukie and I want to leave him out of it . . . 'missing in action.' No point in letting on that the Boss got shot by one of his own. That's no kind of ending. I was hoping you'd go along with us."

"Yes," I said, "I will."

"Thanks. I thought you would."

"I'm doing it for his sake . . . the Boss's . . . or maybe for

Lucy's. But I have a feeling that you're asking for Eccles; could that be so?"

"Maybe," he sighed. "Yes."

"Would you mind telling me why?"

"Mr. Morrison, I wouldn't know where to start. We all got our reasons. There's reasons for everything we do, and everything that happens to us. I believe that."

"And Eccles' reasons?"

"He wanted to be great. He wasn't alone. There's a lot of that going around. I guess you know."

"And for that . . . that's why he . . ."

Biddle raised up his hands; he would hear no more.

"You just write the Boss up a hero one more time. Make it nice. And let it go."

"Hello, Edwin," Lucy said. It was dark in the gazebo. I could hardly make out where she was sitting. We did not embrace.

"Sit down," she said. "I'm not crying now. But I have been and I don't want you to see me."

"I understand."

"Dukie made me cry. That was the hardest thing so far. Seeking Dukie. I went through it all dry-eyed, till Dukie."

"He wants to go to Arlington. I spoke to General Gottschalk. Was that all right?"

"Yes. Do you know something, Edwin? It took until now for me to find out that the buffalo soldiers had a nickname for me. All these years, all the way back to Arizona. They called me the Queen of Sheba. Eccles started it. I never knew."

"What are you going to do, Luce?"

"Jaime Navarro wants me to stay. As long as I like, he says. I'll always have a home here. It won't take him very long to propose."

"No!"

"I'll be gone. I'll go back to Arlington with Henry and then . . . I don't know . . . I think I want to be by myself for a while. A long while, possibly . . ."

"I thought you had been."

"No. I was always out there with him. He knew it, too. He

carried the burden of my dreams. Ours. That's not a burden I want to transfer to anyone else, Edwin. I believe I'll carry that load myself."

I heard her out, knowing that our time had passed. There was no chance to talk about us.

"I'm sorry I left you like that. On New Year's Eve. I'm truly sorry."

"Don't bother apologizing. I understand. There are other men like you. And other women like me. But there was only one of him. And now . . . now he's gone."

She stopped, and for a moment I thought that I was going to see her cry. But when she resumed she wasn't weeping. She was wondering.

"Not today . . . not tomorrow . . . but sometime I'm going to sit down and try to understand it all . . ."

"Understand . . . what . . . ?"

"What happened. I believed, Edwin, in you and him. In us. In our country, too. That we could never go wrong. Never be wrong . . . never do wrong . . . Now . . ." She shrugged and turned to me. "At least you survived."

"Yes . . . that's me . . . survived to tell the tale."

I knew she didn't believe me, didn't believe I'd tell the tale. Her expression said as much. She had no reason to believe me.

"I've got to go now. What are your plans?"

"Plans? Well, I'm leaving, too. For South Africa. The Boer War."

"*Another* war?"

"Yes. I'm a war correspondent."

"You poor man," she said. And then she said, "Goodbye."

EPILOGUE

THE STATUE: MILTON, INDIANA, 1913

Travel to my hometown of Milton, Indiana, today or fifty years from today, and you will find a statue of my best friend, Major Henry Lawson, in the heart of the town square. There he sits, an equestrian figure, larger than life, pulling up on reins, stabbing ahead with his sword, as if to pounce on a dandelion interrupting the flow of municipal lawn.

At first glance, the statue looks no different from its dozens, hundreds, of counterparts that patrol parks, guard courthouses, protect libraries across America: a nineteenth-century man-on-a-horse, sword drawn, rushing into battle. But though the scene suggests the Civil War, the man on the horse is middle-aged, and Lawson was only a beardless boy, an unmounted underage infantryman in 1865. Another thing: Lawson is wearing his trademark, the full-length yellow rain slicker, so incongruously like those worn by school crossing guards to this very day, yet this did not become his style until late in his career, in the

Philippines. So there is more guile in the statue than meets the eye, elements of a lifetime combined in one tableau. Yet it is all somehow true, and all Lawson: the headlong charge, the disregard of danger, the lifelong search for a worthy opponent, which —for the enemy is not part of the statue—he never quite found.

Fashions change, in the cut of a coat, the trimming of a beard, the design of a house. Fashions change in people also, and the Henry Lawson I knew was already out of date—adventurous, heroic, romantic—when, in July 1913, I traveled to Milton, Indiana, for the last time. I had been commissioned to deliver remarks at the dedication of the town's memorial to its most famous son. (The invitation assured me that I was "the second most famous.") I remember sitting in a train that cut across farmland north of Indianapolis and wondering what to tell and what to omit. It wasn't the first time I had to make such decisions about Henry Lawson. Here are some scraps of the oratory I composed aboard the train that carried me home.

> . . . Some of you knew the man before he was a statue, in the bivouacs and on the battlefields of the South, the fatal deserts of the Southwest, the contested hillsides of the Philippines. To the sight of this mounted warrior you can add a thousand other scenes: the carefree farm boy skipping through this very square, pole in hand, gone fishin'! The amateur horseman. The despairing algebra student. The young soldier, the first volunteer, the returning hero!
>
> . . . And yet, as years roll by and generations pass, there will be those who know only the statue. Today they are a youthful minority, tomorrow an adult majority, and someday, ah, some inevitable, unanimous day, the statue will be all that Milton knows of Henry Lawson. What then, my friends, will people make of him? Is he our Hoosier Ozymandias? Will this figure we dedicate be a kind of Stonehenge, alien and mystifying to all who pass? . . .

Of course not, my speech assured them, not if the story passed from father to son, not if books were read and ideals preserved, not if all sorts of impossible and probably undesirable things happened. A tomb is a tomb, no matter that the body lies in Arlington, Virginia, and the headstone rears its bulk in Milton, Indiana. Time hollows out the mightiest of monuments as surely as it slays the strongest of men. I could have told them that, I thought, but no. Not with the whole town listening, listening with the kind of desperate interest people in small left-out places show in what becomes of local youths who venture out into the world. Pride mingled with resentment in a place like Milton. Oh, there was awe for his accomplishments—Medal of Honor at Stone Mountain, cavalry command in the Apache campaigns, hero's death in the Philippines—but there was envy also. He was from here, like us. He played ball, fished, went to the same schools. So why didn't he turn out like us? Or—and this was the real question—why didn't we turn out like him? They claimed him as a native son, one of their own. They were entitled to. Yet all the while they knew in their hearts that he was an exception, one of a kind, and no kin at all . . .

I finished drafting my speech, eloquent and insincere, as the train pulled into town. That night I found myself staring out a window of the Milton House, our hometown's only hotel. Once it had seemed like a wonderful place. To sit in the Milton House dining room was my young reporter's dream. Now I saw it was only a small-town hotel frequented by scruffy back-country salesmen and travelers on their way to Indianapolis who read day-late newspapers in the downstairs lobby.

I glanced out the window, like some drummer sizing up new territory. Yet I came from here. These streets—empty now, and draped with yards of listless bunting—were mine. I wanted to walk them, one last time. I stepped quietly out onto the veranda facing the courthouse square and heard a noise that stopped me dead. Only one man on earth could snore like that.

It was Paul W. Koch, Lawson's long-time aide-de-camp. No need to worry about waking him. I walked over and looked down at him. He was white-haired now. A blanket covered his legs and it hurt me to see that he was sleeping in a wheelchair, not a rocker, and that his shoes had heels which would stay like new forever. At his side was a cup of coffee, gone cold, and a cigar turned into ashes.

"Hello, Koch," I whispered.

I reached inside my jacket, pulled out a couple of Havanas, dropped them in his lap, and backed away. A ribbon on his bathrobe announced that he was a "guest of honor." Koch probably said it reminded him of a "damn dog show." I could hear him saying something like that.

I blame old Koch for what happened next. The sight of him had moved me. I could feel it—one of the few times in life I could truthfully say I felt something in my heart—a pain, and a thrill, and a summons. Leaving Koch in his wheelchair, I headed out onto the town square. I headed for Henry Lawson.

Furtive, I walked the four sides of the square, the outside sidewalk. Some youths were sitting on a bench in front of a new movie house. I nodded good evening. They stared at me, country stares, not rude but blank. Next, the inside sidewalk, perimeter of the square itself, like a confidential agent who feared a trap. At last, I cut into the square, down an aisle where dew was gathering on ranks of wooden chairs. Summer lightning crackled overhead, electricity filled the air, and there was Lawson's statue, draped in bunting, bound with cords, like Gulliver come to Lilliput. I circled the monument once, twice, three times, the whole pattern of my life repeated, while thunder rumbled overhead, like reports of a mighty battle, something with cannons and cavalry, something that charged across the sky and ended gloriously.

I was sitting in the front row, a place reserved for close family, important mourners, and I heard my voice.

"Hello, Boss," I said, and the sound, the very sound, destroyed me. I don't know how long I wept. Was I crying, whispering, imagining? I would like to think that it was inside my head, but remembering it, I hear voices. My voice. And his.

"What is it, Eddie?" he asked, and the rain's first drops were falling.

I said I was sorry about how things had turned out. I felt it was my fault, if I had done more, done less, done nothing, things would've turned out better. He asked why.

It was coming back to Milton, I responded, and sensing how things had come apart for all of us, with him gone and a vast distance between Lucy and myself, and knowing that it would stay that way forever, there was no counting on time to repair things, to heal what was dead and dying. It was little things. It was seeing Koch in a wheelchair, fallen asleep while keeping watch on the statue, and that a Mr. Diller had come all the way from California and that a certain Sergeant John Duquesne was staying with a colored family on a nearby farm, and they had all come, from out of retirement and nursing homes, trailing relatives, marching proudly, to a final encampment that was breaking my heart.

Things happen, he said, and you shouldn't blame yourself. Not after so long, especially. "I've been dead a long time now."

You died far away, I countered, you died early and in vain, and don't tell me that it's over, Boss, because as long as I'm alive, it's not over, because here's one man who keeps carrying around the past, but he can't change it. Can't change it. But there's nights I feel so close to you, Boss, you're so much around. Here. Tonight. Bruising the rain out of the thunderclouds, I hope it's you up there, riding in the sky. Is it you I hear?

The raindrops were the size of silver dollars, one here, one there; they sounded like footsteps among the empty chairs.

"Boss, I'm sorry." Good. Conversational level. Something you could hear across a room, but still not loud enough. "I'M SORRY." Loud enough for my speech tomorrow. That is what my whole speech should be, two words, *I'M SORRY*.

I arose and headed back down the aisle. In the bushes, somebody giggled. Kids from in front of the movie spying on me, no doubt, chasing off across the grass. I didn't care. The heavy rain wasn't far off now and it was headed our way. Halfway out of the park, aisle seat, someone was sitting, some motionless someone who had watched me pace, seen me cry, heard me shout.

"Oh my God!" I said. "Lucy?"

She raised her head.

"I'm sorry, too," she said.

It was the first we'd talked since that parting in Manila. The next day, I'd watched the *George Meade* sail out of Manila Bay, homeward-bound. I was on another ship myself, which sailed a little later, in another direction, to another war. "*Another* war." Lucy sounded so pitying when she said it, as if a life sentence had been passed on me: I was condemned to continue living as I had lived, sentenced not to change. "*Another* war." There had been lots more wars. Then it had been Manila to Mafeking. And tomorrow: Milton to Veracruz. What I had been, I still was.

I had heard from her only perfunctorily in the years between. Most of the news came from people who had heard about her and, knowing of my connection with the Lawson story, passed on what they knew. She had married again, in Washington, in 1905. I gathered her husband, a manufacturer of farming equipment, had been a civil commissioner in the government of the Philippines and later served in the Cabinet of President Taft. He had died, I heard, and left Lucy quite well off, which Lawson had not done. She lived in New York and Bar Harbor and other places. This was her first trip back to Milton.

The rain was serious now. I took her by the arm and, sensing that the hotel would be inappropriate, found shelter for us in the covered bandstand which high school musicians would occupy the next morning.

I seated her on a folding chair and sat down beside her. It was pouring now, a proper July drenching, with fireworks overhead, so that we saw each other in flashes, an image here, an image there.

"I didn't want to see you, Edwin," she confessed.

"Why, Luce?"

"I was afraid of it . . . that it would all come back . . . and that I couldn't stand it."

"Not all the memories are bad . . ."

"No. But the good ones can hurt, too."

A timely flash of lightning showed me her face and I saw she was looking at me the way she used to look: those same green eyes which knew me so well and had known me forever. A knowledge which supported and destroyed love. Perhaps it was better she had married a stranger.

"Anyway, it all comes back, no matter what," she said. "He's really here tonight, isn't he? It all comes back, very strong. Stronger than I can bear for very long. Do you feel it, too?"

"My God!" I cried. "You heard me, didn't you? I was talking to him!"

"I keep thinking of all the things we wanted . . ."

"Luce . . . you remember the time we talked . . . the last time?"

"Yes . . ."

"You said that sooner or later you . . . you were going to figure it out . . . what happened . . . where we . . . went off the track . . ."

"Yes . . ."

"Well . . . did you . . . ?"

"No, Edwin," she answered, with a firmness that suggested she thought it was wrong of me to hold her to that distant promise to herself. "When I think about it . . . I remember . . . the good times . . . the grandness of him . . . his sayings. 'Yeah . . . well . . . so.' The rides we took together. The good times. Don't begrudge me that."

She glanced back at the shrouded statue, rain dripping off its canvas moorings.

"I don't regret loving him . . ." She faced me again. "He belongs up there. He deserves it. I think we all have gotten what we deserved. And the things we didn't get . . . well, they weren't worthy of us. Or we weren't worthy of them. And now it's over."

The rain had slackened. She arose and we walked across the park. The air was clean and charged, the grass was glistening. You could smell the earth. It felt like home again. Too soon, we were at the sidewalk in front of the Milton House.

"We have lots of catching up to do," I said.

She laughed or cried, I don't know. A little of both, I suppose. She kissed me on the forehead, on the lips.

"No, we don't," she said, and went upstairs.

And so we spent our last night, together and apart in the town we had set out from with such strength and innocence and to which we had now returned, for the last time. Strength and innocence: that was us. It's a peculiar combination, peculiarly American, unstable, powerful, fatal. It carried us a long way from home and when we came back we were weaker than we had been, and less innocent, and changed forever.

At dawn on my last morning in Milton—my last, forever—I

walked out of town, along River Road, to where Carter Hammond's house still presided over the junction of the Wabash and Lenape. Lucy's birthplace was a convalescent home, county-run, and though it was early, a half dozen shuffling figures occupied the porch that her father had loved. They were poor and sick, but I envied them that porch.

I'd have given a lot to walk up those steps again and take a seat and smell the wood, the way it smelled in summertime. My name assured me of a polite puzzled reception, a cup of coffee, and a tour of the premises. But the more I thought of it, the more fatuous such a visit became. Jaime Navarro was right: a house did indeed belong to the people who lived in it. It was too late for me to claim occupancy. Yet Carter Hammond had been right, righter than the rest of us who had washed around the world on a wave of American power that receded as suddenly as it surged. I remembered, as a lesson too late for the learning, a line of Samuel Johnson's that the end of all ambition is to be happy at home.

Late in the morning, the sky cleared, the sun blasted, and the humidity returned. Hotel guests mopped their brows at breakfast. I went to my room to pack. A band was tuning up somewhere, starting the festivities. Crowds of people filed into the park, filling up the folding chairs. About half of them I knew: Lawson's teachers, neighbors, boyhood chums. Down on the sidewalk, Paul Koch was making a commotion while Dukie pushed his wheelchair. Then I saw Lucy join them. She greeted Dukie warmly, still the Queen of Sheba, and bent over to hug Koch, who cheered up rapidly. Watching them from my window, it felt to me like we all lived here together.

It was . . . it is . . . it will always be impossible to believe that our adventure had ended, though there were endings all around me. No! my heart protested. Nonetheless, I put on my suit and tucked away my speech. Like a man attending his own funeral, I walked down the stairs and across the street, into the park, to dedicate the statue.